THE
Starry
KNIGHT

KNIGHT PUBLISHING BOOK 2

L.B. MARTIN

COPYRIGHT

The Starry Knight

© 2023, L.B. Martin, and its affiliates and assigns and licensors.

Brantley Greenwald is affiliated with L.B. Martin.

Edited by Terry Hooker, Blue Dahlia Publishing House, LLC

Cover Art by Taylor Dawn, SWEET 15 DESIGNS, LLC

E-book & Paperback: Danvers Designs

"Art is to console those who are broken by life."

-Vincent Van Gogh

DEDICATION

To all my ladies out there who want their men to throw them up against a wall, this one is for you. Now be a *good girl* and turn the page.

PLAYLIST

- *Slipped Away – Avril Lavigne*
- *Broken – Jonah Kagen*
- *Heal – Tom Odell*
- *Dancing With Your Ghost – Sasha Alex Sloan*
- *Need You Now (How Many Times) – Plumb*
- *Everybody Wants To Rule The World – Lorde*
- *Ceilings – Lizzy McAlpine*
- *My Immortal – Evanescence*
- *Easy To Love – Bryce Savage*
- *If You Want Love – NF*
- *Lovely – Billie Eilish & Khalid*
- *Bad Things – MGK & Camila Cabello*
- *Feelings Are Fatal – mxmtoon*

- *This Is Me Trying – Taylor Swift*
- *Control – Zoe Wees*
- *At My Best (feat. Hailee Steinfield) – MGK*
- *Dandelions – Ruth B.*
- *Play With Fire (Feat. Yacht Money) – Sam Tinnesz*
- *Emo Girl – Machine Gun Kelly & WILLOW*
- *The Devil Wears Lace – Steven Rodriguez*
- *Bird Set Free – Sia*
- *Dirtier Thoughts – Nation Haven*
- *Champagne & Sunshine – PLVTINUM & Tarro*
- *Breathe – Kansh*
- *Sparks – Coldplay*
- *Past Lives – DJ Agos*

- *The High – Bryce Savage*
- *I Don't Want Wanna Live Forever (Fifty Shades Darker) – ZAYN & Taylor Swift*
- *Lost Boy – Ruth B.*

CONTENT WARNINGS

This book contains references to themes of gun violence, death on page, death from cancer off page, mental illness, PTSD, anxiety attacks, brief discussion of rape and physical violence. Some scenes in this novel may be extremely upsetting, therefore, reader discretion is advised.

Some sexual scenes involve breath play, spanking, praise and breeding kinks. This novel is a complete work of fiction and should not be used as a BDSM resource. Practice safe sex, you naughty vixens!

Prologue   1

One   11

Two   27

Three   35

Four   41

Five   51

Six   59

Seven   67

Eight   71

Nine   83

Ten   93

Eleven   101

Twelve   113

Thirteen   125

Fourteen   139

Fifteen   147

Sixteen   157

Seventeen   171

Eighteen   181

Nineteen   199

Twenty   211

Twenty One   221

Twenty Two   233

Twenty Three   237

Twenty Four   247

Twenty Five   257

Twenty Six   267

Twenty Seven   281

Twenty Eight   293

Twenty Nine   309

Thirty   321

Thirty One   329

Thirty Two   339

Thirty Three   355

Thirty Four   365

Thirty-Five   375

Epilogue   385

More By LB Martin   389

About the Author   391

Mental Health Awareness   393

PROLOGUE

1 year ago...

Stormy

*B*ANG!

The sound reverberates from the walls into my skull. I wake in panic mode, not knowing if I dreamt the noise or not.

Then I hear it. The screams. The yelling. Sounds of scuffling chairs across hardwood floors. Someone calls out to dial 911. In the darkness of the room I stumble to the door, the only light breaking through is coming from behind the closed door. Turning the handle, I can't comprehend what I'm seeing, it feels like I'm looking at an alternate universe. It must be. I can't be in the right place. All sounds fall away as I look at everyone running around. All this motion yet no one seems to go anywhere. I'm hit in the face by the pungent fumes of gun powder. It creeps into my senses as I close my eyes, a sense of doom falling over me like a cape. Opening my eyes. I see him. Bodies crowd the space, but I know it's him.

Whether it's instinct or our connected souls, I can feel him slipping from me.

I make my way to the kitchen and fall to my knees when I see his beautiful face looking back at me. The room fades away and it's just he and I. I grasp his hand, it feel clammy in mine. A tear slips from his eye mixing with the blood splattered across his face. The reality of what's going on in the room surges back to me, I am surrounded by utter pandemonium. His brother is on the phone with the police. His mother is shouting orders to me and everyone around us. Directions on what to do. She's a retired nurse, old habits and all that. I don't move. I can't. I'm glued to the spot—just staring. Confusion clouds my mind as I glance up. What the hell happened here? Why am I holding my dying husband's hand?

He's not dying. I'm just being dramatic, right?

"Storm, please don't worry. I love you, Always," he stammers with just a hint of smile as he looks up at me. The words are hard to make out, the damage to his jaw and cheek making it hard for him to speak

Tears begin to flood down my cheeks hearing those raspy words leave his bloodied mouth. *Can I wake up from this nightmare now? I've had enough. Someone wake me up.*

"Don't you dare be saying goodbye to me. Don't you dare. You promised me. Always. This isn't always," I scream the words at him as I close my eyes. I squeeze his hand harder, willing my life force to make his stronger. This can't be it. We had so many plans. Future plans. Plans that don't involve my husband lying on a cold floor with a gunshot through his neck.

He doesn't respond to my hysteria. I open my eyes only to see the second the life fades from his. Gone in an instant. Seizing his body to mine, I no longer care who or what is happening around us. I pull him closer, clinging to him. I need to feel his body heat against mine. To know he'll be okay. This is just a fucking nightmare, and I'll wake up. I have to wake up.

Someone grabs me from behind, pinning my arms down, they drag me away from his lifeless body. His eyes are still on me, staring through me. He's not really there anymore. I break free from my captor and fight my way back to his side only to be removed more forcibly. The police and EMTs have arrived, but they don't understand that he promised me. He promised always and forever. He vowed it. We vowed together. This isn't forever, it can't be. They don't understand. Someone is holding me back, people in various uniforms try to resuscitate him. I feel the increasing pressure on my arms as fingers dig into me, I know marks will be left in their wake.

They cut his shirt open. It's one I made for him. I see the Flash's face cut to shreds as the shirt is removed. It's fitting really. Gone in a flash. The words ricochet through my mind.

"Clear," someone calls. Blaine's body jolts. They shake their heads in unison after attempting several more times.

I'm stunned into silence. I'm in shock. Or am I asleep? Is this a dream? A nightmare? *Can I fucking wake up now?*

Blaine's hoisted onto a gurney and rolled out of the house. I fight with all my strength to get to him, but I'm kept rooted to the spot. His brother is holding me back. His fingers still digging into my arms.

I look around the room at the disaster before me. Blood stains the floor where he laid. His mother is crying in his father's arms. My sister-in-law is standing there as lifeless as Blaine was. She's not moving a muscle, just staring off into space. Michael, Blaine's brother, loosens his hold on me once the ambulance is gone. I fall to the floor and crawl to the spot where he was. Laying my head down in the cool sticky mess, I see my hands covered in blood. The thought occurs to me, this is the most beautiful but deadly shade of red. I curl into myself, and let sweet oblivion take me into the darkness.

Earlier that day...

"Come with us, Stormy. Don't you want to try out your new Ruger?" Blaine pleads for me to come with him and his family to the shooting range. "It's either that or my mom will take you out shopping," he sing-songs, using the last arrow in his arsenal. He knows I'd hate to go shopping, not because I dislike shopping itself, but the stores she would drag me to aren't my cup of tea.

"Fine." I say aggravatedly. "Let me get dressed. Make sure to pack me a pair of those noise canceling headphones," I leave him to pack up the bags. Stepping into the room we're using for our stay at his parents' house, I cringe at the array of knickknacks in this ultra small room.

I slap on a pair of jeans and a T-shirt, then braid my hair into two sections to frame my face. I decide to clean up a bit, I clean up the thrown clothes and shoes, placing them back in our luggage, then make the bed. I look around and sigh with relief knowing we'll be leaving here tomorrow. I head back to the living room where I see everyone getting ready to head to the range. There are several duffel bags loaded with guns, ammo, headphones, targets. Everything that anyone would need for a fun day.

Blaine, his father, brother, nephew, and I are all going. Everything gets loaded into two cars, and we make our way to our destination. Upon arrival, we set everything up and go through all the different weapons. We have a great time seeing who is the best shot using all the different pistols and rifles we brought. Blaine's always impressed by how well I can shoot a pistol. I beam with pride when he goes around showing everyone my targets.

Once the Florida heat really starts to kick in, we pack the entirety of our equipment up and drive back to Blaine's parents' house. When Blaine and I are alone in the car, I decide to broach the same topic we seem to fight about constantly.

"Thanks for inviting me out here today. It was fun." I begin the conversation as Blaine navigates through traffic.

"Of course. I want you wherever I am. It wouldn't have been as fun had you not come," he replies without taking his eyes off the road, his hand resting on my thigh. Nervous about what I'm going to say next, then just spit it out.

"I was thinking I could take some online courses while we are on tour. That way when it's over I can go to school full-time. I think I found a good university that will work with our hectic schedule. I reached out to them, and they are eager to get me enrolled. What do you think?" I rush out, hands shaking in my lap, knowing we always fight about me going to school. He wants my focus to be one hundred percent on the band, and I want to do something else with my life. We started this band in high school, never dreaming it would go anywhere. I didn't want to become an overnight sensation. I wanted to graduate and go to art school.

Unfortunately, we were picked up by a talent agent at a small show one night, and the rest is history.

"Storm don't start with this again. We signed with the record label. They would want all your attention on the band. Not to mention, that's the only thing *I* want you focused on. As the manager and lead guitarist, I won't permit you to spread yourself to thin. This isn't up for debate. You aren't going to art school. We've all had to sacrifice things for this endeavor. It will pay off. End of discussion."

I take a deep breath, trying to rein in my temper, "First off, how dare you talk to me like I'm just a member of the band. I am your fucking wife. Remember? Or has this instant fame gone to your head making you forgot that tiny detail? Second, I didn't want to be famous, but heaven forbid you consider anything I want out of life. You were so different in high school, Blaine. You actually cared about me and my wants. Now all you care about is Damaged Jacks. Maybe I should just quit, and you can find another lead vocalist," I yell this last part as I cross my arms over my heaving chest. I look at the scenery passing us by as we drive down the road. I have so many thoughts running through my head, I don't think I can voice them all. The most prominent thought is that Blaine has been treating me more and more like property rather than a wife lately.

Blaine slams his hand into the steering wheel and growls, "Of course, I know you're my wife dammit. Don't even start with that shit. Right now, the band comes first. Let's get through this tour. Then we'll see where we stand with you going to art school. And that's all I'm going to say about it." He turns onto the road where the house is located. I thought we were done talking, but Blaine has one more thing to add, "We aren't continuing this conversation inside. I don't want their opinions on the matter. How about you head to the room to read a book while we take care of cleaning the guns. We planned on sitting around the table and making a night of it." He opens his door and slams it hard before stomping into the house.

I take a few moments to catch my breath, but once I emerge from the car, only Sean, Blaine's nephew, is outside grabbing some of the bags. I nod my head to him and walk into the house. I hear the men setting everything up, I quickly turn right, heading straight to our bedroom to get cleaned up.

After getting cleaned up, I step out of the room, I see that dinner is ready. I would normally sit down to eat with the family, especially since it's our last night here, but I'm not in the mood to play the happy wife. I make myself a plate and head back to the room, excusing myself with a migraine. Tonight's the last night we'll be staying here, tomorrow we start the world tour.

I sit on the bed, thinking about what my life was like before all this world tour craziness. Blaine and I became best friends in middle school. We bonded over our love of music and art, growing closer and closer until our friendship turned romantic. We spent a lot of time together and it made sense for us to date as well. There wasn't ever a particular spark between us. More like comfort.

We started the band back in high school and named it Damaged Jacks. Jacks after Blaine's last name. It was just for fun, a way to pass the time until we graduated. In the beginning, I would sing along to Blaine's guitar. We eventually added more musicians; a drummer, bass guitarist, and a keyboardist. We practiced in different garages throughout our high school years, then we started playing our songs in small pubs and bars in the area. One night we were playing our regular set and a talent agent happened to be in the audience. He offered us a chance to play for his record label and before we knew it, our songs were being played on the radio. We spent months in a recording studio putting together our first album. Once that was complete, there was a whirlwind of local shows, interviews and ultimately planning a tour.

We were so excited by the radio plays, we then spent months in the recording studio. With the tour right around the corner, we decided to spend the week before we leave with his parents. They're our only family here and we knew we wouldn't see them for a while. My parents had passed a few years back in a car accident. As they were leaving my graduation a drunk driver crossed over into their lane. They all died on impact including the drunk driver.

It was the worst day of my life. But I didn't get time to grieve. The band always came first, then Blaine decided we should get married. That way I would have a family since I was alone now. At the time, it seemed like the right thing to do. We rushed the wedding and purchased a place to live within weeks. It was more of a marriage of convenience, but I went along with it, I know Blaine was only trying to do what was best for me. I'm not sure it was the right decision, though. I love him with my whole heart, but it's a different kind of love. We're more best friends and roommates than lovers.

After the band got signed to a record label, Blaine changed. He wasn't the same carefree boy I once knew. He became controlling and more concerned about the band than me. Blaine welcomed the spotlight that was thrown at us, while I tried to fade into the darkness. I'm not looking forward to this tour like the rest of the band. Sure, being famous has its perks, but the added stress doesn't make it worth it. Of course, I can't talk about any of this with Blaine, he has a way of changing our discussions in favor of himself. I sigh as I lie on the bed, looking up at the ceiling. We leave tomorrow so I need to face the facts and put on a smile for the world to see.

The first stop on our tour is going to be New York City. Blaine and I have always wanted to go there together. I am excited to see the city. We'll have a couple days of sightseeing before getting down to business.

Remembering my dirty plate from dinner, I stand from the bed, stretching to get the kinks out of my back before grabbing it and heading down to return it to the kitchen. I tell the men good night and give Blaine a kiss on the top of his head. They have everything set up to dismantle and clean the guns we used so they will be ready for the next time. When I get back to the room, I finish packing our things, leaving out a change of clothes for tomorrow. Once I'm satisfied everything is where it needs to be, I climb into bed. Sleep comes easy with the stressful, long day I had. Never in my life could I imagine that the next time I woke I'd be witnessing the worst thing I'd ever seen, my husband dying on the kitchen floor.

ONE

Stormy

"**M**oving sucks ass," I mutter under my breath as I pile another huge box from the moving van onto the street. My mind wanders as I lift boxes, it's been one hell of a year. I went into a state of shock after witnessing Blaine's death which forced me into an extensive therapy program that made me deal with my parents' and husband's death. The therapist was able to get me out of my commitment to the band by stating I was mentally unstable, which if course was true. There was no way I would have been able to go on tour with a band I started with my late husband. Some days I didn't think I'd be able to go on at all, much less sing in front of a crowd. I can't deny I miss the adrenaline rush, though, I know in my heart I could never go back to it I don't think I'll ever sing again. Even listening to the radio is painful. Music just doesn't illicit the same kind of euphoric emotions it once did.

After completing the therapy program, I took off. I knew I wanted to come to New York. That was always in the cards. Plus, I wanted to attend art school and they have one of the best ones in the country. With no real ties to Florida, I sold our house, packed up most of my belongings, and set off for the Big Apple. Fortunately, I was able to find a roommate through the university's website since I don't know anyone in the city. I emailed her once. So, who knows what I'm walking in to.

"Hey there," a voice booms behind me causing me to drop my current box on the sidewalk, I turn to put a face to the voice. I'm momentarily at a loss for words. This woman's head looks like a fucking Picasso painting. Well, more specifically, her hair. I've never seen so many unnatural colors on one head in my life. "I'm Lana. You must be Stormy. I'm so happy to finally meet you." She runs over and wraps her arms around me like a boa constrictor. *Fuck my life, she's a hugger.* Ever since the night my life stopped, I like to keep to myself, and I definitely don't hug people. Especially ones I don't know.

"Heh, yep that's me. Nice to meet you." I awkwardly manage to squeak out before she releases me. I feel like I might have made a mistake, this is not going to go well. I take a moment to try to catch my breath and move my gaze down to her clothes which are as bright as her head. I don't think we could be any more different if we tried.

"I've been just dying for you to get here. I know I already said it but I'm just so excited to finally put a face to the name. Here let me help you with these!" She grabs the box out of my hand, while continuing to talk a mile a minute. "Your parents didn't come to help you move in?" Lana asks as she heaves a large box around in her arms, trying to get a more comfortable grip.

"They couldn't make it. They're dead, so, you know, it's just me," I reply without looking. I've finally rendered her speechless. A feat I didn't think possible.

"Oh my God, I am so, so sorry. I didn't know. That's so terrible. Gah, I can be so insensitive. I shouldn't have even asked. Oh, of course they'd be here if they could. Please forgive me. I'm so sorry, Stormy. I didn't want our first meeting to be like this. I want us to be the best of friends, then I go and put my foot in my mouth," Lana rushes out, dropping my box to the ground and coming back over to me for what I suspect would be another hug. I hold the box for dear life. I notice she looks at me like she wants to cry, which might be worse than a hug.

"Look, it's not a big deal. Don't beat yourself up about it," I see tears in her eyes as I say this. *Fuck, I'm not prepared for this kind of emotion.* I start second guessing my choices, I should have tried to get a place without a roommate, but I didn't want to spend more of the inheritance my parents left me or the life insurance I got from Blaine's death on housing. I'm already paying for school and this apartment and everything else, I'll need to get a job soon so that I never have to worry about money. I hear Lana take a deep breath and it brings me back to the present.

"Still, I'm very sorry for your loss. I won't bring it up again," she says in a much more reserved tone. "Let's get these boxes in before it starts to rain." Thankfully, Lana doesn't ask any questions just picks up the box she had dropped, and heads inside. I follow along behind her, wishing the whole packing and unpacking along with the introduction part was already over. I'm tired of moving and I'm only twenty-two years old. How many more times am I going to have to do this? I think to myself, maybe next time I'll hire movers. This shit is for the birds.

Once all my belongings are inside, Lana gives me a tour of my new apartment. It's bigger than I thought it would be and I'm so thankful for that. I like my own space and being crammed in with this ball of energy isn't my idea of a good time.

"This is our bathroom. We have this shower and a nice clawfoot tub. Don't you love those?" I nod my head as she goes on pointing out things I can already see with my own eyes. I continue to acknowledge her with a nod while I look around for myself.

The bathroom is nice and big. There are two sinks, so we won't have to share. There seems to be adequate cabinet and drawer space as well, so we won't have crap out all over the counters. I want to keep things nice and tidy, and I truly hope that Lana isn't a slob. It might just send me over the edge if she is.

Heading out of the bathroom, she takes me back to the living room that we had passed through when we brought my boxes in. I didn't get a chance to look around because we were trying to beat the rain. Luckily for us, this apartment came partially furnished. Neither of us had to bring any large furniture, which is great. I can imagine myself and Lana trying to bring in a mattress or couch. Even with the help of the elevator, it would have been disastrous.

The living room is nice and spacious with a gray L-shaped couch facing a large bank of floor-to-ceiling windows. This might be my favorite part of the apartment; I think especially since being on the tenth floor gives us that advantage. Once I step back from the windows, I see there are floor lamps on either side of the couch and a modern black coffee table sitting on a white shag rug that looks softer than silk. There isn't anything on the walls with the exception of one painting off to the side. I move closer to get a better look. I can tell instantly that this is an original. I search the bottom to find the signature and am taken aback when I see Lana's initials on it. I figured it came with the apartment, but she hung this herself. I am more intrigued by this woman now. If she can paint something like this, she has depth further than her crazy exterior.

"Oh, we can take that down if you want. I was just trying to get some color on these walls." Lana comes up beside me reaching to take the painting down while I am still devouring this work of art. I can't believe something this deep came out of this thin, crazy outgoing girl next to me.

I put my hands on her to stop her, "I like this here. I don't want to take it down," I promise. I don't feel like going into detail about how much I love it. Perhaps when we get to know each other better. She pulls me along to the kitchen, showing me all the appliances and where everything is. It's not as though I can see it with my own eyes.

She turns and shrugs, "So, that's basically it. I know you probably want to unpack and get yourself situated. I was thinking we could order in tonight and hangout in the living room. You know, to get to know each other if you want? It'll be my treat!" she exclaims. I would rather be alone. It's been a long day, and I really don't care to tell my life story to a stranger, but she won't be a stranger long. We'll be living together for the foreseeable future. I think she can tell I'm pondering a response because she's quick to start talking again., "It will be fun. Please," she pleads.

"Sure," I reply faking a smile just as she claps her hands together smiling like I just brought her a new puppy.

"This will be great. Do you like Chinese? That's what I was thinking about getting us," she adds talking a mile a minute.

"Yeah, that's fine. Just let me know when," I respond as I start walking to my room. She stops me before I get too far.

"Before I forget, what's your number? I can text you when I'm about to order. Plus, we need each other's numbers anyway, so we can keep in touch during the day." Lana chuckles to herself as she gets her phone out, and I contemplate giving her a fake number for the time being. I decide against it but only because I think she would cry if I did. I don't want that to happen again. Besides, she would probably barge through my door to let me know the number was wrong. She finally leaves me in peace to unpack. I am thankful for the reprieve from all the talking that girl can do. I hope she's starting to realize I'm not as bubbly a person as she is. At least, not anymore. Not since the accidents that took the people I loved from me. I doubt I could ever be happy like that again. I'm basically on meds to numb the pain of my life.

I sit down on my unmade queen-sized bed and look at all the boxes surrounding me. An overwhelming sensation washes over me and I feel like a fish out of water. Maybe I shouldn't have made such a huge move from Florida to New York. Doing this all alone is starting to freak me out. I shake my head and smash those thoughts down. Mustering the strength to get up, I start unpacking. As I stand to shake the cobwebs from my brain my phone chimes several times. I reach into my bag to retrieve it.

Unknown:

> This is Lana. Just thought you needed mine as well.

Unknown:

> I am so excited to have you here.

Unknown:

> What do you want me to order you from the Chinese place down the street?

Fuck! It's already starting. I knew I should have given her a fake number. I truly hope she grows on me because right now I'm ready to throw all my boxes back in the moving van and find another place to live. Or maybe kick her out because I am quite fond of this apartment already. I smile to myself thinking about what she would do if I asked her to move out. After changing her name in my phone, I text her back.

Stormy:

> Almond chicken with white rice and no egg roll.

Picasso:

> You don't want fried rice or an egg roll? Are you crazy?

Oh, she doesn't want to open that can of worms. She doesn't need to know my level of crazy yet.

Stormy:

> Allergic to eggs.

Picasso:

What? How do you live?

Picasso:

I'm sorry again. That was insensitive of me.

I need to wrap this conversation up or I think we'll sit here and text back and forth all night even though we're in the same fucking apartment.

Stormy:

I never really liked eggs to begin with. Then I had a bad reaction once and found out I was allergic to them. No big deal. Going to unpack now.

Just when I think I've finally shut her up, another message comes through. I put my phone down without reading it because I am running out of energy with her. I open the closest box to me and begin to unpack. The room has beautiful built-in bookshelves, which I love. All my smutty books are going to look perfect in them. Romance novels are my escape from this world, and I have tons of them. I empty one box, placing each book on the shelves, then take a step back to admire my work. My phone chimes again, and I feel guilty I didn't check her last message. I don't want her to think I'm a bitch, I prefer her find that out as fact if needed. After breaking down the empty box, I sigh and check her latest messages.

Picasso:

Let me know if you need help.

Picasso:

> I know moving can be stressful. I am here if you need me.

One simple sentence but it's rendered me speechless. This girl doesn't know anything about me, and I haven't exactly been welcoming. But she would still come in here and help me unpack. Maybe I judged her too quickly. I mean, physically she is the total opposite of me. Think Enid versus Wednesday Addams. The only exception is that I bleached my black hair, then dyed it silver. It's naturally black and people were able to recognize me from the band. I didn't want that anymore. I wanted to be my own person when I came to New York, so I changed it. It's not like Superman. If people look closely enough, they can still see me. I mean my face used to be plastered all over the media, but changing my hair gave me a sense of peace. They still play our version of songs on the radio. Another reason why I don't listen to music. I don't know what I would do if I were to hear one of our songs right now. The new band recorded an album and went on tour, but the radio still plays the ones I'm in. I tear my mind away from those thoughts as I look at the rest of the boxes I have left to unpack. I decide to text Lana back.

Stormy:

> I'm starving. Let's go ahead and order.

Picasso:

> Yes! Meet me in the living room!

Here we go. I wonder how much she should know about my past. There is so much I could tell her, I don't really know what

I should say. I decide to gloss over the band stuff and tell her everything else. I pull my long hair into a messy bun and make my way to the living room.

After we finish the delicious Chinese dinner, I felt like I had gotten to know Lana a lot better. I've got to say, I liked her more now than I did earlier. She's very outgoing and chipper, but she isn't fake about it. She truly is a happy person and I find myself wishing I could be as carefree as she.

"You know, you look so familiar to me," Lana remarks, as I begin cleaning up our empty containers. I knew something like this would come up eventually but not this soon. How could changing my hair be enough for people not to recognize me? I don't know whether to laugh or cry. I could go ahead and get it out there, so she doesn't find out from someone else. But I just want to be Stormy for a little bit longer. Just plain Stormy that came to New York to attend art school. I take the trash to the kitchen and return hoping she doesn't keep pressing the issue.

"You're probably going to laugh, but you look like the lead singer from Damaged Jacks. Well, actually, the old lead singer. Please tell me you know who that band is. They're the best; they were even better when she was with them. I heard she went to rehab after the lead guitarist was killed. I don't think that was the case though, but who knows, right? I mean the tabloids will tell us anything." Lana finishes her spiel and finally takes a breath. The air leaves my lungs, and for a moment I don't think I can do this. I don't think I can tell her. I stand still in shock, wanting to run but having nowhere to hide. My eyes widen in fear and all I want to do is run back to the safety of my room.

"Is everything okay? Did I say something wrong?" She questions as I walk around the sectional and take my seat on the couch. I look up at the ceiling while taking a large gulp of wine. When my glass is empty, I place it on the table, I try not to look at Lana because of the tears filling my eyes.

"I-I haven't heard of them. I don't really listen to the radio all that much." A tear rolls down my cheek. I try to hide the evidence, but Lana sees me wipe it away. As I jump up from the couch and make my way to my bedroom, Lana is there grasping my arm and turning me to face her.

"Holy shit. It can't be. I knew you looked familiar, but never in a million years would I think it was true. It is, isn't it? I'm sorry for bringing it up. I'm just on a roll with sticking my foot in my mouth around you. Are you okay? Do you want to talk about it?" She fires off the questions quickly.

I shake my head pleadingly, "No, I don't really want to talk about it. Lana, please let me go," I feel a panic attack coming on. I have only been here a few hours and already someone knows who I am. I knew I wouldn't be able to pull this off.

"I would never tell anyone, you know? You can trust me, Stormy. I haven't always had the easiest life either, so I can somewhat imagine the pain you're going through. If you need anything at all, I'll be here," she says trying to console me. She releases her grasp on me, and I sigh in relief.

"Lana, the media doesn't know where I am. Since I never used my real name with the band, I'm able to use it now. But I can't let them find me. I can't go back into the spotlight with everything that I went through, Lana. I'm sure you read or saw videos about how Blaine died. Well, I was there that night. It was horrible and everything you can imagine from a nightmare. The death was ruled an accidental gunshot wound to the head. My nephew was the one that took the shot, but he did it unknowingly. He didn't know the gun was loaded and he was playing with it. My therapist was able to get me out of the band based on my mental state." I am full on crying now. Lana wraps her arms around me. This time I don't cringe but welcome the embrace.

"Please, please don't tell anyone. I left that part of my life back in Florida. I'm here to start over. They can't find me. They just can't." I slide to the floor and pull my knees up to my chest. Rocking back and forth because I can no longer hold it in. I've been cut open and my past is bleeding out onto the floor around me. A part of me died that night with Blaine. I don't think she can ever be resuscitated.

Lana falls to her knees beside me with a worried expression on her face. "Is there something I can do for you? Do you need anything else?" she asks as she rubs circles over my back. The sensation is oddly comforting and brings me back to the present.

"C-can you go get my purse? I have some medicine in there I can take." I'm barely able to murmur to her, but fortunately she hears me. She takes off like a shot, leaving me in the middle of the hall, I take a moment to do the breathing exercises my therapist taught me. It's hard when you're right in the middle of an episode but sometimes I'm able to calm myself without having to always rely on medication to get me through. I admit that I use my medicine as a crutch. It melts away the panic, so I don't have to.

Lana comes sprinting back with my purse. She gives it over and with shaking hands, I search through the bag for my medicine bottle. I grasp it and pull the container out into my hand. I try but fail to open it and Lana gently takes it from my shaking fingers. She opens it but not before I see her look at the label. Anger radiates through me at her intrusion. I snatch the bottle back, grabbing a tablet and swallowing it without any water. I close the bottle and shove it away deep inside my purse.

"It's a prescription. It's not illegal. I don't know what you're thinking, but plenty of people suffer from anxiety, Lana. Maybe I should just find another place to live," I rant breathlessly. I get mean and angry when I'm in the middle of a panic attack. Sometimes I just rock back and forth crying, but other times I can't help but spew filth that I immediately regret and never apologize for.

"Whoa, slow down. I'm not judging you if that's what you think. I'm sorry I looked at the label. That wasn't any of my business. I'm just worried about you," she responds, holding up her hands in defense.

"Well, there's no reason to be. I'll be f-fine in a minute." I'm already tired from the move and the anxiety takes a lot of energy from my body as well. I just want to crawl into bed and sleep, forgetting this ever happened.

"I don't want to upset you further, but can you take that medicine with wine?" Lana questions.

"I said I'll be fine. I just need to get some sleep," I lie. I'm not fine, but it's an untruth I'm used to telling by now. I'm broken, but will tell you I'm fine. I'm hurting, but I don't want to break down, letting people see what's really going on inside me. I hate that I let her see a crack in my armor. I try to stand up but flop back down on my ass. Lana stands, pulling me to my feet. She quietly walks me to my room, I feel like I should apologize for the way I behaved but I don't have the energy or the words to tell her. As she opens my door, I wince at the sight of my unmade bed. I think I would pay someone right now to go through my boxes and find my sheets because I am so tired. I think Lana reads my mind because she starts going through my boxes until she finds the one that says, "Bedroom linens." She begins making the bed and I let her. I don't know how long it's been since someone took care of me but it's nice. Once she finishes up, I fall face first into the pillows and am asleep before she can even turn off the bedside lamp.

I wake to the smell of coffee brewing. The bed feels unfamiliar, and for a moment I don't remember where I am. Then the events of last night come crashing into my mind. I open my eyes to very bright sunlight streaming through the windows. Unfortunately, there are no drapes and I did not have time to put any up. I groan at the pain in my head and throw my arm over my eyes. Just as I roll over to try and go back to sleep, there's a knock on my door. I know it's Lana, and I don't want to face her in the light of day. Who knows what she thinks about me. She probably wants me out of here ASAP. That would probably be my first reaction instead of what I said to her last night.

"Come in," I murmur. All I see is bright colors as she opens my door. Once my eyes adjust to the intensity of light in the room, I can see the lively-eyed Lana walking in with two mugs. From the smell of it, they are both filled with coffee.

"I thought you could use some coffee. I didn't know how you take it though." She hands me the mug and there's no malice in her voice, only concern. That can't be right. No one has shown me this much kindness in years, and I don't deserve it after the way I behaved.

"Black is fine. Thank you. You didn't have to, especially after the way I acted last night. I understand completely if you want me out of your hair," I respond taking a sip of the steaming coffee.

"Stormy, we all have bad days. I don't fault you at all for last night. I can see that you're going through a lot, hopefully you'll let me in so we can help each other. I don't want another new roommate. I believe we can make this work. But we must be open with each other. That means me as well, which is hard for me," she explains, sitting on the edge of my bed.

"Thank you for understanding. I knew I needed to tell you the truth. It actually feels like a relief that someone knows. I hate having to be in hiding. But after everything, the media never got the exclusive interview they wanted." I take another sip of the coffee and savor the taste. "You know, I was married to Blaine. Not many people know that. So, I not only lost my husband that day but my best friend and bandmate. I just couldn't handle it. I only checked into rehab to get the extensive therapy I needed. I wasn't on drugs or anything. A lot of people think that, and I've never corrected them." I hesitate for a moment. "I'm sorry if I am bringing you

25

down," I murmur as I wipe my tears on the long sleeve under shirt I have on.

"Oh hush. We're getting to know each other and that means the down and dirty, nitty gritty shit that makes us who we are," Lana explains, and I can't help but crack a small smile. Picasso is growing on me.

"Thank you. I never open up like this to anyone, but I feel like I can trust you, Lana," I utter softly.

"You definitely can. So, onto a happier topic. You mentioned last night that you needed to find a job. I work for a catering company and it's easy money. We actually have a gig this weekend if you're interested. My boss is always looking for more servers. I can talk to her if you want me to."

"That would be great. I do have waitressing experience, so that should be a plus. Let me know what she says. I think I'm going to get some more sleep. I'm exhausted from yesterday." Last night took a lot out of me. Well, all day yesterday took a lot out of me, actually. Driving the moving van from Florida to New York is no joke. I stopped for the night half-way but it was still exhausting.

"I'll text her later and let you know. Thank you for trusting me enough to tell me who you really are. It means a lot." Lana gives me a hug. Then she stands and walks out of my room, closing the door behind her.

I place the mug on my nightstand, cover my face with the blanket to block out the sun, and go back to sleep feeling much more peaceful than I did last night.

TWO

Sebastian

"Elijah, I said I needed last quarter's sales records. Not the guest list to the investor fundraiser for this weekend," I state to my brother's frazzled executive assistant. He's been running around this office like a chicken with his damn head cut off since Miles has been on his honeymoon in Ireland. Actually, the whole office has been a shit show since Miles left. I truly don't understand how he juggled so many things at once. As the Chief Operating Officer, or COO, my area of expertise is finance, facts, numbers, a beginning, and an end to the day. I don't typically see workdays like these, where things are up for discussion. Things like deciding what wine to serve at fundraiser, I don't give a fuck about that kind of stuff. Miles does that. But here I am trying to do my job and Miles' at the same time, pulling fucking twelve-hour shifts in the process. I have a month of this shit to deal with. On top of that my assistant has gone out on maternity leave, leaving me to fend for myself. She was supposed to line up someone else in her place, but Tracy went into labor before she expected to. So, I was left with Elijah. Poor Elijah looks like he might fall over at any second. He isn't used to me and my ways of working. I think my brother has been a bit lax with the dude, to be honest, because he can't handle anything I throw at him. It just piles up on his desk. Then he gives it back to me along with more work that he's somehow added to the mess along the way. There's got to be a better solution than this. Picking up the phone, I dial Human Resources. Maybe they have someone they can send up here to be my other assistant.

"H.R. This is Mary speaking, how may I help you today?"

"Mary, are you having a lovely day?" I ask, my question dripping with sweetness.

"What do you want now, Sebastian?" Mary snaps. She knows me all too well.

"Well, since you asked so nicely, I was wondering if we have anyone that can come fill the role of my assistant until Tracy returns?" I reply with a grin I'm sure she can hear through the phone. Mary has been here since my father was CEO and knows all about the shenanigans Miles and I used to pull. I guess you could call her our work mother. She tries her best to keep me in line, but that's too hard a task for most.

"Do you think we have extra people just twiddling their fingers waiting for you to call and need someone? Of course, we don't. I'll have to put out an ad this afternoon and hopefully get someone in here by Monday. Think you and Elijah can hold it down until then? I need to get back to all the work that's accumulated since your brother left!" she exclaims, and I hear her exasperation over the phone.

"Thank you, Mary. What would I do without you? Oh, and will you make sure they're competent? I don't have time to hold someone's hand while they learn the ropes," I request.

"Do you think I would get someone that couldn't handle you? We need a lion tamer in here," she retorts with a chuckle.

"I'm not that bad, Mary. Give me some credit," I plead.

"Yeah, yeah. I suppose. I'll get this ad together and send it to you for approval before I post it," she states.

"Thank you, Mary. You're the best!" I express myself in the sweetest voice I can muster, before I hang up the phone.

With that taken care of, I breathe a sigh of relief. Hopefully, things will turn around here soon. I loathe having to ask someone else for help, but the truth is, without Miles here things have turned to shit. Leaning back in my chair with my hands behind my head, I gaze out of the floor-to-ceiling windows in my office. Being on the twentieth floor I get a good glimpse of the horizon and the setting sun. I've worked through another lunch. No wonder I am feeling especially hangry towards Elijah today. I make a mental note to give the guy some extra vacation days when Miles returns.

Turning back around to my desk, I see all the details about the fundraiser that *still* need to be approved. Sighing, I pick up the phone and make all the necessary arrangements. Once everything is settled, I close my laptop down and pack up my things for the evening. I can't stay here all night again. My mother used to always tell me, "It'll all get done. No need to stress about it." And that's exactly what I have been doing, stressing! I going to work myself to death at this rate. I get up from the desk and go to the walk-in closet that I had installed when we bought this building. Removing my suit, I put on the clothes I wore here this morning: jeans and a t-shirt. Grabbing my leather jacket, I leave my office and find a frazzled Elijah at his desk, scribbling notes at an unnatural pace.

"Slow down there, Elijah. Your hand is going to break off." Having not heard me open my door, he jumps at my booming voice.

"I'm just trying to get this all done, sir," he responds.

"Let's get out of here. This work will still be here tomorrow waiting for us. I don't want to spend another long night here," I reply.

"Are you sure, sir?" he questions.

"Positive. Pack your stuff and get out of here. I'll see you tomorrow, bright and early," I remark.

As I walk toward the bank of elevators, I pull out my phone and order takeout. I can pick it up on my way home, saving me the time of having to fix something when I get there. In the elevator, I press the garage button. I rode my bike in today so no need to wait for a car. Normally, I have Nicolas or Thomas, our family chauffeurs give me a ride, but today I wanted to feel the open road at my fingertips. I don't always get a chance to ride, so I took advantage of the weather and hopped on.

I step into the garage, I notice most of our employees have cleared out, which is to be expected. My motorcycle is one of the only vehicles left down here. It's parked close to the doors, that's a perk of being a boss. As I walk towards my black Ducati Diavel, adrenaline begins coursing through my body. I love to ride, to feel the air rush past me as I fly through the streets of New York City. Throwing on my leather jacket, I unclasp my helmet from the back of the bike. Making sure the Bluetooth in my helmet is connected, I pocket my phone. As I sling my leg over the bike I start the engine, feeling the purr come to life under my body. Excitement flows through me as I kick the bike into gear and race out the gates of Knight Publishing Company. I set off to pick up dinner and then home, where I hope to have a relaxing evening.

Stormy

My eyes spring open and my heart feels as though it's beating out of my chest. I wake to a cold sweat and for just a moment, I remember the horrible dream I was having. It was the night Blaine died in my arms. I rub my hands down my face and then back up to my eyes where tears had begun to emerge. Throwing the covers off my heated body, I swing my legs over the bed and sit up hoping this will wake me up further to erase the dream and the memories. I check my watch and see I slept all day. I haven't done that in a long time. I needed it though. I was emotionally and physically drained from the move and the panic attack. I look at all the boxes stacked in my room and wish they were already empty. I fucking hate moving. I hate having to unpack in a new place and having to decide where I want to put everything. I sigh to myself and stand. I walk over to the boxes and search for the one marked "clothes". Pulling out something to wear, I then go in search of my toiletries. A shower would be magical right now. Thankfully, I am neurotic about labeling, or I wouldn't be able to find anything in all these boxes.

Grabbing everything I need, I open my door and peer out. Not that I'm trying to sneak around but I'd rather shower and get myself together before the colorful Lana makes an appearance. I don't see or hear her so I walk down the hallway to the bathroom, finding it empty. Sighing in relief, I walk in and lock the door behind me. As I place my clothes on the counter I see myself in the mirror and notice the dark circles under my eyes. Even with all the sleep in the world, I don't think I'll ever get rid of those. They've been my constant companion since Blaine passed away. I hate the reflection staring back at me. Turning away from the mirror, I start the shower and let the steam fill the room before I step in and wash all my sadness away.

Once out, I wipe the steam off the mirror and am thankful to see some of the color has returned to my cheeks. I brush my teeth and then my hair. Not feeling like drying it, I grab my dirty laundry and unlock the door. As it opens, I jump back when I see Picasso right in front of me. She's in a new set of colorful clothes with paint spattered all over them.

"I didn't mean to startle you. I was just about to knock when the door opened," she admits.

"No worries, I didn't see you earlier, so I figured you had gone out," I reply with a small shake in my voice. In all honesty, she scared the shit out of me.

"Nope. I wanted to be here when you got up in case you needed anything. I did go grocery shopping after coffee, but I figured you would sleep through that. So, how are you feeling?" she inquires.

"Better. The shower definitely helped. Let me go put these clothes up and I'll come back out," I reply.

"Okay," Lana responds as she turns around and walks towards the living room.

I throw my clothes in the hamper in my room and slip on my Chuck's. Grabbing my phone, I take one last look at the looming boxes and close my door. As I head toward the living room, I hear the TV going. Again, I take in the nice open space. I think this will be my second favorite room once mine is finished. Lana peaks up from the couch as she sees me approaching.

"Hey girl. I was thinking that we could go out tonight and get some dinner. My treat!" she exclaims as she places her phone down on the couch.

"I'm not letting you pay twice in a row. It'll be my treat tonight. Let me grab my bag," I retreat to my room, grabbing my purse and making sure my anxiety meds are still in there. Once I confirm, I sling the purse across my shoulders and make my way back out to Lana. My first night out and about in New York City. This should be interesting.

"By the way, I spoke to my catering boss and she's more than happy to bring you on board, starting with this big fundraiser this weekend. We can go by and get your uniform tomorrow," Lana mentions as we head out the door of our apartment.

"Thank you for setting that up. I hope waitressing is like riding a bike," I reply. I admit that I'm a little nervous because it's been a couple years since I've done it. But I need to get my life started here and what better way than to have a job lined up. The thought gives me butterflies. Maybe I really can do this. Maybe I can be the Stormy Brooks I want to be. "So, where are we heading tonight?"

I question as we get into the elevator and make our way down to the street.

"There is a cool bar up the street with awesome food. Mostly younger crowds hang out there because of the artsy atmosphere," Lana answers. "We can walk there from here. That way we won't have to Uber back after we've had a few." I nod in agreement as we set off down the street. The cool air on my face feels nice and fresh after spending the whole day in the apartment. I take a deep breath and follow Lana to our destination.

THREE

Sebastian

I t's already fucking Saturday and the fundraiser begins in less than four hours. Shit is hitting the fan all over the place. My phone begins ringing again as it has been all morning, look down at the caller ID and see Miles' face smiling up at me. "Fuck!" I mutter to myself as I scrub my hand over my eyes. I slide my thumb across the screen to answer his Facetime.

"Hey bro, aren't you supposed to be honeymooning?" I question before he can ask me how things are going here.

"We are. We just got to Dublin and Lizzie is ecstatic. How's everything back home?" Miles asks before I can comment on Dublin. He's calling to check up on me.

Of course, he is.

"Fucking fantastic. Ya know, we should throw these parties all the time. They aren't stressful at all," I say sarcastically.

Miles laughs, "I'm sure you have everything under control. How's Elijah managing?"

"I don't think he's slept since you guys left. He jumps every time I come near him. It's starting to give me a complex. I'm not trying to be a dick, but he seems to think I'm the devil himself," I roll my eyes at the phone and Miles just chuckles at the shit I am going through.

"He's used to me. I don't have the temper that you have, well, unless provoked. Plus, you have the tattooed bad boy vibe going on. He isn't used to you. Anyways, just wanted to make sure everything is ready for tonight. I don't have to remind you that this is an important event for the company. Since I'm not there, you are the leader of KPC. Please act like it. Marcy will be there just in case something gets out of control," He goes on and on.

"Thanks for the vote of confidence, big bro," I reply dryly.

"I do believe in you. I wouldn't have left if I didn't think you could handle it. So, quit your little pity party and get shit done. You're a Knight. You got this. I took extra precautions with having our public relations rep there with you." He chuckles as he says this.

"Well thanks for believing in me," I murmur darkly. "Listen, I've missed like ten calls since we have been talking. Tell Lizzie hi for me."

"Alright, alright. Call me if you need me. Love you, Seb," he replies.

"Yeah, yeah, love you too bro." I end the call and throw the phone on my bed. I'm not looking back at that shit until I do some cardio. I need to get some of this stress under control. Grabbing some clothes, I walk down the stairs to my exercise room. I jump on the treadmill and put my Earpods in, cranking up the volume. I speed the machine until I'm at a full run. My playlist signals to me when I need to speed up or slow down, I made it with the treadmill in mind and it keeps my pace well. I run through the playlist for thirty minutes and then move on to the slower cool down tracks at the end. Jumping off the machine, I grab my towel and wipe the sweat from my face and neck. The workout might've helped my stress a little bit, but it skyrockets back to the top when I get back to see my phone has thirty missed calls. Most of them are from Elijah. He's freaking out about the investor fundraiser tonight. I'm definitely not the one to comfort him. I'm more of a get it done and move on type of person. I don't dwell on the things that I can't change. Elijah on the other hand, is a perfectionist. He wants everything run by me and approved by me though. That isn't necessarily a bad thing, but I want him to believe in himself and not need me to hold his hand every step of the way. He needs to take his own initiative and trust his gut.

As I stare down at the calls, I'm reminded why I hate these stupid parties in the first place. Miles is the one that deals with this shit normally, not me. I don't want to be the one that arranges party decorations, or caterers to use, or anything else. Tell me where and when I need to show up, and that's what I'll do.

If only Mary would've gotten me an assistant already, I wouldn't have to deal with this shit. Hopefully on Monday I'll have a new person on my team and Elijah can take a breather.

I toss my phone back on the comforter and walk into my en suite bathroom. The lights instantly turn on as I step inside, a feature I wanted throughout my penthouse. I like hands-free technology. I take a moment and sync up my Bluetooth speak to my phone a miscellaneous playlist begins blaring through my speakers as I jump in the shower. The showerheads come to life at the perfect temperature I've set them to. It's amazing what money can buy.

37

Soaping up my body, I think about the night ahead. My brother and I normally don't bring dates to these shindigs, but I hope there's someone there that I can take home, it's been a long and stressful week and I could use the release. I rinse my body and step out of the shower, as the motion censored showerheads cut off.

Grabbing a towel, I run it across my hair several times and then wrap it around my waist. The heat in the bathroom steamed up the mirrors, so I have to wipe my hand over one to see what I'm doing as I shave my face. The past week I've been sporting a short beard, but that ends tonight. Once I'm done, I dry off my face, clean the sink, and brush my teeth.

Returning to my room, I step into my closet and pull out tonight's tux and hang it on the door. Before I can even think of getting dressed, I need a drink. Having a small wet bar in the corner of my room has its advantages. I head that way and pour myself two fingers of whiskey which I down in one gulp. The burn is one that I've come to love. I haven't always been a whiskey fan, but it was our father's drink of choice and he passed that love down to his sons. I pour another and walk back to my closet, placing my glass down on my dresser. I check myself in the mirror, I'm not going to deny that my time in the gym pays off. I admire the tattoos on my chest and arms, making a mental note to call and make an appointment for another. I just can't get enough of them. Ink is addictive, but also meaningful. I don't get tattoos just to get them. They all represent something. Over my heart is the Knight family crest and under is my father's name. That's just one of the many.

I stop my perusal and begin getting dressed. Throwing the towel into the bin, I pull on a pair of black briefs. I'm about to put on my pants when my phone rings again. *Fuck. If I make it through*

38

the night without throwing my phone into the Hudson, it's going to be a miracle.

"Sebastian Knight speaking," I answer.

"Yes sir, this is David with the Riverfront venue. We have you booked for this evening's festivities. I'm just calling to let you know that the caterers have arrived, and the decorators just left. Everything is under control, sir," the owner of the venue replies.

"Thank you, David, for seeing to that. I will be arriving when the guests do. Please make sure the caterers know the proper protocol for not conversing with the guests," I state, as I press the phone between my ear and shoulder, while I continue to dress.

"Yes, sir. The staff is up to date with all the information and protocols. I just had a meeting with them," David supplies.

"Good to hear, David. Make sure security is at all entrances," I respond.

"They have completed a sweep of the property and are already in place, sir," he answers back.

"Excellent. I'll leave you to it then," I reply as I disconnect the call.

I set my phone down next to my drink, swapping it for my glass. Taking a large sip, I swirl the amber liquid around my mouth before it runs down my throat. I can't wait to get this night over with, Miles owes me big-time. Setting my drink down, I finish getting dressed. I can't help but think tonight something is going to happen. Not sure if it's going to be good or bad but something. I'm sure of it.

Fuck me, I hate these things.

39

FOUR

Stormy

A knock comes from my door. "Are you finished getting dressed?" Lana questions. I take a look at my appearance in my floor length mirror, the crisp white shirt and black slacks look foreign to me. Not to mention the black tie that I am sporting makes me feel like I am dressing up for Halloween as Michael Jackson or something. Maybe I should breakout in the *"Thriller"* dance right here.

"Yeah, I'm done. You can come in," I respond to Lana. She walks in wearing the same uniform. It's an odd look on her, especially since it isn't full of colors and paint splatters. I chuckle at the sight. At least she still has her crazy hair that allows her personality to peek through.

"It fits great. I know it's ugly but it's only for a couple hours," she says.

"It's fine. Just not used to wearing something so formal. Not a big deal. Can I put my hair in a ponytail?" I ask because I would really hate to have to put it in a nice bun. Then I'd feel like a mix between a butler and a lunch lady. I cringe at the thought.

41

"A ponytail is fine. I have to clip mine back since it's not long enough to fit into a rubber band." She comes over to the mirror and fixes her makeup while I brush my long hair into a ponytail. Even in a ponytail it's still long enough to fall over my shoulder, they might make me put it in a bun after all.

"I'm a little nervous," I admit. That's not something I would usually tell anyone, but I feel like Lana and I have reached a level in our relationship where I can tell her things like that and I won't be judged.

"I was too with my first event, but it went fine. And I'll be right there with you if you have any questions." Lana steps back from the mirror and squeezes my shoulder.

"You're right. I've got this. Thanks again for getting me this gig. I don't want to live on my savings," I say as I spray some of my fly aways down.

"Girl, stop thanking me. It wasn't a problem at all. I was happy to help. Plus, it'll make work more fun. Sometimes I'm bored to death," Lana remarks with a cringe.

"Okay, I think I'm ready," I state as I giggle at her.

"Awesome. Grab an extra pair of clothes, so we can go out afterwards. I promise we'll need it," she announces as she walks out of my room. Quickly, I grab another set of clothes and my Chuck's, stuffing everything into an overnight bag. Taking one last look in the mirror, I decide this is the best it's going to get, and I head out too.

As our Uber drops us at the venue I have to take some deep breaths. I don't know why I'm so nervous. It's probably being thrust into a large, packed setting that has me on edge. I used to like crowds and I wanted to be the center of attention, but not anymore. I hope I get to be more of a wallflower tonight and that nothing brings any attention to me. This is only my third night in the city, and I don't want anyone else finding out who I really am.

"Girl, are you okay? I was talking to you," Lana asks as she moves in front of me, looking into my eyes.

"Yeah, sorry. Must have zoned out there for a minute," I smile nervously as I reply.

"It's going to be fine. Gina is going to love you. Let's go get our orders for the night." Lana pulls me along beside her as we enter the catering tent. She walks us toward a large woman who looks to be in her early fifties with short black hair. I only see the back of her because she's scolding two other waiters for something. Her tone makes me think we won't get along like Lana believes. I might not be at this job for a while like I was planning. I have a penchant for talking back, since I was told what to do most of my life. I grew my own voice after Blaine died.

"Gina, this is Stormy, the girl I was telling you about." Lana gets Gina's attention after she finishes with the other servers. "Stormy, this is Gina, she's been my boss for a year now."

"Nice to meet you, ma'am. Thank you for giving me this opportunity." I hold out my hand for her to shake but she dismisses me.

"Yeah, yeah. Just get your orders and don't fuck anything up. This is a big event, and the company we are working for is one of the largest in the city." Gina shuffles away as I stand there in shock with my hand still outstretched for her to shake.

"Wow. She isn't normally like that, I swear. She must just be stressed out right now. I know this is a big night for the company. We got an email about it. It's a big publishing company that's hosting authors and investors tonight. Anyway, I'm sorry about her," Lana remarks.

"No worries. I've been around people like her. I'm going to stay out of her line of fire though," I reply.

"That's probably a good idea," she comments. "Let's go get our orders, so we can get ready for the night."

Lana leads me over to another person with a clipboard who apparently made the list on where everyone will be placed tonight. There's a detailed drawing of the floor inside the venue. Lana's and my section are close to each other. We get our aprons on and start pouring the champagne into these beautiful crystal flutes. Once they're full, it's our time to leave the tent and serve the attendees. I take a deep breath and lift the tray. *I can do this.*

The servers are in a line as we walk into the venue, but we veer off to our respective positions once we get inside. I can't help but ogle all the beautiful people around me. These gowns are to die for, I wish I could trade places with one of these women. Even though our band signed with a record label, we never attended a party like this. I think there were some scheduled but then everything fell apart and here I am serving these people instead of being one of them.

It is what it is. I can't change the past and everything seems to happen for a reason.

As I walk around to different sections of guests that are standing and mingling, my tray of champagne flutes dwindles until I have to return to the tent to pour more. I fill my tray again and do another trip with a full tray of shining flutes. This time I pay more attention to the other side of the room. There is a man over there that is the epitome of hot. He's a tall drink of water. I can only see his profile, but he is absolutely gorgeous. I can see a hint of tattoos creeping up the side of his neck, and I wonder who he is. A lot of people seem to be vying for his attention, so he must be someone important. I'm sure he wouldn't look twice at the help like me, but it doesn't stop my perusal of him. With that thought, I finish my rounds and take my empty tray back to the tent outside.

Appetizers are next and I have to wait for the plates to be completed before I'm able to take them inside. The man I saw earlier comes out from the back entrance we are using and is on his cell phone arguing with someone by the looks of it. His body language is rigid, and I can tell he's pissed off about something. For some reason, I feel this pull toward him. I want to go over and help him with whatever he's upset with. It's an odd feeling and I'm not sure where it's coming from because I certainly haven't had any feelings for anyone since Blaine passed away. He isn't my type at all and yet, he seems like my perfect type. He's like a walking oxymoron for me. I love his roguish tattooed style, but his tux screams money. I'm not looking for anyone especially entitled pricks. He ends his call, pocketing his phone, then scrubbing his other hand down his face. As I'm about to walk over there, another man walks up behind him and leads him back inside but not before he looks my way with a look of fire in his gaze. His emerald, green eyes could be seen from a mile away. *Phew, that look could burn me up from the inside out. Why do I feel the need to get closer to him? I don't have the faintest idea who he is, but hot damn, I've always liked to play with fire.*

45

Sebastian

I've been putting out figurative fires left and right all night. I want five seconds of peace before I'm pulled away again. When I stepped outside earlier to take a call, I could feel eyes on me, but it wasn't until I got off the phone that I had a chance to see those exotic yellow eyes. The pull between us was electric, but Elijah came to take me back inside. I wanted to keep my eyes on the gorgeous little vixen, but I was thrust back into this god-awful fundraiser.

"Mr. Thompson wants to speak with you about investing in the company," Elijah says as he leads me back inside.

"Fine. I'll speak with him. Lead the way," I mutter, not really caring where I am being led unless it was back in the other direction.

As I sit and talk with Jared Thompson from Thompson and Simmons Investments, my mind trails off to the yellow-eyed beauty. When I look up, I see her long silver hair out of the corner of my eye. I turn my head just in time to see her presenting the last dish on her tray to Mary, the head of HR. As she turns to leave, she catches sight of me, and a slight blush creeps up her cheeks before she is gone again.

"Excuse me, gentlemen, there's something I need to tend to," I say to the men at the table. As I rise from my seat, I button my tux, then walk through the throng of people. Quickly, I follow the mysterious woman, while dodging party attendees at every turn. Soon, I find myself exiting the same way she did. Walking across the lawn, I can hear the chatter back in the venue as well as the clanking of cooking utensils in the catering tent. As I turn the corner to the opening of the tent, I see the vixen barreling straight for me balancing a tray filled with pasta dishes. Time slows as I see plates flying through the air toward me. They crash together, leaving a mess in their wake.

"Fuck," I yell out as I look down at my once crisp white shirt that's now turned red with marinara sauce. It looks like a murder via pasta took place out here. My anger spirals out of control because this is the last straw of the night. I can't take it anymore. Instead of walking away, like I should, I let the word vomit flow even though I know I'll regret it later. "Don't you look where you're fucking going?" I shout.

"Excuse me? You were the one that came barging in here. You ran into me!" she growls back at me.

"It's part of your job to look out for people and *not* run into them," I exclaim as I take my jacket off and toss it to the ground.

"Yeah, and it's your job to attend the party, *not* disturb the catering," she volleys back at me. Her once honey yellow eyes have turned dark with anger.

"It's my responsibility to see to all areas of this fundr—" I am cut off mid-sentence when the chef comes out and sees the mess between me and the girl.

"New girl, get this shit cleaned up at once," Gina lays into the woman before me. Her eyes stay trained on mine for a moment longer, the anger growing, then she looks to Gina.

"I was just about to get on that, but this gentleman decided to prolong my standing here, in pasta sauce, instead," the little vixen responds to Gina, and I can see figurative smoke coming out of the chef's ears. I would chuckle at the scene if I weren't covered in tonight's dinner.

"Don't you dare talk to me like that, you little brat. You're fired!" The saucy woman rolls her yellow eyes and storms off around the corner. I'm left standing there with Gina. "I'm so sorry, sir. I will have this cleaned up in no time, and I will personally make sure that your tux gets laundered as soon as possible," she blurts out when she sees the extent of the damage by coming closer to the crime scene.

"That won't be necessary. I shouldn't have been back here to begin with. It was my fault that this incident occurred." I try and reason with Gina. I don't want the stunning woman to get fired over this. I knew I should have just walked away instead of making the scene worse, but that's my pattern. I always make a scene when I shouldn't. I look around, hoping that no one is wiser about this event, but I see Mary watching from the entranceway with a scornful look on her face. My mother would look at me the same if she'd heard how I'd just spoken to a lady.

"Please, sir, I insist. It was that insolent girl's fault that you're wearing tonight's dish. It was her first night. I shouldn't have hired her in the first place," Gina remarks.

"I'll have my assistant take this tux to the cleaners as soon as possible. You don't need to do anything further. I'll leave you to get the rest of the entrees out," I say as I turn and walk over to Mary, picking up my suit jacket on the way.

"My, my, my. I never thought I would see the day when I was so disappointed in you. You know that incident was all your fault. What were you even doing out here to begin with?" Mary inquires, I sense the underlying fury toward me. Before I can answer, Marcy, our PR representative, is outside trying to do damage control.

"I've got a new tux on the way. Elijah left as soon as he saw and informed me what was going on out here," Marcy states.

"Thank you. I suppose I do need a new tux." I glance back over to the mess across the lawn, and I see the woman I wanted to get to know on her hands and knees picking up the pieces of the plates that broke on contact with the ground. I hear her yelp and my heart pangs at the thought that she cut herself on the glass plates. I'm about to go over to her when Mary catches me by the arm.

"Don't you think you've done enough? I'll go over and make sure she's okay. I heard the way the chef was speaking to her, as well as what you said. At least she held her own when you were spewing verbal garbage at her. The girl has a backbone," Mary announces as she trots over toward the woman now wrapping her hand in a towel. The more I see her in pain, the more I want to go to her and apologize for being such a dick. She didn't deserve that. I should have just waited until after the event to find her, but now I've gone and fucked everything up. I knew tonight was going to be a total shit show.

I leave Marcy while she works on her phone, typing away, and walk behind the venue to the river. I take my phone from my pocket and throw it into the Hudson. I take a deep breath of fresh air and stare off into the distance. *Fuck, what a mess I made.* Never did I think I'd be the one to cause the problems tonight.

FIVE

Stormy

What a total jackass. I should've known that his looks were too good to be true. With the way he treated this mishap, I would hate to see what happened if a real problem arose. I don't even know why he was coming back here to begin with. Guests haven't found themselves back here all evening, and then, all of a sudden, there he was coming into the tent where I had a tray full of entrees. Where is Lana when you need her? I hate that I went and got myself fired on the first night. Hopefully, this won't affect her employment. Gina is a massive bitch, just like I suspected, and she seems like she would retaliate against her, even though she did nothing wrong.

"Hello, dear. I saw what happened. Are you alright?" I startle at the sound of a voice because I was too deep in my thoughts to realize anyone had walked over. "I'm sorry. I didn't mean to scare you. I am Mary," she explains.

"Oh, hi. I'm okay. Just cleaning up this mess. Thank you for coming over to check on me," I stammer and get back to picking up the pieces of glass. I expect Mary to walk away now but she's still standing there staring down at me.

"I see you cut yourself. Do you need to have it looked at? I can get a doctor out here if needed," she insists.

I glance at my hand, "I haven't really looked at it. I wrapped it up as soon as it happened, then got back down here to clean this up." I point to the chaos on the lawn.

"Don't you worry about that. I'll get someone to come finish up. Now, let me see your hand, child," Mary asserts. I get up from the ground to show her my hand.

"Stormy," I utter. "My name is Stormy." She unwraps my hand, and I look away from the sight of the blood coating it. It takes me back to that night, and I have to fight hard not to let my mind wander back to that dark place.

"Stormy. That's a beautiful and very unique name." she smiles at me, "I believe you need stitches, Stormy. I'll call a doctor to come out here for you." Mary puts the rag back into the palm of my hand and closes my fingers over it tightly.

"Oh, thank you, but you don't have to do that. I can get it checked out when I leave here. It's not a big deal," I reply, but Mary isn't listening to me. She's already on her phone getting someone out here as soon as possible.

"Since this happened at our party, I need you looked at while you're still at the venue," she implores. The look she gives me lets me know there is no arguing about this

"I didn't realize this was your party, ma'am. I am so sorry for this mess. Please don't penalize Gina. The fault is all mine," I beseech.

"I saw everything. I know this wasn't your fault, but I admire you for saying so. You know, I heard Gina yell that you were fired.

You wouldn't happen to be looking for something in an office setting, would you?" Mary inquires.

"Actually, that sounds far more appealing than being a waitress. Do you have an opening?" I query.

"As a matter of fact, I do." She pulls out a business card that I suspect she came over here to give me in the first place. I don't know for sure but the ease that she whipped it out of her gown gives me a sense that there was more than her just wanting to know if I was alright. She hands it over. The beautiful gold lettering reflects off the twinkling lights above our heads. "Come see me Monday morning, and we'll get you settled in." Mary smiles.

"You don't want to interview me first?" I question. "I might not be the right person for the job."

"Very well. Are you good with working at a computer?" she quizzes. Everyone is good with a computer nowadays. I hardly feel like it's a reason for hiring. Nevertheless, I respond.

"Yes, ma'am, of course. That won't be a problem."

"Then that's perfect because I know you can handle everything else." I don't have time to ask what she means by that because the doctor comes out and begins examining my hand. Lana steps out of the venue and finds her place beside me.

"I heard what happened. Are you okay?" Lana asks.

"I'm fine, but I hope I didn't get you in trouble for bringing me. Gina is pissed," I acknowledge.

"Don't worry about it. I'll talk to her," Lana advises.

"No, that's okay. I actually have another job lined up." I look over to Mary and she winks at me.

"Wow, you move fast. I'll need those details girl!" Lana exclaims.

"I'll tell you everything after I can get out of here." I wince from the pain of the doctor assessing my hand.

"Okay, Miss, you're definitely going to need stitches. I need you to go wash your arm down to your hand. We need to get this sauce off you before I can do anything. I'll be over here when you're finished." He gestures to a table being set up behind the venue. *Man, these people go all out to avoid a lawsuit* is all I can think when I see everything they are doing for me.

Mary even got some men that look like security guards, to clean up the rest of the glass pieces from the ground. Its humorous seeing these large men picking up dainty pieces of china.

"I'll be right back," I say as I enter the tent, grabbing my bag and walking toward the bathrooms. Before I can even think about washing myself I must get out of these god-awful clothes. I'm thankful that Lana told me to bring a spare set even if this isn't what she quite what she had in mind. I'm trying to remove this stupid uniform without getting blood everywhere but I'm sure they won't want this one back. I think it's stained beyond repair. That thought brings me back to the man that started this whole shit show of a night. I'm sure his thousands of dollar suit is completely ruined. I sit for a moment to wonder if I feel bad for him. The answer is no, I don't. Still, I can't deny the fire I saw in his eyes was almost a turn on. If it wasn't for the poison coming out of his mouth, I might have been interested. That would be a feat in itself since I haven't thought about anyone like that in a very long time. I am thankful I don't let people walk all over me anymore. I did a lot of growing up in just a year.

A moment later, I'm walking out of the bathroom leaving behind that stupid uniform in the trashcan.

"You good?" Lana questions when she catches up to me.

"Yeah, just have to go get sewn up, then I am getting out of here. Or do you want me to wait for you?" I query. I hope she doesn't want me to stay. I don't want to run into that man or Gina again, I've had enough of them to last me a good while.

"No, I'll finish up here and meet you back at home. You need to get there and rest your hand anyway," she reassures, giving me a hug, then heads back into the venue to clean up the dishes.

I walk over to the doctor and try my best to keep the tears at bay as he stitches up my palm. I grit my teeth and try to think about anything other than what's going on right now. Once he's finished, he gives me directions on cleaning the wound and redressing the area.

"Thank you, sir. And thank you, Mary, for everything. I will see you on Monday." I use my good hand to pull out my phone from my bag. I order an Uber as I walk toward the front of the venue. The twinge of pain in my hand reminds me again of the man from tonight. I wonder what he was doing here. He must do business with Mary's company. I pull out the business card again and see it says Knight Publishing Company.

It might be kind of fun to work for a publisher. I wonder if I get to read any of the books, I would love to read romance manuscripts as they come through. What a cool job that would be! Looks like everything is turning out to be okay. the Uber arrives and as I drive away from the Riverfront venue, I'm excited to see what Monday holds. A second brand new start for me.

Sebastian

Well, that was a fucking disaster of a fundraiser. Thankfully, the guests were none the wiser about the incident outside at the catering tent. Elijah came through with another tux for me and about a pound of cologne to get rid of the pasta smell, I still smell like marinara even now as I walk into my penthouse. Instead of heading straight to the shower, I go to my wet bar to pour another whiskey. I think with everything that happened, alcohol first, then shower time. Maybe even at the same time.

Discarding my jacket on the couch, I flop down with my drink and turn on the television. Pulling my laptop from the coffee table, I email Elijah informing him he needs to get me a new iPhone tomorrow, since my anger got the best of me and mine is now at the bottom of the Hudson River. His reply is immediate with a, "Yes, sir." With that taken care of, at least I don't have to worry about more calls until tomorrow. I'm sure Miles has tried to call and ask how tonight went. He's just going to have to wait until tomorrow for an update, or never.

Fuck, I can't believe I spoke that way to the gorgeous little hellcat. I can't believe she talked to me like that. Didn't she know who I was? She was a spirited little thing.

I scrub my hand over my face. I don't want to think about tonight anymore. I down the rest of my whiskey as I rise from the couch and make my way toward the en suite to take a shower. I want to wash this figurative and literal mess off me. Tomorrow is a new day, and then Monday morning I will have a new assistant.

Things will get back to order in the office and everything will work out. That's all I think after I shower, then I crash onto my bed and pass right out. The day was too exhausting to stay awake any longer.

SIX

Stormy

I t's a dreary, autumn day when I wake the next morning. I hear
the rain beating on the window in my bedroom before I even
open my eyes. I love rainy days. They seem to wash away the pain
and anguish from the day before. Except today, I can definitely still
feel the pain thumping away in my hand. I shift in bed and see that
some blood seeped through the bandages. This acts as a reminder
of what a shitty night I had. If it wasn't for that man I would be
lying here enjoying the sound of the rain. Instead, I make my way
to the bathroom with the bandages I picked up from the store last
night. After changing the bandages, I go back to my room in search
of some ibuprofen. I pop open the lid and shake out the amount
that the doctor told me to take and wash them down with the
water next to my bed. Knowing I won't be able to finish unpacking
in this condition, I go to the kitchen to grab some frozen peas to
keep on my palm for the swelling. I make myself some coffee and
toast one handed and bring it back to my bedroom. Pulling my
Kindle from my bag, I toss it on the bed. There's nothing better
to do on a rainy day than to read smut. Sitting on my bed, I slide

my legs back under the covers. I down my coffee and toast while I scroll through my Kindle deciding on what to read. I stop when I remember purchasing *Neon Gods* by Katee Robert. I am a sucker for her books. I snuggle in and put the peas on my palm while I escape to Olympus.

Six hours later, I turn to the last page in the book. I grasp the Kindle to my chest and smile at the happily ever after of Hades and Persephone. I check the time on my watch and can't believe I spent the entire day reading. I loved every minute of it though, but now I've got to get ready to start a new job tomorrow. That reminds me, I need to go buy some office attire. Clueless over where I should shop, I walk to Lana's room because I know she will be able to steer me in the right direction.

I knock on her door. "Lana, are you in there?" I ask.

"Yeah, come on in," she replies. I open the door and am momentarily speechless at all the beautiful paintings she has adorning her walls. I walk up to the closest one and study it.

"Did you paint all of these?" I inquire as I examine the different techniques she used.

"I did. I started painting and drawing when I was in elementary school, it kind of transformed into an obsession," Lana responds.

"You definitely need to bring some of these into the rest of the apartment. We need some color on our walls," I remark. "But that's not why I came in here. I was just getting sidetracked by your work.

I need to go shopping for some clothes to wear to my new job," I explain as I look over to her.

"Oh fun! It's in an office, right? I know just the place to go. Mind if I tag along? I love shopping!" she exclaims.

"Of course, I don't mind. Besides, I'm going to need some help picking stuff out. I'm more of a jeans and chucks sort of girl," I express.

"There's nothing wrong with that. I like your emo/skater thing you have going on, but that's not going to work for this new job," she states.

"Definitely not. I'll go get dressed and meet you in the living room. Sound good?" I ask.

"I just need to get some shoes on, so it won't take me long," Lana answers.

"Okay. Be right back." I head back to my room, throw on some holey jeans, a band t-shirt and pull my hair into a long, silver ponytail. I slide my feet into my shoes and grab my bag and jacket since it's still raining a bit. Setting my things down on the couch, I run to the bathroom to brush my teeth. Once I'm done, Lana is in the living room waiting for me.

"I also want to get some decorations for the apartment. Think we'll have time?" I ask Lana.

"We should. Let's do your clothes first since that's most important and then we'll see what time it is. We can eat out or pick up something and eat here." Putting on my jacket, I grab my bag and sling it across my body. We're out of the apartment and down by the curb hailing a cab just a few minutes later.

Once one comes to a stop in front of us, we jump inside.

"Where are you ladies heading?" the cab driver asks. Lana looks at me and smiles.

"Shabby Chic in SoHo," she tells the man, then off we go.

"I've never heard of that place," I mention as the driver pulls out into traffic.

"It's a great place for the office attire you need but also has the styles that you'll love. It's one of my favorite places to splurge," Lana answers. I nod my head and watch the passing scenes from my window.

When we arrive, we pay the driver and step out onto the busy streets of New York City. Even with the rain, people are packed on the sidewalks. Lana grabs my hand as we dart through the cluster of people.

Once we're inside, I feel like I need to shake like a dog to get all the rain off me. I'm sure we look like a bunch of drowned rats. One of the saleswomen turns her nose up at us but the other comes over and offers us her help.

"What can I help you ladies with?" she inquires as she looks from Lana to me.

"I need a new wardrobe for a job that starts tomorrow. I waited until the last minute, so any help is appreciated," I explain. I hate having the attention on me, especially when I feel like I don't belong.

"That's not a problem. My name is Samantha, by the way. What type of clothes are you needing?" she questions.

"Well, I need office attire but without losing my personality. I don't want stuffy, boring clothes," I respond.

"You came to the right place. Let me take your coats and you can start looking around," she says with a smile.

The next few hours fly by as we both try on tons and tons of different outfits. Most of everything I tried on, I loved. My credit card won't love it, but I sure do. Once we leave, Lana persuades me to go next door for more shoes. I can't lie, I'm intrigued to see all the high-end shoes. My eyes immediately fall on a pair of delectably glossy black patent leather Louboutin's with their iconic red sole. My mouth waters at the sight. I know I shouldn't get these, but I'll be damned if I can turn away now that I set my sights on them. Up until today I have been very conservative with my savings, but I think it's time for me to have a bit of fun.

"Are you seriously going to get those?" Lana questions as she points to the box in my hands. I look at her with a guilty grin, and she laughs.

"I'm pretty sure I *need* them," I exaggerate.

"Yeah, yeah," she mutters in response.

"You're the one that insisted we come in here. I would have been happy at a Converse store," I tell her, chuckling to myself. "I think I have everything I need for tomorrow. Want to grab some dinner to take home? My hand is starting to throb a bit, so I won't be able to carry all these bags around."

"Sure. What are you in the mood for?" Lana asks, as we make our way to the cash register.

"Pizza or Mexican sounds good," I reply. I set the box of shoes down next to the saleswoman at the register. *Man, if looks could kill. Why the hell is she looking at me like I offended her.*

"Ma'am," she hisses, "are you sure you meant to grab *this* pair of shoes? There is a clearance section I'm sure would be more to your liking." *Oh, hell no she didn't.*

"Actually, these are perfect for me. And you know what? Do they come in another color? I would love a second pair," I seethe as the woman gasps.

"S-sure. They also come in beige. I'll go get them," she stutters, then struts off to grab the other pair of shoes.

"I can't believe she just said that to you," Lana comments.

"Yeah, well she did and sucks for her, but she won't be getting this commission either. I'm going to ask for another associate to check us out. I don't put up with shitty people anymore," I say just as the awful woman comes back holding the second pair of shoes.

"Here you go. These are the beige ones. Would you like these as well?" she asks.

"As a matter of fact, I would love them. But before you ring me up, I would like a different associate to help us. You understand, right? I'm sure there is someone you can help in the clearance section," I gesture toward the far corner of the store.

"I apologize. Of course, let me get someone for you." The woman walks away and I hope I never have to see her again. I hate it when people think they are better than other people. I won't ever come to this store again.

"You are my new hero," Lana states. "Too bad we don't wear the same size shoes." She smiles and quirks a brow at my boxes.

Once the new associate checks us out, Lana and I leave the store. We get a cab relatively quickly and pile our millions of bags into the trunk. I don't know how we are going to get all this and dinner up to our apartment, but it's safe to say that I think I've had my exercise for the day with all the walking we've done. We decide to have pizza delivered, so we head straight home. The cab driver drops us off on the curb of our apartment and helps us get the bags out of the trunk. When we get into the apartment, Lana and I collapse on the couch in a fit of giggles. I don't remember the last time I felt this light. I hope it means things are turning around for me.

SEVEN

Sebastian

Elijah brings me my knew phone after setting it up for me. I needed an upgrade anyway. I suppose I could have gone about it better than throwing it into the river, but such is life. When I turn on the device, I see several missed calls and messages from Miles, those are the only ones I'm paying attention to. I open the messenger app and begin reading.

Miles:

> How was the fundraiser?

Miles:

> Heard from Marcy. Call me.

Miles:

> Sebastian, if you keep ignoring me, I will come back from Ireland and kick your ass. Then you will have to explain to Lizzie why we had to leave early.

The last message was sent about an hour ago. I better call him even though I would rather text. He picks up on the first ring.

"Where the hell have you been?" Miles shouts. I have to pull the phone away from my ear, so I don't go deaf.

"Calm your tits, bro. I had an eventful night and in a dumb moment, I threw my phone into the river. Elijah just dropped this new one off," I answer.

"Why the hell would you throw your phone into the Hudson?" Miles is still shouting.

"Because it was a shit show of a night and I literally couldn't take anymore. Enough about that. The fundraiser was fine. The behind the scenes wasn't as smooth, but the guests were none the wiser," I reply.

"Marcy already informed me that you ran into some girl and she spilled her tray all over you. Then apparently you went on to berate her where anyone could hear." Fuck, I was hoping to avoid this story. I hear Miles take a few breaths as he calms himself some, but I can tell that at any moment he may start back up again.

"It was an accident. I had been running around all night long fixing things and it was my last straw. Everything is fine. So, how is Ireland?" I try to change the subject, but Miles isn't having it.

"It's been great but that's not what we're talking about right now." Miles continues, "Marcy said Mary told her that the girl cut her hand pretty bad. Did you know that?" Fuck, she did? I knew I should have gone back over there and apologized, but my pride and Mary kept me from doing it.

"No, I didn't know. I walked away from the incident so I wouldn't say more that I would regret," I say.

"If only there was something that keeps you from saying stupid shit. Like a brain! Seriously, do I need to come back? If you can't handle it..." Miles continues, but I interrupt him.

"No! I have everything under control. Besides, Mary will have me a new assistant tomorrow so everything should get back to normal," I assure.

"Fine, then I'll leave you to prepare for the week. You might want to see if Mary got this girl's information and at least send her some 'I'm sorry flowers' or something. It sounds like you were a real dick to her." Miles' description, though accurate, makes me feel like shit because I know I acted horribly. I'm too old to be acting that childish but to be fair, she was dishing it right back at me. I felt like I had my own sparring partner, which let me be able to get some of my aggression out on her. Unfortunately, she didn't deserve that. I can't say it wasn't hot seeing a woman stand up to me. I liked it a little too much.

"I'll see if I can get in touch with the girl. You're right, she didn't deserve the wrath I spewed at her," I state.

"Glad we got that settled. Get some rest, and I'll check in again this week. Love you, bro."

"Okay, love you, too." I hang up the phone and slip it into my pocket.

Walking over to my wet bar in the living room, I pour myself a whiskey and take it out to my balcony. I enjoy watching the sun set from up here. Most of the time, I get home way past sunset but when I'm here I take advantage of having the perfect balcony. I take a sip of my whiskey and close my eyes, swirling the liquid around in my mouth. When I open them, I see the colors in the sky twirling together, making a masterpiece before my eyes.

After all the rain we had today, I didn't think the sunset would be this magnificent. Fortunately, it stopped just in time to create this canvas. I sit on the couch under the covered part of my balcony and take another sip of my drink. I need to talk to Mary tomorrow about the girl from the venue. My heart aches at the thought of the physical and mental pain I put her through. Miles is right. I need to do something for her. She was gorgeous and I was trying to talk to her before everything fell apart. Maybe she would let me take her out as an apology. I finish my drink and take one last look at the sky before I head back into my penthouse.

Tomorrow is a new day. I vow to be a better human being than I was yesterday. *Mostly.*

EIGHT

Stormy

I t's Monday morning and of course I'm running around the apartment trying to get ready on time. I'd hate to disappoint Mary and be late for my first day, especially after all the care she gave to me on Saturday. Lana and I stayed up late hanging up all my new clothes and organizing everything. She even helped with my remaining boxes claiming that I needed help with my hand being all cut up. However, I'm happy my room now looks like my own and not just a temporary residence.

I knew it would be hard to wake up early today, so I went ahead and picked out what I would be wearing. I shimmy on a tight black pencil skirt the best I can with the use of only one hand. It falls just above my knees and I add a white button up shirt with cap sleeves. Reaching into my closet, I pull out the black Louboutin high heels and put them on. Checking myself in my floor length mirror, I'm impressed with my appearance. My hair is straightened and falling loosely down my back, my makeup is on point with a smoky eye shadow I picked to match my outfit. I grab my new purse and make sure that my anxiety medication is in there, better to have it than need it and not have it. I clutch my Harry Potter Patronus Pandora necklace where it lays around my neck and take a deep breath. This pendant, like the spell, keeps me safe. Or rather I have the peace of mind that it will.

"Stormy, aren't you dressed yet?" Lana calls from somewhere in the apartment.

"Almost," I yell back. I grab my new black knee length coat from behind the door and throw it over my shoulders. As I walk out of my room, I see Lana standing by the front door with a to-go cup of coffee.

"I made this for you since I didn't think you had the time." She hands me the insulated mug and the aroma from the coffee instantly calms me. *I can do this.* As I look at the mug, I see a quote that's always been a favorite of mine.

"I dream my painting and I paint my dream."
-Vincent Van Gogh

"Thank you, Lana. This is actually one of my favorite quotes," I reveal as I turn the mug around in my hands. It has one of his famous paintings in the background. "I might steal this mug."

"I bought it for you to start your new job. Coffee is like ambrosia to the gods in the office world," Picasso chuckles to herself at her joke. I can't help but crack a smile as well.

"You're right. I'm glad you're my roommate, Lana," I lean in to give her a quick hug. "I'll text you later and let you know how it's going. Oh, don't forget today is the day to schedule classes. My time frame is around lunch so it shouldn't be a problem. I'm sure

I can use a computer at work. Hold this for a minute." I hand her the mug to put my jacket on.

"My time frame is this morning. I'll let you know what all I get into so maybe we can have some of the same classes," she mentions as I button up the peacoat. She hands the mug back to me and smiles.

"I'll see you later. I have to go, or I'll be late. I don't want to lose two jobs in the span of a few days," I reply.

"Don't worry about Saturday, it was that asshole's fault, not yours," she yells as I step out into the dank hallway. I nod in response. Even though I shouldn't, I can't help the butterflies fluttering around in my stomach at the thought of that tall, handsome asshole. Maybe it's a sign that I'm ready to move on with my life.

I get down to the street and hail a taxi as it passes by. I slide in and give the driver the address. I settle into the seat and take my first sip of coffee, the warmth spreads through my body. The first sip is always the best. It's almost like a Holy experience. As we weave in and out of the traffic of the crowded streets of New York, a wave of nerves hit me. I can't believe I moved halfway across the country less than a week ago and now here I am about to start a fancy office job. Well, it might not be fancy. I could be a glorified coffee girl. Mary didn't really tell me what I would be doing, she almost seemed to leave those details out on purpose. I try and push those negative thoughts away and concentrate on the positives. I got a new job. I am registering for classes today. My roommate is growing on me. I might even go as far as to say I like her. Things are looking up.

The cab driver pulls up to the sidewalk and parks. I look out the window at the huge building before me. I'm used to skyscrapers, somewhat, but driving by them and entering one is a big difference. The butterflies in my stomach had died down and now they are one big swirling dervish. After paying the driver, I open the door, the chill in the air seems to have gotten worse. Maybe it's just the frigid climate around the ominous building. For a moment, I contemplate turning around and getting back into the cab, but he already took off. I subconsciously grab my necklace and make my way inside the building.

Once I get close enough, a doorman opens the door for me to enter. This place is definitely fancier than I thought. I should've done some research before I came. As I look around, people are milling about doing different tasks. I head to the receptionist hoping Mary has let them know I am coming.

"Hello, how can I help you?" the smiling brunette behind the counter asks.

"Hi. I'm here to see Mary. She gave me this card. I'm Stormy Brooks." I slide the card over to her.

"Of course. She's waiting for you on the eighteenth floor. Just go up the elevator and tell the woman at the front desk there that you have an appointment with Mary. Here's your card back. It was nice meeting you. I'm Olivia," she informs me as I pocket the card.

"You as well. Thank you," I reply, then turn on my heels and walk to the bank of elevators on the far side of the wall. I'm thankful I am a pro at walking in heels since that's all I bought to go with my clothes. Being short all my life, I got used to them early on to give myself some height. I'm not terribly short but being 5'4 when everyone around me seemed to get a second growth spurt, I had to do something to improve my self-esteem. So, heels it was.

I press the up button for the elevator and wait. I take this time to really look around. The décor is modern and there are various styles of paintings I want to inspect closer when I get the time. This company seems to buy their artwork from local artists, which is a huge green check for me. I love that they are supporting local instead of buying abroad. I'd love to see my pieces in a building like this, but they aren't the same esthetic as they have going here. Mine are more on the emotional side.

The elevator dings, and I turn quickly, colliding with a hard, masculine surface. The man grips my elbows, ensuring I stay upright. My hands clasp the leather jacket he's wearing. His manly cologne floods my senses. Sandalwood, vanilla, and outdoorsy leather were combined to wreak havoc on any female. His cologne and his grip on my arms make me want to melt into him, but then I realize this is a total stranger I'm standing here holding. Embarrassment sneaks up my spine, and I drop my hands from his chest.

"I'm so sorry, I was looking at the art and waiting for the elevator. I didn't see you there," I mutter as I clear the hair that's fallen into my face. I look up at the man, and my heart drops. "You," is the only thing I utter before I back away from him. It's *him*. The man from the fundraiser on Saturday. The man that cussed me out, causing me to get fired. Not that I particularly liked that job, but hell. This asshat is right in front of me. But damn is he fine as hell up close. Saturday he was in a black tux that displayed his toned body perfection. But now he's wearing jeans with a biker jacket and I'm pretty sure my ovaries just exploded. He's sex on a stick, and I would eat him all day long. *Damn, where are these thoughts coming from?*

"What are you doing here?" He questions as he looks me up and down. He has a look in his eyes that I can't decipher. I don't know whether to be pleased with him checking me out or pissed that he has the audacity. I'm leaning towards the latter.

"I'm here to see Mary," I respond as I try to step around him but he puts his body in the way of elevator and me. "Excuse me, I need to get through. If you don't mind." I gesture toward the open elevator that's waiting for me.

A few people move around us and into the elevator the doors closing behind them. The fire in my veins ignites and I'm so close to knocking this man out. I can't believe he, of all people, is standing in front of me right now. I was okay to never see him again. I was actually hoping for that due to the rage he induces in me. I can see people are staring at us now and this is definitely not how I wanted my first day to go.

I step around him and hit the elevator button again. This time when it comes, I'll be ready.

"Why do you need to see Mary?" he continues. The courage of this man must be astronomical because he clearly hasn't seen a woman lose her shit.

"That's actually none of your business." The elevator dings and I shove him out of the way enough to enter. He trails right in after me. I press the button for floor eighteen, he leans back in the corner with his arms crossed over each other. As I'm about to say something else to the jackass, I see a beautiful painting in the elevator with us. Without a word, I walk over to it and observe the minute details the artist used. I can feel the uplifting emotions pouring out of it. Already, I feel better than I did five minutes ago.

I'm startled out of my perusal of the painting as his confident and sensuous voice rings through the cart.

"So, you were about to tell me why you're here to see Mary," he inquires again.

"Actually, I don't think I was," I bite out.

"Look, about Saturday—" He looks down at his shoes, and then sets his sights on my bandaged hand. An expression crosses his face and for a moment he looks sorry. "Your hand is injured," he states more to himself than me. He doesn't get a chance to finish because the doors to the elevator open and I'm out of them the next second. I walk straight up to the receptionist on this floor.

"Hi. I have an appointment with Mary," I inform her. "Can you let her know that Stormy Brooks is here?"

"Sure." She picks up her phone and calls Mary letting her know I've arrived. The next second the hairs on the back of my neck start standing on end. I know he's behind me. Can't this joker take a hint.

Before I have the chance to turn around and give him another piece of my mind, Mary walks out of her office and beams at me.

"It's so good to see you again, dear. How is your hand holding up?" she queries.

"It's alright, I guess. It shouldn't keep me from working if that's what you're worried about," I respond.

"That's not what I was thinking at all. I want you to take it easy until those stitches come out. I see you've officially met Sebastian." She gestures toward the man behind me.

"Actually, we haven't met. I ran into him downstairs, and he insisted on following me up here," I reply with a little snark in my voice. He comes up beside me as I look up at him, he must be at least 6'4. He looks at me for a moment, then at Mary.

"Mary, please tell me this isn't what I think it is," he murmurs as he nods his head toward me.

"I'm not sure what you're thinking, Sebastian, but I brought this young lady in for a job since you got her fired from her other one," she remarks.

"Come with me, darling. We need to get some paperwork filled out." She points toward her office.

"Mary, can I have a word with you?" Sebastian huffs out.

"You'll have to wait, my dear. I need to get Stormy settled in as your assistant." A wave of shock rolls across me, I hope I didn't hear her correctly. There is no way I can work for this bosshole.

"E-excuse me? I don't think that's the best idea. We don't exactly get along, Mary. Didn't you see us on Saturday?" I question. Grasping at any thread I can. There is no way this will work out, but I've already spent so much money on new clothes and shoes. My mind starts to spiral, I start thinking of worst-case scenarios. A lovely side effect of all my past trauma.

"Of course it is my dear. Just go on in there and wait. I'll be along in a moment." I turn back to look at Sebastian, he looks just as shocked as me. I nod to Mary as I walk into her office. I remove my jacket and take a seat. Looking around her space makes me feel at home. She has children's drawings hung up and her decorations resemble something my own mother would've had. The atmosphere puts me more at ease than I was a few moments ago. I take several deep breaths. I pull my phone out, I need to look up Sebastian, see what he does here and why he's so important that he needs an assistant. Before I get the chance, Mary walks in and shuts her door. She still has that smile on her face, so I'm guessing Sebastian wasn't mean to her.

"Now that I got that taken care of, we can get your paperwork done." Mary sits in her chair and pulls out a manilla envelope placing it in front of me.

"Mary, thank you for helping me out Saturday and bringing me here for a job, but there is no way he and I can work together." I go to stand but Mary stops me.

"Just listen, honey. I knew there was no way I could get you here if I you told who you'd be working for. That's why I left that little part out. But what I do know is, you are perfect for this job. You won't let Sebastian walk all over you. You can stand up for yourself and with him, that's going to be needed sometimes. He isn't the monster you're imagining. I told him how wrong he was to speak to you like that on Saturday, and believe it or not, I know he felt bad about it later. He has a hot head and sometimes things just fly out of his mouth without a filter. But he is a fair employer, and he's a good man. He desperately needs an assistant. His is on maternity leave. Not to mention his brother, Miles, is on his honeymoon for the next few weeks, so that leaves Sebastian completely in charge," she continues. My brain short circuits when she says that Sebastian is in charge. I recall a set of oil paintings in the lobby of Miles and Sebastian Knight. I thought there were some similarities there, but I wasn't sure where I'd seen them before. Now here I am in the asshole's own publishing empire, being asked to work for him. "I'm just asking you to give him a chance. If it doesn't work out, then I'll find someone else, *and* I'll write you a letter of recommendation. It's a win-win situation, Stormy."

I've dealt with men like him before. Even Blaine used to walk all over me from time to time. I hate thinking negative things about Blaine, especially since he died when we were still in an argument over whether I'd get to attend college while touring with the band.

"This is just a lot to take in, Mary. Thank you for putting so much faith in me. I think I can do this. I can deal with him. He's nothing I haven't dealt with before," I reply with a smile.

"That's the spirit I saw from you on Saturday. You'll fit in perfectly here!" She exclaims, clapping her hands together. "Alright, fill out this paperwork and I'll show you to your desk. It's on the twentieth floor, but if you ever need anything, don't hesitate to call or come pay me a visit."

I smile up at this motherly woman of whom I've already grown fond of. Pulling the stack of papers from the envelope I get to work filling them out. Mary steps out for a moment to make some copies of my license and social security card. While she's gone, I take a moment to text Lana.

Stormy:

You aren't going to believe who I'm working for.

It only takes her a second to respond.

Picasso:

Who???

Stormy:

The guy from Saturday night. Apparently, he and his brother own this place. His name is Sebastian Knight.

Picasso:

> OMG! Shut up! Let me send you this news article about him! Call me whenever you get a break! I need to know everything!

Stormy:

> I'll call soon.

Just then, the news article that she was talking about comes up. The article states he is the most eligible playboy bachelor in New York City. Of course he is. I let out a deep sigh and put my phone back in my purse. This may be harder than I already think it's going to be. When Mary returns, I've already completed the necessary paperwork.

"All done?" She beams.

"Yes ma'am. Here is everything you need." I hand her the envelope with all of my information.

"Perfect, let's go get your ID card to get you to the twentieth floor and I will show you where everything is."

I stand, grabbing my bag and jacket, and follow Mary out of her office. For better or worse, I just signed my name on the dotted line to work for a maniac that yells at innocent women that spill pasta sauce on themselves and others. I just hope I'm as strong as Mary seems to think I am.

NINE

Sebastian

What the actual fuck did I walk into today. Seeing *her* in the entranceway to my building had me doing a double take. She's even more gorgeous and frustrating in the light of day than she was this past weekend. I came into the office with the mind set of talking to Mary to see if she had the woman's contact information or something, so I could send flowers, never in a million years did I imagine her being hired at my company, and as my executive assistant no less. Once I realized why she was there, I pulled Mary aside.

"Mary, this isn't going to work. You saw the way we were at the fundraiser." The words I spewed at her come to mind, but I push them away to continue this conversation.

"What I saw was a strong woman that would stand her ground against you. She's perfect for this position." Mary smiles slyly. I try to come up with another reason why this woman shouldn't be my assistant, but my mind goes blank. I contemplate her name, Stormy. It fits her personality perfectly. Storms can be beautiful disasters and I have a feeling that one's coming. The perfect storm.

I relent on the subject because I know Mary means well and I really do need a new assistant. Elijah can't cut it working for me. I just hope Stormy can forgive me for the way I treated her. From her earlier actions, it seems I have my work cut out for me.

"I'll leave you to it then. Apparently you know what you are doing. I'll be in my office if you need me." Mary waves me off and heads towards her office. Just before she closes the door, I see a glimpse of sexy as fuck legs crossed at the ankle. This is going to be harder than I thought. *Why does she have to be so attractive?* I definitely can't go there now. I scrub my hand down my face and walk to the bank of elevators that'll take me to my floor.

Once I get to my office, Elijah comes running in with my coffee. "So, Mary hired another assistant for me, you will be able to take a breather." The look of sheer relief on his face tells me how hard I have been working him. I'd almost feel bad, but it *is* his job. "She'll be up here once Mary is finished with her. Will you make sure Tracy's desk is ready for her? Also, thank you for getting my coffee, Elijah." I take the cup from his hands and take a sip.

"No problem, sir. I'll get to it. As far as your schedule today, you only have one meeting at twelve. It's with the Thompson and Simmons investments since you weren't able to finish that conversation Saturday. Would you like me to attend to take notes?" Elijah questions.

"No, that won't be necessary. I'll get Sto- I mean the new assistant to sit in on the meeting with me. She needs to learn the ropes anyways. Also, help her out if she needs some assistance with the computer programs," I reply as I take my laptop out of my bag and boot it up.

"Not a problem. I will get started with Tracy's desk. I believe she left it in a mess." He turns and walks out of my office, closing the door behind him. I walk to my closet and find a suit to put on. As much as I enjoy wearing my biker attire, I am the boss. I need to look the part. I pull out a navy suit and take it to my adjoining bathroom to change.

When I come back out, I hang up the clothes that I wore here and shut the closet. Sitting down I pull up my emails and groan at how many there are. I need these to be filtered before they get to me. I don't have time to sit here and read all this shit when I guarantee that most of it can be handled by other staff members. I scroll through them and only open a handful. I'll have Stormy go through these. Thinking of her gives me a warm feeling in my chest. Absentmindedly, I rub the area. I push her out of my mind and get to work.

A knock at my door brings me out of the trance I was in while I was working. I check my watch and figure it's probably Elijah reminding me about meeting in ten minutes.

"Come in," I instruct.

As the door opens, I am momentarily speechless at the sight of Stormy in my doorway. She's wearing a snug black skirt with a white buttoned up shirt tucked in. I see the ink she has running down one of her arms. I never noticed she had tattoos, of course both times I have seen her she was wearing long sleeves. When I saw her this morning, she had on a long jacket that left her attire out of view. I try to get a good look at the ink, but I'm too far away to see all the details. I look up and get the full view of her, I'm taken aback by her beauty. Her silver locks fall down her back with some parted and falling just beside her arm.

"Sorry to interrupt, but Mary said lunch started at twelve and I wanted to see if you needed anything before I clock out," she states in a matter-of-fact way. I can feel her anger radiating off her. She hates me.

"Actually, lunch will be late today. We have a meeting to get to in about five minutes. I need you in there with me to take notes. I'm sure Elijah showed you how I like them done." I rise from my seat and button my suit.

"Elijah didn't mention a meeting today and there isn't one on your calendar." Stormy pulls out the iPad we give our executive assistants and scrolls through it. I'm sure she is double checking her facts. The thing is though, this meeting was scheduled this morning and I'm sure Elijah just forgot to add it to the calendar.

"It's a last-minute meeting and I need you there. You will be free to take a lunch after," I explain.

She stands tall but nibbles on the side of her lip giving her away. I can tell she is uncomfortable even though she is trying hard not to show it.

"I actually have something that needs to be done at twelve," she says looking at me straight in the eyes.

"It'll have to wait," I respond as I grab my computer. I don't really need her; I could get Elijah to take notes today, but she needs to know that I'm the boss and things like this pop up from time to time. I'm sure she doesn't have anything too important that needs to be done right now.

"*Sir*," she emphasizes, "I have something that has been planned for weeks. I can't reschedule," she asserts.

"Do you want a job or not Ms. Brooks? This is part of the job. Leave your badge on the desk if you can't handle it." I don't know why I am being a dick to her again. She just pulls it out of me. I really don't want her to leave. I have resigned myself to the knowledge of her working here, even though it's only been one day. I looked into her information that Mary forwarded to me this morning. That's how I came to know her last name. I wanted to find out more about her, but there is a chunk of time missing in her resumé. I'm not sure what she has been up to in the last two years. It's puzzling. I round the corner of my desk and ask, "So, what will it be?" She crosses her arms across her chest the best she can while still holding the iPad. I see the fire flicker in her yellow eyes. They are the most extraordinary color eyes I have ever seen. I thought they were beautiful the night of the fundraiser but that was in the darkness with flickers of twinkling lights above us. In the light of day, they illuminate her face.

"I guess I don't really have a choice, but since I have two minutes I need to make a phone call. I will meet you in the conference room." She turns on her heels and leaves me staring after her. The back of her skirt has a slit in it, and I can see where she has some type of tattoos on the backs of her thighs, right under her ass. I know I shouldn't be looking, but I can't help to check her out as she angrily stomps away from me. My cock appreciates the view. I groan as I adjust myself and head toward the conference room. As I pass by the back of her desk I hear bits and pieces of her phone call.

"He's being a dick and insists he needs me in a meeting right this minute. I need you to go online and register for my classes. I have them written on my desk in my room. I'll send you my login information." "Yes, thank you so much!" "I would have died if I didn't get into the classes I wanted. I'll see you tonight."

Now I feel like a real prick. I saw on her resumé that she attended college in Florida, but she didn't complete it. I suppose she is trying to do that here and I wouldn't let her get on the computer to register for her classes. I remember those days of trying to get the classes that I needed and being furious when they filled up before I got to them. I'm about to tell her she can skip this meeting, but she goes and opens her mouth.

"I'm ready, your Majesty," she says cheekily. How is it that Elijah acts terrified of me, but this girl sees me as her sparring partner. I guess Mary was right. She probably is a perfect fit for this job. I chuckle at her jab at me and lead her to the conference room. The urge to place my hand on the small of her back as we walk is intense.

Once we make it inside the conference room, I show Stormy to her seat and then take my seat next to her. She puts down the notebook, pen, and iPad she was carrying and places them all perfectly in front of her. The pen is ever so slightly out of alignment with the rest, and she uses her pinky to make it line up correctly. So, she has OCD about some things. Maybe that's why she doesn't let people walk all over her. I sit there and study her for a moment until I hear Jared Thompson's boisterous voice coming down the hallway. I stand and ready myself for this meeting. Jared's a few years my senior and likes to tell people how he amassed his fortune, when in reality it was his father's money. An hour with him and I want to blow my brains out. Hopefully, he can stay on topic today and we can get this over with. He enters the room and instead of greeting me, he zeroes in on Stormy and I can see the sleezy way he is looking at her. It makes my fists clench at my side.

"Jared, long time no see." Implying how I just saw him Saturday. I stretch my hand out for him to shake and to bring the attention back to me. He at least returns my gesture and takes my hand for a moment before his attention is back on her.

"Nice to see you again, Knight. And who is this stunning creature?" He says as he holds out his hand for Stormy to take.

"Stormy Brooks, sir. I will be sitting in on this meeting." Even with a snake like Jared, she keeps herself composed but I can't help but notice that she has gotten closer to me while she shook his hand.

"This is my new executive assistant, Ms. Brooks. Why don't we all have a seat and get down to business?" I gesture to the table across from me for Jared to sit, but he chooses the chair right in front of Stormy. What a slimy jackass.

I start the meeting and continue to talk while Jared's attention is clearly not on me. I catch a glance at Stormy to see if she has sighted Jared's not so subtle perusal of her. Her body language tells me she indeed has noticed. Her arms are closed in on her and she is hunched over the desk taking notes. There is a slight twinge of pink on her cheeks. Anyone could tell that she is uncomfortable, but Jared can't take a hint. My fists tighten more at my side until the clicker for the screen projection is at risk of being cracked in two. I have to do something about this.

"Jared, at any time do you plan on listening to what I have to say? You were the one who insisted that we scheduled this meeting. If not, then you are wasting both of our time." I know I shouldn't speak to a potential investor like that, but I'm also going to take care of my employees. If he is this sleezy, then I don't want to work with him anyways. Miles would agree with me.

"Whoa there, Sebastian. Aren't you supposed to be schmoozing me? I mean it's my money you want." He takes a breath and winks at Stormy. She visibly shutters and looks at me. It's that look that makes me wrap this meeting up.

"Actually, I think this meeting has come to an end. If you would please show yourself out," I assert.

"You've got to be kidding me, Knight. What will big brother say when he learns you lost a major account?" Jared stands, his face turning red.

"Oh, we don't think of you as a major account. And Miles backs me up one hundred percent of the time, especially if it involves our employees. Now, I've asked you to leave. Do I need to call for security to escort you from the premises?" I ask.

"No need. You will regret this, Knight." Jared obviously doesn't like being talked down to and he doesn't like being denied. But over my dead body would he touch Stormy. She's *mine.*

What the fuck? She isn't mine. I don't know where the hell that came from. She's *not* mine. But saying that to myself makes me want to see red. *What the hell is wrong with me?*

Jared leaves the conference room and I hear a small sigh of relief come from Stormy. "I'm sorry he was making you uncomfortable. There is no excuse for that. I'm sorry I didn't notice it sooner," I state, as I take my seat next to her.

"Thank you for getting rid of him, although I hate that you lost his company's money," she responds.

"No need to thank me. Honestly, the guy has always been a sleazeball. I've had enough of him and his dirty money," I reply as she nods her approval.

"If you don't need me any longer, can I take my lunch break?" She asks as she looks from her watch to me.

"Sure. When you get finished, come to my office so we can go over schedules, emails, and things of the like."

"Thank you!" She exclaims and she has her things bundled up and in her arms as she nearly runs from the room. I check my watch as well and see that she probably still has time to get into her class scheduling. Packing up my laptop, I leave the conference room and head back to my office. I pass Stormy along the way with her fingers flying over her keyboard. From a distance I can see SVA on the screen. So, she is taking classes at the School of Visual Arts in New York City. No wonder she was examining the painting downstairs. I wonder if her schedule is going to affect her work schedule. I decide to drop my laptop off in my office and I walk toward the elevators. I need to get out of here because Stormy just does something strange to me. I feel the need to be close to her, and I immensely enjoy verbally sparring with her. She's messing me all up.

TEN

Stormy

*P**hew.* I was able to get all the classes I wanted. I needed most of them to be online or at night since I have this job now and it all worked out. I sit back in my chair and let out a deep breath.

Stormy:

I got all the classes that I wanted!

It takes Lana a few minutes to respond. In the meantime, I check my watch and see that I have enough time to run down to the ground level cafeteria that's in this building. My stomach rumbles in acknowledgment.

Picasso:

That's so great! I got everything except The Abstract Image class. Did you get that one?

I did, and I think there was still spots available. It's a night class. Not sure if you wanted that or not.

Check and see. I'm going to go get some lunch.

I grab my purse and drop my phone in. Walking toward the elevator, I see Elijah heading the same way from the other side of the floor. He introduced himself this morning after I was finished with Mary and he helped me figure out the programs they use for scheduling and such. He was a huge help and super nice. However, I don't see how he lasted a second working for Sebastian. I'm surprised he wasn't eaten alive. He warned me about Sebastian but what he doesn't know is that I can handle that man any day. He pisses me off, but at the end of the day he isn't going to walk all over me like he did Elijah. I don't care what he's used to.

"Hey, going downstairs?" Elijah asks once he catches up to me. He's probably five or so inches taller than me with my heels on and pretty thin. He wears circle black rimmed glasses which accentuate his green eyes. He reminds me of Harry Potter, in the books not the movies version. This interests me because I have a full sleeve of tattoos dedicated to that book series.

"Yeah, I'm starved. Heading down to the café," I reply after I hit the down button.

"I'll join you if you don't mind," he suggests.

"That's fine. I don't have tons of time. I was just going to grab something and come right back up," I state as the elevator doors open. We walk in and he presses the ground button.

"How's your first day going?" Elijah queries.

"It's been fine so far. There was an uncomfortable meeting with Jared Thompson but other than that the computer work is a piece of cake. I used to schedule things all the time when I was in – I mean, when I was younger and in college." My cheeks heat up and I look away from Elijah before he notices. I almost told a complete stranger about my past. *What the hell is wrong with me?* Hopefully, he won't fixate with the wording mishap I just had.

"Wow, it took me a while to figure everything out. Plus, you are working for the ogre. I'm seriously sorry that you have to work for him. I'll help out anytime I can," he states.

"Thank you, but I can handle him. I grew up with a lot of guys around, so I know how to deal with a particularly stubborn one." Blaine was always stubborn and sometimes downright mean to me. It wasn't always like that, but once we became famous, he wanted everything to be his way. Nothing was ever up for discussion. It's strange to think of myself as a widow. But that's what I am, even if our marriage was one of convenience. I loved him, but I wasn't in love with him anymore. I'm not sure when it happened, I just fell out of love at some point.

The elevator doors open and Elijah gestures for me to go first. He follows me out and we walk toward the cafeteria.

"Are you alright?" He asks. "Seemed like I lost you for a minute in the elevator."

"Oh yeah, yeah. I just was thinking of some things I need to get done today." I had a whole walk down memory lane while I was in the elevator. *Good job making people believe you aren't weird, Stormy.*

"Oh good. I thought it was because I asked you out." I stop walking and look at Elijah with a puzzled look. "I guess you zoned out before that. Heh." He rakes his hand through his black hair and stares back at me.

I start walking again. "I'm sorry, Elijah. I have been under a lot of stress lately. I haven't even been in New York for a week yet. I'm still trying to get my bearings." I try to convey my disinterest without hurting his feelings. In all honesty, I don't think he would be able to handle me. Between my past and my anxiety, I don't think he would be capable to be the rock that I need. He is too sweet to give me the tough love that I need sometimes.

"No worries. Maybe we can grab a drink after work sometime." He is persistent. I'll give him that.

We order our food and wait the few minutes it takes to prepare. Elijah tries to pay for mine, but I decline the offer. I'm going to have to tell him flat out that I'm not interested. Obviously, he didn't get the hint. I hate being put in this situation. We grab our meals and head back toward the bank of elevators.

"Do you know where these paintings came from?" I ask Elijah, as I look at a different one I hadn't seen before.

"I think Miles acquired them from a local gallery when he and his brother took over the company after their father passed away," he says.

"They're stunning," I say as I inspect the painting in front of me.

"Yes, you are." Elijah says with a flush of pink on his cheeks. I kind of want to slap him for being so forward with me and only knowing me for a few hours.

"Elijah, you're sweet, but I'm-" before I can finish my sentence, Sebastian is behind us and finishing it for me.

"She just started working here a few hours ago. Learn how to read body language, Elijah. She isn't interested." Well, that's one way to put it, but now Elijah is the color of a tomato. He mumbles something about forgetting his drink from the cafeteria and takes off in that direction.

"What the hell? That was rude. I had it under control," I state, as the elevator doors open and we walk in. Sebastian swipes his card to take us to the twentieth floor.

"He didn't need to be talking to you like that. You already had one sleazeball come on to you today. You didn't need another one," he grits out.

"Elijah isn't a sleazeball. He was just taking a chance. Albeit not a good one but" I trail off. I'm not sure why I'm defending him, his actions did piss me off but it's better than agreeing with Sebastian. Actually, I don't know which is a better course of action. They both piss me off. Where does he come off thinking he can save me twice in one day when he threw me under the bus on Saturday.

"He needs to work on being a better member of the team than trying, and failing, at hitting on the new employee," Sebastian grinds his jaw as he finishes the last part of his statement. If I didn't know any better, I would say that he was jealous, but I know that's not true.

"Fuck you. You" but before I can finish, Sebastian has me pinned up against the elevator wall.

He grips a handful of my hair as he whispers into the shell of my ear, "What was that you wanted me to do to you?" He smirks as heat blooms on my cheeks. This motherfucker thinks he can get a rise out of me, but he has another thing coming. Yes, he is insanely hot. Too hot for his own good, actually. But he isn't going to get what he wants. I'm fresh meat around here and he wants to claim me first. It's all a game to men. He lets go of me and my head tingles from the pain of being pulled but oddly enough I have to hold in a moan at the sensation.

"Do you do this to all women? It's probably why you're still single," I tell him as I straighten my body.

"How do you know I'm single? Have you been looking into me?" He asks with a side grin.

"No, that's not what I was – Oh just forget it." I step away from him to the other side of the elevator.

I have nothing more to say to this man. He has a retort for anything that can come out of my mouth. We stand in tense silence as the elevator climbs the floors. I don't want to face Sebastian, but I am rewarded by his appearance in the mirror in front of me. He's a lot taller than me, even in heels and he wears impeccably tailored suits that fit him like a glove. I'm sure he has a personal shopper, I can't fathom seeing Sebastian doing mundane tasks like common people. He acts snobby and better than every other person in a room. But he is a looker. His thick dark brown hair falls gently over his forehead and his smoldering green eyes could rival any model in New York City. His chiseled jaw and defined cheek bones must be a family trait if the portraits downstairs are anything to go by. His family has impeccable genes. You can tell he works out, but he isn't huge. He looks more like Ryan Reynolds. Maybe Sebastian is Deadpool, they are both assholes. He's a beautiful fuckboy that keeps messing with the wrong girl.

The elevator reaches the twentieth floor and I dash out with my lunch in hand. I set my sandwich down on my desk and throw my purse into an empty drawer. It's only one o' clock and I'm ready to leave this place. I still have to go into Sebastian's office after lunch and go over some shit that Elijah probably already taught me. I sigh thinking, no reason in dreading something that has to happen no matter what. I eat quickly and pull out my phone.

Stormy:

Want to get art supplies tonight? I need to get my mind off this place.

Picasso:

You don't have to ask me twice. That's my favorite kind of shopping, but I will be getting home late tonight. Can we do a raincheck?

Stormy:

Sure. No worries.

I sigh again and put my phone away. Gathering the iPad and a notebook, I get up and head to the handsome devil's office. I take a deep breath and knock on his door.

"Come in." His deep gravelly voice travels to my side of the door and down to my clit. Hmm, that's a new development. *What the hell is wrong with me?* I shift uncomfortably in my heels and enter the man's cave.

ELEVEN

Sebastian

The meeting with Stormy was short and uneventful, ironically. I went through my schedule and told her to forward me only important emails to which she said she already knew how. Fuck me, she's a firecracker, it's an attractive quality. I never know what's going to come out of her pretty little mouth. Fuck, that mouth of hers. I want to see it wrapped around my cock leaving red lipstick all down it. Just the thought has me adjusting myself under my desk. I can't be attracted to an employee, but I also can't deny that I want to know more about her. It's a mind fuck.

The week passes quickly enough. Stormy and I get on for the most part. She takes special measure to make sure she isn't alone with me unless she has to be. It's Thursday afternoon and I'm wrapping things up for the day when an alert pops up on my phone warning me of an impending storm. *Shit, I rode my bike today.* It's going to be a wet trip home. I check my watch and see it's near closing time anyways. I'm going to go ahead and get out of here and hopefully avoid the worst of it. Standing from my desk, I close my laptop with the proposal I was working on and walk to my closet to retrieve the clothes I wore to work today. Stripping out of my suit, I pull on my jeans and boots. I replace my undershirt with a black Henley and my leather jacket over top. I put my laptop in my bag, along with some reports that I need to go over tonight. No rest for the wicked, I suppose. I shoot a text to Elijah telling him he can leave when he finishes up whatever he is working on. I'll tell Stormy she can leave when I pass by her desk.

I open my office door and am graced by the sight of Stormy leaning over her desk looking for something. I can't help but to stare for a moment because she has a spectacular ass. Although, an argument could be made that her whole body is wrapped in a spectacular package. I scrub my hand over my face and walk towards her.

"There's a storm coming in, so you can go ahead and leave for the day." Stormy jumps at my sudden appearance near her but composes herself quickly.

"Yeah, thanks. It's already raining pretty hard out there," she states as she studies the wall of floor-to-ceiling windows looking out over the city. It looks like getting out of here before the storm arrived was a moot point. It's already here.

"I'll see you bright and early tomorrow, Ms. Brooks." I stride past her holding my helmet under one arm and my bag slinged over the other. Waiting for the elevator seems to take longer than usual, but it probably not, it's probably just me wanting to get home before this weather gets too dangerous for a motorcycle. Finally, it arrives, and I step in hitting the garage floor.

I hop on my bike and rev the engine a few times to get it warmed up. I'm not looking forward to getting soaked, it's too late now. I should've called Thomas to come pick me up, but I didn't want to interrupt him spending time with his wife, since her less than savory prognosis came back about her cancer.

Leaving the garage, I look left then right and see a very wet silver-haired goddess standing on the side of the street. She's trying to hail a cab, they all keep speeding right past her. She looks down at her bandaged hand and I hear a "Shit" leave her mouth. I don't know when I let my foot off the brake but somehow I end up right in front of her and I can't help but appreciate how the rain is falling on her head and down her face. She looks like a siren, here to steer men to their deaths. I remove my helmet and set it aside.

"What are you doing out here?" I shout over the downpour.

"What does it look like? I'm waiting for a cab," she yells back at me.

"No cabs are going to stop in this weather. Hop on and I'll give you a ride." The words tumble from my mouth before I can stop them, they're out.

"I'm not getting on that thing with you. Are you crazy?" she shouts. I look up at the angry storm about to parade down on us and I know I have to get her out of here even if I have to lift her and put her on the bike myself. I reach inside my saddle bag and pull out an extra helmet that I keep with me. I get off the bike and stand right in front of her. She looks up at me with those doe eyes still full of fire. In one move, I take the helmet and place it on her head. "Hey! I said I'm not going anywhere with you, you psycho!"

She exclaims while juggling her purse and trying to get the helmet off without using the injured hand.

I ignore her protests and bring the hand in question down to me so I can examine it closer. I see blood seeping through the bandages. I would bet money that she ripped some of her stitches out when she was waving her hand in the air and trying to hail a cab. I have to get this taken care of immediately. I feel another twinge in my chest at the sight of her in pain making me rub my hand over my heart to steady the unpleasant feeling. The warmth from her hand spreads up my arm.

"Get your ass on this bike, Stormy. You're hurt. I need to get you home and I can't do that with you being stubborn." She looks down the road, probably for a cab to come and save her. When one doesn't magically appear, she looks back down at her hand that I'm still holding.

"Fine. But I've never been on one of these before." She points to the bike. I have to fight back a smile that she will be doing something with me for the first time.

"All you need to do is hang on. Think you can handle that?" I ask not wanting an answer just wanting to see her reaction. "Also, the helmets are connected via Bluetooth so you can talk to me if you need to." I put mine back on and look at her. She looks hot as hell in my helmet. I close the glass visor on hers to keep the rain out and show her how to get onto my bike. After a little maneuvering, we are heading down the street. "We need to stop at Walgreen's Pharmacy to get some more bandages and things for your hand," I say through the speaker.

"That's not necessary. I think I still have some stuff at home." I roll my eyes at her insistence of being difficult. Most woman would fall over themselves to get this close to me, Stormy acts like it is a hardship to have to do it. Maybe she really does hate me. I mean we didn't meet under great terms. There is one thing I know for sure, that it's a fine line between love and hate. And fuck me, I don't hate her.

Stormy

My hands are wrapped around Sebastian as tight as they can go without giving him internal damage. I don't think the best time to try riding a motorcycle for the first time should be during a thunderstorm. I may be wrong, but all I can think about is sliding off to my death. *A little dramatic, I know.* It's hard to think straight with the warmth from his back pressing in on me. I can't help but to sink into him a little more.

His voice purrs over the engine, "I'm stopping at a pharmacy up the road for more bandages."

It takes me a moment to realize what he said. "Wait. No, no. That's not necessary. I-I'm fine," I stutter as a chill seeps down my spine from the freezing rain soaking through my clothes.

I hear him chuckle through the speaker. "It wasn't a question, Gandalf."

"Whatever. You know he was badass," I mutter to myself. Rolling my eyes I concentrate on using my remaining strength for holding on to Sebastian instead of throwing back quips. A few minutes pass before we are turning into a pharmacy parking lot. Sebastian parks and cuts the engine. He parked where there was an overhang so the rain isn't pelting us as badly.

"You're going to have to let me go if we want to get off this bike." He murmurs and heat flames my cheeks. Thank goodness I am still wearing this damned helmet. I pull my arms back as he slides off the bike, removing his helmet as he goes. He holds his hand out for me to take and I'm momentarily shocked by his sweet gesture. I take it and slide off the bike the best I can in heels and a skirt without having a Britney Spears moment. *No one is seeing my underwear today, folks.* Once I'm sturdy on my feet, Sebastian pulls me closer and removes the strap of my helmet for me and tugs it over my head. Our eyes meet and for a heated moment while everything around us stills. Then he opens his mouth. "You know, if I didn't know any better, I would say that you like me a little."

Of course, he would ruin the moment by opening his mouth. "I guess you don't know any better then," I reply as I march inside the store leaving him with a satisfied smirk on his face. He knows he gets to me, it's a dangerous game he's playing. I need to be more on guard when I'm around him. He's a playboy and now my boss. I can't go there. *I won't go there.*

I walk through the aisles until I find the first aid section. I look down at my hand and cringe at the blood seeping through the bandages. The throbbing intensified after holding onto Sebastian for dear life. This wound is in the worst spot for healing purposes. It's hard to not move the palm of your hand. I guess I need to wrap it tighter to restrict movement. I take a deep breath to calm the nerves threatening to spill out. *It's just a surface cut. You are fine, Stormy.* A tear begins to fall but I wipe it away.

Sebastian finds me in the aisle and starts throwing items into the hand-held basket.

"I don't need all this," I inform him, he ignores me and continues grabbing different kinds of bandages and ointments and tossing them into the basket.

"There. I think that's all we need." He motions to the basket. "Unless you need something else from here?" I shake my head and he takes my uninjured hand and walks us to the front of the store. His hand is warm and comforting for some reason and mine fits perfectly inside his. The thought is jarring, so I lift my hand from his as he places the basket on the conveyor belt. That's when I realize that I left my wallet on the bike.

"I need to run out and get my wallet. I'll be right back." I tell him as I start toward the front doors.

He moves quickly, grabbing me around the waist and hauling me back against him. The breath gets knocked from my lungs as I smack against his hard frame. The sudden movement has me taking a step to right myself. The feel of my back pressed against his muscular body sends shivers up my spine. Goosebumps erupt over my skin as he leans over and whispers in my ear. "I've got this." He holds me against his body, his large hand splaying over my midsection while we're checking out. He somehow pays with one hand and grabs the bags. "Now be a good girl and get back on the bike," he murmurs in a low husky voice as he lets me go. I stand on my wobbly legs for a moment as the thought of what he just said washes over me. I think my brain short circuited when he said, "good girl." No one has ever called me that. Fuck, why do

I want to obey him? Why do I want to hear him say it again? My legs move of their own accord toward Sebastian. As he's packing the bags into his bike he looks over his shoulder at me with a grin on his face. That bastard knows what he does to me. Somehow, somewhere along the way, he got under my skin.

The storm has gotten worse in the little time we were in the store. "Looks like we are in for quite a ride. Don't let go of me," he says firmly as he places the helmet back on my head. He takes his time attaching the straps like he wants to make sure everything is secure. "Here take my jacket. You're shivering."

"I'm not taking your jacket. You need that." I shake my head and try to move past him. Again, he stops me.

"You need to stop doing that, Stormy." His face is stern as he talks. "I said take my jacket. I'll be fine. You're the one that isn't used to this kind of weather," he reiterates and takes his jacket off and slings it around my shoulders. The heat immediately envelops me, and his cologne permeates my senses. I close my eyes as the leather, sandalwood and vanilla scent invades my mind.

"Thank you," I mutter. It's all I can say. Sebastian gets on the bike, with me following suit, squeezing him tightly. He pulls out of the parking lot and straight into the traffic. With the light traffic and his penchant for speeding, it doesn't take long for us to get to my apartment. He pulls into a vacant spot and shuts off the bike. He slides off the seat. Then without missing a beat he grabs me, placing me standing in front of him. I tug off my helmet while he is doing the same. The rain beats down harder on us as we stand there. I know I have to make a run for it, so I slip out of my heels and hold them along with my purse.

"Thank you for the ride. I -" before I can finish, he cuts in.

"Come on. I have to fix your hand," he shouts through the sound of thunder overhead. This isn't the place to argue. I want to get inside, I guess he shouldn't be riding in this kind of weather. But I wasn't expecting him to come up to my apartment. I hold on to my stuff and take off through the parking lot. My feet splash in the puddles as I run. If this wasn't a bad storm, I would be taking this opportunity to be dancing around in it. I love the rain. I feel like it cleanses my soul.

Sebastian runs up beside me, grabbing my hand. He smiles down at me while we are running, letting out a laugh. I want to hold on to this feeling. It's a freeing feeling.

We finally make it to the lobby of my apartment. I look over to see a very wet, tall, and handsome version of Sebastian. His clothes stick to his skin, outlining the amazing muscles I knew he had. I probably look like a drowned rat compared to him. I'm sure my makeup is running in all directions.

"You really don't have to help me with my hand. I can handle it." I look down at where the bandages were. They must have come undone in the rain and my palm is slowly bleeding onto the floor. Some of the stitches popped open, letting me see how deep the cut really was. My stomach flips at the sight. Seeing all the fresh blood on my hand takes me back to the night Blaine was shot. I begin to tremble when I remember the red sticky mess of my late husband. I try really hard to will my thoughts to absolutely anything else, but I slide to the floor clutching my hand. I'm losing this battle. Panic is taking over. The lobby transforms into the scene from the kitchen that night as a sob escapes my lips. Eyes closed tightly; I squeeze my hand allowing the pain to faintly tether me to the present.

Sebastian is right there with me, pulling me to his chest. I can't get any words out to tell him what is going on. My mind is fucking with me. I can see Blaine lying there before me. This feels like I am experiencing that night all over again. Just like that night I can feel someone's hands wrapped around my waist, pulling me away. Tears stream down my face, mixing with rain and makeup.

"I'm right here," Sebastian soothes as he pushes strands of my hair from my face. He grabs my face and forces me to look him in the eyes. "I'm right here. Take a deep breath with me. In through your nose and out through your mouth." I try to mimic his breathing actions, but the images keep playing through my mind. "Stormy, listen to me. You have to slow your breathing. You're going to hyperventilate. Now, deep breaths in and out," he commands. "That's it. Just like that. Take another one. You have to keep breathing, Stormy. Listen to my voice. I've got you." I try to keep up with his breathing pattern. I watch as he inhales, and I do the same. He exhales and all the air leaves my lungs. "Now tell me three things you see." I look at him for a moment, puzzled, but I do what he says.

"I-I see you." I breathe out. I try to look around while my head is still grasped between his hands. "I see my ruined shoes." I partly laugh out. "I see blood." My breath hitches when I look back at my hand. I'm close to going back under, but Sebastian is right there to bring me back.

"Good girl. Don't look at your hand. Look at me. Tell me three things you smell." Again, I look at him sardonically, but I try to concentrate on what I smell.

"I smell leather. And your cologne. Sandalwood and vanilla, I think. And I smell the dirty lobby smell." He grins at my answers,

I can't help but to return it. A sob gets caught in my throat as I try to explain what just happened. I feel so vulnerable and raw. The adrenaline coursing through my body wants me to take flight, get out of here to hide away from all the pain. "I-I'm okay, now. I'm so sorry you had to see-"

"Shh, come here." He pulls us up from the ground and tugs me into a tight embrace. I can't help but to lean in close to him. His smell and warmth grounds me. "Don't ever apologize for that," he demands.

"But how did you know?" I murmur. *How the hell did he know what was happening to me? How did he know how to stop it from going any further?*

"My cousin, Sam, has PTSD from the military," he explains. "I've been around him when he was having a flash back and I could see the same expression on you. He once told me how his therapist said to ground himself during an episode. Naming three things you can see and three things you can smell. You can keep going and name other things around you. It helps bring you back to the present," he breathes out, into the side of my ear. Another tremble runs through me as his hot breath caresses my skin.

I'm shivering all over now. Whether it's from my soaked clothing or coming down from the panic attack. "Thank you," is all I manage to say.

"Let's get you to your apartment." Sebastian picks up my discarded shoes and purse, plus all the shopping bags. He takes my hand as we walk towards the elevator. Maybe my first impression of Sebastian was wrong. Maybe he isn't the colossal asshat that I thought he was. However, I still have to remember the news article Lana sent me about him. He's a playboy and I can't give my heart to someone that's going to throw me away. I've been through way too much for that. I have to keep my guard up around him. *Yeah, final last words.*

TWELVE

Sebastian

As we walk into Stormy's apartment, she shrugs out of my jacket and hangs it by the door. The moment it's hung I think it looks good in that spot. Then I wonder where the hell that came from. I do admit I want to know more about this mysterious vixen before me and what demons she's fighting. She was about to go into full blown panic mode when she saw the blood on her hand. Seeing the blood struck something within her and she went to a dark place. I'm just glad I was able to get her through it. An event like that binds people together. I feel closer to her now. That shared experience shot a tether between us that I don't think I want to sever.

"Where is your bathroom? We need to clean your hand." I drop her shoes and purse to the floor.

"Thank you for the ride and everything, but I can take care of my hand myself." She still is trying to fight me on this. Little does she know that this isn't a battle that she is going to win.

"Is that right? You're right-handed, Stormy. How are you going to manage to get these closures on your palm? Can you stop being

113

a pain in the ass for five seconds and let someone help you?" I grab her left hand and tug her to me. She lets out a gasp as I push her up against the wall and press my body into hers.

"I-I can do it, Sebastian," she replies breathlessly. She licks her lips and looks up at me towering over her. She tries to push me away, but I stand unaffected.

I lean down, my face level with hers, "I think you need someone to do it for you. Who takes care of you, Stormy? Hmm? You need to let people in." She rolls her eyes and tries to duck around me but I'm there hauling her back to the wall. This time I keep one hand on her waist and the other on her face. She's got nowhere to go. She has to submit to me.

"Sebastian, I-" I slam my lips down on hers, shutting up that sassy little mouth. We stand motionless for a moment, until she finally succumbs and pulls me closer. She rises on her toes, I pick her up and her legs automatically circle around my waist. I push her back against the wall and cup her face while I devour her mouth. She lets out a low moan, allowing my tongue access to hers.

She pulls back for a moment. "Stop. We can't do this. You're my boss, Sebastian." I chuckle as I move a strand of her hair from her face.

"I'm not your boss right now, Angel." I kiss her again. Passion fuels our mouths as we consume each other. She tastes like strawberries and pure sweetness. I could kiss her for hours, but I need to bandage her hand. I just need to break the kiss, but I'm not ready to give up the taste of Stormy yet. She's so fucking sweet. She's unlike anyone I have ever met. I pull away for just a moment.

"Bathroom?" I question, as I kiss down the side of her neck. Licking and nipping as I go. The smell of her perfume is sexy as fuck. I don't know what it is. Something floral but mixed with a flavor that is all Stormy. It's a heady combination.

"Second door to the right," she groans out as I massage her ass in my hands. I look up and move in the direction of the bathroom. We slam against the door and without breaking the kiss she reaches down, feeling for the doorknob. She turns it and flicks on the lights as we enter. I set her on the counter and push myself between her legs. Her skirt rides up even more and I bet anything she's wet. I can feel her heat pressing against me. Breaking the kiss, I pull back and see her swollen, red lips.

"We need to get out of these wet clothes." She nods her head in agreement, but that's not going to do. "I need your words, Stormy." I whisper into her ear. I can see goosebumps run along her arms when I get this close to her. A smile crosses my face at the way I affect her.

"Yes. Turn on the shower, Sebastian," she breathes out. I don't have to be told twice. I pull away from her to open the glass door and turn the shower on hot. I don't want her catching a cold because she was out in the freezing rain for so long. As much as I want her out of her clothes because I need to fuck her, they also need to come off so she can get into something warm. It's an odd sensation, caring that way about someone. I have this overwhelming feeling to protect this woman.

Steam begins to rise around us. I walk back over to Stormy, still sitting on the counter. She hasn't taken her eyes off me the whole time I was away from her. I'd say she wants me just as badly as I want her.

"Are you sure, Stormy?" I question. I want to make sure she isn't going to regret this later.

She bites her bottom lip and nods again. "Yes, Sebastian, please." I close the door and lock it. I don't hesitate and start undressing her. I can see her purple bra showing through her drenched white shirt.

"Arms up." She raises her arms above her head and a little slice of her tummy shows. I grasp both sides of her shirt and slowly raise it up her body. I throw it to the side once it's off and I press my lips to hers again. I needed to taste her. I pull her forward so I can reach around and unhook her bra. It falls from her shoulders, I take a step back to take in the perfect sight that is Stormy. She is a fucking goddess sitting here. I want to worship her body the way it deserves. I grab her chin in my hand and bring it up until she's looking at me. "Do you know how gorgeous you are? Do you know how hard I've tried to stay away from you? I can't anymore. I need to be inside you." She tries to look away, I hold firm onto her chin. I can see the inexperience written across her face, but that doesn't stop me. I lean down taking one nipple into my mouth while I tweak the other with my fingers. She grips my hair and pushes her chest out for me to get better leverage. I wrap my arm around her, pulling her body closer to mine. Her soft skin brushes against mine.

"Yes," she moans out. I move my mouth to show attention to the other nipple. I gently bite and pull it between my teeth. She clenches my hair tighter, letting me know she likes a bit of pain with her pleasure. She might not realize it, but I do. I realized it the day in the elevator. I could see it in her eyes when I pulled her hair.

"Your turn," she smirks, as she takes the bottom of my shirt and tugs it up my body as far as she can, I take my hand and strip the rest of it away. She moves her uninjured hand along my chest and down my abs. She tries to unbuckle my belt, I help move it along. I whip my belt out and throw it off to the side. It clinks against the tile floor. I unbutton my jeans and let her push them down. My hard cock springs free and a small gulp comes from her. I chuckle at her expression. I know what she is thinking, but it will fucking fit.

I gently pull her from the counter and place her on the cool tile. She unzips her skirt and lets it fall away. She's left in a matching purple thong. I can see her plump ass in the mirror, I want to turn her around and spank it. My hand print would be a nice addition to her smooth milky flesh. I also see the tattoos that I thought I saw the other day. They look like matching bows underneath her ass cheeks. I'll have to get a good look at them later.

I slide down to my knees before her. I look up and see the fire in her eyes like the night of the fundraiser, only this time I'm going to play with that fire. I kiss a path down from her breasts to her belly button as I slide my hands down her silky skin. I want to feel and taste everything on this woman. It's a strong feeling to finally get something I have wanted since the first time I laid eyes on her. I hook my fingers in her thong and pull it down her legs. It pools on the floor with the rest of our discarded clothing.

"Fuck, you're killing me, Angel. Are you wet for me?" She whimpers as I trail my fingers up her inner thigh to her cunt. "Is this needy little pussy ready to be ravaged by me, because once I start, mmm, I'm not going to stop," I say as she shivers in my hands.

"Please," she whimpers. I spread her legs further apart and lean in, smelling her arousal. I lick a path from her center to her clit. She places her hands on my shoulders as I dive in further. Not getting the view I want; I lift her leg and throw it over my shoulder. The sudden movement makes her squeal. Now I have a better sight of her juicy pussy. I go in for another taste and it's even better than the last. She tastes like sweet nectar from the gods. I could eat from her all day.

"That feels so good," she utters as she rocks into my face. I pick up my pace lapping at her juices and circling her clit with my tongue. Adding a finger, she moans and thrust herself on me. I add a second finger and she squeezes me hard as I lick and pound into her. It only takes a moment before she is shattering right before me. "Yes, yes!" She moans. I continue to lick and suck her clit as her release washes through her. It's a beautiful sight to behold. I lick my lips, tasting her sweetness one last time before I drop her leg back to the floor.

I stand and grasp her waist walking us into the shower. The hot water sprays us as we step in. The heat feels good against my cool skin. But even without the shower, Stormy is heating me up from the inside out.

"What do you want, Stormy?" I ask as her pussy rocks against my hard cock. It would be easy to slide right inside of her from this angle.

"I want you." Is all she says before she crashes her lips down on mine. It's like magic to my fucking ears. Never in a million years did I think Stormy would utter those words to me, but here we are. I push her up against the glass and trail my hand over her bare pussy. She moans as I slide one finger inside her. Fuck she is so tight and so wet. I slide in a second finger, using my thumb to circle her clit. She begins riding my fingers, fighting for her own orgasm again.

118

"Yes, right there!" she exclaims as I pump my fingers in and out of her tight little hole. It doesn't take long for her to come all over my hand. It's pure bliss I see on her face.

"Fuck, that was so hot." I lean my head against hers as she continues to come down from her high. "Please tell me you are on birth control." She looks puzzled for a moment until recognition dawns on her face. I don't *ever* fuck without condoms but there is something about her that makes me *need* to get inside her bare.

"I-I am. But I've never-" That's all I want to hear. We'll be each other's first in that department. I don't know why that makes me so happy. I just want to claim her like a fucking caveman. To put my print on her. To mark her as my own. The thought is insane and irrational, but it doesn't make it less true. I am captivated by this little vixen.

"I'm clean. You can trust me on that," I reassure her.

"Okay. I've only been with one other person." I knew she was mostly innocent. For a moment I want to find that other guy and beat the shit out of him for touching what's mine. *What the actual fuck is wrong with me? Why do I keep having these bizarre emotions with her? Is this what my brother was always going on about?* The fuck with that. This is just a one-off thing. Like everyone else I fuck. She will be out of my system after tonight, then I can go back to my normal ways. That thought sours my stomach.

"Don't worry. I'll take care of you." I take one hand from her ass and line my cock up to her entrance. She is so drenched that I coat myself in her wetness and plunge into her with one swift motion.

A scream erupts from her mouth. I begrudgingly stand there motionless, letting her adjust to my size. I push her back up against the glass and take her chin in my hand, bringing her lips to meet mine. We both grow desperate as we ravage each other with our mouths. Stormy pulls my face closer to hers and begins to move up and down my shaft. *Thank fuck.* I couldn't wait much longer.

"Fuck, you are so tight. Hang on." I demand. She braces her hands on my shoulders as I begin to pound into her. Her face soon morphs into one of pleasure.

"Oh, Sebastian. Yes!" she chants over and over.

"Say my name when you come. I want everyone in this building to hear who makes you feel this good." Her nails dig into my shoulders, I'm sure leaving marks. I slap her ass hard. An audible gasp slips from her sweet little mouth. I knew she would like some pain. She rocks in tandem with my thrusts and soon she is at her peak again. I feel her walls clamp down on me and it's everything I can do to hold off longer.

"Sebastian!" she yells. And a smile tugs at the corner of my mouth.

"That's right, Angel." I keep thrusting in harder and harder with every motion. I start to feel the tingle at the base of my spine, I know I won't last much longer. I start rubbing her clit in rough circles, causing her to jolt in my arms.

"I can't. Not again," she whines into my chest.

"You will." I smack the other ass cheek and that fire returns to her eyes. So, that's what my girl needed. She needed an awakening. I take her nipple in my finger, pinching and pulling until she is writhing on my dick again. This time when she comes, I do too.

"Fuuuck," I yell as jet after jet of my come dumps into Stormy's tight little pussy. I begin to slow my strokes as she starts to go limp in my arms from exhaustion. Our juices slide down my balls and into the drain below us. I pull out of her and set her on her feet.

Holding her up until she gets her balance, I lean down and take her mouth. It's raw, intense, and sweet. *How can a kiss be sweet?* But that's how it feels with her in my arms.

She breaks away from me first. "That was intense." I kiss her soft lips again.

"Let's shower so we can get out of here." I don't want to admit how intense that was for me as well. It's the best sex I've ever had, and it wasn't even the kinky fuckery that I'm normally into. I don't have the guts to investigate that further. I grab the shampoo bottle squeezing some into the palm of my hand. "Turn around." I command. I spread the shampoo through her long hair and massage her scalp. I tell myself I am helping her because her hand is injured, but that's not the whole truth. I find that I want to do this simple thing for her. *What the hell is wrong with me?* No one takes care of her. I know her independence is important to her, but I can also tell she's never been properly cared for.

"You don't have to wash my hair, you know?" She peaks over her shoulder at me, I concentrate on the task at hand. I pull the shower head off and begin rinsing her hair, making sure to get all the shampoo out. I repeat the process with her conditioner while she washes her body. I wanted to do that too, but the water is already starting to get cool. Once we are both rinsed, Stormy turns the water off. She goes to open the door, I pull her back for a moment. I don't want this to be over yet. I don't want the spell to be broken when that door opens. I pull her into my arms, kissing her feverishly. She returns it with the same ferocity. She pulls back with a smile on her face, and I find that I want to be the reason for all her smiles.

"Can I get the towels, now?" she queries. I release her from my grasp and nod. Not trusting my words right now. "Good, I'm getting cold," she says as she turns to open the door.

Once we are dried off, I tie the towel around my waist. Stormy wraps hers around her body. I wish she was still naked before me.

"Do you want me to put your clothes in the dryer?" She asks.

"Let me." I gather my drenched clothes from the floor and follow her out of the bathroom. I throw my clothes into the machine, hitting the start button. "We need to get back in there to fix your hand," I point out. The bleeding has slowed. *Thank fuck.* I would have felt like a bastard if she was bleeding the entire time we were in the shower.

"Oh yeah. Okay." She walks back to the bathroom. I head to the door where I dropped the bags from the pharmacy before meeting her back in the bathroom.

She looks down at her hand. "Fuck. This looks bad."

"Get up on the counter. We need to stop the bleeding." I help her up and grab the bags, dumping all the contents on the counter with her. I wash my hands first before I touch her hand.

"I'm going to wash this." I take her injured hand and run it under the water. She cringes, looking away. She must not like the sight of blood. "Do you have a wash cloth?"

"Yeah, in that drawer," she gestures to the one to my left. I open it and grab one. I turn off the water, pat dry her hand, then place the cloth in her palm.

"Squeeze this until I tell you to open your hand." I instruct. I look through the things on the counter, finding the butterfly closures. Opening the package, I take out a few of the temporary closures. "Okay, open up."

"Where did you learn to do all this?" she inquires.

"I actually took a few medical classes in college. I wasn't sure what I wanted to do. I knew I was expected to work in the family business, but I didn't always want to. I wanted to help people." I look at her beautiful yellow eyes getting lost in what I was doing for a moment. I clear my throat and look back to her hand, applying the small bandages over the cut to make the skin come back together. This is the next best thing besides more sutures or even super glue. She wiggles a bit on the counter, her face contorts into a pained expression. "Am I hurting you?"

"It's okay. It needs to be done. Tell me more." I think my talking takes her mind off the pain, if that's the case I will talk all night if it makes her feel better. I have this desire to protect her and to take her pain away. Not that I don't think she can do that on her own, but I feel like she has been carrying too much, I want to lift some of the burden for her.

"So, I took these medical classes and one of them was wound care. That's why I took you to the pharmacy. I didn't think you would have everything that was needed," I admit.

"You didn't have to do all that." I look back up at her, seeing the vulnerability that she hides.

"I wanted to. Is that okay?" I keep my eyes on her until she answers me.

"It is," she replies. "Thank you. It means a lot."

I turn my gaze back to her hand and finish wrapping it up to immobilize it. The more she moves it, the easier it will be to open those sutures back open, making the wound never heal properly.

"I'm glad that I could help." I don't mean with just her hand. I think she understands my meaning.

123

"Downstairs I was going into a panic attack, you were able to pull me out of it. No one has been able to step in like that and bring me back. I feel a little embarrassed that my boss saw that side of me," she mutters the last part to herself, looking down.

"Stormy, look at me." I pull her chin up until her eyes are on me. "I told you, I'm not your boss right now." I run my thumb over her plump bottom lip and lean in closer, placing my other hand on her waist. She takes a deep breath, her eyes never stray from mine. I crash my lips down on hers. She's so soft and sweet. I can still taste her strawberry ChapStick, I want to lick it all off. A soft moan escapes her parted lips allowing me access to the rest of her mouth. My tongue tangles with hers and her pure sweetness invades my mouth. I pull her body to the edge of the counter, her legs part to let me through. She wraps her legs around my waist, pulling our bodies together.

Stormy pulls back a bit and whispers, "I think I need to get dressed."

"Aw, where is the fun in that. I can't get dressed yet. You don't want me to feel left out do you?" I ask with a smile on my face.

"Did you really think that would work?" She laughs and it's like music to my ears. I shake my head no as she pushes me back and hops off the counter. "Can we at least get out of here?"

"Lead the way." I don't know where she is heading, but I'm coming to realize I would blindly follow her anywhere. A fucking scary thought. Surely, it was just because the sex was incredible, right? Fuck if I know. That fucking fine line. I definitely don't hate her. Does that mean? *Fuck me.*

THIRTEEN

Stormy

*H**oly shit.* This can't be happening. Sebastian Knight is in my apartment, just fucked me against the shower, took care of my hand, and is now coming to my bedroom. *Is this real life?* I'm definitely not like those supermodel types he's normally seen with. But I can't help but feel special with the way he looks at me. Like he's really seeing me. He has this possessive quality about him that makes me think he would make a great partner if he were ever to settle down.

I open the door to my bedroom and usher him inside. I flip the switch that turns on the lamp, not wanting the bright lights from the ceiling right now. Sebastian breaks away from me and begins looking around my room. I lean against my dresser watching him observe. I feel more naked right now than I did in the shower. Bedrooms are incredibly intimate to me. I try to see the room from his eyes, wondering how he sees it.

He stops in front of a self-portrait I painted last year after the accident. "You were in pain. When did you paint this?" he asks, studying the canvas. It's not a question that I was in pain. He can see the anguish I was feeling when I painted that piece.

"I painted that about a year ago," I reply. He nods in response and continues to peruse the rest of the paintings I have leaning against the wall.

"Stormy, these are exceptional. Some of these could be used for book covers. Have you ever thought of doing that?" he questions. I shake my head. He looks at me and smiles. A fucking dimple comes out and I melt on sight. I don't think I have ever seen him truly smile before, only smirk.

"Thanks. I'll have to keep that in mind," I murmur, pulling the towel closer to my body. I've never really shown people my art. I'm not sure I would have shown Sebastian if they didn't happen to be in here. I've always painted what I was feeling in that moment. I'm very much an expressionist painter. I always have been. It's my equivalent to journaling I believe.

He moves on from the paintings to my bookshelf and heat flames my cheeks. He's about to see all the smut I read, which is a lot. "Looks like someone enjoys the romance genre." He grins as he takes one of the books from the shelf. "You know, I read somewhere that people tend to read romance to live out their fantasies. What are your fantasies, Stormy?" He queries, closing the book and putting it back in place. He crosses the room in a few strides to stand before me in his towel. "Tell me and maybe I can make them come true." He places both hands on the side of the dresser, boxing me in. Leaning down, he brushes his mouth against the shell of my ear. "I want to know what makes you so hot and needy when you are reading these books. Do you want to be dominated? Bound and at my mercy? Do you think about mixing pain with pleasure because I already know you like it." Chills run up my spine at his contact. I have no idea how to respond. He basically hit the nail on the head. He read me like one of my fucking books.

"I think I want what a lot of women want," I murmur.

"And what is that?" he asks.

"I want to be able to shut off my brain for five seconds and not have to worry about anything. I want to be at the mercy of a man who knows that he's doing. I love what I read in those books, but I want it to come to life. I want to know I'll be taken care of physically, mentally and emotionally." I don't know how that admission escaped my lips, but I don't care. I'm tired of knowing what I want and not going after it. Sebastian gave me a gift, asking me what I wanted. No one ever has.

"I knew you were a natural submissive," he whispers, "even though you're a feisty little thing. You just want to give up all that control, don't you? You need someone to help you carry the load that you are holding onto." He grazes my cheek as he puts some hair behind my ear.

"Yes," I breathe. He stands up from the dresser, towering over me. I can't help but check out the ink covering his perfect body. I didn't get a good look at it earlier but now he is on display in front of me. I want to capture his body in a painting. I don't think I could do it justice, though. He looks like a Greek god. With his chiseled muscles and sculpted body. It's as if Eros, son of Aphrodite, is standing before me.

"Do you trust me?" The question brings me back to the present. *Do I trust him? I shouldn't*. But oddly enough, I find myself nodding yes in response. He takes my hand in his and leads me to the bed. He pulls the towel from my body, tossing it to the floor. My first instinct is to cover myself, but Sebastian isn't having it. "Don't hide yourself from me. You are so sexy, Stormy, and I want to see your body." Moving my hands to my sides, I stand a little straighter looking at him. "Mmm, do you have any idea what you do to me?" I look down and see that his cock is trying to free itself from the confines of the towel. Feeling confident, I grasp the material and toss it to the side keeping my eyes locked on his. I see the heat building as he lets go of any restraint.

Sebastian cups my face with both hands, dragging his thumb over my bottom lip. Leaning down, he ghosts his lips over mine. Back and forth until the tension is too much, leaving the only way to relieve it is to have his lips firmly on me. I press into him, standing on my tippy toes. He smashes his lips down on mine. Our bodies come together as his tongue delves into my mouth. Butterflies erupt in my stomach at the feeling of this man pressed against me. The way this man kisses me is like nothing I have ever experienced before. Never in my life has a kiss felt possessive, but that's the way Sebastian makes it feel. Like he would go feral if he couldn't have his lips on mine. He tangles one hand in my hair tentatively until I moan out from the feeling. His hold tightens and my scalp burns, but he was right, I become ravenous. I want to mount this man more than I want my next breath.

He breaks away after nipping my bottom lip. "On your knees, Angel." I hesitate for a moment but when I look in his eyes, I see the dominance there and I suddenly don't want to disappoint him. I drop to my knees before him as I await my next instruction. I stare at his full length in front of me, I can't believe his huge size ever fit inside me. "Take me in your hand." My hand instantly finds his cock and he moans from the contact. I never did this with Blaine. I didn't have the desire to. I find that I really want to pleasure Sebastian. I want him to feel drunk with desire. I lean forward, licking the tip, tasting his salty pre-come before it hits the floor. "Mm, fuck, you're an eager little thing, aren't you? I don't think I told you to use your mouth yet, but I guess you couldn't help yourself." He smirks down at me. His cock throbs as I slide my hand from base to tip and back down. "Your hand feels so good wrapped around me, I want to feel your throat. Open up, Angel." I only get a moment before he thrusts inside my mouth. The pain from straining to open wide enough and the pull on my wet hair is wildly titillating. Tears begin to prick at my eyes, still, I don't want to stop. I want his whole cock in my mouth, even if that seems impossible. Sebastian angles my head looking up to him. "Hollow out your cheeks and breathe through your nose. Take me all the way." I whimper at his dirty mouth. I want more of it. *I need it.* He pumps his hips back and forth. I eventually take him all the way. "You take me so well." He purrs. The beating my throat is taking makes me slick between my legs. I reach between my thighs, parting my wet folds. I moan around his cock, and he groans in appreciation. "Since you are touching yourself without permission, I'm going to have to punish you," he groans as he watches my fingers graze my wet pussy. Heat spreads through my body at the thought of him punishing me.

Sebastian's thrusts become ragged, I know he's close. My tongue flattens and I use it to lick around him as he withdrawals from my mouth. "Fuck, Stormy, swallow me down, Angel." He grits out, holding my head in place with both of his hands cupping my cheeks. Jets of come spray my mouth making me have to keep swallowing to make sure I get it all. I have never been this turned on in my life. I didn't know giving pleasure like this could make me so wet, I nearly come just from the pure bliss I see on Sebastian's face. When he pulls out, he's still hard and looks like he is ready to go again.

"That was hot. You're such a good girl, taking me all the way like that," He reaches down, pulling me to my feet. He leans down bringing his lips to mine. His tongue tangles with my own and I know he can taste himself. He pulls back a bit and asks, "Was that your first blow job?" Heat flames my cheeks knowing that I may have done a terrible job.

"It was. I'm sorry-" He stops me from continuing by placing his finger over my mouth.

"It was amazing. You have nothing to be sorry about. You did everything I told you and it was epic. You can practice on me anytime you want," he jokes. Relief fills me and I smile at him. His gorgeous green eyes bore into mine.

"Get on the bed, Stormy," he demands. I sit on the edge of the bed looking up at him. "In the middle," he instructs. I nod tentatively, moving backwards until I am lying in the middle of the bed. My heart is thrumming in my chest wondering what this man has in store for me. Unease snakes its way up my body, and I'm left wondering if I can be strong enough to endure whatever he has to offer. "Close your eyes," he commands. My eyes stay on him for a moment then I decide to obey his demand. I hear him move away from the bed and a rustling sound. I am so tempted to open my eyes to see what he is doing but I hold strong, taking a deep breath. In the next moment, the bed dips and I can feel him hovering over my body. "This is to make sure you keep them closed." I don't understand his meaning until I feel a silky fabric fall over my eyes. He lifts my head and ties it. "Have you ever been blind-folded?" he asks.

"N-no," I stutter out.

"Breathe, Stormy." I take another deep breath and he begins again. "Now I need you to pick a safe word." I've read about this. Using a safe word is like failsafe. If I use the word, all activities stop immediately. I ponder for a moment and then a smile tugs at my mouth.

"Gandalf," I respond. It's what the bastard called me on the bike earlier. No doubt it was because of the silver color of my hair, but I can't help but to throw it back at him. I hear him chuckle and it's like a melody I don't want to ever stop hearing.

"Gandalf it is. Say that and everything stops, no questions asked," he whispers in my ear. Another tremble runs through my body. "Now, relax." I feel him crawling down my body and it has my hands itching to cover myself. I'm not fat but I'm not skinny either. I have love handles that seem to stay no matter what exercises and diets I try. I've come to terms with them but that doesn't mean I feel comfortable naked in front of a man like Sebastian. I'm blindfolded and I can't see if there is disgust or appreciation in his face. I just have to lay here and take it. Maybe I wasn't cut out for this kind of sex. Maybe I need to stick to dollar store vanilla sex. Blaine always told me to watch what I ate because I was going to be in front of thousands of people and they wouldn't always have something nice to say about my body. I think that's when my body awareness started. "Come back to me, Stormy. Get out of your head."

"How did you know?" I ask, lifting my hands to feel the fabric covering my eyes.

"I could feel your body tense. Live in this moment. Not any others. Just be here with me." I feel him climb back up my body, in an instant his lips are on mine. Our mouths move in tandem, making me forget about the blindfold. I focus all my energy on the feelings this man evokes from me. Sebastian moves from my mouth to trail kisses along my jawline then moves down my neck. He kisses, nips, then licks his way down to my collar bone. My center floods with sensations. He trails a hand up my body to caress one breast. My nipples pebble at the attention. His mouth trails down to the other, pulling the nipple in his mouth. He pulls with his hand while lightly biting with his mouth. My body begins writhing on the bed, needing him to touch me more, to give me more.

"You like that, don't you?" He continues with his attention to my nipples. He bites down harder, I yell out then groan as he soothes it over with his tongue. I feel like I could come from this alone.

"Yes, oh fuck. Yes!" I exclaim. He bites and sucks a path down my body, no doubt leaving behind marks. He nips both hip bones before settling between my legs. Anticipation builds and the struggle to pull up my blindfold and look is strong. I grip the sheets instead, trying to ground myself in the moment.

"Don't be shy, Angel, spread these gorgeous legs for me." I suck in a breath at his words but do what he says. I let my trembling legs fall open for him. I wait for a sign of disapproval but all I hear is a moan escape his lips. "Damn you are so wet. Is this ripe little cunt wet for me?"

A mumbled "yes" comes out as he begins trailing his mouth up my inner thigh. He gets so close to my pussy then repeats his actions on my other thigh. The anticipation is killing me. I want to pull his gorgeous head and put him where I want him. "Please, Sebastian," I whine as he gets close again, this time breathing right over my core so I can feel his breath on me. It's not enough. I need more.

"What do you want? You need to tell me." He takes his fingers and lazily rubs them over my mound then back up to my stomach, avoiding the place I want him most.

I let out a nervous chuckle. I'm not used to being this forward. I'm not sure I can tell him what I want. "I-I need your mouth on me," I stutter out.

"Where?" A one-word question that has me biting my bottom lip.

Fuck it. This is what I want. "I need your mouth on my pussy," I say in a rush. The air leaves my lungs as I wait for his reply.

"That's my good girl, telling me what you want." He blows cool air across my heated flesh as he descends on my pussy like a man starved. His shoulders hold my legs apart as he eats me, licking from my center to my clit. "Mm, you taste so sweet." He groans as he goes in for another taste. All of my senses are on high alert after taking away my vision. It's like he somehow heightened everything, especially since I don't know what's coming next. Sebastian thrusts two fingers inside me, curving them to tweak that sweet spot. I push my hips up to meet his movements, but he uses his other hand to push down on my stomach, grounding me to the bed. I feel him add another finger and my pleasure skyrockets.

All of a sudden, he removes his fingers. But before I can protest, I'm flipped over on my stomach. Sebastian pulls my ass into the air, thrusting his cock deep inside me. He grabs my hips and continues to pound into my aching pussy. He slaps my ass hard on both sides.

"That's for touching this pussy without being told to," he growls.

"Sebastian," I hiss as he stretches me more and more with every pump of his cock.

"You take me so well, Angel. You're such a good fucking girl. I'm going to ruin you for every other man." I gush at his words. He leans over grabbing a fist of my hair and pulls it tight. The burn of my scalp turns to pleasure the more he fucks me. My orgasm builds and builds until I am thrown over the edge of oblivion. My pussy clenches down on his cock, making him growl out in response. "You like being a good girl don't you? You want to be my good little slut?" A whimper escapes my mouth as I continue to climb higher and higher in ecstasy. "Answer me," he commands.

"Yes. Fuck. Yes, I want to be your good girl." He pulls almost completely out until only the head of his cock is inside me. Then he slams his hips forward almost pushing me flat against the bed.

He leans over me as he continues to thrust, ghosting his lips over my shoulder. "This pussy feels so good wrapped around me." He whispers in my ear. I can't help but sob at his words. I've never been talked to like this. *I've never been fucked like this.* He reaches around me to circle my clit.

"I can't. Not again," Is all I can say.

"You can and you will or next time I won't let you come at all." He pulls my hair harder, making tears stream down my face. He picks up his pace, continuing working my clit until I am screaming out his name. Before I even start to come down, I hear him growl, "Fuck, baby, that's it. Come hard for me. I want to feel you come on my cock," he grits out and I feel his ropes of come spurting inside me.

"Oh god, yes!" My pussy continues to clamp down on him, milking everything out of his cock.

"Not God, Angel, call me Daddy." I don't know why that's so hot, but it is.

"Daddy!" I scream into my pillow as I slowly come down from my high. His thrusts slow as he releases my hair.

"That was-" I start.

"Fucking amazing," he finishes. Instead of pulling out, he rolls us to our sides. Sebastian pulls the blindfold from my eyes, letting me see that he used my Ravenclaw tie to cover my eyes. He kisses along the column of my neck. "You're incredible," he whispers into the shell of my ear. He wipes the tears from my cheeks and turns my chin toward him. He looks me in the eyes for a moment before his lips meet mine. It's a sweet, intoxicating kiss. This man and his skills will never cease to amaze me. He can turn me into a puddle with how he works his lips with mine. The way he works his cock is a whole different story. *Is all sex like this? Of course it's not.* There is something about Sebastian and our chemistry that ignites my shattered heart.

He pulls away from me, his cock slipping from my folds. "Let me clean you up." Before I can protest, he's off the bed and coming back with a towel in hand. He rolls me to my back and spreads my legs, wiping away our mess. He throws the towel into the hamper, before joining me back in bed. I pull the covers back and slide inside the cool sheets. Sebastian follows suit then pulls my body back against his. He skims his fingers down my body then back up, leaving goosebumps in his wake.

"You didn't use the safe word." He acknowledges.

"Did you think I would?" I ask.

"No, I didn't. I knew what you needed, I'm just happy you let yourself experience it," he remarks.

I quirk my eyebrow at his statement. "You think you know me?"

He nods, pushing a piece of hair from my face. "I'm starting to." My heartbeat picks up, I don't know how to respond to that. I can't take this experience for anything more than it was. Just two people having sex. I know that's all it means to him. He knows how to say all the right things to women, I mean that's how he got dubbed Most Eligible Playboy in Manhattan. But still, for a moment I can pretend that there is something deeper between us. "I like your ink. I'm a Harry Potter fan, as well. I especially love the little bows under your ass." He remarks. I playfully smack him in the chest.

"What house are you in?" I question, skating over the bows tattoo remark. I don't want to tell him that I got them on a dare and how much Blaine thought it made me look like a hooker. But I still love them.

"Gryffindor, of course," he replies.

"Scandalous. A Gryffindor sleeping with a Ravenclaw. Call the Daily Prophet." We both let out a laugh and it feels good with him. It feels easy. Maybe his wasn't more than sex. Somehow, it doesn't feel like it.

A yawn escapes my lips and Sebastian chuckles to himself. "Get some sleep." I nod my head and close my eyes, resting my head on his chest. He leans up kissing my forehead, making me melt inside.

I'm playing with fire, knowing I'll be burned. But damn, what a scar it will make.

FOURTEEN

Sebastian

I wake to the sound of cars honking in the distance. Looking at my watch, I see it's four thirty in the morning. I never spend the night with women that I sleep with, but I couldn't resist pulling Stormy's soft body against mine and falling asleep. Things got so heated between us that we both passed out. I look over at her gorgeous sleeping form. Her long silver hair shimmers in the moonlight and her exquisite body seems to shine in the darkness. She looks like a goddess herself, rivaling the perfect Aphrodite. My chest aches at the sight. I can't help but wonder if this is how Miles felt about Lizzie. He seemed bewitched by her from the start. Fear clogs my throat, and I suddenly can't breathe. I can't do this. I can't be in a relationship. I don't know the first thing about them. I don't want to hurt her. I would never forgive myself. She's been through enough without me adding to it. I know she has, even if she hasn't told me. I could see it in some of her paintings. Stormy's been through serious pain in her life.

I slip out of bed quietly, avoiding waking her. I look around the room until I spot a discarded towel on the floor. Hurriedly, I tie it around my waist and open her bedroom door. I take one more look at the sleeping beauty in bed. I could slip back in behind her like nothing ever happened. My brain and heart are at war with each other. In the end my brain wins out. I close her door behind me as I tiptoe down the hall to the laundry area. I grab my clothes and make my way to the bathroom. Before I can open the door, it opens from the other side. A loud gasp comes from who I suppose is Stormy's roommate.

"What the hell?" she squeaks, holding her hand to her chest.

"I'm sorry. I was just getting my clothes from the dryer. I didn't mean to startle you." I hold up my clothes to show her proof, hoping like hell my towel stays tied. "I'm Sebastian." I shuffle the clothes to one hand to free up the other. She takes it hesitantly.

"I know who you are. Why are you sneaking around at," she looks at her watch, "four forty-five in the morning?" she asks in a whisper.

"I need to get back to my place before work." It's not a total lie. I do need a shower and clothes, although I do have a closet at work full of suits. She doesn't need to know that.

"Mhm and did you tell Stormy you were leaving?" she asks. Now folding her arms over her chest.

"I didn't want to wake her," I lie. More like I was being a coward and now I'm getting called out for it.

"Riiight. Don't you dare hurt that girl. You have no idea what kind of shit she has been through." I ponder that for a moment and wonder what exactly happened to Stormy. Before I can ask any questions, she responds again. "You really need to think about what you want because she isn't a one-night stand kind of girl. I'm sure you know that." She turns and walks away, closing the door behind her. I'm left alone in the hallway holding my clothes. I look at Stormy's door and then to the bathroom, trying to figure out which move to make. *Fuck, why is this so hard.* I hit it and quit it all the time. How is Stormy any different? *She just is.* It's what my heart keeps telling me. My brain determines this is a good time to be indecisive on a matter. I'm never indecisive. *Fuck!*

I take one step in the direction I decide to go then I hear a ding. I pause mid step and hear my phone ringing. No one would be calling me right now unless it was an emergency. I follow the sound and realize I left my phone in the bathroom. Picking it up, I see Miles' face on the screen and my stomach drops.

"Hey bro, what's wrong?" I ask.

"Seb, it's Marie. She's on life support right now. She took a turn for the worse and Thomas took her to the hospital. They are keeping her stable until everyone can get there. Thomas needs you there for him, bro. Lizzie and I are bringing the jet home. I already woke the crew, they are getting everything ready for us." I sit and listen as Miles goes on about his travel plans. My gut wrenches at the thought of Thomas losing his wife. I can't imagine the pain he is in right now.

"What hospital? I'm getting dressed right now." I pull on my boxers and pants, holding the phone between my ear and shoulder.

"She's at Mount Sinai." Good. That's not too far from here.

"Okay. I'll get there and let you know more information. You and Lizzie be safe."

"You too. Love you bro."

"Love you too." I hang up and slide the phone in my pocket. As I pull my shirt over my head, I spot my belt on the floor and grab it. Looking around, I check to see if there is anything I'm forgetting. I jog from the bathroom to the front door, grabbing my jacket from the hanger. It's still wet, but it will have to do. I pull on my boots and grab my keys, taking one look back at Stormy's room. I open the front door, locking it as I do and close it behind me. Trying to focus on the task at hand, I can't help but think about Stormy and what she is going to think when she wakes up alone in a few hours. I push that thought away as I start my bike. Securing my helmet, I pull out of the parking lot and head toward the hospital. It's crazy how life can change from one day to the next. I hope I get there in time. Thomas needs me right now.

Stormy

Buzz. Buzz. Buzz. I reach my hand up and slap at my phone until the heinous noise stops. My hand slides over to the side of the bed and I find it cool against my skin. I think I knew he wouldn't be here when I woke this morning. I wanted to believe he would be here but the article I read pops into my mind. I know I shouldn't believe everything I read; I know that more than most. Reporters never got my story correct when I was in the band. It should be comforting that I know things can be thrown out of proportion but in the end, I am still waking up to an empty bed this morning.

Rolling out of bed, I check my phone for any messages and then I remember that we never exchanged numbers. Of course we didn't. I sigh as I scrub my hand over my face. I throw on my robe and leave my room. The walk to the bathroom is filled with thoughts of last night. I've never been blindfolded before, surprisingly it didn't scare me. I actually trusted Sebastian which is a huge step for me. I almost want to call my therapist but then again, I doubt she wants to hear about my sex life. A chuckle escapes me at what her response would be.

I turn on the shower and wait for it to heat up while I brush my teeth. Looking into the mirror, I look different. I think that's what a thorough fucking will do to you. I wrap my hand in a plastic bag, so it won't get wet in the shower. Discarding the robe, I step into the steaming, hot water. The memories of being thrust up against the wall in here makes me flush with need. Sebastian was so demanding, yet gentle. He and Blaine couldn't be more different in that department. I never knew sex could be so electric. Of course, I've seen movies and porn but that was all acting. This was real, and intense, and it was better than anything I've ever experienced. I never have felt more of a connection with someone. Even though I can't decide if I still hate him, there definitely is chemistry there.

I've wasted enough water daydreaming, so I wash quickly and get out. I wrap my hair in a towel and throw my robe back on. Opening the door to the bathroom, I'm hit with cooler air, and I sinch my robe tighter around my body. I make my way to the kitchen and see that coffee has already been made. As I reach for a mug, I hear Lana come in behind me.

"Someone had an interesting night," she singsongs as she gets a mug for herself.

I crinkle my nose, hoping she didn't hear too much. I also don't want her to think that this is a regular thing for me. I think my emotions were so heightened from the panic attack that I wasn't thinking straight.

"Please tell me you didn't hear anything," I plead. I pour myself a cup of coffee and reach for the creamer that she pulled from the refrigerator.

"I didn't hear anything. I just literally ran into him in the middle of the night," she remarks as she finishes making her cup. I take in what she said. He was fleeing in the middle of the night. I should've known. He came here and got what he wanted. I shouldn't feel so used but I do. We didn't say what last night meant but I should have known it would mean more to me than to him. I feel tears prick my eyes and I don't know why other than I sometimes cry when I get angry. And that's what I am.

"I guess he was fleeing the scene before I woke up," I reply, taking a sip on the hot coffee. I savor the taste before I swallow it down but thinking about Sebastian makes it sour in my mouth. I'll be damned if I let a man come between me and coffee. I shake my head at the thought.

"I'm not really sure. He had his clothes in his hand but then I heard him on the phone, and it sounded urgent. He left soon after he hung up. I wasn't trying to eavesdrop," she holds up her hands, "or maybe I was. I didn't want him to hurt you. By the way, I thought we hated him?" she questions. I look down at my mug trying to come up with the best answer.

"I do or did. I don't know. Everything happened so fast," I express.

"How did he even end up in our apartment?" she asks.

"Ugh, it's a long story. Basically, he saw me waiting for a cab in the pouring rain, so he offered me a ride on his motorcycle.

Obviously, I said no multiple times, but he wasn't having it. Also, my stitches opened up and I was bleeding, so I didn't really have a choice. Then he stopped by a pharmacy and got supplies that *he* would need to bandage me up." I let all that sink in and take another sip of coffee. "He followed me into the lobby, and I ended up having a panic attack from seeing the blood on my hand. He somehow was able to talk me through it. He came up to the apartment and the rest is history," I explain. She's sitting on one of the kitchen stools listening intently like it's the best news she's heard.

"Wow, I don't really know what to say. He was such an ass to you at the fundraiser and even at work," she notes.

"Oh, I know. I still don't know how I feel about everything. But I'm pretty sure it was a one-off type of deal. I hope it's not uncomfortable at work," I cringe at the thought. "Anyways, I have to get ready. Oh, and the rain ruined my new shoes," I motion to them by the door.

"No! Not the Louboutins!" she exclaims.

"Yep. Not going to lie, I don't know what I'm more upset by. The fact that Sebastian wasn't here this morning or my ruined shoes," I laugh and it feels good to be this lighthearted after everything that's happened.

"Definitely the shoes, girl." Lana takes one in her hand and looks it over. "But I have an idea for these. Can I give them a makeover?" There is no telling what she is going to do to them, but they can't be worn how they are right now.

"Sure. Do your thing." I check my watch and see that I'm running behind from this little chat. "I've got to go."

"We can get the art supplies tonight if you want to," she suggests.

"Yeah, that works. I'll message you later," she nods her head as we split ways, going to our bedrooms.

I set my coffee down while looking through my closet for what I want to wear today. Picking up my phone, I check what the weather is going to be like. Chilly and still a bit wet. I grab a long-sleeved black wrap around dress with some black high heeled booties. With my clothes picked out, I dry and straighten my hair. Once that's finally done, I sit in front of my floor length mirror to put on my makeup. I wish I had a vanity table, but it's not a big deal to sit on the floor.

I get up and dress, looking into the mirror to make sure everything looks alright. My hair drapes down my back, it's a stark contrast from the black dress. I look closer in the mirror and realize it's time for me to bleach and dye my roots again. Since I have naturally dark hair, it doesn't take long for my roots to begin to show.

I grab a jacket from my closet along with a black purse. The one I normally use is still wet, hopefully not ruined. My keys are by the door along with my wet bag. I stop on the way out to move my wallet and meds to the new purse, then I'm out the door. I decide it's a good thing Sebastian isn't here this morning because I don't want to have anything to do with him. I hate the fact that I'm attracted to him in the first place. I hate that he was the best sex I've ever had. For fuck's sake. I try really hard to believe what I'm telling myself. I try and fail. *Fuck my life.*

FIFTEEN

Sebastian

H ours have ticked by as I sit here at the hospital. Thomas was distraught when I arrived, but I've since been able to calm him down some. I can't imagine the pain he's going through. He's always talked about Marie with a huge smile on his face. She's the love of his life. I'm in the waiting room, which is fitting because it's a waiting game now. They say there's nothing to be done but to make sure she is comfortable in her final hours.

Miles wasn't exactly sure what caused Marie's health to plummet so drastically but once I arrived at the hospital, I learned she had a brainstem stroke. Apparently, it was severe enough to significantly damage her brain. Now her brain is unable to function in a way that sustains life. She was able to be placed on life support long enough for a few family members to say goodbye. Thomas and Marie never had children of their own, Miles and I have always been treated as such.

Thomas comes into the waiting room with tears streaming down his face. I jump up instantly and go to him.

147

"S-she's finally at rest now. She's no longer battling cancer. Heaven is her new home." He murmurs into my shoulder as I hold him. I can't stop the tears that threaten to spill from my own eyes. I loved her like a mother. I pull him in closer and pat his back.

"She isn't suffering anymore." I whisper. I wish Miles was already here. He's so much better at dealing with situations like this. I just feel sad and uncomfortable. I want to make things better for Thomas but there isn't anything I can do except take care of the funeral plans for him. That's exactly what I'm going to do. Once Thomas breaks away from me, I tell him my plans. "I'll take care of everything. I don't want you to have to worry about a thing. Is there anything specific you wanted for her funeral?" I ask.

He shakes his head and looks at me. "You don't have to do anything. I can figure it all out."

"It's the least I can do. Marie was like a mother to me. I want to do this for you. You've been through enough," I respond.

"Thank you. I really appreciate it. She loved lilies, all kinds," he remarks.

"Consider it done. We'll have all the lilies we can get. Now I think you need some rest. Do you want to stay at my apartment? I don't want you to be alone," I state.

"Oh, no that's okay. My brother and his wife will be in town later today. I think I'll just head home and get some sleep." I nod my head, pulling out my phone to have an Uber come pick him up. I don't want him driving right now. I'll have to make plans later to come back here and get the Bently. I lead Thomas to the front of the hospital to wait for his ride.

"I ordered you an Uber, so you won't have to drive," I tell him as we stand at the entrance to the emergency room.

"Thank you, son, for everything. Marie and I always had a soft spot for you boys," he conveys.

"I know. We loved her like our own mother. She'll be truly missed." The car comes to a halt in front of us and I help Thomas inside. Double checking the address, I shut the door and watch as he rides off. I check my watch, it's ten in the morning. I decide to head into the office since there is a funeral I need to plan. I have no clue where to start with that but I'm sure Stormy can make a few calls and get everything settled. *Stormy.* My thoughts have been consumed since I left her apartment this morning, I haven't had the chance to call the office or even think about her. But now as I stand here, I'm left with the realization that I need to be near her right now.

I hop on my bike and speed out of the parking lot toward Knight Publishing Company. About thirty minutes later, I'm pulling into the underground garage of the company. The traffic was terrible as usual, it took me longer to get here. I park, placing my helmet on the seat. I stand at the elevator waiting for it to open as my phone chimes.

Miles:

How is he?

Sebastian:

He's tired, so I sent him home in an Uber. He was at least at peace knowing she was no longer suffering.

Miles:

> Lizzie and I will be flying in tonight, so I probably won't see you until tomorrow morning.

Sebastian:

> I told Thomas that we would take care of the funeral arrangements. I just arrived at the office so that I could get started on that.

Miles:

> Good. I'll help tomorrow.

I pocket my phone as I climb into the elevator, pushing the twentieth floor and swiping my card. I find myself nervous to see Stormy. I've never had this reaction to a woman, especially one I've already slept with. Normally I'm a one and done kind of guy but the thought of doing that to Stormy makes my heart ache.

The elevator dings as the doors open. I step off and instantly spot Stormy across the room. It's like she is this beacon of light promising to bring me back to her if I lose my way. I begin walking in her direction as Elijah steps up to her desk. He leans over, speaking softly into Stormy's ear and I don't miss the way she leans away from him, ever so slightly. She's trying to be polite but that's the last thing I'm about to be. I already told him in enough words to leave her alone. I guess he didn't get the hint. He needs to keep away from what's mine. I chose not to dwell on the fact that I have called her mine twice in the span of twenty-four hours. I'll revisit that tidbit later.

"Elijah, I thought I told you to leave Ms. Brooks alone." They both jump at my booming voice, having not seen me arrive.

"I-I was just helping her with your schedule," he remarks, I look to Stormy who rolls her eyes at him. So, that's not what he was doing. I'm sure he was trying to ask her out again.

"Sure," I reply, "Stormy can I see you in my office?" She looks at me and her face reddens. Grabbing the iPad, she stands and follows me. "Close the door behind you," I instruct as I take a seat behind my desk. I still have on my clothes from yesterday, but I don't give a fuck what I look like today. I'm exhausted and emotionally drained from this morning. Plus, I don't have any meetings today where I need to look presentable.

Stormy takes a seat in front of my desk, I can't keep my eyes from lingering on her chest. Her dress is a black low-cut thing that I want to tear from her body. My cock strains against my pants, showing its appreciation. Her long flowing hair drapes around her as she looks to me for further instructions.

"I need help with something. It's time sensitive so everything else can be put on hold for the moment," I explain.

She looks unsure but unlocks the iPad, waiting to hear more. "Okay. What can I do?" she asks with a hint of blush creeping up her face. I need to talk to her about last night but now isn't the time. I have to get the funeral preparations underway.

"I need help planning a funeral," I remark looking down at my laptop as I boot it up. When I look back at Stormy her face has paled. Her lips have parted, making a slight oval shape.

"I, um, yeah, okay," she fumbles a bit then looks down at her lap. She wrings her fingers together. I'm about to ask her what's wrong when she composes herself enough with a deep breath and looks at me. "What do you need me to do?" she asks.

"A family friend passed away and I told her husband that we'd take care of everything. We'll be using Posey Funeral Home but as far as the date, flowers, etc. I need your help." She nods her head solemnly for a moment then begins typing away. "Oh, and we need to use lilies. Every kind you can find. It was her favorite."

"Will this be an open casket or is she being cremated?" she inquires without lifting her head. I hadn't thought about those kinds of details. I'll have to call Thomas and see what he wanted for Marie. Maybe they talked about what she wanted since she was so ill. For a moment I think maybe Stormy has had to go through this before. She's asked me something that I'd have never thought to ask. I want her to explain but I have to get this done as soon as possible.

"I'll have to make a call and find out. In the meantime, just get done what you can." She nods her head and stands from her seat. Before she leaves I need to mention last night but I'm not sure what to say. "About last night," I begin.

"Don't worry about it. I'll get right on this, *boss*." she replies. *Ouch.*

"I wasn't finished with our meeting, *Ms. Brooks.* Please have a seat." If looks could kill, I'd be dead in my seat. She plops back down in the seat. "I need to go over my schedule for next week. All meetings need to be pushed back to the following week. My hours will vary for the next week as we get everything settled for Thomas. That reminds me, I need meals sent to him, as well. I'll email you a list of his diet restrictions," I thrum my pen on the desk, thinking about what else needs to be done. Stormy looks up from taking notes, waiting for me to continue. "Can you think of anything else that needs to be done in regard to the funeral?" I ask. She bounces the iPad on her knee for a moment and then responds. "The newspaper needs to be notified and something has to be written about the deceased. It needs to involve remaining family members and then you can mention what she was like while she was alive. You need to decide if people can send flowers or if you want a donation set in place in her honor. Also, you need to get with Thomas and see if he wants to add the funeral arrangements in the paper or if you want to keep those details under wraps for a more intimate setting." Stormy looks back down to her lap, I can't help but wonder who she knew that passed away. I'm all but certain now that she's had to do this before. She's too young to have learned this information other than having to do it for herself. I feel like I have cracked a code to the things she keeps locked away. Before I can say anything further, she speaks again. "Is there anything else that I can do for you?" she ask formally, and I shake my head.

"I'll let you know if there is anything else. Also, I need your cell phone number in case I'm not at the office and I need something. I'll send word to HR that you will be working overtime this next week. That doesn't necessarily mean here at the office, but I need you available." She takes a pen and notepad from my desk, writing her number on it and sliding it back over to me. We sit for a moment in silence. She locks eyes with me, I can see the fire burning within them.

"Will that be all?" She inquires with a bite to her tone as she levels her shoulders.

I stand and walk around the desk, leaning against it. She takes a deep breath and averts her gaze from me. "No, it's not all." I lean in, placing my hands on either side of her chair. I'm done being her boss. Now, I'm Sebastian and there are some things she needs to understand. "I want to talk about last night." She turns to face me, our mouths inches apart.

"There isn't anything to discuss. It was a mistake. I was high on adrenaline after everything happened. That's all," she declares, crossing her arms over her chest. The move making them more pronounced than they already were.

"Let's get one thing straight, Angel," I whisper into the shell of her ear. "I may be your boss right now but don't forget who made you come last night until you passed out from pleasure." I suck her lobe into my mouth for a moment and release it. Goosebumps erupt over her chest flowing up the column of her neck. A satisfied smile spreads across my face at her visceral reaction to me. I lean back to see her face. Pink floods her cheeks, I'm sure it's not the only thing flooded.

"I'm not your plaything, Sebastian. You had your one night. Don't think I don't know your reputation," she presses her hand into my chest to move me away, but I stand firm.

"Did I give you any indication that last night was a one-time thing?" I question.

"As a matter of fact, you did. You snuck out in the middle of the night. Lana mentioned she saw you," she hisses.

I grab a fist of her hair and pull her head back for her to look in my eyes. "Did she tell you that I spent the entire time from leaving your apartment to here now at the hospital with a dear friend while he was losing his wife? Did you not recognize that I'm in the same clothes that I was last night?" I growl out, seeing her eyes become pools of lava. I've never seen the yellow so vibrant.

She places her hand over mine in her hair trying to get me to let go. "Don't pretend like you were leaving for a noble reason. It was a coincidence that your phone rang and gave you an out to leave."

"You think you know everything, don't you?" I lift her chin with my thumb, so her eyes can't leave mine. "Well, I think your ass needs my hand print on it. Daddy needs to punish his little slut." She gasps out as the words leave my mouth. I remove my hands from her body and lean back against the desk. I got the point across that I needed to. If she thinks she is done with me then she is in for a surprise. "Now, we will get back to this discussion later. I need you to get started on the things we talked about." I walk around to my side of the desk, taking my seat as Stormy's eyes bore into me. I don't look up as she stands, opens the door and closes it behind her. I know that little spitfire is upset with me, but I couldn't have her thinking that I didn't want to continue whatever this is between us. Stormy challenges me at every turn and she isn't getting away from me easily. I haven't felt this fire inside me before. I'll be damned if it gets stomped out.

Leaning back in my chair, I look out through my floor-to-ceiling windows at the overcast sky. I scrub my hands over my face and smile to myself when I remember the way Stormy looked at me like she wanted to punch me. She's a whirlwind of emotions, a hurricane looking to wreak havoc on my soul. Something tells me that I've got my work cut out for me if I want Stormy in my life. *Challenge accepted*.

Sixteen

Stormy

I feel like everyone can see my red tinged cheeks as I leave Sebastian's office. I head straight for the comfort of my desk. Of course, Elijah is waiting there for me. He's really starting to grate on my nerves.

"I was coming to check on you. Mr. Knight seemed like he was in a bad mood this morning. Is there anything I can help you with?" Elijah asks, looking at me like a lovesick puppy.

"No, everything's fine. He needed me to work on something for him." It's not my place to tell people about the funeral I'm planning for Sebastian. His little stunt in his office made me forget about the funeral but now that I'm back at my desk, I'm nauseated at the thought of planning another one. I had to plan my parents', then I helped with Blaine's. I didn't think I would have to do this again, but here I am.

"Alright, well you know where to find me if you need me." I nod my head and get to work at my computer. Eventually, he gives up and walks away. I let out a deep sigh. I need to have a conversation with him to let him know that I'm not interested. I thought I already had but apparently he didn't listen. The next time I won't be as nice. I push that thought away, getting to work.

The rest of the work day is uneventful. Sebastian stayed in his office until he left a little bit ago. I finished up with his schedule and got things underway for the funeral arrangements. I'm still waiting to hear from Sebastian on a few things so I know how to continue. When he got my number it was under the guise that he needed it for work, but I bet he uses it for more than that. Especially with how he reacted this morning in his office.

Shutting down my computer for the day, I grab my purse and jacket. As the elevators open, I step in and hit the lobby floor. Thank God it's not raining today. My boots clink against the marble flooring as I walk to the double doors leading to the city. The security guard opens the door and I step out into the crisp New York City air.

Hailing a cab, I jump in and give him my address. My phone vibrates in my jacket. I pull it from my pocket and see it's Lana.

Picasso:

> Are we still on to get art supplies tonight? I'm home.

I type an immediate reply.

Stormy:

Absolutely, I could use it. Dinner, too?

Picasso:

Yes! I'm starved!

Picasso:

Hurry up and get home!

Stormy:

Calm your tits. I'm on the way. Be there soon!

I slide my phone back into my pocket, smiling as I look out the window at all the people walking on this chilly afternoon. I love this city as much as I knew I would. Out of nowhere, I hear a sound that freezes me down to my soul. I look on in horror as the cab driver shifts to turn it up. And there, on the radio, is Damaged Jacks. The old Damaged Jacks that I used to be in. That's me on the radio singing my heart out to our number one hit song. I feel like the air in the cab is being sucked out and I can't gasp enough to get oxygen into my lungs.

"S-sir, can we turn the radio off?" I knock at the plastic partition between us, but he can't hear me over the blaring music. I knock louder and he finally looks in his rearview mirror at me.

"What's up, doll face? Don't you puke in my cab. You don't look so good," he mutters barely audible over the music. Fucking twatwaffle.

159

"Can we turn the radio off?" I ask again, showing more force than I feel. I just want to get out of this spiraling vortex before it sucks me in.

"No can do. The old thing doesn't turn off. Just the volume works." He announces but it's too late. The damage is done. My hands are shaking by the time he lets me off in front of my apartment. I haven't heard that music in over a year. After the song was finished, the DJ went on to tell the audience that he wished he knew what happened to the lead singer of the band after the guitarist died. Apparently, they are still searching for me.

I pull out my prescription, tossing a tablet back without water. Swallowing hard, I get the medicine down my throat. I walk into the apartment, slamming the door behind me. Lana comes out of her room, seeing the expression on my face she has to know something is wrong. I shake my head, making my way to my bedroom. Before I can close the door, she pops her head in.

"Okay, what happened? You were fine like twenty minutes ago," she said explains.

I shake my head, turning away from her. I pull my hair at the sides and let out a scream. I can feel Lana come up behind me, wrapping me in her arms. I fall back against her, we slide to the floor.

"Was it that asshole? I'll give him a piece of my mind," she says. Finally finding my voice, I tell her about the car ride.

"Shit. I'm so sorry. That has to be a punch to the gut," I nod my head at the mental picture. That's exactly what it felt like.

"I need to get out of here. Let's go get drinks somewhere," I state as I stand up from the floor.

"Yeah, sure, whatever you want. Do you want to go like that or change?" She asks. I look down at my dress and I know I just want to be comfortable.

"I'm going to put on some jeans," I tell her as I begin rummaging through my drawers.

"Okay, let me go change really quickly," She's out of the room the next second.

I stand there looking at myself in the mirror. I have to purge myself of the old Stormy. I'm not that girl anymore. I'm not a member of Damaged Jacks. I'm just a girl trying to make it in the big city with my paintings, not music.

I change into jeans and a black, long-sleeved sweater. I hold onto my pendant for a moment before I release it and it falls back to my chest. I pull on my Converse shoes and brush my hair.

"I'm ready." Lana calls from the other room. I take one last look before grabbing my purse and jacket.

"Me too. So, where are you taking me?" I ask.

"Only the best place around here, The Tipsy Tap." I laugh at the name and nod my head, following her out the door.

Twenty minutes later, we pay for our Uber and step onto the streets of busy New York City. Lana takes my hand, ushering me inside the bar. Of course, they have fucking karaoke tonight. I avert my eyes, heading straight for the bar. I raise my hand for the handsome bartender to come over. I scan the darkened bar. There seems to be a good bit of people here tonight. The person singing right now is butchering *"Oops I did it again"* by Britney Spears. It makes me cringe just from all the singing lessons I took over the years. My teachers would roll over in their graves if they heard this shit.

"I'm sorry. I didn't think they would have karaoke tonight. I thought that was just an early weekday thing." Lana declares.

"No worries. What do you want to drink? Shots first?" I question.

"Sure, let's do tequila shots, then I want a beer, Corona." I nod as the bartender approaches.

"What can I get you ladies?" He slings his towel over his shoulder and looks us up and down, not being discreet at all. He's no longer handsome, more cringy than anything.

"We need four shots of tequila, she wants a Corona, and I'll take a Long Island iced tea," I lean over the bar and shout. I don't miss his eyes lingering on my breasts. I sigh to myself and pull out my ID for him to check. Lana pulls hers out as well, we both show him then put them away.

"Thank you, ladies. I'll get those drinks right over." I nod, waiting impatiently to get my mouth on some liquor. I know I shouldn't be drinking but I give very few fucks right now. I want to get shitfaced and forget all about the last few days.

The bartender brings us the shots first. "What should we toast to?" I ask Lana as I grab the salt.

"How about to totally awesome roommates?" She shrugs and I laugh.

"To roommates!" We clink our shots together, hit the counter and toss them back. Sucking the lime in my mouth, I reach for the second round. I pass Lana hers and we toss the second back easier than the first. The liquor burns my throat on the way down, but the lime is the perfect chaser. I contemplate doing more shots, but I don't want to get drunk in a few minutes and have to leave. I can already feel the tingle in my limbs.

"Here you go ladies." The bartender is back and handing us our drinks. The hairs on the back of my neck stand on end as a familiar voice echoes into my ear.

"Well, fancy seeing you here, kitten. I've been thinking about you," he whispers for only me to hear. I turn to see Lana flirting with the bartender, not paying attention to what's going on with me. I take a large sip of my drink and turn to face Jared fucking Thompson, the asshole from the meeting the other day.

"Mr. Thompson," I acknowledge with a nod.

"Call me Jared, kitten. Where is the big, bad Sebastian Knight? Not here to save you from me again? He was pissing all over you, claiming you in front of me." He stumbles closer. I move at the last moment, and he hits the bar counter with a thud. He chuckles darkly, a scary expression forms on his face.

"I don't need someone to save me from you." I utter with more confidence than I feel.

"Ha ha, you should be smarter than that. I'll be taking you home with me tonight and claiming your sweet little ass for myself." He says stepping closer, blocking my escape. He grabs onto my waist, pulling me flush against his body.

"No thank you. Now, get your slimy hands off me," I seethe.

"That's no way to talk to your elders, you brat." It's purely reflex what comes next. I drop my drink to the floor, using the distraction to grab ahold of Jared's shoulder and kick him in the nuts. He's on the floor a second later, writhing in pain. The commotion caus-es a few people to look but they turn away. I guess they figured he passed out drunk. Lana rushes over to me as I step around Jared's pathetic body on the ground. I've never been more thankful that I took that stupid self-defense class. I thought it was a waste of time but it sure as fuck came in handy.

"What the hell just happened?" Lana questions. I shrug my shoulders and walk back up to the bartender.

"He just passed out and took my drink with him. Mind making me another?" I look at Lana and she's staring at Jared on the floor. Maybe he did pass out after all. A smile tugs at my lips and I couldn't be prouder of myself.

"Not a problem." He moves about the bar making me anoth-er drink. I'm already feeling the effects of the shots. I shouldn't be drinking more, but after what just happened, I need another distraction. He comes back with a fresh drink and sets it in front of me.

"Thank you." I give him my card to keep the tab open and we move away, looking for a table. Lana points to the corner and I follow behind her, glancing again at the woman on stage. I chuckle and contemplate if I should get up there and let loose.

"That guy looked like a creep back there. Are you okay?" she asks.

"Yeah, just some asshat. Anyways, I was thinking maybe I want to get up there and sing something." Lana looks at me over her beer, shocked.

"Are you serious right now?" she asks.

"Hell yes! I need to get out of my head, and I need to get over this shit I have with the old band. I want to be free and happy," I confess, slamming my drink down on the table.

"I think you need to slow down on your drinks!" she exclaims.

"No, no, no! I don't feel a thing," I lie. "Let's go look at the book of songs. Do you want to sing?"

"Hell no! I don't do karaoke! But I'll sit here and cheer you on for sure," Lana shrugs her shoulders but maybe I'll be able to get her to sing later. I hop up from our booth and skip back to the bar. The bartender was watching me the whole time so he's at the end of the bar when I get over to him.

"Can I see the song book?" I ask with a sway of my hips. Thankfully, the next person to take the stage can sing in the right keys. They sound like they come here just for this opportunity.

"Here you go, darlin'," He drawls. I can't place his accent, but I know he isn't from here. Hmm, just like me. I'm a transplant. I slide the book over in front of me and begin looking through the pages. I don't really know what I'm looking for. I guess I'll know it when I see it. I feel a buzz in my pocket. Wondering if it's Lana telling me what to sing, I pull it out.

Unknown:

> This is Sebastian. I got some more information for you.

I roll my eyes. Of course, he would text me right now. I contemplate ignoring him, but I know that will just lead to more messages. I go to type, but the keys come up a bit blurry. I hesitate for a moment wondering what I should say.

> Stormy isn't available right now.

I save his number in my phone, and I laugh.

Daddy:

> Stormy, what are you doing?

Stormy:

> I'm living my life! Lana and I needed drinks. Well, more me, but I can't fly solo so here we are. Oh, I ran into your ol' pal Jared. He's the real winner, that one.

Daddy:

> Stormy, where the hell are you? Did he touch you?

I laugh at his stern voice I can hear as I read his text.

Daddy:

> Tell me where you are, Angel.

Stormy:

> Why? Are you going to come and sing with me? I forgot what this place is called. Tipsy Topsy Turvy something or other. Got to go.

Daddy:

> I'm coming for you.

I slide my phone back in my pocket without registering what he just said. I motion for the bartender to come back, and he nods his head. I take a large gulp of my tea and relish the taste. I haven't had one of these in a long time. In the back of my head, I know this is a bad idea. I shouldn't be drinking this much after taking anxiety medication. But it doesn't stop me. I don't want this weight on my shoulders tonight. The bartender comes back over when I'm deep in thought.

"Did you decide on a song?" he asks.

"*My Immortal* by Evanescence," I point to the song number and hand him the book. He nods and I scoot off the bar stool and head back toward Lana.

"Did you pick out a song?" she asks.

"Yes, but I'm not telling you. You'll have to wait and see." I take another sip of my drink and realize that I finished it at some point.

"Alright. I'm going to get another beer; do you want anything?" I think for a minute and nod my head.

"Another round of shots and water. I probably shouldn't drink too much more. I took medicine right after I got out of the cab." Her anger flares. I take a mental note that I don't think I've ever seen her get angry. I'm not really sure why she is right now. We were having a good time.

"Stormy! You could get sick! You probably will!" she screeches.

"Lana, I'm fine. Look at me. I feel fine. Just one more shot and I'll switch to water. I promise." She shrugs and heads off toward the bar. I feel my pocket vibrate again but I don't pull it out. I know it is probably Sebastian again. Why can't I have some fun? No one wants me to have some fun and let my hair down for once. I don't want to feel anything right now. The next second, my name is being called to go up on stage. For a moment, I think this is a terrible idea, but I push through. I'm not going to let the past dictate my future. I walk up to the stage and take the mic, introducing myself.

"Hi. I'm Stormy and this is Evanescence." The music starts out low and I close my eyes and sing. I forget about all the people watching me and just concentrate on the lyrics. They mean something to me, that's why I picked this song. I open my eyes as the chorus plays. Sebastian is sitting right before me and I'm glad he isn't interrupting my song. I close my eyes again and belt out the rest of the song.

Once I finish, I receive a standing ovation. Not sure that I really earned it, but it's better than anyone else got. I place the mic back on the stand and Sebastian is there helping me off the stage. He interlaces our hands together, pulling me to the back of the bar where Lana is sitting. A camera flash brings me out of my stupor, I shield my eyes from the glare. Another goes off, Sebastian is taking me by the waist out of the bar. The cold air bites my exposed skin and I look back to make sure Lana is right there with us. I sigh in relief when I see her jogging behind.

"What was that all about? I was just singing a song! I have a tab open," I shout at Sebastian.

"You were drawing a fucking crowd, that's what you were doing," he retorts.

"Why the hell do you care?" He slams his lips over mine and for a moment I think it's just to shut me up, but I can't help but to lean into him as he ravages my mouth. I moan out and grasp onto his shirt, tugging him closer. Another shot is taken of us, I don't understand what's going on. Sebastian breaks the kiss to confront the man with the camera.

"Delete those pictures. *Now*." Sebastian yells at the man. All too late, I realize what I have done. People will see those pictures of me and know where I am. Fuck, how could I be so stupid. I go to punch the man, but I'm pulled back into a hard chest. Sebastian held me back. I'm so angry. I don't feel so well. My limbs feel heavy, and my vision starts to blur. All too quickly I'm surrounded by blackness, being pulled under.

SEVENTEEN

Sebastian

What the fuck? I look to Stormy's roommate who doesn't look that drunk. How much more could Stormy have had? I hold her limp body in my arms as I make my way to the car.

"How much did she have to drink?" I angrily question her roommate, wondering why she didn't look out for her better.

"Not that much, but" she hesitates for a moment and looks around. "She took anxiety medication before we left. I don't think she is supposed to drink alcohol with it," she replies, wringing her hands together.

"You let her fucking drink?" I yell. My voice booms in the parking lot. We get to my car, and I open the passenger door, laying Stormy inside. I buckle her in and reach for her purse.

"She didn't tell me until she had already downed a few shots and a Long Island iced tea," she pleads but I'm busy looking through Stormy's purse for the medication she took. I find the bottle and read the label: Clonazepam. *Fuck.*

"I'm taking her to my apartment. My doctor will meet us there. Can you call Uber? I don't want to waste any more time than I

171

need to. Go back into the bar, close her tab and wait until the car arrives. Text Stormy's phone and I'll give you updates," I command, not waiting for a reply.

"Yes, please take care of her," she says after I close the passenger door.

I run around to the driver's side and slide behind the wheel. Stormy's head is resting against the cool window of the car. Immediately I pull up my contacts to call Dr. Peterson. The line rings through the speakers of the car as I pull out of the parking lot.

"Yes, Mr. Knight, what can I do for you?" he asks groggily.

"I need you to meet me at my apartment. My," I pause for a moment searching for the right word for her. "Girlfriend needs to be seen. She went out drinking tonight after taking some anxiety medication and she passed out in my arms." I pull into traffic and honk my horn for people to get out of the way. Slowly, the cars begin moving to the side as I make my way through. In no time, we're on the highway heading to my apartment.

"I'll get my things together and meet you there. Is she breathing alright?" I look over at Stormy to see her chest rising and falling at a normal pace.

"Yes, she is. I'll be at my apartment in ten minutes." I hang up the phone and look back to Stormy. I've never felt so much fear for another person in my entire life. I can't lose her, not when I just found her. Miles calls when we are a few minutes from my apartment, I deny the call, not entirely sure what I would tell him. I'm sure he's calling to tell me they're back in New York. I can call him later tomorrow.

I pull into my gated garage, shift into park, and leave the car running. I run around to the passenger side door, carefully opening it so Stormy doesn't get too jostled. Unbuckling her belt, I lift her small body into my arms and carry her through the lobby to my personal elevator.

"Park the car for me Frank," I call out to the man behind the security desk. "Also, Dr. Peterson is on the way. Let him up."

"Of course, yes sir," he responds as he rounds the corner and goes to tend to my car. The elevator doors open, I rush in pressing my button behind me.

"Please stay with me, Stormy." I whisper in her ear. She shifts for a moment and my heart soars that she'll be okay. Her breathing continues to be steady which reassures me for now. As the doors open up, I sprint into my apartment, the lights illuminating each room that I step foot. I've never been more thankful for automatic lights in my life. I take Stormy to my bedroom, laying her on my bed. She looks so tiny compared to the king-sized bed. I sit beside her for a moment, just staring at the goddess before me. After pushing a stray piece of hair from her face, I go to the bathroom to retrieve a wet washcloth. Placing it on her forehead, I run my knuckles over her cheek, feeling her smooth skin.

"Sebastian, I'm here," Dr Peterson calls from the elevator.

"In my room," I shout back. I pull the medication bottle from my pocket and hand it to him when he comes into view.

"She took one of these before she went out drinking. Her roommate said she didn't mention it until after she'd been drinking," I say in a rush.

"Alright, step aside, son. Go get yourself a bottle of water and let me examine her. I'll call you back here in a moment."

"No, absolutely not. I'm not leaving her."

"You're hovering in the way. I need my space to make sure she's going to be okay. Trust me," he says a bit more forcibly.

"Argh," I groan out and leave the room. I walk through my apartment to the kitchen. Grabbing water from the fridge, I take a seat on the couch. I find that I can't stay still. I need to keep moving to expel some of this nervous energy I have coursing through me. I retrieve Stormy's phone from her purse and see my missed messages on her screen. I huff out a laugh when I see the name she has set for me. "Daddy." What a firecracker, that one. I don't know what it is about her, but she ignites something deep inside me.

I sit back down to look for the message thread between her and her roommate. The only other thread other than ours is with Picasso. I chuckle to myself because I know for a fact that's her. Her hair is the color of every shade of paint imaginable.

I pull up the messages and let her know that the doctor's here looking her over. What a nightmare. And the paparazzi that were there made everything a hundred times worse. I sit up abruptly thinking about the man taking the pictures. Stormy freaked out when she realized what was happening. Does she not like being photographed or is there something bigger going on that I'm not aware of? Whatever it is, I need to call Marcy, our PR rep, and let her know some photos will be surfacing soon. I rest my head against the cool leather sofa, scrubbing my hand down my face. I pull out my phone and send her a text.

Sebastian:

Just a heads up, there might be some photos surfacing of me and woman tonight.

Her response is almost immediate. I would laugh if it wasn't so serious.

Marcy:

> What the hell have you gotten into this time? I was hoping for a quiet weekend.

Sebastian:

> I was picking a friend up from a bar and people started taking pictures of us together. There might be some of her passed out in my arms. I need them taken down immediately. She seemed pretty upset about it.

Marcy:

> I'll do what I can, but I can't promise some haven't already been leaked.

Sebastian:

> Thank you, Marcy, I owe you.

Marcy:

> Of course, you do. I was getting bored with the Knight brothers. Thanks for stirring up some shit so I can get my hands dirty. What's the woman's name?

Sebastian:

> Stormy Brooks.

Marcy:

> I'll let you know if I see anything.

I toss my phone on the sofa and rub my hands over my face. What a nightmare of a day. I'm going to need a fucking vacation after this.

"Sebastian," The doctor calls out my name, I'm up and heading for my room a moment later.

"Is she okay?" I ask, veering over his shoulder.

"She'll be fine. I hooked her up to an IV to get some fluids in her. She is breathing normally, which is what I was concerned about. Since both the medication and the alcohol can cause difficulty breathing. I put a pulse oximeter on her finger, it should be left there throughout the night. It will sound an alarm if she begins to not get enough oxygen. I believe she just passed out from over exertion along with the combined medication and alcohol. I don't believe she is any danger," He expresses with a contented sigh. "I'm going to continue monitoring her for another hour or so. I need to let the fluids get into her system before I remove the IV."

"Thank you, Steve. I owe you one," I clap him on the shoulder and step around him into the room. Stormy looks angelic lying there on my bed. I head to my closet and pull out some workout clothes. I need to get some of this pent-up energy out of me or I'll never be able to sleep.

"I'm going down to the gym if that's alright? Help yourself to anything you want."

"Oh, I noticed Ms. Brooks has a bandaged hand. Should I take a look at that?" he asks.

"Actually, that would be great. She cut her palm on glass. She had some stitches put in but some of them opened up the other night." I mention, thinking back to the night when I first had Stormy pressed up against the shower. I shake my head to get the images of her naked from my head. I need to focus on getting her better before I can do that to her again.

"Okay, I will check it out. Hey, are you doing okay?" Dr Peterson asks.

I shrug my shoulders. "I just have a lot on my plate at the moment." He nods his head in understanding.

"I'll be here when you get back," He goes to Stormy and begins to unwrap her hand. I turn and walk from the room down the stairs to my gym. The lights illuminate all the exercise equipment that I have. I drop my clothes on the bench after I shed them from my body. After I redress in my workout clothes, I walk up to my free-standing punching bag. Sliding on my gloves, I begin pounding away at the bag. Each punch melts away some of the stress I have building inside me. After I exhaust myself with the punching bag, I jump on the treadmill. Setting the speed to a jog, I try to keep my focus solely on the task at hand. The pounding of my feet on the machine grounds me to the moment and it helps. Once I finish, I'm physically and mentally exhausted. All I want to do is shower and climb in bed. I grab a towel to wipe my face then grab my old clothes, leaving the gym. I walk back to the main level of the apartment headed toward my bedroom. Steve is sitting in the corner of my room on a leather chair that my interior designer insisted I needed. I guess it can come in handy.

"How's she doing?" I gesture to Stormy as I wipe the towel down my face.

"She's going to be fine. I'll go ahead and take the IV out and I'll get out of here," He stands, putting away the paperwork he was looking over. "Make sure she gets plenty of rest. I imagine she will have a nasty hangover in the morning. I left some Motrin on the nightstand for her to take when she wakes. I'll call and check in with you in the morning." He removes the IV and leaves a small bandage on her arm.

"Thank you again for coming on such short notice. She scared me when she passed out in my arms," I think back to tonight and a chill runs up my spine.

"You did the right thing. Now, try and get some rest as well," he remarks.

"Will do." I reply as he leaves the room. Soon I hear the front door close behind him. I turn from him and walk over to where Stormy is lying on my bed. She looks good in here. If only it were under different circumstances. I take a seat beside her, building questions in my mind of things we need to discuss when she comes to. I want to know what the hell she was thinking. She was fine at work this afternoon, so something must have happened to her to set her off after she left. I can't help but to tighten my fists at the thought of someone hurting her. I hear her phone chime from the living room, I know it must be her roommate checking on her. I get up and grab the phone, responding to the message as I walk back.

Picasso:

Is she alright?

Stormy:

Yes. The doctor just left. He said she would be fine. He hooked her up to an IV drip and said she needed rest. Do you have any idea what happened to her to cause her to need the medicine?

Bubbles appear and then disappear. Over and over until she finally responds.

Picasso:

> I think you need to ask her about that.

Stormy:

> Oh, I definitely will when she wakes up.

Picasso:

> Don't give her a hard time. She went through a lot, even if she tells you she is fine.

I stare at the screen for a moment, not knowing how to respond. I want to call my private investigator to do an extensive background check, but maybe I should wait for her to tell me. *The fuck with that.* I need to know if she is in danger or what she is hiding. I place Stormy's phone on my dresser and retrieve mine from the living room, shooting off a text to my PI. I need to know everything about Stormy Brooks. She's hiding something and it's time for all the cards to be set on the table.

I check on Stormy again and I decide to shower before I curl in behind her. I just need to rinse this day from my mind, not to mention all the sweat I just worked up. The shower feels amazing on my muscles. The heat seeps into my body and I feel relaxed once I'm finished. I step out of the shower as the steam billows out around me. Pulling on a pair of boxers, I settle in behind Stormy. Tomorrow I'll get answers. I kiss her forehead and wrap my arm around her waist. Even though she's asleep, she snuggles into me, making a soft whimpering sound. I check to make sure she is alright before turning off the bedside lamp.

"I'll see you in the morning, Angel. You scared me tonight. And tomorrow, I want to know everything." I kiss her again and close my eyes listening to her breathing. The stark realization hits me that I would do anything for this woman. A woman that I barely know anything about. Stormy has already gotten under my skin. *Can I be what she needs?*

EIGHTEEN

Stormy

I wake from a harrowing dream. One that took me to the past and made me relive my worst nightmares. I couldn't escape it. I was there again, begging Blaine not to go. Movement on the bed has me cracking open my eyes to see who's there. What I find it both startling and insanely hot. Sebastian lies asleep beside me in what I presume is his bed. It's huge and definitely not mine. I take a moment to look at my surroundings, I'm dumbfounded as to how I got here. Last night is hazy to say the least.

I slap my hand over my face as images of last night surface in my mind. Fuck, I was not myself. I was exactly who I was a year ago, drinking to numb the pain. I know the cab ride triggered my past trauma, but I never meant to take it this far.

I try to slide out of bed, but I'm hoisted into place by a large hand wrapped around my waist.

A low husky growl comes from beside my ear, "Good morning, Angel."

"Good morning, Sebastian. What am I doing here?" I ask. Trying to make sense of everything.

"You mixed meds and alcohol together making you pass out in my arms. Thank fuck I was there," he says with a groan as he pulls me back against him. "Now be a good girl and go back to sleep. I'm not ready to wake up yet," he murmurs softly. A tingling sensation shoots through my body at his words. How can he get me this worked up a crack thirty in the morning?

"I have to use the restroom. So, if you'll please let me go," he opens his eyes to look at me. It looks like emeralds shining back. He lifts his arm, releasing me from his grasp. I walk into his bathroom and the lights come on automatically. The floor is oddly warm as well. *Are you kidding me? He has heated flooring!* Wow, how the rich live. I shut the door behind me and do my business. Washing my hands, I look in the mirror and am horrified by the person staring back at me. I can't believe he didn't throw me out of bed looking like this. I find some soap and wash my face, ridding myself of the smeared black mascara. I realize that I have new bandages on my hand as well as one on my forearm. *Seriously, what the hell happened last night? Did he seriously take care of me?* That counters everything I thought I knew about him. I know he's going to want to talk about what happened last night, I'm not sure I can tell him everything. I don't know what he would think of me, knowing I'm a widow, was in a rock band, changed my hair color and moved to a different state to escape the sympathy stares. I sigh to myself. This isn't going to be a fun conversation.

I open the drawers looking for a spare toothbrush. There is no way I'm going back out there with tequila breath. Ugh, gross. I feel gross. I think my pores are bleeding liquor. I need a shower, greasy food, Motrin, and water. Not necessarily in that order but all of it, nonetheless. I give up my pursuit of a toothbrush and peak my head out of the door. I watch Sebastian as he sleeps, my heart-beat drums in my chest. He elicits this flame inside me.

"Are you going to keep staring or come back to bed?" he chuckles softly.

"I was looking for a spare toothbrush. Anything really. I'll use my finger if I have to." I cringe at the thought.

He grunts and throws his legs over the side of the bed. I'm greeted with one hundred percent perfection. I could just swoon from his sculpted chest alone. Add in his beautiful face and his infuriatingly stubborn mouth and I melt. And let's not forget the tattoos. They are my weakness. That reminds me that I want to ask him about them sometime.

He comes up to me leaning over to kiss my forehead. A sweet gesture that makes me wonder what the hell is going on. He moves around me and pads to the bathroom opening the only drawer I didn't and retrieves a toothbrush still in the package.

"Thank you," I take it from him and brush my teeth, enjoy-ing the cool mint flavor. Now on to my list of things I need to feel better. I'll have to wait until I get home for the shower since I don't have any clean clothes here. That leaves me with the two easiest, water and meds. This headache needs to go away.

I walk back to the bedroom and see exactly what I wanted, waiting for me beside the bed. Sebastian is there sitting on the edge, looking right at me. I can't decipher the look, but I know it's full of questions. He leans over grabbing the water and pills, handing them to me.

"Here, take these. They will help with the headache that I'm sure you have," I nod, accepting the items. I down the pills and drink the entire bottle of water. My throat felt like the Sahara Desert.

"Thank you," I murmur as I wipe a drip of water from my lips.

"Come sit." Ugh, I knew it. The dreaded talk like he really is my daddy. The thought both excites and infuriates me. This is my life, and I can do what I want. We aren't dating. I don't know why he is acting like this.

"Actually, I just wanted to say thank you for last night." I go to pick up my discarded jeans and sweater folded on the dresser, but he beats me to it.

"Oh no you don't." He grabs my hips and lifts me to his chest, bringing me back to bed.

"Sebastian, let me go." I squirm in his grasp. He throws me to the bed on my belly. Before I can turn myself around, he is there behind me pulling my hips up to his body. Without warning he spanks my ass hard. I yelp out and he smooths his hand over the pain. I think that's it, but he changes sides, spanking me even harder this time. He rubs the inflamed skin and flips me until I'm lying on my back. Staring up at him, I see a blaze in his eyes.

"I told you to sit down, Angel. I don't want to tell you twice next time or your punishment will be more severe." My core floods at his words. I can't believe after everything I have been through; I like being submissive to a man. *This man* of all people.

"I'm on the bed. Now what do you want," I question with a tinge of irritation.

"You better watch that bratty mouth of yours. I want to talk about last night." I try to shift away from him. I don't want to talk about this. I don't want to bring up the past. I hate going to that dark, lonely place.

"Last night was nothing. You aren't my father. Now let me up. I need to get home." I try to push his chest, but he sits firm on his knees.

"No, I'm not your father, but someone needs to be," he retorts, pulling my body back to facing him.

"Fuck you. You don't know anything about me. I don't need a father or a *daddy*," I snap back.

"I disagree and I believe you listed me in your phone as Daddy. Now, tell me what the fuck happened last night. I know you took meds and then proceeded to get drunk. The combination made you pass out in my arms. If I wasn't there, you would have hit the ground. Do you think your drunk roommate would have been able to get you home safely?" He asks with a low growl to his tone. I know he's right, but I don't want to admit it. I don't really know how to respond. I'm thankful he was there, but I don't even know how he knew where I was in the first place.

"How did you know where I was?" I ask in a huff.

"You said you were at Tipsy Topsy Turvy. I knew only one bar with the word Tipsy in it. I got there as fast as I could because I knew you were drunk," he replies.

"I just don't understand why you care."

"I just do dammit." His words are final, and they shut me up. I guess I never really had anyone that cared like that. Even my parents were absent, making me have to grow up before my time. Before I'm able to respond, his phone rings. "We aren't done." He grunts as he gets off the bed and answers the phone.

I feel like my past and present are about to collide. The anxiety begins to build in my stomach, and I have the urge run. I sit up on the bed and look at Sebastian as he walks over to the other nightstand to get his phone.

"Fuck." Is all he says before he answers his phone, looking at me with a stern expression. Yep, he is about to find out everything. I want to hide under the covers or better yet actually run. Maybe move to another state and try to start over again. I cover my face in my hands as the tears begin to slide down my cheeks. This is really happening.

Today I have a virtual appointment with my psychiatrist/therapist. I totally forgot all about it. My phone alarm chimes that the appointment starts in five minutes. It's been about a month since I spoke to her. She knew I was moving to New York and agreed to continue seeing me virtually. I really didn't want to find another doctor and have to go through the process of talking through all my shit again. Detailing everything I went through was hard enough the first time with Dr. Heffington. That's not something I want to experience again. Pulling my phone from my pocket, I find a quiet area in the apartment to talk. I sign in and wait in the virtual waiting room. Things like this make me appreciate technology. I never liked being the center of attention in the band and getting my face plastered all over media sites but this kind of technology where I can speak with my doctor in Florida is pretty cool. I don't have to wait long before my call moves from the waiting room to her office. And then she is there on the screen in front of me. I wipe my tears away hoping she doesn't instantly spot them.

"It's good to see you, Stormy. How was the move? Have you been crying?" She questions.

"It wasn't too bad. Obviously I hate the unpacking aspect, but my new roommate helped me out. There is just a lot going on at the moment. Maybe we should reschedule," I mention.

"Is that what you really want? How about you tell me what's going on? Is your roommate giving you problems?" Dr. Heffington asks.

"No, it's not her. She is pretty much the opposite of me in every way. She is full of life and color while I am more of a black and white character. She's trying to get me to open up more and I actually told her about who I am and mostly everything that happened. I went out last night and people got pictures of me and now I'm sure they know who I am and where I am." I explain.

"That was a big step telling your roommate about your past. It took months for you to open up to me. I'm proud of you for trusting someone else with your secrets. As for the tabloids, you knew that would happen eventually. Right?" she questions.

"I figured I would've had more time. I wanted to just be Stormy Brooks for a bit longer. It didn't take them long to find me. It's weird. As for Lana, I am too actually. I had no intention of telling her, but she recognized me after a while, and I didn't want to lie to her. Plus, she just seems like a person I can trust. She's generous and kind. I lucked out with her being my roommate," I reply.

"Excellent news. So, how have you been feeling other than this bit with the media? I mean you packed up and moved all the way up the coast. Have you heard from your in-laws?" she queries.

"I changed my phone number before I left so that none of my old shit could follow me up here. You're the only person from Florida that has my new number," I remark.

"I think it's good to get a fresh start after everything you have been through, but I wonder if maybe you should reach out to the Jacks' and let them know you are alright? I would be worried if you just disappeared on me," she responds.

"Well, I wouldn't disappear on you. But they don't care where I am. You know they turned on me after Blaine's death. They thought I only married him for the insurance money which I didn't even know he had signed up for. It's just better to leave them in the dust. Plus, now that the press knows where I am; they'll find me. They want that money," I say.

"They've been very difficult through all this. I don't want you to be all alone in the world. You need a support system. I'm hoping that your new roommate can be part of that for you. You said her name was Lana?" she asks.

"Yes, her name is Lana, but I put her in my phone as Picasso because that's what her head looks like, a Picasso painting. When I tell you that she has every color in her hair, I mean it. But it expresses her personality perfectly. I like her," I tell my doctor. She writes something down in her notes and looks back at the video.

"So, have you found a job yet? I know you were concerned about that," she mentions.

"Well, yes. I did but then I got fired the same night. But I ended up getting offered another one the same night," I reply with a laugh.

"You got fired on your first night? What was the job?" she asks.

"Well, Lana works for this catering company, and they were serving a large fundraiser. They needed extra employees so when she called her boss, I got the job instantly. When we got there, the owner, Gina, was already in a pissy mood so it didn't help that some man ran into me and caused me to spill all the plates on my tray. We weren't in the main venue, so no one really saw it happen but apparently, he is this billionaire and it was his fundraiser for his publishing company. I didn't know who he was at the time and we both had a few choice words to call each other. Gina over heard and saw what happened so she fired me on the spot," I sigh, looking out my window then back to Dr. Heffington. "Anyways, I ended up cutting my hand pretty badly while I was cleaning up the glassware, the HR for the publishing company came up to me and got a doctor out there to put stitches in and everything. It was all kind of bizarre. Then she offered me a job. I didn't know it was going to be for the arrogant man I had just confronted but it was. When I got there Monday morning, we arrived at the same time, I managed to run into him this time. Neither one of us apologized as we continued to berate each other," I shake my head through the phone, and she does the same. "Anyways, the HR woman, Mary, hired me because she saw the way I talked to Sebastian the night of the fundraiser and she said she knew I'd be able to handle him if I worked there," I finish.

"Wow, that was an eventful first week. Is Sebastian still giving you trouble? Is he difficult to work for?" she questions.

"Not really. I can handle him. He's no different than any other man. And once you learn to handle one you can handle them all. There is this other assistant there that was filling in until they were able to get someone in there. Elijah is a whole other story. He won't leave me alone. He's asked me out several times and I have declined. Now when he isn't busy, which seems like all the time, he's hanging out at my desk. I'm going to have to come up with another way of saying I'm not interested since my words seem to have no meaning," I confess.

"Have you reported him? Sounds like this Mary woman likes you and I'm sure she would like to keep you around. If she found out that someone was bothering you, I'm sure she would do something about it or at the very least have a talk with him," she suggests.

"I was thinking about that too. If he keeps on, then I will report him because he is driving me insane and it's making me not want to go into the office. I don't want to hate the job," I reply.

"So, other than all that, how is your medications working? Are you still having to take the clonazepam?" I cringe because I knew she was going to bring this up and I don't want to tell her about my night out.

"I've taken it a couple times since I've been here. I don't take it every day like I used to when everything happened. But I did have an incident with it," I look at her and frown.

"You might as well tell me, Stormy. I will get it out of you one way or another," she asserts. I see her stern face on my phone, I know I have no other option than to tell her what happened.

"Well, I was in a cab coming home from work and a song from Damaged Jacks came on. It was one of the older ones where I was singing. The cab driver immediately turned it up and I banged on the partition to get his attention but by the time I did, the damage was done. I had to sit there and listen. It brought back those terrible images of that night from the kitchen floor. Anyways, once he dropped me off in front of my apartment, I took out the medicine and swallowed it without any water or anything. Once I got into the apartment, Lana could tell something was wrong. I'd texted her that I was on the way home and I was fine, so she knew that something happened between then and when I got home. She held me as I got upset explaining what happened and then out of nowhere, I declared that we needed to go out for drinks," I say in a low voice, not wanting her to hear how I reverted back to my old ways that night.

"Stormy, you know better than that. Please tell me you didn't get drunk on the medication. If you keep abusing it, I won't prescribe it anymore," she declares.

"Lana took me to a karaoke bar, to be fair she didn't realize that they would have karaoke that night and she didn't know that I had taken medication. Anyways, we had a couple shots, and I had another drink. I ended up on stage singing. Then Sebastian came, which is a good thing because I ended up passing out on the street. I know it's terrible and I'm sorry. I haven't taken the medicine since," I claim.

"Why would Sebastian come to get you. Is there something going on between you and him?" she asks. I don't really know how to answer. Yes, there is but what exactly I don't know?

"I slept with him the other night. It was raining and he gave me a ride home. He came up to help me with my hand which I told him I didn't need him to, but he insisted then one thing led to another. I know it's terrible. Blaine has only been gone just over a year. Tell me I'm a terrible person," I insist.

"Stormy, calm down. No one is saying that you're a terrible person. How long it takes to get over someone is specific to that person. You weren't really romantically involved with Blaine even though you were married. You were more of best friends and roommates than lovers. As for sleeping with your boss, I wouldn't say that's the smartest move. You don't know what will happen between one another so it could cause some strain at work. But I'm sure you can handle it," She asserts.

"The thing is I wasn't going to sleep with him. I still basically hated him. But then he helped me through panic attack episode, and I didn't have to take any medicine. It was amazing. He was able to ground me to the moment and pull me back before I slipped further away. He used a technique that I wasn't familiar with, but he said that his cousin who has PTSD told him about it. Sebastian got me to name three things I could see and smell. It got me thinking more on that and less on what I was panicking about," I answer.

"That's a great technique to have in your arsenal. I feel ashamed that I didn't teach you that while you were staying here. Using your senses and naming things you can see, feel, hear and smell are great ways to ground yourself to the present. It can be hard to do if you are already too deep in a panic episode but that's great he was able to help you with that. I'd say he isn't so bad after all. Maybe you just got off on the wrong foot." She explains. "Now with this drinking and taking your medication, that is a big no no. I don't want to hear you doing that again. Thank you for trusting me enough to tell me but that's strike two. If you do something irresponsible again then I'm going to take that prescription away from you. Do you understand?" she questions.

"Yes, ma'am. I'm sorry that I did it. It was stupid and reckless, and I could've come out worse than I did. Thank you for holding me accountable," I say.

"So, I didn't know whether to bring this up or not, but I've seen a picture with an article with you and this man. It had you passed out in his arms. I was glad that we had this appointment today so

I could figure out what's going on. That's Sebastian, correct?" she asks.

"Yes, that's him. He came there to check on me," I respond.

"That doesn't sound like just a hookup to me. Are you sure he doesn't really care about you?" I have to sit and think for a minute. Sebastian acts like he cares for me, but he's also known to have a line of women. I don't really know what's true.

"I'm not sure. I guess time will tell," I murmur.

"Don't push him away, Stormy. I know you. You're already trying to think of the best way to escape him. He could be good for you. He's already committed to taking care of your hand and your panic attacks. I wouldn't dust that under the rug. Not all men are equipped to handle such things and if he's doing it willingly, then I would say he has feelings for you. But you don't need to take my word for it. You need to talk to him about it. I could meet with both of you if you want me to," She insists.

"I don't know. I'll let you know. He's a billionaire, Dr. Heffington. He could have anyone he wants. I've seen the type of girls he's normally with and they don't look like me. I don't want to get my hopes up but also, I still think we have a love/hate relationship. We are both extremely hardheaded and we still haven't apologized for the things we have said to each other," I respond.

"Remember that going through a situation like that panic attack can bond people together. Chemicals in the brain don't distinguish between the adrenaline of falling in love or a fight or flight episode. It's possible that what started out as enemies has developed into something deeper than either of you expected. I see the fear in your eyes. Not everyone is going to leave you like Blaine and your parents. You were dealt a shitty hand in life but that doesn't mean that you can't turn it around. You have to trust people. If you want trust you have to give some away. Talk to Sebastian, Stormy."

"Thank you for everything. I'll talk to him. I don't know when, but I will."

"Well, I have kept you for long enough. Make sure you talk to this man before you run away and don't mix anymore medication with alcohol. Same time in two weeks?" she asks. I nod my head as she writes the appointment down.

"Thank you for always believing in me even when no one else did. I'm glad to have you as a doctor," I reply before we get off the phone.

"You are more than welcome. We'll talk again soon," she says as I hang up and look out the window at all the clouds flying over. I wonder what I should say to Sebastian. I don't want to be the first to bring up what we are. I don't want to look needy. I sigh and put my phone away. Things with men are always so complicated.

Sebastian

"How bad is it?" I ask Marcy. She never calls, just texts. I know something is going on if she is calling me.

"You and Ms. Brooks are plastered all over the media. But that's not all, are you sitting down?" Fucking hell this can't be good. I walk over to my chair in the corner and sit, keeping my eyes on

Stormy in case she tries to bolt. She's got her face covered and I would bet that tears are cascading down her face. She is talking with someone on the phone.

"Tell me," I demand.

"Stormy Brooks is also known as Stormy Jacks. Do you know who that is?" The name seems familiar to me, but I can't place it. Why did she lie about her last name?

"She was the lead singer of Damaged Jacks until a year ago when tragedy struck the band. The lead guitarist was killed." I let that sink in. I've heard that band name. They are all over the radio. Now that I think about it, when she was singing last night I felt like she could have a career in it. And she has. Why is she lying to me and to everyone? "I take it by your silence that you didn't know any of that?" Marcy questions.

I clear my throat that suddenly feels dry. "No, I didn't. Tell me the rest. I know there is more," I insist.

"She was married to the lead guitarist, who was shot at his parent's residence. Apparently, it was accidental by the nephew. She was there and witnessed him dying. She went into a rehab facility soon after. The media has been trying to find her ever since. She's a big deal in the music industry and record labels want her. She died her hair, and she is going by her maiden name." It takes me a moment to understand everything that Marcy is telling me. I knew something bad happened in her past, but I could never imagine that she saw her husband dying. A sudden bolt of jealousy surges through me at the thought of her loving another man. "I was able to dig into her background and found all this out. Her parents' also passed away in a car accident about a year before that. They we going to her graduation and were struck by a drunk driver. The poor thing has been through more than you can imagine."

"I don't really know what to say." I look back up from the floor and see that Stormy and her clothes have disappeared. "I have to go. Try and get the photos taken down. Do whatever it takes."

"Wait! Don't leave your apartment, there are paparazzi out there. We are trying to get the police there, but they aren't going fast enough. You need to stay put until this blows over. They know you know her, plus you're like a New York celebrity. Both of you together are making headlines. They'll harass both of you. I'm doing everything I can." Fuck, she is going to be bombarded. I jump up and grab a pair of sweats, tugging them on. I run out of my room and down the hall to the front door that just closed. I open it quickly and see the elevator doors closing.

"Stormy! Stop! You can't leave." But it's too late. The elevator doors close and I see it making its way down. "Fuck! Damnit!" I think fast, running to the stairs, I take them two at a time, hoping I will make it there before she does, but I live on the top floor. I realize that I still have my phone clutched in my hands and I put it to my ear to tell Marcy what's going on.

"Marcy, Stormy was here, she just sprinted from my apartment. She's going down the elevator and will be bombarded if there are paparazzi everywhere. She fucking suffers from panic attacks, Marcy. Fuck." I don't know if it's the adrenaline or the sheer will to save her from such horrible things that makes me get to the ground floor around the same time the elevator opens. But just as Marcy said, there are photographers everywhere. Stormy's eyes meet mine and I see the sheer panic there. I run and grab her in my arms.

"It's okay. It's okay. Let's get out of here," I whisper into the shell of her ear, trying to calm her and myself at the same time. She nods into my chest, I barely register the flashes going off. I grab her in my arms, and she wraps her legs around me, as I press the button for the elevator. It opens immediately and I jump in. Pressing the button to close the door, I can still see the flashes going off in the distance, but I have Stormy clinging to me for dear life. She is my main focus right now. I know they got the pictures they came here for. A disheveled woman and a man in just pants doesn't paint us in the best light. Marcy is going to have a field day with everything. *Marcy!*

"Sorry Marcy, I got her. We're going back to my apartment. They saw us. I'm sorry your job just got ten times harder. I've to go. Let me know if anything else comes up," I say into the phone.

"Will do. Take care of that poor girl, she needs it." Marcy hangs up and I pocket my phone.

I pull Stormy closer to me and she tightens her hold on me.

"I'm so sorry." She whimpers. I can feel her tears running down my chest and my heart aches at the pain she is going through.

"You don't need to apologize. We will get everything resolved." I murmur, trying to keep myself calm when all I feel is rage flowing through me. The audacity of people that feel the need to harass innocents to get photographs of them astounds me. I grip her hips tighter and she yelps but I just need to feel her, to ground myself. I need to be present to help her, not furious that people are storming my building. I take a deep breath and look down into the yellow tear-filled pools of Stormy's eyes and I know without a doubt that I am in love with her. I don't know when it happened or how, but she is mine. I don't care about her past, I just want to be her future.

197

Nineteen

Sebastian

We get back into the apartment, I set Stormy on the couch making sure to wrap her in a blanket. She pulls her knees up to her chest as she continues to tremble. I crouch down in front of her and cup her face in my hands. My thumb wipes away her tears even as they continue to spill. I look at this gorgeous creature in front of me and I just want to protect her.

"You don't have to talk about anything right now. I want you to know I'm right here for you. Do you want to shower? It will help you feel better," I state. I lean up and kiss her forehead and it just feels right. Having her here feels right. Having her in my arms, my bed, and my apartment makes everything feel complete. I can't explain it, I don't want to. I'm coming to realize that Stormy is my person. I don't want to ever see her go and I definitely don't want to see her run from me again. I need to have a talk with her.

"Why are you being so nice about all this? I didn't tell you about my past and now it's caught up with me and I'm dragging you down with me." She looks so lost that the fire in her eyes has faded.

I hate to see her like this. I want my wild hurricane back. I want that smart ass keeping me on my toes.

"It's true, everything breaks down and goes haywire when you're involved and it's the best place I've ever been. You're my perfect storm." She gasps and looks at me with wonder in her eyes. I rub the remaining tears away. I think she's finally realizing that she can trust me to hold up the weights she has been carrying around for so long. The ones I know she has been shouldering alone.

"No one has ever said anything like that to me. I'm a mess, Sebastian. I-" I shush her with a kiss. I wrap my hand around her hair and pull it tight, holding her close to me. She moans and I take that invitation for my tongue to delve into her mouth. She tastes like my toothpaste and her strawberry ChapStick. It's an addicting flavor. One that is all Stormy. I pull back to gaze into her eyes. I see some of the fire is back.

"Bathroom, now, Angel," she smiles and nods her head.

"As long as you come with me," she taunts, giving me a devilish smile, which makes my heart soar. She's coming back to me.

Standing up, I push the blanket from her shoulders and push her knees down. She looks up through her lashes while reaching for me. I pick her up from the couch, she crosses her legs behind my waist while wrapping her arms around my neck. She then leans in and takes my lips in hers. It's soft and sweet like she is telling me she is okay with everything. With me. With us. I carry her to the bathroom, placing her on the counter. After starting the shower, I turn and see she's already discarded her sweater and shoes. She's sitting there in a white camisole, bra, and jeans. With a shy smile on her face, she lifts her arms, looking at me expectingly. I pull up the camisole, slowly grazing her milky sweet skin. Leaning forward she unhooks her bra allowing me to drag it down her arms and throw it into the pile of clothes on the floor.

"Do you know how absolutely stunning you are?" I ask, genuinely curious. A blush creeps up her cheeks. I don't think she has ever been appreciated like this. I want to worship her body the way it deserves. I lean into the crook of her neck and inhale the scent that is all Stormy. A floral mixture of something else, maybe vanilla. It's a heady scent and makes me drunk on her. I kiss up the column of her neck until I get to her ear. "You are amazing and I'm going to remind you until you believe me." I nip her ear and she trembles beneath my touch.

"Please, Daddy, I need you," she murmurs. Those words light the fire inside me and I can't get her pants off fast enough. I lift her from the counter, placing her on her feet. I push her jeans and underwear down her legs so she can step out of them. I push my pants and boxers down in one go, stepping out. My hard cock springs free, wanting to be where it belongs, in Stormy's sweet pussy.

I grab her waist and carry her to the shower. A small gasp escapes her lips as I bring her closer to me. It tells me exactly how she wants to be touched. How she wants to be caressed. I push her back under the spray and little droplets of water collect on her lashes. I clench her waist tighter, a shiver runs through her. I know what I do to her. Her body doesn't lie. She wants me just as badly as I want her. Stormy looks to me, I can see the willingness to obey every command I am about to utter. I lean down to kiss her soft lips before letting her down slowly. Her pussy rubbing along my length on the way down. I go to my knees in front of her. The perfect visual of me worshiping her.

"Put your leg over my shoulder." She does as I say while I run my hand up her thigh making her shiver at my touch. I hold her steady with my other hand as I plunge one finger inside her tight channel. She throws her head back allowing the spray of the jets to flow down her breasts making me harder than I have ever been. She makes me want to squeeze all the pleasure out of her that I can. I never really cared before about other women, as long as I got off. Women were disposable to me. But now I've found that rare needle in a haystack. The one in a million that was made just for me.

I add two more fingers, wanting her to get there faster. My thumb circles her clit, it doesn't take long before she is exploding before me. A perfect sight to behold.

"Yes, yes! Daddy!" she yells out as she comes all over my hand. I continue thrusting inside her, making her orgasm last longer. As she comes down, I place her leg back on the floor, standing up and holding her steady. I take her lips in mine in a ravenous kiss. I pull her against me so she can feel the evidence of my arousal pressed against her stomach. She reaches down between us to grab my cock. The sensations of her hand and the hot water running over me has me hissing out.

"Get up here, Angel." I command, as she jumps into my arms. Her legs tighten around my waist. "Put me inside you." Her hand slides down my chest slowly then moves between us to grab me and put me at her entrance. As soon as I'm there, I thrust inside of her. "Fuck, you are so tight, baby!" I pin her against the wall and pound her harder and harder. She moans out and calls my name several times. Well, she calls out Daddy. And that's exactly what I am. I will take care of all her needs, starting with this. I am responsible for all her pleasure.

"You feel so good inside me. Don't stop!" she exclaims.

"Never," I respond with a grunt. I continue to thrust into her, bringing her to another climax, her walls clamping down on me. Rubbing her clit harder as she screams out. I set her down on shaky legs, pulling out of her. "Turn around. Hands on the wall, Angel." She does as I command, and I thrust back inside of her, going deeper from this angle. "One day I'm going to take this ass. How's that sound? Do you want me to fuck your ass, baby?"

"Yes, please, yes! I've never-" She doesn't finish her sentence because that's all I needed to hear. I'll be her first in her ass. The thought shoots my orgasm rocketing through my body. I continue to pump into her tight little hole until I'm completely spent. I lean over her, interlacing our fingers together. I kiss down her neck and over her shoulder, not wanting us to part just yet. I want to stay inside her forever. The thought should scare me, but it doesn't. It excites me.

"I don't know what you do to me. I can't get enough of you," I whisper into her ear. She turns her head letting me capture her lips with mine. A slow seductive kiss. I want her to feel what I feel. I want her to know I love her even if I can't say the words yet.

"I can't get enough either." She murmurs against my mouth. She looks up at me and I see it there. She feels the same way, but she is also scared of getting hurt. Kissing her cheek, I pull out to turn her around.

"Who's your Daddy?" I ask as I clench her waist, pulling her close to me.

"You are. Only you." She breathes out.

"Good girl, now trust me to take care of you. Every part of you."
She looks away for a moment and I think she might reject me. My
heart is in my throat as I await a reply. She looks back at me with
tears in her eyes. She smiles and I melt on the spot.

"I trust you." I hug her, wanting to feel all of her touching me. I
wrap my hands in her hair, massaging her head. We stand like that
for a while until the water begins to cool.

"I think we better shower and get out of here before the water is
completely cold." I say.

We take turns bathing each other, then step out of the shower.
I hand her a heated towel and get one for myself. Grabbing an
extra one for her hair, I throw it on her head and chuckle at her
expression.

"Hey!" she squeals as I pull her close. I can't get enough of this
woman. I need to touch her. I need her with every fiber of my
being. I didn't think it was possible to fall for someone this quickly,
but it happened at some point. There's no going back.

"What? I need to touch you." She smiles at my confession.

"Well then put your hands to work and dry me off. Your floor
might be heated but the rest of my body is cold." She squirms,
trying to get completely covered by the towel.

"I can fix that." I wink at her.

"God, you're incorrigible." She rolls her eyes at me.

"Hey, I'm just trying to help." I pick her up and throw her over
my shoulder. She screams and laughs at the same time. I run to the
bedroom, throwing her on the bed. She flops a few times, laughing
the whole time.

"I'm going to get your bed all wet with my hair." She states, like
I care what she does to my bed. I couldn't care less. I throw her the

towel wrapped around me and she covers her eyes like she hasn't seen me this naked several times now.

"Why are you covering your eyes? You know you like it!" I jump in the bed right beside her, causing her to bounce again. I grab her body, putting us both under the covers. "Stop wriggling. I'm trying to warm you up."

"Let me at least wrap my hair in this towel first." She does just that then snuggles in beside me. I could get used to this. Having Stormy in my arms just feels right. Like she was the jagged little puzzle piece I needed to fit with. Just like my father would tell us when we were kids, "If it's right, you know."

"Shit, what about work?" She shoots up and looks at me.

I chuckle. "I'll tell your boss that you called in sick," I wink at her, she playfully punches me in the chest.

"That's not funny. Everyone will know something is up between us." She worries her bottom lip. I pull her chin toward me so she's looking at me.

"I don't give a fuck what people think. You are mine. Anyone can know," I say in all seriousness.

"Elijah is going to flip out. He won't leave me alone," She utters but tries to look away when she sees the anger bubbling up inside me. That motherfucker has been hitting on her all this time even when I told him in no certain terms to leave her alone. I sit up, ready to get my phone to call my brother and let him know that I'm about to fire his assistant. "Hey, it's okay. I can handle him. You don't have to fight all my battles."

I cup her cheeks. "That's what I'm here for. I want to do that for you. Besides, you shouldn't be uncomfortable at work. That's sexual harassment and I won't stand for it." She rubs her hand down my chest and back up, trying to soothe me.

"We'll deal with that later. How about a nap?" She falls backwards onto the bed, her breasts bouncing along with her. Leaning over I pull a nipple into my mouth, while I slide my hand over her smooth skin. I move to the other nipple, giving it a little tug with my teeth. "Mm, Daddy did you hear me say something other than nap?" she teases. I look up at her, giving her a devilish smile.

"Nap can mean other things, Angel." I profess. I slip my hand between her legs and find that she is soaked. I crawl over her until I am holding myself on top of her. I kiss a trail down her collar bone, over her breasts, down to her belly button and over to each hip bone before I continue downwards. I smell her sexy as fuck arousal and I can't wait to get another taste. "Open up for me. Let me see you."

She does as I say. I am greeted with the most perfect ripe pussy I've ever seen. "I need my breakfast," I say with a smirk. She rolls her eyes until I lick from her center to her clit. She lets out a loud moan as she writhes on the bed. I continue to eat my fill until she is chanting my name. Hearing her call me Daddy does something to me. I want to see her cunt dripping with my seed. I want to see her belly swell, knowing she is carrying my child with her. I never in my life thought I would want that. But I want it with Stormy. I want it all. I think of adding my name to hers and I chuckle thinking of Stormy Knight. She's going to hate it and I'll love it even more. I add two fingers to her as I continue to lick and nibble away. I hold down her hips to the bed, so she can't go anywhere. She has to take the pleasure I'm giving her.

"Daddy!" she screams and I think the other tenants in this building might be able to hear her. I climb up her body and slam my cock inside her. I kiss her so she can taste herself on me. I feel her orgasm ricochet through her body, I thrust in and out of her wet pussy. I can already feel my climax barreling through me. She turns me on so much, just eating her out was enough to make me come. I thrust into her over and over, each more punishing than the last. I want my seed to make it through even if she is taking birth control. For a moment I wonder if she carries it in her purse or if she will be skipping a day today. Hope springs in my heart, I want to tie her to me in as many ways as I can. I come in a rush, thinking of her pregnant with my child. I probably should talk to her about it but fuck that. I will always take care of her. Jets and jets of my come hit her womb and I will the little swimmers to do their job.

"Fuck, Angel, you feel amazing squeezing my cock. You take me so well."

"Your cock is so big and fills me up, Daddy. I love it." Pride soars through me at her words. I pump in one last time and keep my cock firmly in place, hoping those little fuckers stay in there.

"Keep saying things like that and you definitely won't get that nap." I kiss the tip of her nose and roll off her, reluctantly. "Stay there." I shove to my feet, getting a wash cloth from the bathroom to clean her up. When I get back, I see she did as she was told and stayed there. I smile at my little vixen listening to what her Daddy told her to do. I wipe around her thighs then scoop some of my come and push it back into her. She gives me a quizzical look.

"What are you doing?" I shrug my shoulders and continue pushing it back inside her. "I'm on birth control, you know?" She looks at me like I have lost my damn mind and maybe I have. I finish cleaning her up and throw the rag over my shoulder.

"What kind of birth control are you on? The pill?" I question. I don't want to have to get Dr. Peterson over here to remove birth control if she has a permanent one. I'll do it, but then she will know that's what I want before I'm ready to tell her.

"Yes, the pill. Why? I'm not going to get pregnant if that's what you are worried about. I take it religiously." She replies and I wonder again if she has it in her purse. I don't remember seeing it when I went in there looking for her anxiety meds.

"Well, we can't leave the apartment for a while so unless you carry it with you..." I trail off, letting her come to the same conclusion I'm thinking.

"Fuck, I have to leave. I don't have it with me. I didn't think I would be staying somewhere last night. You have to take me home, Sebastian." She sits up, biting her bottom lip and wringing her hands together.

"Calm down, Angel. Everything will be fine." I put my hand over hers, not wanting her to reinjure it. I try to reassure her, knowing damn well that we aren't leaving this apartment with all the paparazzi lingering. Maybe later this afternoon, but I'm sure they know where she lives by now. I need to get up and take care of this. As much as I would love to keep fucking Stormy, I need to get rid of these people, to find out what scandal they are spilling. Miles is probably having a fit. I need to go find my phone. Fuck, I don't want to pop this bubble we are in. "I need to go find my phone to see what is going on with everything. You can take a nap if you want to. I'll get you some clothes to put on, too," I add.

"Thank you." I grab some sweats and a Princeton t-shirt and toss it to Stormy. She gets up and pulls on the clothes, I have never seen a sight better than Stormy in my clothes. They are way too big for her, but she looks so fucking sexy with my sweats rolled up and a huge tee. "Why are you looking at me like that?" she asks.

I shrug, "I just like seeing you in my clothes." I turn and head to the living room where I think I dropped my phone earlier. I find it on the couch and see I have several missed calls from Miles and Marcy. *Fuck. This can't be good.* I press on Marcy's name first, hoping she has some good news for me. I told Stormy I would protect her, but I need to know what I'm up against.

TWENTY

Stormy

What a whirlwind of twenty-four hours. So much has happened. I know I need to talk to Sebastian about everything from my past. From the look on his face when he got the call, he already knows a lot. I'm sure he has questions. I walk into the bathroom, gathering my clothes. I need to be ready when he says I can leave. My chest aches at the thought of leaving him. He's growing on me. I don't think he is the play-boy that everyone painted him as. I know better than anyone that the tabloids can blow things out of proportion. Or maybe with me he is different. A girl can dream.

Classes start today and I have my first one tonight. I don't want people following me when I'm on campus though. I shouldn't have gone to that bar last night, but it's done and over with. Now I have to live with the consequences.

"Fuck." I mutter to myself. I sure got myself in deep. I'm sure I have been plastered all over the internet by now. I'm scared to even look at my phone. I need to call Lana and tell her I am okay.

Shit, she's probably worried. I go to my purse in the living room to retrieve my phone and I hear Sebastian on the phone.

"She's not like that. She's innocent in all this. Stormy was just at the wrong place at the wrong time." He spits into his phone. His back is to me so he doesn't know I can hear him. I wonder what awful things are being said about me. I grab my phone and head back to his bedroom. I don't want to hear anymore. I dial Lana's number and wait for her to pick up.

"Thank God, you're alive! I was so worried," she nearly yells into the phone. I have to move it away from my ear before I go deaf.

"I'm fine. Just a headache, but other than that I am okay. Everyone found out, Lana," I confess, with a tear slipping down my cheek.

"I know, honey. There are people camped out here waiting for you," she states, with an aggravated sigh.

"I'm so sorry I dragged you into this. I didn't mean to. I screwed everything up." I cry into the phone. "What am I going to do?" I ask, needing some type of advice or guidance.

"I'm not really sure. I think if you make a statement or interview then they will maybe leave you alone. They want to know what really happened with your husband's death. At least that's what the internet is saying. They also said that you like famous men, that you traded Blaine for Sebastian," I gasp at the news.

"Let me go so I can look up everything people are saying. I hope I can make it home today, but there are people camped out here too," I reply.

"Just take care of yourself. I'm fine. These people don't bother me and if they do, they can get acquainted with my fists," Lana chuckles on the other end of the phone.

I smile, "Thank you. I'll text you later when I know something."

"Bye, Stormy," Lana replies as the line goes dead. I pull up the internet browser on my phone and type in my name. Immediately tons of news articles pop up. Some calling me a whore for making out with Sebastian on a darkened street corner. One picture is me passed out in Sebastian's arms and it says I'm an alcoholic and drug abuser. There are pictures from this morning, with me looking disheveled and Sebastian in just sweats. Fuck this all paints me in a terrible light. I'm never going to be able to show my face in this city again. I click on one article in particular.

L.B. MARTIN

Stormy Jacks Finally Found!

Is she hiding because she killed her husband?

Stormy Jacks was finally found in New York City outside of the bar, The Tipsy Tap. She was hanging onto billionaire, playboy, Sebastian Knight. Jacks has been missing from the picture since her husband, Blaine Jacks of Damaged Jacks, was found dead in his family home. No comments were made at the time of the death and there haven't been any since. The funeral was private, but we know she was in attendance. Would a murderer attend the funeral of her husband?

The autopsy reported that Blaine Jacks was killed by an accidental gunshot to the head, but we have reports that the two were seen arguing earlier that day. We reached out to Blaine's family this morning and they implied that she was guilty, but they haven't filed charges against her. She received a large sum from the life insurance of Blaine then she fled Florida without anyone's knowledge and dyed her hair in hopes to be unrecognizable.

Fortunately for us, she participated in karaoke at this bar and her voice was instantly recognized by the bartender, Travis Gray. He sent in photographs and a video recording of the performance. You can see the video below. If Jacks is innocent, why is she hiding?

More information is coming soon.

WWW.TABLOIDGOSSIP.COM

Fuck. My. Life. Of course, they would say I was guilty. They didn't want their precious nephew to get in trouble. He was the one that picked up the gun and played with it. He didn't know it was loaded, he fired the shot right at Blaine. No one knows the truth other than the people that were there. At the time, I didn't press charges because he was just a kid, only fifteen. I didn't want to ruin his life. It was my father-in-law's fault for leaving a loaded and chambered gun lying around. He should have known better. And now they're implying it was my fault? What the hell is wrong with them? It's bad enough that they turned on me as soon as Blaine was in the ground. They wanted the money from his life insurance, and they said that's the only reason I married him in the first place. I didn't even know he had a life insurance policy until the attorney contacted me after Blaine's death. They can have the money if that will make them leave me alone.

I take a deep breath, trying not to spiral out of control. I glance down at my wet bandaged hand and remember the blood there. I was asleep that night when it happened, for fucks sake. The gun shot woke me up and I wobbled to the door half asleep. Then I saw him there on the floor covered in blood.

I tear the Band-Aids off my hand. It's mostly healed anyways, and I don't want them there anymore. I need to get out of this apartment. I feel like I can't breathe. The air is being sucked out of my lungs and I feel like I'm going to have a heart attack. My chest tightens and all my muscles begin to spasm. Sweat begins streaming down my face, mixing with the tears. I fall to the floor, dropping my phone in the process. I pull my knees up to my chest and rock back and forth, trying to breathe but I can't. My lungs aren't working. *Am I dying?* This is it. I'm going to die right here.

The thought makes me want to vomit. I can feel it coming up my throat. The acid burns and I really think my heart might explode. I need my medicine, but I can't get it. I grip my knees tighter and try to think of three things like Sebastian taught me, but I can't. All I can hear is my own heart beating. It sounds like it might burst. *Three things, Stormy, think.* But I can't. I can't do anything but sit here and wait. Wait for what exactly, I don't know. I close my eyes, trying to picture anywhere but that kitchen floor. His lifeless ocean blue eyes staring through my soul. I was right there with him. My best friend. Gone in a flash. Tears stream down my face faster and faster, leaving Sebastian's shirt wet.

Suddenly, I'm pulled back with firm arms. I get pressed up against a hard body and I sink into the warmth. "I'm here, Angel. Listen to my voice. Come back to me. Take a deep breath." He puts his large hand on my chest. "When I push down, breathe out when I let up, breathe in. Now, let's do it. In." He lifts his hand so I can breathe in then he presses down on my chest. "Now, out. Keep going." He continues releasing me and then pressing down on my chest until my breathing has mostly evened out. "Now, open those eyes and tell me three things you see." I open my eyes and blink a few times to get rid of the blurry tears.

"I need my medicine, Sebastian. I can't do this without it." I argue.

"You don't need that shit, Stormy. You have me. Now, tell me three things you see."

"I-I s-see your bed. The dr-dresser and windows." I wipe my eyes, trying to clear up my vision.

"Good girl." He whispers into the shell of my ear. "Now, tell me what you feel."

"I feel you. I feel your warmth around me. I feel your hands on me." I close my eyes and concentrate on the feel of being wrapped up by Sebastian. He got on the floor for me and brought me back. Somehow he can always reach me, no matter how far gone I am. His voice is like a tether I hold on to for dear life. I pull and pull on his rope just as he does, and we meet in the middle. The world could be going up in flames around us but as long as he was connected to me, I wouldn't burn. I bury myself in him, hoping he can feel just how much I need him. He's my rock. It's a startling realization, but nevertheless, it's true. He's the only thing that can bring me back. He's my new medicine and I think I might be addicted.

"There you go, I'm right here." He squeezes his arms tighter around me and I melt into him a little more. He feels safe. More importantly, I feel safe in his arms. I grab ahold of his arms and pull them tighter around me. I can't get close enough. Resting my head on his shoulder, he leans over and kisses my cheek, forehead, then finally my lips. He tastes like my sweetest salvation. His hand cups my cheek and he dives deeper until our souls are tangling together. He pulls back and whispers, "All you have to do is call me. I'll be there." He rests his forehead against mine, looking into my eyes. His lustrous green eyes bore into mine and for a moment I believe that he would be there for me. I realize at some point I fell for this gorgeous man in front of me. I don't know how it happened, but it did. Then I remember that no one ever stays. They eventually vanish into thin air. I pull away from his magnetic connection. I need to get my shit together figuratively and literally. I can't stay here; I've already done enough damage. Just like he said, everything goes haywire when I'm around. I can't stay here and get crushed; I don't think I would recover from that. With everything I've been through, losing Sebastian would be the hardest.

"Thank you," I say awkwardly. I hate that he keeps seeing me so vulnerable. I grab my phone and see the article is still on the screen. I scoff but before I can close it, Sebastian has my phone in his hands. He sighs as he reads it. His face gets madder with every passing second, until I'm sure he will explode. I try to take it from him. "It's nothing, really. I just came across it and it upset me."

"It's not nothing. It's painting you as a murderer. These are serious allegations," He looks up from the phone. I shrug, looking away from his penetrating gaze.

"It's not true, you know. I wasn't even in the room when it happened," I shift away from him and try to get up.

"Hey, I believe you. Why don't you tell me what happened? I have only heard from other sources, and I need to hear the truth from your lips." He pulls me back against him and I go freely.

"How do you know it will be the truth?" I question.

"Because I believe you. I don't think you would lie to me, right?" he asks.

"I wouldn't," I agree. "Okay, I haven't told this story to anyone other than my therapist and Lana."

I start at the beginning when Blaine and I were in school together. I want him to get the full picture in its entirety. I tell him everything, not leaving out a single detail. Some parts are uncomfortable, and I can feel him tense under me when I mention marrying Blaine, but he relaxes when I explain the circumstances around it. I continue all the way up to when I blacked out on the floor after they had taken his body away. I tell him who is really responsible and how they want money and that I want to give it to them if it will make them quiet these rumors. He's silent the whole time, just listening to everything I have to say. A few tears slip past my eyes when I remember certain parts, but he is there to soothe me and to urge me to continue. Once I'm finished, I'm exhausted. I close my eyes, taking a deep breath I'm proud of myself for getting through that story. He shifts on the floor, standing up and bending over to pick me up. I don't protest as he puts me in his bed and covers me up.

"I'm here now, Angel. You aren't alone anymore." He whispers. He cuddles in behind me and I fall asleep to his soothing words.

TWENTY ONE

Sebastian

I can't imagine everything Stormy has been through. She is the strongest person I know. She's been through more than I'll ever know. It's what gives her an edge. You can't burn a woman who wears her pain like armor. I brush the hair from her face and stare at the beauty before me. Her lashes flutter as she sleeps, making me smile to myself. I like having her here with me. I don't want her to leave, especially with everything going on. She's safer here with me. Everyone knows where she is now, this isn't going to blow over soon. I think back to her singing on stage last night, she was a natural. I wonder if she wants that lifestyle. My life is here in New York. I don't know what I would do if she wanted to go on tour. She has the talent for it. She mentioned that she didn't want to after Blaine's death, but what if she would like to do that now? Could I let her go? My phone buzzes in my pocket and I groan. It's been going off all day. I had to task Elijah with completing the arrangements for the funeral. There is just so much going on at the same time. I pull out my phone and see its Miles. I gently shift off the bed, leaving Stormy to rest. I cover her body in my blankets and walk to my door, shutting it behind me.

Once I get to the living room, he's already hung up, so I call him back.

"Well, it's about time you answered," he barks through the phone.

"Calm down. In case you haven't seen the news, I have been dealing with some shit today," I reply as I sit on my couch.

"Yeah, I see that. Marcy called me." I roll my eyes. Miles is always on my case about making headlines. "This woman you are harboring needs to go back to her place. She isn't bringing good publicity to us." I scoff at his remark.

"She isn't going anywhere," I growl into the phone.

"What the fuck is your deal? I know you, the forever bachelor, hasn't caught feelings," he taunts.

"Shut the hell up, Miles. Now isn't the time to get into this. She's staying here until she's safe or maybe forever, who knows?" I cringe at my admittance. I didn't want him to know because I knew he would give me hell. He told me when he met Lizzie that he couldn't wait until I was in the same boat. Well, it didn't take long for me to find that perfect storm.

"You have to be kidding me. You like her. You actually like her." It isn't a question.

"I do," I reply, not wanting to add any more to that statement.

"Well, shit. She must be something special to have caught your attention. Does she feel the same way?" he asks.

"I feel like she does. I also know she doesn't trust easy. I don't know how to make her believe I want her," I confess. I need my brother for this. He's my best friend after all.

"Lizzie was like that in the beginning. I had to constantly re-assure her that I wasn't going anywhere. She eventually came to believe it. This woman seems like she has been through a lot so don't fuck with her if you aren't one hundred percent sure," Miles points out.

"How did you know Lizzie was the one?" I ask.

He sighs, "I just knew. It was this feeling inside me whenever I saw her or was around her. My chest aches when she isn't near. I'm more in love with her today than I was yesterday. I'm in a constant state of amazement that she chose me. I can't see a life worth living without her in it. That's how you know," He professes.

"You know, Stormy was the woman at the fundraiser that I ran in to. I was following her because I wanted to ask her out. I saw her across the room, and I knew I needed to meet her. Obviously, our first encounter was less than ideal. Even our second meeting was a disaster. Mary brought her in and hired her as my assistant," I shake my head with a smile. I now know what Mary was doing. I just didn't see it until now. She must have known we would be good together, if we were ever able to stop fighting. I continue, "But I have always had this pull towards her and maybe that's why our emotions were so high every time we came in contact with each other. Even now, she gives me a hard time. She's right there to put me in my place anytime I get too cocky." I state, wanting to be with her in bed even more now.

"Dude, I didn't know she was the same woman. It all makes sense now. I never knew you to blow up so bad. You've got it bad, don't you?" he questions.

"Yeah, I do. Now is the hard part, getting her to believe me," I utter.

"She needs to hang out with Lizzie. Sounds like the girl needs some people on her side," he remarks.

"Yeah, she only has her roommate. Other than that, she has no one." I shake my head. Sad for her.

"Let me talk to Lizzie and see when we can get together. Obviously, it has to be when things die down a bit. Oh, that reminds me of why I called. Wait, did you say she is your assistant?" He asks.

"Yeah, Mary hired her after she saw her getting fired for my actions. We literally ran into each other again on her first day at the company. It's been an interesting battle ever since," I smirk, thinking back to all our arguments. Even when we got in a heated debate, I wanted that fiery little vixen.

"Well, damn. We are going to have to send out a companywide memo about your relationship so there isn't any sexual harassment allegations. I'll get Elijah to do it," he asserts.

"No. Absolutely not. He's the one that should have a sexual harassment case brought against him for how he's been making Stormy feel at work. She's turned him down several times and he hasn't taken the hint. I even addressed the issue, and he continues hanging all over her." I seethe.

"That doesn't seem like Elijah. Are you sure?" Miles questions and my anger boils over at the fact that I am being asked this.

"Yes, I'm sure, damnit. When did you start questioning me?" I growl.

"Calm down, Seb. I wasn't questioning you like that. I just never knew Elijah to be anything but respectful. I will take care of him. I'll need a detailed report from both of you to cover our bases. Send it to Mary so she can file it away. I guess I'll need her to get me a new assistant, too," he chuckles. "So, back to the reason for my call.

What are you going to do about the press?" I think for a moment. Stormy mentioned that she thinks her late husband's family wants money. Maybe that will get them off her back.

"I have a few ideas. I'll let you know if I need any help, but I think I have it under control. And Marcy is working on getting the police to patrol around here so they can't camp out."

"Alright, well let me know if I can help with the funeral arrangements."

"Actually, that is something you can do. Can you get with Elijah and finalize everything? He got everything from Stormy's desk, so he has all the information. It can be his last assignment." I smile to myself. I'm happy to be getting rid of that fucker. Anyone that makes Stormy uncomfortable is an enemy of mine.

"Yeah, no problem. Take care of your girl. Love you, bro."

"Love you, too." I drop the phone beside me and scrub my hands over my face. I need to find out how to get in touch with Blaine's parents. I pull up my PI's number and shoot him a text.

Sebastian:

> I need the contact information for Blaine Jack's family in Florida.

Jackson:

> I'll send it right over. Be careful, they might take you for more than you think.

Sebastian:

Thanks for all the info on Stormy. She actually ended up telling me everything. As far as the Jacks', they aren't going to get a cent unless they sign something my attorney will draw up. They aren't getting more than I deem necessary to leave her alone.

Jackson:

Good. Let me know if you need anything else.

Sebastian:

Will do.

Should I include Stormy in this? I don't want her to be angry that I went behind her back, but I also don't want her to have to deal with this. *Fuck.* I'll decide later, right now there is someone I need to be with. I walk back to my room, cracking open the door to find my sleeping Angel just as I left her. Pulling off my sweats, I slide in behind her snuggling in close. I want to feel her soft body pressed against mine. She smells like my body soap, I smile because I feel like I've claimed her with my scent. I nuzzle into her neck, breathing her in. She shifts in my embrace, pushing herself back against me closing any gap between our bodies so they become as one.

"Sebastian," She whispers.

"I'm right here, Angel," I murmur.

"Why do you call me, Angel?" she asks sleepily.

"For one, your eyes are so bright, they look like halos. And second," I kiss the side of her neck, "second is because you emit this shine that never seems to dull even though you have been through the harshest of days. Never lose your shine, Stormy."

She turns her head and I see a single tear stream down her cheek, I catch it with my thumb. "Don't cry, my sweet girl."

"They aren't sad tears. I just," she begins, "I never thought I would be comfortable showing someone the most vulnerable parts of me, but you see me at my worst and still want to be with me. You even saw my paintings and didn't run. Those are splashes of color from my soul put on canvas." She confesses.

"Look at me. I want all of you. I want to know every corner of your soul. I told you there isn't any place I'd rather be, and I meant it." I lean over capturing her lips in mine, savoring her unique taste. I never want to forget this moment. It feels profound, like she is finally accepting me into her life. And I'll be damned if I screw it up.

"Thank you." She mutters against my lips. "Thank you for not being who I thought you were, for being everything I didn't know I needed. You feel like home with a heartbeat. If that makes any sense. Maybe I'm rambling." I lean over her body, looking down into her eyes.

"You don't ever have to thank me." I pause for a moment not sure if I should say it or not. But looking into her eyes, I can see she feels the same, even if she doesn't know it yet. I can wait for her to realize it, but I need her to know. "Stormy, I love you. We may have had a rough go in the beginning, but you have ingrained yourself into my soul. I may not be the hero in your stories, but I would burn the world for you." A gasp escapes her beautiful lips, and more tears begin streaming down her face. She reaches up to cups my cheek in her hand.

"Sebastian, I knew there was a connection with you at the fundraiser. I saw you across the room and I just wanted to be near you. I felt as though there was a tether pulling us together. I think Mary saw something similar that night and that's why she gave me the job to work with you." She takes a breath, blinking back a few tears. "I thought I hated you, but that was never the case. Somehow, I think I always knew that our souls were made of the same thing and were calling to each other." She pulls her hand down, grasping my arm. She's waiting for a reply, but she doesn't know that she just told me the best thing I have ever heard in my life. It could only be better if she told me she loved me. I think she does but is having a harder time telling me and I understand that. I truly do. I will give her all the time she needs to come to terms with her love for me. And I will do everything in my power to help her realize it.

I roll off of her, bringing her with me so that she is straddling my waist. "Fuck, I don't deserve you." I pull her head down to mine and smash my lips to hers. It isn't sexy, its frantic, like if I don't imprint this woman on me, she will vanish into thin air. "I need you," I murmur before I begin ravaging her lips again. She nods her head but doesn't break the connection. Her towel, that was wrapped in her hair, falls to the side and I push it off the bed.

Skimming my hands down her waist, I pull on my shirt she's wearing, bringing it up her body while trailing my hands along her luscious curves. I break the kiss long enough to tear the shirt over her head and then I dive back in. Stormy begins rocking back and forth along my hard shaft, making me groan from the heat of her pussy. I can feel it through all the layers between us and I know she is wet for me.

I grab the rolled down sweats. "I need these off of you, Angel." Pulling them down, she raises her ass in the air allowing me to move them further down, but I need them completely off. She helps with getting her legs out then we are back at it. Moans leave our mouths as we tangle together, not stopping for air. I pull back only for a moment, and I see the hunger in her eyes. Mine must reflect the same. "Take my boxers off," I command. She shifts down my body kissing and licking as she goes. The sensation makes me harder than I've ever been in my life. She comes to my boxers and looks up at me with mischief in her eyes. Taking the band in her hand, she ever so slowly pulls them down my body. My cock bounds free from its confines, more than ready for her. If I don't get inside her soon, I might snap. Throwing my boxers over her shoulders, she inches back up my body, her eyes never leaving mine. She stops at my throbbing shaft, taking it in her hand as she licks the head. I hiss out from the pleasure it evokes. She takes me in her mouth fully and I groan from the sensations. I lean up grabbing her waist, pulling her until she is sitting on me. "There will be time for that later. I need to be inside this tight pussy." I push three fingers inside her, making sure she is ready. She is soaking wet. She's more than ready. She is about to explode like I am.

Stormy lifts up as I slide my fingers from her, she lines me up with her entrance. Ever so slowly she pushes herself down on me. I push myself up against the headboard to give me better access to her mouth. She lifts up and slams back down on me going faster and harder with each stroke. I love watching her find her own pleasure with my cock inside her. The look of total bliss on her face as she slides up and down my aching cock is mesmerizing. I cup her face and kiss her deeply, hopefully showing her the love I proclaimed earlier. I need her to believe me and to trust that I will always be here for her.

"Fuck you feel so good. You're mine, Stormy. Mine. Do you hear me? I want you to say it." I grit out as I begin matching her thrust for thrust. Her breasts bounce with every movement. I want to take them in my mouth, but I want to watch her more.

"I'm yours, Daddy. Yours," She swears. She closes her eyes and throws her head back. I know she is getting close, I want to see her when I tear her to pieces.

"Look at me," I demand. "Keep those gorgeous eyes on me when you come on my cock." She nods her head and focuses her eyes on me. Placing her hands on my shoulders for leverage, she grinds her hips down into me. I move my hand to play with her clit. Just the contact is all it takes to throw her over the edge. Her movements become jerky as she continues to ride me, I grasp her hips and thrust up and down for her. She cries out from pleasure.

"Yes, yes, yes," She chants over and over. Her eyes are still locked on mine as her walls continue to convulse around me.

"Tell me who owns this pussy," I grunt out, feeling my own release coming.

"It's yours, Daddy." Hearing the words slip from her mouth is my undoing. I buck into her wildly until I'm shooting my load inside her waiting womb. I slow my movements but continue to thrust in and out, riding the pleasure as is courses through me. Before I can say anything, she crashes her lips down on mine. I grab a fist of hair, pulling her body closer to mine. I wrap my other arm around her body keeping her where I want her. Pushing us away from the headboard, I lay down bringing her with me. I want her body on mine.

"You are perfect, you know that?" She shakes her head in disagreement.

"You are the only one that thinks that," she states.

"I'm the only one that matters." Stormy bites her bottom lip and nods in agreement. She tries to roll off me, but I keep her firmly in place. "Stay." She doesn't fight me but rests her head on my chest. Leaning up, I kiss the top of her head. "I love you, Angel. Get some sleep." I want us to fall asleep like this forever, with me still inside her. I pull the covers over us and make sure she is comfortable. Within minutes, I can feel her soft breaths against my chest. Knowing she is safe and asleep in my arms, I let sleep carry me off as well.

TWENTY TWO

Stormy

I wake still caged in Sebastian's safe arms. I know he's awake as well because he is hard inside me and thrusting softly. A small gasp escapes my lips at the pleasure he is giving me. Never has sex been this good. Not that I have had much experience, but Sebastian takes it to a whole new level. Every time it feels more electric, more intimate. I can't describe it. Without any warning, Sebastian flips us over, never leaving my pussy.

"Good afternoon, Angel," he whispers into the shell of my ear as he slowing pumps in and out of me. This is making love. Slow and sensual.

I smile up at him. "Can you just always stay inside me?" I joke.

"Does it feel that good, baby?" He asks with a smirk on his face.

"Yes, so good. I guess I will have to get a dick replica making kit for when I'm not with you," I tease him as his eyes turn serious.

"Fuck no you won't. The only thing allowed in this pussy is me." He begins pounding harder making me realize that I am sore from earlier, or maybe the time before that. I wince and turn my eyes from his gaze. "Am I hurting you?" He slows, almost stopping completely.

"No, I'm just a little sore." He kisses my mouth then moves along my jaw and down my neck. His cock slips from my entrance and I whine from the loss.

"Don't worry. I will take care of you," he coos as he continues his descent down my body. Nipping and licking, then kissing, all the way down to my aching pussy. Sebastian pushes my legs apart with his shoulders, keeping me in place. "Does this little pussy need some extra loving?" A sob escapes my lips as I nod in response.

"Yes, Daddy, make it feel better, please," I plead.

"Well since you are being such a good girl..." He trails off as he takes a mouthful of my cunt in his mouth. *Fuck me.* Everything he does to me feels incredible. It's like he has a roadmap of my body, and he knows exactly what stops to make and when to detour. He continues devouring my pussy as I thread my fingers through his hair, pulling him closer to me. I can't help but ride his face. I feel dirty but when I hear him groan, it spurs me on more. His tongue strokes me in long, slow licks, like he is dying and this is his last meal that he wants to savor. Sebastian's eyes look to mine, I see the intensity in them. He adds a finger slowly and curls it at just the right spot and I shoot off like a rocket.

"That's it, come for me," he whispers loud enough that I hear. He continues licking and sucking me through my release until I am a sweaty mess on his bed. He lifts his head, and I can see my arousal smeared across his face. He licks his lips and gives me a grin. "You taste like the fruit of the gods. I could eat this pussy all day," he smirks.

He leans up, sitting on his knees. I can see his angry hard cock and I feel bad that he didn't get off. He sees me looking. "Don't worry about me. I'll be okay. This is just what you do to me." Even with his comment, I want to see him chasing his orgasm.

"I want you to come on me. Mark me," I murmur. I swear his eyes turn from their beautiful shade of green to molten lava.

"You want me to jack myself?" He questions as he grabs his cock. "It won't take long with the way you're looking at me," he confesses.

"I want to see." He spreads my legs further squeezing between them, sliding his cock along my slit. His cock becomes slippery with my juices, it's the most erotic thing I've ever seen. He continues pumping his cock as I look on.

"You're exquisite, Angel. Lying there in my bed like it was made just for you." I lean up and place my hand over his.

"Let me." he moves his hand and hisses as I grasp him tightly, my hand doesn't reach all the way around, but he doesn't seem to mind. The opposite actually.

"That's it. Just like that," he urges and pride blooms in my chest at his words. I want to be able to please him the same as he does me. I don't want him to tire of me because I can't do what other girls can do for him. "Come back to me, baby." I shake my head and look at him. I don't know how he always knows when my brain takes me somewhere else. I double my efforts and I'm rewarded with his moans. "I'm going to come." He breathes out seconds before releasing himself on my stomach. He thrusts into my hand, stopping as his pleasure barrels through him. Once he's finished. He leans over me, taking my mouth in his.

"That was incredible." He murmurs against my lips. He breaks away and smears his come all over my stomach, then he writes the word 'mine' in it. I roll my eyes but smile at his devilish grin. He then gathers it together and presses into my pussy. I look at him quizzically, but he doesn't stop. Sebastian continues to thrust his come into my pussy. "Don't look at me like that. This is where it belongs."

I take in his words not really believing what he is saying but this is the second time he has done this. Maybe he has some breeding kink? Or does he really want me pregnant? He asked me about my birth control again this morning and for a moment I panic that I haven't taken it today. Then my stomach growls. My face blushes because it sounded like a monster. I cover my face with my hand, but he removes it, looking down at me.

"Looks like Daddy isn't taking good care of his baby girl. I need to feed you." He gets up, grabbing a towel to wipe up the mess on my stomach, leaving the mess he made in my pussy. He throws me the clothes I had on, and I scoot off the bed and dress.

"I'll meet you in the kitchen. I just need to freshen up." He nods and I take off to his bathroom. The lights come on by themselves again and I don't know if I will ever get used to that. I try to make myself presentable. I look around for a brush but only find a comb. It will have to do. I have so many tangles from not brushing it after our shower this morning. Once I get them out, I look in the mirror and see a light on my face that I have never seen before. It's like I am glowing from the inside out. I smile as I see some love marks on my skin. Leaving the bathroom, I feel lighter than in have in years. Everything is going to be okay. Nothing can bring me down when I have Sebastian by my side.

TWENTY THREE

Stormy

O nce I get to the kitchen, Sebastian has two large sandwiches prepared. Shock rolls through me at the sight. They look like gourmet sandwiches. For some reason I saw him as this spoiled little rich boy that had a chef.

"Wow, you can cook. Or make sandwiches at least," I tease, as I take my plate from him.

"I can do a lot more than that, thank you." He swats my ass, making me jump. "My grandmother is Italian, so she made sure her grandsons knew how to cook," Sebastian explains. I take my plate to the table and sit down. He follows behind and sits next to me.

"Thank you for this," I murmur as I take a bite. Pure heaven explodes in my mouth. "This is delicious."

"It's nothing," he says taking a large bite.

"Have the paparazzi cleared out?" I ask as I continue to down my sandwich. I was starving. I didn't realize how much until I started eating.

"Yes, I believe so."

"Oh, that's great. I need to get home to get ready for class tonight." I explain, hoping that he won't have a problem with me leaving. I gobble my sandwich, not caring if it isn't ladylike.

He drops his sandwich onto his plate and looks at me with an expression I can't quite decipher.

"Um, no. You aren't leaving," He states as he picks up his sandwich and takes another bite.

"What the hell do you mean, I'm not leaving? Classes started today. This is the whole reason I came to New York to attend SVA! I have to be there!" I exclaim moving my plate away because I'm no longer hungry.

"You're plastered all over newspapers and the internet. Do you really think it's okay to go out there now that everyone knows where you are?" He questions.

"I'm not going to stop living because some shitty people decided to sell my picture to the tabloids. I'm going to that class, and you can't stop me," I shout as I rise from my seat and stomp away to his bedroom to put my clothes from yesterday back on. I pick up my phone to order an Uber as Sebastian comes in swiping my phone from me. "What is your problem? You can't keep me locked in your ivory tower, Sebastian," I yell. I'm trying to be calm about this but it's not working out very well. Not with the anger simmering in my system.

He looks down at my phone and sees what I was doing. "I'll be damned if you leave here in an Uber, Stormy. I'll take you to your apartment and then to class. Then we'll figure out a security detail for you," I scoff at his thinking he can control my life. I'm not going to have security following me around everywhere.

"What exactly do you think will happen to me? It's not like I'm still in the band. This will be old news by the end of the week," I state.

"Ha, I doubt that. You were part of one of the largest bands in the country and you think this will just blow over?" He questions. His face morphing into one of anger. If he's angry then he should feel the anxiety rolling through me.

"Don't mock me. I know what I was in. The keyword there is 'was.' I never went on tour. They replaced me," I huff out.

"Have you read any more articles? Maybe about the ones where the fans weren't happy that you quit like you did. The ones that bought tickets and didn't get a chance to see you. How about the article that talked about you being a murderer? You think it's a good idea to leave the safety of this apartment for some class," He knew the moment he fucked up. I can see it on his face. He scrubs his hand over his face and lets out a loud sigh.

"Some class? SOME CLASS? This is my life, Sebastian. This is my passion. I want to do this for a living one day. I want to go to school. I want to learn new techniques." Tears begin to prick at the sides of my eyes. Not because I'm sad, I cry when I get extremely angry sometimes. It feels like a weakness, and I definitely don't want to come across like that right now. This relationship, or whatever it is, isn't going to work if he wants to control every aspect of my life.

"I'm sorry. I didn't mean to call it some class. I just want you safe," He grabs my hand, leading me to the bed. I almost pull my hand from his, but that would be childish. I follow him as he settles on the bed. "Look at me. I'm sorry, alright. I just don't want you to get hurt. This is a new feeling for me, wanting to protect someone." I sigh because I know he is right. I just can't be scared to live. I won't let another man keep me from my dreams. That's the first thing I thought of when he said I couldn't go. Blaine would have said the same thing. Well, he did say the same thing and it had nothing to do with my safety.

I brush stray hair from his forehead. "I understand where you're coming from, but we have to come to some sort of compromise. I'm not letting another man dictate my life." I cringe at the way that sounded. I'm not trying to compare the two of them. This is a romantic relationship and with Blaine it wasn't.

"I can't believe you just compared me to your late husband," He snarls and I know I made a mistake. We are going around in circles, not getting any decisions accomplished.

"You know I didn't mean it like that. I'm just scared." I put my head in my hands, letting out a frustrated sigh. I don't know how we are going to compromise on this. Should we even be fighting about something like this, this early in a relationship? Maybe this isn't going to work out. My stomach recoils at the thought. Sebastian gets up and crouches on his knees before me.

"Hey," he says, trying to get my attention, "I'll drive you and we can talk about this later okay?" I nod my head as he cups my cheek. "I can't lose you when I just found you." He whispers. A lump clogs my throat and I understand what he is saying, even if I don't agree with him one hundred percent. "Go ahead and get dressed and I'll clean up the kitchen." He stands, leaning over to take my lips in his. It's soft yet dominant, telling me that he is still in charge. We will see about that. I can take care of myself.

We get to my apartment and Lana nearly tackles me at the door.

"I've been so worried about you! Don't do that to me again," She declares waiting on me to agree.

"I won't, I promise. It was just a shitty day and I let it get the best of me. Lana, this is Sebastian. Sebastian, this is Lana. I know y'all have met but I didn't know if it was ever officially." They shake each other's hand and murmur their greetings. Lana gives me a skeptical look but wipes it off her face before Sebastian has a chance to catch on. "So, how were your classes today?" I ask, trying to change the subject.

"Good, mainly just going over the syllabus and expectations. You have class tonight, don't you?" she questions.

"Yeah, that's why I'm here. I needed to change and get my things for class." I check my watch and see that we need to get out of here soon if I'm going to get to the campus on time. I'd rather be early than late any day. "I actually need to get going. We will catch up soon."

Sebastian follows me to my room and shuts the door behind himself. Going to my drawers, I take out some clothes and throw them on my bed. I quickly change, trying not to meet Sebastian's heated gaze when he looks my way. We definitely don't have time for that. And I don't want Lana to hear us. Once I'm dressed, I walk over to my mirror and sit in front of it.

"Why are you sitting on the floor?" He asks, as he sits on my bed.

"I don't have a vanity area to put on my makeup, so I sit down here and do it. Not a big deal." He scoffs but doesn't say anything else. I put on the least amount of makeup I can and still look presentable. Then I braid my hair because I don't have the time to straighten it. I get up and walk over to my desk, grabbing my messenger bag and making sure I have everything I need. This is a sketching class so I doubt I will be needing much. "Alright, I think I'm ready." I look up at Sebastian who is staring at me. "What?" I ask.

"You need to pack some clothes to come back to my place tonight. Whatever you will need for a couple days until I can get movers over here to pack everything up." I wait for him to laugh or say just kidding but it never comes.

"What? What are you talking about?" I ask legitimately confused.

"You are coming to live with me. I thought that would be obvious," he says in all seriousness, and I still can't tell if he's joking.

"I wasn't planning on it. I figured you would drop me back off here." I gesture to my bedroom.

"Stormy, pack your shit or I will just take you shopping tomorrow. Regardless, you are coming home with me," he commands.

"Did you just decide that for me? Without asking me? What about Lana? I'm her roommate. I pay half the bills here. Plus, how do we even know we will last? If we don't, I'll be screwed." Sebastian jumps up from the bed. In two strides he is right in front of me, pinning me up against the wall. He takes my hands, securing them above my head. A moan slips from my mouth as he leans forward, breathing on my neck.

"Do I need to remind you who is in charge here? You're being a little brat and I have no qualms about putting you over my knee right here, letting Lana hear how bad you are being." I whimper from his words and my pussy clenches thinking about the last spankings I got. "Now be a good girl and get your things together." He drops my arms but continues boxing me in. Taking my face in his hands, his lips collide with mine in a punishing kiss. He didn't just kiss me, he claimed ownership. Once he backs away, I am basically mush. It takes me a moment to remember what exactly I was supposed to be doing.

"I'll get clothes for a couple days, then I'm coming back here. You aren't going to tell me where I'll live." I duck around him as he tries to pin me again. Grabbing my luggage from the closet, I toss in some work clothes, shoes, makeup, and anything else I think I'll need. Sebastian zips it up and grabs my hand, leading me out my door. "Wait! I need to grab my birth control." I try to turn around but his grasp on me tightens. "I'm serious, Sebastian. Let go." He just grunts and reluctantly lets me go.

I tell Lana that I won't be back for a couple days, and she looks from me to Sebastian and then nods her head.

"Text me," she replies as we head out the front door.

"I will," I respond, shutting the door behind me.

The drive to campus is quiet but Sebastian reaches over taking my hand in his. A simple yet sweet gesture. His warmth spreads up my arm and I wonder why I am fighting him on everything. I want to be independent, but I also want him. Surely, he can see the position he's putting me in. I can't leave Lana high and dry. She's depending on me financially. Sebastian squeezes my hand, taking me from my thoughts.

"What's going on in that head of yours?" he questions.

"Just thinking about everything going on," I reply as I look out the window.

"I want you to move in with me. Not because of everything that's happening with the tabloids but because I truly want you with me." I turn away from the window to look at him. He's being genuine. He promised to protect me, and I can't deny the pull I have toward him. He's like my anchor in rough waters.

"I'll have to think about it Sebastian. I have Lana to think about. If we were getting married or something, I probably wouldn't hesitate, but we're just getting to know each other. I'm scared. I still want my independence." He clenches his jaw. I'm sure because he's not used to being told no.

"So, you're wanting a ring?" he asks.

"No. That's not what I'm saying. You have to look at this from my perspective," I plead.

"You said you were scared we are going to break up. I'm not going anywhere, Angel. You're not going to be able to get rid of me. You can't deny we have this chemistry that can't be described by anything other than epic. I was meant to run into you that night, even if I was a jackass about it," he confesses, making me smile.

"You really were an asshat that night," I laugh and so does he.

We pull onto campus and Sebastian cuts the engine. "Come here for a minute." He gestures to his lap. I look around and then at the time, knowing I need to get out of here. But this man can make me do things I never thought. Unbuckling, I slide over the middle console and straddle his lap. He cups my face and brings his closer to mine. "I love you, Stormy Brooks. I will spend the rest of forever trying to convince you. Can you trust me?" he asks as he rubs his thumb in circles over my cheek.

I don't hesitate. "Yes, I trust you. Of course, I do." I place my forehead on his and close my eyes, taking in the feel of him beneath him.

"Then please do this for me. I want you there. No, I *need* you there." He ghosts his lips over mine and I tremble beneath his touch.

"Okay."

"Okay?" He asks, with a smile on his face.

"Yeah, let's do it. I still have to pay Lana and I feel super guilty about leaving her, but I do want to be with you too. Now, I have to get to class." I lean in giving him a quick kiss, but he isn't having it and pulls me in deeper. I grasp his shirt in my hands wanting that closer connection as well.

"Now, get your sexy ass to class."

"Now you can say you're dating a college student, old man." I giggle and try to climb back over to my seat, but he pulls me back hard and I land on his very hard cock. I can't help but to rub myself against him.

"Hey, I'm only thirty. But that deserves a punishment for later, Angel. Just wait and see what I have planned for you." His smirk lights a fire in my belly.

"You'll have to catch me first!" I exclaim, climbing into the passenger side of the car. Grabbing my bag, I open the door.

"Text me when class is over. I'll be right here," he reminds me.

"Thank you." I close the door and walk towards the building that my class is in. I have butterflies in my stomach at the thought of moving in with Sebastian, but I want to be spontaneous, I want to live my life. So much has been taken from me that it's time I take something for myself. This new chapter of my life is a blank canvas, and I can't wait to see the masterpiece it becomes.

TWENTY FOUR

Sebastian

Stormy walks though the quad and into the building to the far right. I take note in case something happens and she needs me. I have this bad feeling I can't quite shake. As I crank the car, an incoming call comes through the speakers. Miles' name flashes on the screen.

"What's up brother," I answer.

"The funeral is set for Monday at eleven A.M. Elijah was able to make the necessary arrangements," he states.

"Good, good. Thank you for taking over. I've had my hands full," I explain.

"How is everything going with the press. Has Marcy been able to get things squared away?" Miles asks.

"Well, she was able to get the paparazzi removed from my penthouse. Other than that, the news is out there. There isn't much she can do." I shrug even though he can't see me.

"How is Stormy doing with everything? How is everything going?" He asks.

"She convinced me to let her get out of the apartment and go to class. So, you tell me how it's going." Miles chuckles on the phone.

"Sounds like she is a handful, and she has you wrapped around her little finger," he says.

"That she does. I thought the best thing for her was to stay in the apartment. But no, here I am sitting at the campus waiting for her class to be over." I sigh and rest my head back against the seat. "I just want her to be safe. I can't let anything happen to her. Its driving me crazy. All the feelings and shit is for the birds." Miles full on belly laughs at my admission and I'm about five seconds from hanging up on his ass.

"I told you that I couldn't wait for the day this happened to you. Remember me saying that," He pauses for a moment then continues, "In all seriousness, I know what it's like. I went through this with Lizzie. I was a man possessed when I saw her ex putting his hands on her. Keeping them safe is our number one priority. We got possessive genes from dad."

"I didn't understand you falling for her so fast until it happened to me. But don't get me wrong, she still drives me crazy with the mouth she has on her." Miles laughs again and I join in.

"Man, we have it bad," he replies.

"Yeah, I guess we do," I agree.

"Have you talked to Thomas? I haven't had the time to call him," I admit.

"Yeah, I talked to him earlier today. His brother and his wife got into town and are staying with him which is good because I didn't want him to be alone. I would have offered for him to stay with us, which I still might depending on how long his brother stays."

"Stormy scheduled meals to be delivered to him for the next week. So, he should be good in that department," I state.

"Alright, seems like everything is taken care of for now. I was checking in. Call if you need anything," Miles says, as I hear Lizzie say something in the background. That's probably why he is getting off the phone.

"Will do, bro. Love you, man."

"Hey, I love you too. The feelings will get easier. You just aren't used to having any," he laughs.

"Har Har Har, very funny." I roll my eyes.

"Don't get into any more trouble. We'll have to give Marcy a raise," He remarks.

"I can't promise anything," I smirk.

"Alright then, talk soon." Miles hangs up and I begin scrolling through emails from work. Missing a day has filled up my inbox, not to mention I haven't had Stormy filter through them. After responding to a few, I decide to text Stormy. She probably won't answer, but it's worth a shot.

Sebastian:

How's class going?

I wait several moments before I decide to throw my phone in the passenger seat. Opening the car door, I step out to stretch my legs. I see several people leaving the building that Stormy went in to. Class probably let out early since it's the first day. I lean against the car waiting to see her emerge from the group of people. After a few minutes of not seeing her, I open up the car to retrieve my phone. I hit her number and begin to walk. When the phone clicks on, I hear shuffling and her talking but I can't make out the words.

Then I hear male voices and my blood runs cold. I set off in a jog across the campus, keeping the phone glued to my ear in case she is able to answer.

"Stormy, I'm coming for you!" I shout into the phone and continue my pace. I fly up the stairs and into the empty building. I'm about to turn around when I hear it. A small cry comes from an empty classroom across from me. Sliding up to the door and peeking in, I see Stormy cornered by three men, closing in on her. I try to make out what they are saying.

"You're a small little thing, aren't you? I wouldn't mind seeing her on her knees in front of me. Never had a famous whore suck my dick." The one in the middle says to the other men. My fists clench with anger and I see red. Not waiting for the others to speak, I burst through the door. I see the relief written across her face.

"Hey! Who the hell are you?" One shouts, but I don't acknowledge him. In a few strides, I'm across the room standing before them. Before anyone else can speak, I quickly strike one on the ridge of his nose. Stormy gasps as the man falls to the floor holding his bleeding nose in his hands. "Bitch." I hiss looking down at the piece of shit. When I turn around, the larger of the two men lunges at me, his fist colliding into my ribcage. It slightly rattles and knocks the wind out of me. While I'm bent over, in a quick upper cut motion I shatter his jaw with my elbow. The third one grabs me from behind before I can take a breath. Without thinking, I throw my head backwards hitting his face with the back of my skull. As his hold breaks free, I spin my body to lock him in a choke. In a matter of minutes, his unconscious body falls to the floor.

"Mine." I growl as I look to the broken bitches lying on the floor. Holding my ribs, I stumble over to Stormy who looks like she is seconds away from a panic attack. "Are you okay? Did they touch you?" She only shakes her head no and falls into my arms. With tears streaming down her face, she looks up at me. I pull back enough to grab a hold of her face and crash my lips down on hers. It isn't sweet. It's starved, ravenous, possessive. Sliding my hand back through her hair, I grip it to pull her closer. I can't get enough. If those fuckers had so much as laid a finger on her, I would have killed them.

"Y-You saved me. They were talking about r-raping me, Sebastian." She covers her face in my chest, giving me the urge to finish these men off. Fear and anger ripples through me.

"Look at me." I pull her chin up so she can see how serious I am. "I will always save you. From panic attacks to assailants, you're safe. No one is going to fucking harm what's mine. Do you understand? You're *mine*, Stormy." I say firmly. More tears spring from her eyes as she nods in agreement. I pull her close to me, savoring the feeling of her warmth seeping into me. She's safe, I can calm down now. But I know all too well that I will be wound up all-night thinking about the "what ifs".

Pulling my phone from my pocket, I call the police and they're here within minutes. Statements are given, and the three assholes are hauled off to jail where they await trial. If I have anything to do with it, which I will, they will be spending a long time behind bars.

"How about we get out of here?" I whisper into Stormy's ear, and she nods eagerly.

"Thank you gentlemen. You have my card if you need any more information. I will be escorting Ms. Brooks home," I tell the police. They give us the green light to get out of here and within minutes, we are out in the cold city air. I take a deep breath, letting the cool fill my lungs. I slide my hoodie from my body and hand it to Stormy. She's shivering either from the cold or the adrenaline. Either way, she needs it more than me.

"Thank you," She says barely above a whisper. We get to the car, and I open the door for her. Making sure she is securely in place; I shut the door and walk around to mine. I slide in, holding my side as a grunt escapes me. "You should have gotten checked out. We need to go back over there." Stormy says as she reaches for the door handle.

"Not a chance, Angel. We're going home. If I have to, I'll call Dr. Peterson. He's who looked after you the other night." Leaving the campus, Stormy rests her head against the seat and closes her eyes. I force myself to turn away from the goddess in my seat and focus on the road. What a fucking nightmare tonight has been. I haven't had a peaceful night since Stormy came rushing into my life. I wasn't lying to her when I said she was total chaos. Everything goes erratic when she is involved but there is no place I'd rather be. She is my new obsession. I will go to the ends of the earth for her.

Stormy

Tonight, was a fucking wakeup call that I can't go around the city without a bodyguard. I never in a million years thought I would agree with Sebastian on this but after what I went through, I can't imagine what would have happened had Sebastian not stepped in when he did. A chill runs through me at the thought of those men's hands on me.

Before I know it, we are turning into the garage for the penthouse. Sebastian walks around opening my door and retrieving my luggage. The elevator ride is a quiet one and I wish I knew what was going on in his mind. Is he mad at me because he warned me about leaving? A lump forms in my throat at the thought.

"Are you angry with me because of tonight?" I ask once we reach his apartment. He looks hurt for a moment, making me want to take the words back. He drops my luggage to the floor and cups my face with his hands.

"I would never be angry with you for something like tonight. I was scared and fucking furious at the same time, but not at you. They're lucky they are still alive. It's just," he pauses for a moment and closes his eyes, "I thought they were going to hurt you. I can't let that happen." Sebastian rests his forehead against mine and looks into my eyes. "I love you; I can't be without you." He takes my hand and places it across his chest. "This is yours. It beats for you." He kisses me softly at first and then it becomes starving, like the last meal on Earth is within each other. He pushes me against the wall and firmly pins my hands above my head. Kissing along my jaw and down my neck, I writhe against the wall, needing more.

"Mmm, I love when you do that, Daddy." I murmur. My hands itch to get on his body. I want to run them along his sculpted chest and down. I try to pull them free, but he puts more pressure on the hold. Sebastian's other hand skates down my side, grabbing hold of my waist. He pushes his erection against me, I can feel its warmth on my belly.

"As much as I want to take you right now," He groans into my ear, "I need to make some phone calls. Come with me and I'll show you where you can unpack." I have to fucking pack and unpack all over again. I just did this shit! I hate it so much. It's like how some people feel about doing laundry. Sebastian picks up my luggage and I follow behind.

"Fortunately, I have a second closet in my room that's never been used." He opens the door and ushers me inside. Wow, this closet is larger than normal bedrooms. I look around at the endless shoe racks and know right away that I'm going to need more shoes to fill these up.

"This is amazing, Sebastian. I've never seen a closet this fancy. I don't have nearly enough stuff to fit in here." I tell him, while I look around.

"Then we will go shopping," He states as if it's just that easy.

"No. I'll be fine. Besides I need to hold onto my savings to continue to pay Lana. Shit, I have to tell her the news. I don't think she is going to take it well. I wasn't there very long, but we formed a bond. I feel bad, Sebastian," I confess.

"Look at me," he pulls my body to face him, "This is going to be great. I know we have a few obstacles, but I will take care of everything."

"I don't need you to take care of everything. Me moving in here doesn't change that I can do things for myself."

"Fuck, woman, let someone take care of you for once!" He shouts, making me jump away from him. Tears begin streaming down my face and I can't look at him. "I'm sorry, Angel. I didn't mean to yell. With everything that's happened today, I'm on edge." Sebastian walks over to me, grabbing my hand and leading us out of the closet. He sits on the edge of the bed, patting his lap for me to sit. Straddling him, I look up into his lustrous green eyes, getting lost in their depths. He cups my face and takes a deep breath. "Stormy, this is all new emotions for me. I've never been in love before. I've never had this desire to fiercely protect someone in my life. This is something I'm having to deal with. It's like when the Grinch's heart grew three sizes in one day. I feel like that." I chuckle at his comparison, but I understand everything he is saying.

"I've never felt like this before either. It's hard to not be frightened that it could all go away in the blink of an eye," I admit.

"I'm sorry I snapped at you. You push back against me, and I'm not used to that either. But I love that about you, but on certain occasions I need you to trust me enough that I know what's best. You have been through so much, Angel, let me carry it for a while." I am full on crying now. Never in my life has anyone cared so much for me that they wanted to help me carry my baggage. I can feel the weight being lifted, it's the most surreal sensation. "Don't cry, baby. I was just trying to explain myself to you."

"These are happy tears, I promise. I'll try to be better about relinquishing my control over things. I've just had to depend solely on myself for so long, it will be an adjustment for sure," I confess.

"It's you and me against the world. Don't ever forget that. I'll always choose you. Always." He brings his lips down on mine and I feel like I can't get close enough to him. He barreled into my life and turned it upside down, but I have never felt more complete.

Sebastian pulls away and drops his hands from my face. Wrapping them around me, he pulls me close to his body in a tight embrace. His warmth seeps into my soul and I let out a contented sigh. *He is my dark hero and I'm his chaotic fantasy. Together we are a messy, twisted, magical painting.*

Twenty Five

Sebastian

"How about I draw you a bath so you can relax while I make these phone calls?" I question.

"That actually sounds wonderful. I can't remember the last time I took a bath." I lift Stormy from my lap, setting her on the floor before me. I run my thumb over her cheek, gathering tears.

"Let me get it started for you." I stand and she moves from my path letting me get to the bathroom. I see her go into the closet, probably to get some clothes. Under the sink, I find some bath salts that I bought on a whim one time and never used. Once I got them home, I realized I was being a pussy and put them under the sink. They have been there ever since. Fortunately, they are finally coming in handy. I turn on the faucets and sprinkle in some salts. Once I return to the room, Stormy is coming out of the closet with clothes and toiletries. "It'll only take a few minutes to fill up. You can turn the jets on if you would like. It's kind of like a small hot tub." She rolls her eyes at me, and I laugh. "Got to have the best for my girl. I must have known you were coming when I bought this

257

place. Now, go relax. I'm going to order dinner. Any requests?" I ask.

"Hmm, I don't really have any cravings. Just no eggs. I'm allergic," she explains.

"Wow, really? I've never known anyone allergic to eggs. No scrambled eggs for breakfast then," I joke.

"Yeah, but I never liked them anyways so it's not a big deal. I'm good with just about anything," she replies.

"Alright. I'll come check on you in a little bit." Walking over to her, I brush my lips across her forehead down to her ear. "No touching yourself without me in there." I whisper in the shell of her ear. It has the desired effect because goosebump sprinkle her arms and up her neck. I kiss her there then stand, leaving her wanting more. I hear her take a deep breath as I walk away, and I grin to myself. I shut the door behind me, heading to the living room. My first stop is my wet bar to pour myself a glass of whiskey. I don't want to make this call, but I have to. I need to get them to stop harassing my girl.

I pull out my phone and scroll through the information that Jackson sent me about the Jacks' family. I dial the number and listen to the ring as I take a large gulp of whiskey.

"Hello?" A man answers.

"Yes, I'm looking for Dennis Jacks," I reply.

"Speaking," he says.

"Hello, sir. My name is Sebastian Knight. I am calling on behalf of Stormy Brooks," I begin.

"What does that little tramp want now? Hasn't she taken enough from us?" He stammers on, sounding drunk. If I could punch someone through the phone, it would happen right now.

I try to remain calm to get through this conversation without making things worse for Stormy.

"Actually, sir, I am calling to offer you a settlement in exchange for your permanent silence on anything involving Stormy Brooks. You will sign a statement that says you, as well as your family, will never do another interview and an NDA on the money you receive," I explain, gripping the phone so hard, I'm surprised it doesn't crack under the pressure. "You will also never contact Ms. Brooks in the future."

"How much are we talking? I could be persuaded for a hundred grand," He sputters. I roll my eyes and down the rest of my drink.

"Fifty," I reply angrily.

"One hundred or it's no deal," He responds.

"Alright, you must not need any money. Sorry for interrupting you. If you change your mind, you can call me back at this number." I wait a moment before I hang up because I know he will be singing a different tune in a minute.

"Wait, wait. We can work this out," His slimy voice comes through the phone. I smile because I know I called his bluff.

"Fifty grand then?" I question.

"How about seventy-five?" he counters.

"No thank you. I told you the amount. It's more than generous and more than the insurance settlement Ms. Brooks received," I snap back, letting my anger peep through.

"Alright fine. Fifty grand it is, but I want it in cash," he returns.

"Deal. I will have my attorney draw up the paperwork and someone will be in touch shortly. This deal will be null and void if you talk to the press anytime between now and receiving the payment, signature, or no. Also, on the day you receive payment, you will make an official statement that Ms. Brooks was innocent throughout this whole ordeal," I acknowledge.

"Fine. You have a deal," he agrees.

"Thank you for your time." I hang up and toss my phone to the couch, rubbing my aching temples. What a fucking nightmare of in-laws she's had to deal with. I can't believe after everything she has been put through, that people will still continue to treat her poorly. Even supposed family.

I pour myself another drink and pick my phone up, shooting off a text to my lawyer to arrange the needed paperwork. I won't be going down there, but a representative of the firm will, and they'll make sure the statement is given.

With all that done, I call Marcy. It only rings once before she answers.

"Please tell me this is a good phone call and not one that's going to make me bang my head against the wall," She pleads.

"Well, it's good to hear from you as well," I retort. "This is actually not terrible news but news, nonetheless. Stormy and I were involved in an altercation on the SVA campus earlier this evening."

"Lord help me, you truly are the problem child. Go on, tell me," She replies, and I have to chuckle.

"Three men tried to rape her after her class and on campus. I simply came to the rescue in time. I sent them all to the hospital with a ticket straight to jail after they are released. I wanted you to know in case there happened to be any bystanders. I don't think there were. We were in an empty classroom," I explain.

"You Knight brothers go all alpha when you have a woman, don't you. Damn. Too bad you don't have another brother," She jokes.

"We do have a cousin. I should introduce you sometime." My mind wanders to Samuel, and I think they might actually hit it off. I'll have to arrange that once everything settles down.

"Where has he been hiding and how come he doesn't cause as much trouble as you two?" she asks.

"He's been in Afghanistan for several years. He's only been back in the states for a couple months," I clarify.

"Oh, a military man. You definitely need to set me up. But in the meantime, I'll make sure you and Stormy stay out of the tabloids. Lord knows you don't need any more coverage," she says.

"Oh, and also just so you know, I will be paying the Jacks' family to keep quiet from now going forward."

"Please tell me that he will be signing something?" she asks.

"Of course, my attorney is already on it. I just wanted to let you know that we shouldn't be hearing anymore from them, if they know what's good for them," I reply.

"Good to know. Keep me posted on when that's happening. And please stay out of trouble and pass that along to your brother, as well. I know he is back in town." She says.

"Will do. Thank you, Marcy." I hang up, taking another large gulp of my drink. I still need to call my mother and tell her everything that's going on. I have several missed calls from her, and I haven't had the time to get back with her. I guess it's now or never. I dial her number and listen as it rings.

"Well, if it isn't my baby boy. Where the hell have you been? I've been calling you. I had to call Miles and get the scoop of that was going on. So, tell me about this girl," She rattles off. I knew that's what she wanted to talk about. She has been asking me for years when I was going to settle down.

"Well, hello to you, too, Mother," I mutter.

"I'm sorry darling. This is just big news that you finally found someone to make you settle down. I didn't think it would ever happen," She remarks.

"Well, long story short, I literally ran into Stormy the night of the fundraiser. We had less than pleasant things to say to each other. Then Mary, from work, took it upon herself to hire her as my executive assistant. I guess the rest is history," I reply.

"Aw, I am so happy for you, darling. I can't wait to meet her. I want to have you all over since your brother and Lizzie are back," She mentions.

"That sounds great, Mother. I need to go so I can order us some dinner. I just wanted to give you a quick call. I love you." I agree.

"Thank you. I love you too," she responds. She hangs up and I pocket my phone. I finish off my glass of whiskey, feeling much better about things. I need to go ahead and order dinner so it'll get here by the time Stormy is out of the tub. Thinking of her wet and naked just a room away makes me hard, I wish I was in there with her. I need her. I need her more than I have any other person.

I pull my phone out and pop open a delivery service app, ordering us Thai food for dinner. I order almost one of everything because I don't know what she would like. I need to know these things and I intend to find out all I can about her.

I place my glass in the sink and walk back to my bedroom. I open the door and hear the most melodious sound coming from the bathroom. For a moment I think Stormy has put on music but then I get closer, and I could hear her unique voice ringing through. I stand outside the bathroom door listening to her sing. She sounds happy. I pick up on the lyrics.

"Lovely to be sitting here with you
You're kinda cute, but it's
Raining harder
My shoes are now full of water
Lovely to be rained on with you
It's kinda cute, but it's
So short
Then you're driving me home
And I don't wanna leave
But I have to go
You kiss me in your car
And it feels like the start of a movie I've seen before
Before"

These lyrics take me back to when we were on the bike together in the rain. I wonder if that's what she is thinking as well. I open the door slowly so as not to startle her, but she has her eyes closed and continues to sing. I sit by the tub, trying not to disturb her but wanting to soak in every inch of her, including her perfect voice. I would love it if she was always singing, that would mean she was happy. She finishes the song and lays her head back against the tub. I slide my hand down her slippery thigh. She jolts but sees me and smiles. I continue my descent until I'm at her slick, wet pussy.

As I hold onto the side of the tub, my fingers brush against her sensitive clit. She pushes forward against my hand, angling her body to give me better access.

"You sing like a siren. You called to me, and I came," I express, as I push one finger through her folds, keeping my thumb circling her clit.

"I couldn't help it. I used to sing all the time and then I stopped. You brought the song back to my soul." She closes her eyes and begins riding my finger. I add another and she moans out in pleasure. "Mmm, Daddy, yes. You make me feel so good," she murmurs.

"That's my job, Angel." Picking up my pace, I add a third finger curling them to touch her sweet spot. She grabs on to my forearm for support as she rides my hand.

"Yes! Yes!" She chants over and over until she is shooting off like a rocket before my eyes.

"Look at me when you come." I command. "I want to see those gorgeous pools of yellow on me." Her eyes flutter open and are darkened with pleasure. Her thrusts begin to slow.

"Why don't you get in here with me, Daddy?" She says seductively.

"Not right now, Angel. I came to tell you that dinner will be here soon." She pouts but nods her head. I turn off the jets and retrieve a towel for her. She stands, waiting for me to wrap her up. Her eyes playfully dance with mine. I think she's liking being cared for and I like being the one doing it. I want to take care of all her needs. Pampering and babying her bring me immense pleasure. I pull her out of the tub, placing her on the bath mat. She left her hair in a braid and tied it up so it wouldn't get wet. "Are you feeling more relaxed?" I ask.

"Extremely. I could fall asleep right here," she explains.

"Well, I've got to feed you first. Go ahead and get dressed. What do you think about dinner in bed? We can put on a movie if you like," I suggest.

"That sounds great! I love that idea." Before I can reply, the downstairs doorbell rings letting me know dinner has arrived. I have to go let them in the elevator so they can bring our meal up.

"That will be the food. I'll be right back." I kiss her forehead and jog out the door, down the stairs to the main level. I press the intercom and let them know they can use the elevator. The man comes to the door and I'm there waiting. I tip him extra for his troubles and close the door. Setting the bags down on the kitchen counter, I get out one large tray. I stuff it with the meal, napkins, and drinks. This is going to be a better night than it started out as. I have my girl, safe and sound, a delicious meal, and a bed to fool around in later. What could be better?

TWENTY SIX

Stormy

After I lotion up and get dressed, I hop in the bed, waiting for Sebastian to bring dinner. A few minutes later, he strolls through the door with a large tray of what can only be described as a large feast. I think we could feed ten people with the amount of food he bought.

Sebastian sees me gawking at the tray, "I got some of everything. I didn't know what you would want," he remarks.

"That was sweet of you, but you didn't have to buy the whole restaurant," I laugh out.

"Don't worry about it, we will just have leftovers for days." I cringe at the thought of eating the same thing for days.

"I'm kidding. Here take this while I put on something more comfortable." I take the tray and place it on the bed. Smelling all this food makes my stomach grumble. I glance over to Sebastian at the perfect time to see him sliding off his jeans. His ass should be framed. It's the perfect round, muscular ass that you just want to take a bite out of. He sees me staring and heat flames my cheeks. "Like what you see, baby?" He asks. I just cover my eyes and nod my head. I can hear him laugh, a second later the bed is dipping down with his weight. He scoots beside me and pulls my hands down, kissing them. "You don't have to be embarrassed, Angel. I love that you find me attractive."

"Attactive doesn't even cut it, Sebastian. You could be a model. Even better an underwear model. Every girl would snatch that magazine up in a heartbeat," I confess.

"I don't want every girl to look at me like that. There is only one person that gets that privilege, and she is right beside me. Now, let's dig in. What movie are we watching?" He asks as he takes a pair of chopsticks and breaks them apart.

"I was thinking Harry Potter. Are you up to a marathon?" I question.

"Fuck yes! Let's put it on." He reaches for the remote and pulls it up on the television hanging from the wall.

The movie starts and we dig into the food. Both of us are starving so there is little conversation. He ordered so much, it's hard to decide on what to fill up on. Sebastian eats a little bit of everything. He's like an expert with his chopsticks.

"How do you work these so well?" I hold up the chopsticks. He gives me a wide smile and my heart flutters in my chest.

"Here, you need to hold them like this." He places his hands over mine and helps me grip the sticks correctly. His hold lingers longer than needed and I look to him, right as he captures my lips in his. His lips work expertly against mine, making me want more and more. I want to throw all this food on the floor and let this man take me right here.

"I can't get enough of this mouth, Angel." He says when he comes up for a breath and I have to agree. "We need to finish eating before this food isn't the only thing I'm ravaging." He gives me a wink and goes back to eating. Just like that and I'm left panting over here. He took my breath away. I wonder if he even knows how much he affects me. I go back to eating, using the chopsticks how he instructed but all I can think about is his body on mine. I need him.

"I'm getting full," I tell him. He nods in agreement as he wipes his mouth. "Do you want me to take the leftovers to the kitchen?" I ask.

"Nope. I'll do it really quickly. Get comfy and keep watching the movie. I'll be back in a minute." Sebastian picks up the tray, leaving the bottles of water on the nightstand for later. Once he leaves the room, I jump from the bed and brush my teeth. I don't want Thai food smelling breath when we are cuddling and watching the movie. I take out my braid and let the kinky strands fall around my shoulders and down my back. Fluffing it up a bit, I shrug into the mirror knowing this is the best it's going to look. I get back to the bedroom at the same time as Sebastian is walking in.

"And what were you up to?" he asks.

"I just wanted to brush my teeth before we got all cuddly," I reply with a shrug.

"That's what I was about to do." He comes over to me and swats my ass as I'm walking over to the bed. "I'll be there in a minute," he responds.

"Okay." I jump in the bed and move to the other side where I slept earlier. I'm pretty sure his side of the bed is the one closet to the bathroom. That would make sense. I guess I should probably ask him and not assume. "Hey, Sebastian, which side of the bed do you usually sleep on." He peeks out of the bathroom with his toothbrush hanging from his mouth to look at me. "I don't want to be in your spot," I reply. He laughs and disappears back into the bathroom. I hear the water running and then it cuts off and Sebastian emerges.

"I normally sleep here." Gesturing to the side I figured was his. "But it doesn't matter to me. It's just a bed. Where do you want to sleep? This is our bed now, so you need to be comfortable."

"I'm not taking your spot. Over here is fine for me." I scoot to the furthest side and slide under the sheets.

"Alright, if you're sure." He shrugs and jumps into the bed, causing me to bounce several times. I let out a laugh before settling back into place. Once Sebastian is under the covers, he grabs me by the waist, pulling me closer to him. "But don't think for a minute you are sleeping that far away from me. You're spot will be right here in the middle." He says with all seriousness.

"Okay." Is all I can say with the way he is looking at me. He looks like a wolf about to devour its prey. I smell his mint toothpaste and I have to smile that he had the same thought I did. He leans down and whispers in my ear.

"Ever been fucked with Harry Potter playing in the background?" I shake my head.

"Good." He crawls over me, keeping his green eyes locked on mine. "I need you, Stormy. After everything that happened tonight, I need to be inside you. I need to claim this pussy so everyone knows who it belongs to. I want you to smell like me, so no man dares to come near what's mine." He growls, then smashes his lips to mine. I open up to give him better access. Skating my nails across his back, I feel goosebumps erupt over his skin. He groans out in response, making me dig in harder. His kisses become frantic. He slides his lips over my jaw and down my neck to my collar bone. He pulls down the strap to my tank top, releasing my breast. Taking the nipple in his mouth, I moan and drag my hands up to his hair. When I pull, he bites down harder on me. The sensations go directly to my pussy, like a livewire. He pulls his mouth off my nipple and gives attention to the other side.

"Take my shirt off, Daddy," I say, breathlessly. Sebastian chuckles darkly.

"Do you think you can tell me what to do, Angel?" He looks up at me with a devilish grin. I shake my head, zipping my lips. He takes the fabric in his hands and rips it from my body, throwing the shredded fabric over his shoulder. I gasp at the feeling. I've never had anything ripped from my body, but I'm not saying I hate it. Although I did like that shirt. "Is that better?"

"Yes, thank you." He runs his hands up from my waist to my ribs and back down to my belly. I try to cover myself, still self-conscious about my curves.

"Don't you dare hide from me, Angel. I love every part of you. I've never seen a sexier woman in my life. Now, tell me the safe word."

"Gandalf," I say.

"Good girl. Say that and everything stops. Tell me you trust me." It's not a question per se but more of a reaffirmation.

"I trust you, Sebastian." That's all he needs to hear because he jumps down my body, pulling my shorts with him. He stalks his way back up to me, kissing a path along the way. Then he lays down next to me. I'm not sure what he is doing but then he speaks.

"Sit on Daddy's face, baby." I sit up, looking down at him. He scoots his body so that his head is closer to the headboard. "Do I need to repeat myself?" he growls.

"I don't, I mean I never-" I don't really know what to say. I've never done anything like this before.

"Get up here, now. Put your legs on the side of my head and sit on my face. I want my dessert." I awkwardly crawl up his body and do as he says.

"Sebastian, I'm too heavy. I'll suffocate you," I say once I get my legs where he wants them. My pussy is hovering above his face, I don't think I could be more embarrassed.

"Shut the fuck up and sit on my face like a good girl and hold on to the headboard." I want to retort to his talking to me like that, but I also can't deny how much it turns me on when he's all alpha in the bed. I know I am soaked. Grasping the headboard, I close my eyes and lower myself on his waiting mouth. The instant I make contact, he pulls my clit into his mouth hard. I squeal out in pain but the pleasure snakes its way into my system, making my pussy flood. He does it again, knowing he is getting me worked up. He licks from my entrance to my clit and back again. His tongue works magic on me, it isn't long before I'm rocking my hips against his face. I could be mortified but I crave the release more. "That's it, fuck my face, Angel." He groans from underneath me. The vibrations of his voice against my clit sets me off and I am screaming and baring down trying to pull more pleasure from this release.

"Fuck, Daddy. That feels so good. Fuuuck!" I shout, knowing that if he has neighbors then I'm sure they can hear me. Then I think that they are probably used to the sounds coming from this apartment. The thought sours my stomach and cuts my orgasm short. I go to get off of him, but he grabs ahold of my hips.

"What the hell just happened?" He questions, his eyes boring into mine.

"I'm sorry." I break free of his hold and crawl over to my side of the bed, wrapping myself in blankets and pulling my legs up to my chest. I ruined our night together. He's going to throw me out now. He's going to see how insecure I am, even though I can stand up for myself, it's mostly a front. I still don't think I'm good enough for a man like Sebastian.

He comes over to where I am and rolls me over as the tears stream down my face.

"Hey, what's going on in that head of yours?" he asks softly. I shake my head and try to turn away from him, but he isn't having it. "Stormy, I said what's going on. I felt you tense up, so I know something is bothering you," he says with a little more force.

"I'm sorry. I got so loud, and I was thinking that other people in the building might hear me and then my thoughts jumped to them probably being used to hearing it because of how many girls you probably bring here. I'm so sorry. I didn't mean to ruin everything. If you want to take me home, then I understand." I put my hands over my face, trying to hold the tears in.

"Why do you think I bring a lot of women here? Have I given you that impression?" I shake my head.

"It's just that Lana sent me this news article about you a while back naming you the Most Eligible Playboy Bachelor in New York. And I guess deep down I don't know what you see in me, and I fear you'll grow tired of the excitement that I bring to your life. I know

I don't look like those other women," I confess. Sebastian removes my hands from my face and kisses them before he speaks.

"Listen to me, okay. I know you have had a rough go at life, but I want you to know that I want you with every fiber of my being. You have lit a spark inside me that I didn't know I needed. You, Stormy Brooks, are the only woman I have ever been in love with. As far as the other women, you are the only one that I have ever brought here. I never wanted to sully my home with trash women. You're different. I can't imagine this apartment without you now that you've been in it," he takes a breath and kisses the tears from my cheeks, "Those other women are blank canvases hanging on a wall and I'm walking towards the only painting in the room with true colors on it. You, Stormy, are my true love. Your colors light up my life. I haven't been the same since I met you and I don't want it any other way. Your crazy zest at life and penchant for finding trouble is where I want to be. Beside you, always." I look up at his smiling face and I think I fall even harder for this man.

"I'm sorry I judged you for something I read on the internet. You didn't judge me when everything came out about me. I feel so foolish. Please forgive me."

"It's already forgotten. Now, come here." He lays on the bed and gestured to the middle of the bed where I am supposed to be. I slide over to where he is, and he pulls me into his arms. I wrap my arm around him and squeeze him tight, but he lets out a small grunt of pain. I pull back and can see the pain in his eyes.

"Take off your shirt, let me see your ribs," I tell him.

"I'm fine. They're just a little sensitive," he explains.

"Sebastian! Let me see." I pull his shirt up enough that I can see the purple bruising already forming on his side.

"You probably have a broken rib! We need to get you to the hospital." I jump up and try to get off the bed, but I'm hoisted back by huge arms.

"Oh, no you don't. We aren't going anywhere tonight. If it's still bad tomorrow, then I may call Dr. Peterson. He can stop by when he gets a free minute tomorrow."

"But I feel bad. This happened because of me. How can you be okay with this. What if this happens again and you get hurt worse?" I question.

"Angel, look at me. I'm fine. There isn't anything to worry about and I would do the same thing all over again. I wasn't going to let those men touch you," he says firmly.

"Now, tell me about these Harry Potter tattoos. I know they mean something to you, because you have a matching pendant around your neck of the Patronus." Am I a little stunned that Sebastian Knight knew these were Harry Potter tattoos? Not so much. Am I stunned that he knows what a Patronus is? Definitely.

"I can't believe you know what that is. But, yes, they do mean a great deal to me." I lie back on the bed and cuddle up next to him, being wary of his ribs. "When I was young, Harry Potter was the first series I read. They transported me to Hogwarts. I was able to escape the world around me whenever I cracked open a book. They are magical in a way most people don't know. I read and reread the books over and over throughout the years, each time they wove themselves deeper into my soul. When I turned eighteen, I knew I wanted to represent that home I always escaped to. So, this is a collection of the most meaningful things in Harry Potter. Fawkes, the phoenix, was reborn from his ashes. I always like the thought that we can be reborn from our worst experiences. I got it after Blaine's death," I explain.

Sebastian takes my arm in his hands and kisses from my wrist to my shoulder. "I love this ink on you. Knowing the story makes its all the more special."

"What all do yours represent? I know that's a family crest over your heart and I'm guessing your father's name underneath?" I ask.

"Yes, I got it done after he passed away a couple of years ago. He was a great man and is truly missed," he says.

"I'm sorry for your loss."

"Thank you, Angel."

"What about the rest of your tattoos?"

"The dragon on my back represents all the anger I used to have as a teen and into my early twenties. I used to get in fights all the time. It also represents courage, protection, strength, and power. It took several sessions to complete. Then, I got this Celtic symbol that represents brotherhood. Miles has the same one. The blue in it is his birthstone for December and the yellow is my birth stone for November."

"I like them. I love the dragon. It makes me want another tattoo. They're addicting. So, since your birthday is in November it's coming up then."

"It's November first. When is your birthday?"

"Um," I look at my watch that says it's past midnight, "It's today actually," I state matter-of-factly. Sebastian leans up on his elbow and looks down at me. I can't decipher the look he's giving me.

"Are you kidding me? Why didn't you tell me?" he asks.

"I don't know. It's not a big deal. I haven't really celebrated much over the years," I utter.

"Why the hell not? Who wouldn't want to celebrate you?" he asks as he seems to be getting angry.

"Will you calm down. No wonder you got a dragon on your back. You're going all alpha on me right now. Will you just drop it? It's not a big deal. I'm twenty-three, woohoo," I announce.

"Let's go get tattoos today, then. I have been wanting another one, too," he states.

"Okay, yeah, that sounds like fun."

"I'll call my guy in the morning and see if he has an opening. Normally he'll make time for me."

"Thank you, that will be great. I'll have to think about what I want," I confess.

Sebastian leans over and takes my lips in his. Wrapping my arms around his neck, he deepens the kiss and moves over my body. I can feel his hard length pressing against my belly. I reach between us and stroke his cock through his pants. He groans out and tugs his shirt over his head then leans back down, crashing his lips to mine. I reach my other hand down and try to pull his pants down, but I don't have enough space to get them very far.

"Can you take your pants off?" I ask, wanting to feel his naked body against mine.

"I thought you'd never ask." He rolls off me to remove his pants then he is back on me. "Are you ready for me, Angel? I need to be inside you." He breathes into my ear.

"Yes, please, fuck me, Daddy." I plead.

"Fuck yes, baby. That's what I want to hear," he says as he slams into me. The force pushes me up the bed. He thrusts in harder and deeper the second and third time, not allowing me to adjust to his size. The pain soon turns to pleasure, and I moan out.

"Yes, just like that. You feel amazing," I express.

"Your wet little cunt was made just for me and only me. Tell me who this pussy belongs to."

"It's, yours, Daddy. All of me is yours," I confess.

"Fuck, you're killing me, baby." Sebastian reaches between us and plays with my clit. Rubbing in circles in tandem with the thrust of his hips. My orgasm builds and builds until I can't take it anymore. I go over the edge, my pussy clamping down on his cock. "That's it, come for me, Angel." He continues to draw out my pleasure as he strokes my clit. Once I begin my descent back down, his ministrations slow. Sebastian moves his hand slowly up my leg, picking it up and placing it over his shoulder. The angle hitting a whole new bundle of nerves.

"Yes, I'm going to come again. Don't stop!" I plead.

"Don't forget your safe word," Is all he says before he wraps his large hand around my throat. For a moment, I'm fearful, but I see the love and passion in his eyes, and I know he wouldn't do anything to hurt me. His grasp tightens and I can barely breathe, but he feels so good that I'm about to come again. "Take this cock like the good little slut you are." He growls as his pumps become more frantic. I shatter again around his cock, milking him. "I'm going to fill you up until you are dripping with my seed. I want to see your belly swollen with my child, Stormy. Take this come!" He shouts as jets and jets of come is pumped into my pussy. I can feel every jolt and it makes my orgasm continue along with his. Finally, he drops my leg and collapses on me, barely holding his weight above me.

He kisses along my neck and up my chin then finally on the lips. I can't get enough of his perfect lips on mine. He doesn't pull out of me but continues ever so slowly pumping into me.

"You are incredible, you know that? You did so good. You trusted me, didn't you?" he praises.

"I did. And it's the most explosive orgasm I've ever had," I reply.

He kisses my forehead and whispers, "Happy birthday, Angel. This will be your new birthday tradition at midnight." He kisses my lips with so much love and passion that tears form in the corners of my eyes. He is so good to me. He loves me and I still haven't told him that I love him. I feel like it's a secret that's going to burst from my chest at any moment. I don't know when the right time is.

Sebastian pulls out of me slowly while his eyes are locked on mine. He kisses a path down to my belly and places an extra-long kiss there. Then he scoops our releases up and pushes it back inside me.

"Shit, I forgot to take my pill yesterday. With everything going on, I just forgot. I'm sorry I-" He doesn't let me finish.

"Don't take them anymore. I'm serious, Stormy. I want to see you growing our child. I can't stop imagining it." I know I have shock written across my face. I don't know what to say. That's such a huge step. He knows I don't know what to say so he gets up and retrieves a wash cloth to clean us both up, then he cuddles in behind me. "I love you, Angel. Get some sleep." I think about what he said and asked of me for a while before I fall asleep and the crazy thing is that I'm actually thinking about not taking them, just like he said. I think I fell and hit my head somewhere. I can't believe I would actually ever consider that, but with Sebastian everything feels so different. I fall asleep with his big arm curled around me and the warmth of his body pressed against me. It can't get much better than this.

TWENTY SEVEN

Sebastian

I wake to the alarm I set before I fell asleep last night. Since Stormy decided to drop the bomb on me that it was her birthday, I knew I had to get up and plan something for her today. I slip out of bed, shower quickly, and put on clothes. I leave Stormy to sleep in because there are some things I want to take care of before I wake her. I grab my phone and leave the room, shutting the door behind me.

As I make my way to the kitchen, I scroll through my contacts until I find Zane Covington. His tattoo shop, Broken Halo Tattoo, has been my go-to place for tattoos since I started getting them. I decide to shoot him a text instead of calling in case he is still asleep.

Sebastian:

> Hey man, checking to see if you have any spots available today for me and my girl. It's her birthday. Let me know.

Placing my phone on the counter, I start the coffee maker. It doesn't take long for Zane to get back with me.

281

Zane:

> Hey bro. I have some openings later this evening if that works for you? Around eight would probably be best.

Sebastian:

> That would be great. Thanks man. See you then.

I pocket my phone and pour myself a cup of coffee, adding sugar after. Leaning against the counter, I think about all the ideas I have for Stormy today. I need to get her out of the apartment for a while, so my interior designer can come in and rearrange one of my spare bedrooms. An idea springs to mind. Maybe Lizzie can take Stormy out for lunch and a bout of shopping. That should give me enough time to get everything together. I would usually use my assistant to buy the things I need for the room but since that's Stormy, I will have to do the shopping myself. This should be fun. I pull up my contacts and call Miles. I don't want to wake Lizzie if she is still sleeping.

"What's up bro? You don't normally get up this early unless something's wrong. Please tell me there isn't anything wrong. I can't handle much more," he groans into the phone, and I think I woke him up. Oh well, I don't give a shit. I need his help.

"Today is Stormy's birthday and I need some help. Does Lizzie have any plans today?" I question.

"I don't think so, why?" he asks.

"I wanted to see if she would get Stormy out of the apartment for a while so I can fix up a room for her," I remark.

"I'm sure she would love that. What did you have in mind?" he queries.

"Maybe Lizzie could take her to lunch and then some shopping. Then you can go with me and help me get some things I need at the art supply store," I respond, hoping he is feeling generous enough to help me today.

"Lizzie has been wanting to meet this mystery woman, so I'm sure she would love to. Also, why the hell do you need art supplies?" he asks.

"Because Stormy is an artist and I wanted to turn one of bedrooms into a studio for her. That means I have only a few hours to get everything together," I state.

"Why did you wait until the last minute?" he asks.

"I didn't know today was her birthday until last night. I don't think she would have even told me if I hadn't asked," I express.

"She sounds like Lizzie. She doesn't really care to celebrate her birthday, but I make sure to make it a big deal every year." he claims.

"Exactly. So, will you help your little brother out?" I question.

"Of course, I will. Let me get Lizzie up and make sure she didn't have any plans today. She didn't mention anything yesterday. I can also get her to make a list of things you will need. She's an artist as well. Might be of some help." he answers.

"Yeah, that would be great. I have absolutely no idea where to start. She mostly paints, I know that." I respond. "But she's in art school at SVA, and she has all kinds of different classes."

"Cool. They will have some things in common. Let me wake Lizzie and I will text you back." he suggests.

"Thanks, Miles. Love you."

"Love you too brother."

I pocket my phone and get to work on some breakfast, making sure to avoid eggs. I decide on pancakes, substituting the eggs for bananas. It's a little trick my grandmother taught me when I was younger. The knowledge is finally coming in handy. After mixing the ingredients, I cook them up and plate them with some fruit and powdered sugar. The dish looks pretty good if I do say so myself. I gather the plate, a cup of coffee with cream and sugar, and syrup on the large tray. It's going to be breakfast in bed kind of day for my birthday girl.

I crack the door open and see Stormy is still sound asleep. I place the tray on the bench at the end of the bed and decide to wake her a different way. Sliding under the covers, I crawl until I'm between her legs. I move them further apart; I see the ripe pussy that I can't get enough of. With a flick of my tongue, I groan as I taste her perfect sweet nectar. I continue slowly licking until she begins to softly moan in her sleep. Her legs begin to tremble, and I know she will be awake soon. I pull the blanket down so I can see her when she does. Her eyes flicker open as she lets out another breathy moan. I push in two fingers and see her eyes roll back. As I lick, suck, and thrust my fingers inside her, she begins writhing on the bed.

"Oh, Sebastian. Fuck, Daddy. Right there!" She shouts when I find the rhythm that works best for her. I don't stop. I want her coming on my hand. I love seeing her fall apart and know that I'm the one that brought her to that place.

"Come for me, my Angel." As the words leave my lips, she screams out and comes all over my mouth and hand. I continue my ministrations through her climax until she begins to come down.

I don't want to work her up again. I need to feed her breakfast. "That's my good girl," I praise.

Once she is satisfied, I crawl up her body, kissing along the way. "Good morning, beautiful. I brought you breakfast," I whisper in the shell of her ear. Goosebumps erupt over her skin and it's a beautiful sight.

"Was an orgasm on the menu?" she smirks. It's that quick wit that gets me every time. I love it.

"It was for me. It's my new favorite breakfast." She slaps me on the chest playfully and laughs.

"What was that for?" I question.

"Pussy isn't a nourishing breakfast," she insists.

"I beg to differ." I kiss her mouth so she can taste her sweetness. "Let me get your tray." Hopping off the bed, I retrieve the breakfast tray and place it over her lap. "Happy birthday, Angel," I say as I kiss her forehead. "I made you banana pancakes as to not use eggs." I cut up bananas and strawberries and added them to the side.

"Sebastian, wow, this looks amazing. You really didn't have to do this for me," she says looking at me seriously.

"I wanted to. It wasn't a big deal. Now, eat. I have some plans for you today. How would you like to go shopping with Miles' wife, Lizzie. She is dying to meet you."

"Really? How come?" she asks.

"Because they thought I would be single for the rest of my life, apparently. They want to meet the woman that finally tamed me," I respond.

"I'd hardly say that I tamed you. You're still as ornery as when we first met. I may have just softened the edges a bit." She pours some syrup on her pancakes and takes her first bite. "Mmm, these are delicious. You need to try a bite." She hands me a forkful and I open my mouth for her to feed me. It's a simple act, but so very intimate.

"Those are good. I make some mean pancakes. So, back to plans today. Would you like to go with her?" I ask.

"Sure, I need to know more people in the city. The only people I know are Lana, you, and people at work." She continues eating the pancakes and offering me bites here and there. "What is Lizzie like?"

"She's an author, and she likes to paint as well. At least that's what Miles tells me. But you can go to lunch and shopping and just make a day of it," I explain.

"Wow, an author, that's really cool. What are you going to do all day? Didn't want to hang out with me today?" She asks with a little frown on her face. I can't have that.

"Of course, I do, baby. I have a surprise for you, and I need some time to work it out." Stormy's eyes light up with surprise.

"What are you planning? Now, you have to tell me!" She exclaims. Finishing her last bite, she moves the tray and hops on my lap. "Tell me, Daddy." She says, fluttering her eyes.

"Oh no you don't. You can't get me to spill by being all cute," I say as I kiss her nose.

"Please. You can tell me one hint," She pleads.

"Nope. You're just going to have to wait. Now, go take a shower while I go down to the gym. Sound like a plan?" I ask.

"Fine. I guess I will take a shower all alone then," she pouts.

"Aren't you in a feisty mood this morning. Daddy might have to punish this cute little ass before the day is through." I squeeze her ass in my hands, and she lets out a soft moan. My cock jumps at the sound. I can't fuck her right now no matter how much I want to. We have places to be, and I need to get her out of this apartment. I groan as she starts rubbing her hot pussy against me. Just a quickie wouldn't hurt, right?

I flip her onto her back and pin her hands above her head. Her eyes darken as she realizes what I'm about to do to her. I smash my lips down on her. She tastes like a drug and feels the same way. I'm addicted to her. I don't think I will ever get enough, and I don't want to. I want to crave her every day.

I kick my sweats off. "Open for me, Angel. Spread these perfect legs." She opens and I slide right through. Keeping my hold on her hands, I trail my other hand down her body until I reach her soaking pussy. "Are you ready for me? Does this pussy need to be fed this morning?" She whimpers and nods her head. My cock is hard and aching, needing the release only Stormy can bring. I line myself up at her entrance and thrust in one punishing movement.

Stormy screams out from the sudden penetration but then begins pushing back against me with every pump of my hips. "Fuck you feel incredible. And you take me so well. Doesn't my cock fit perfectly in your tight little pussy?" I question as I continue to pound into her. My orgasm is already building, and I can see the look in her eyes that she is right there with me. "Answer me or I will take it away," I begin to pull out when she screams out.

"You fit perfectly in my pussy. I never want another cock inside me. Only yours."

I laugh darkly. "You won't ever have another dick inside you, baby. I'll kill any fucker who tries." I nip and lick up the column of her neck, leaving my marks behind for all those idiots to see when she is out today. I want everyone to know she is taken. I grasp her throat in my hands and whisper in her ear. "Be a good little girl and come on my cock and you will get a lot of birthday surprises." She whimpers at my words, I can feel her swallow and I tighten my hold. Her face begins turning red, but her eyes are hooded as her orgasm begins to roll through her. I release my hold on throat and begin circling her clit, wanting her pleasure to last longer. She squeezes me so hard that I fall over the edge with her. I continue to thrust into her as I come the most I have in my life. Ropes after ropes release into her cunt as I slow my pace. "Fuck!" I shout at the sheer intensity the sex is between us. I've never had a fuck that was half as good as it is with Stormy. I feel her walls continue to clamp down on me, milking every bit of come that I have out of me.

"Daddy, I want to stay here so you can fuck me all day," she says and I can't blame her. If I didn't already make plans, we wouldn't be leaving this bed today. But alas, it's time for us to get up and get going.

"I wish we could, but we have plans." I kiss her lips, nibbling on her bottom lip in the process. I pull out of her, and I instantly miss her warm, tight hole. I release her hands and they instantly wrap around my head. We continue our make out session like we are a couple of teenagers. I can't pull myself away from her. I kiss along her jaw and down the side of her neck, making my way to her nipples that didn't get any love earlier. I pull one into my mouth and tweak the other with my fingers. Stormy lets out a cry as she slides her fingers through my hair. Pulling me closer to her, she lifts her chest to me making me suck and tug harder. I think she could come just from this stimulation alone. I'll have to dive into that discovery later. I pull my mouth from her nipple with a pop and look up at the gorgeous angel lying in our bed. *Our bed*. That's a heady realization.

"Daddy," She whines. I warned her about whining today. It may be her birthday but I'm still in charge. I flip her to her stomach in one swift move. The action makes her huff out a breath of air. I pull her ass up into the air, kissing it before my hand flies leaving a mark behind. I repeat the action to the other cheek, and she shrieks out in pain. I soothe my hand over her ass before I slap her ass again. Both sides now hold my print and pride blooms in my chest at the sight.

"I told you what would happen if you kept on whining." My cock hardens again at the sight of her in this position, totally at my mercy. I thrust inside of her without warning, and she grasps the blankets beneath her. Fuck, I could live in this pussy.

"Yes, Daddy. I just wanted you again. I can't get enough of you. I've never felt this good." She admits in a murmur. I smile because I know how she feels.

"I know, Angel. I don't want to leave this pussy, but I have to." I reach around her waist and slap her clit.

"Fuck!" she shouts, but moans as I begin rubbing circles with my thumb.

"Is that what my little slut needed?" I question.

"Yes, YES!" she yells as she comes again. Her walls clench down on me tightly like a vise. I move my hands back around to her ass and pull her to me and I continue thrusting in her. My finger finds her virgin hole and I press inside. She clenches down on me.

"Relax, let me in, baby. It'll feel so good." She relaxes some allowing me to pump my finger inside her rosebud.

"Sebastian, it feels so good. I'm going to come again!"

"Me too, baby. Fuck you are so perfect." I come again with a roar. Leaning over, I kiss over her shoulders. Chills spring up in my wake. I collapse onto the bed, bringing her with me. We lie there catching our breaths, no one speaking. I reluctantly pull out of her so I can turn her body toward me. Her face is flushed, and she has never been more stunning as when she is freshly fucked. I push the hair from her face and take her lips into mine. Stormy runs her hands up my chest and I realize I never want to feel another woman touching me. She is it for me. I truly want it to be her and me always.

"Sebastian, I-" but she doesn't finish because my phone begins ringing in my sweats on the floor. I have a feeling of what she was going to say, and I curse my phone for taking the moment away. It's probably Miles confirming everything. Stormy sits up looking spooked. "I guess I need to take that shower if I'm going out." She scoots off the bed and heads toward the bathroom. I curse under my breath, grabbing my phone. I see Miles's name on the screen, and I give him a call back once I hear the shower start. Placing the phone between my shoulder and ear, I put on some gym clothes. I walk downstairs as Miles answers the phone.

"Hey, Lizzie is game for today. She can't wait to meet Stormy," he states.

"Great," Is all I can muster. My mood has drastically plummeted. I want to know what's going on in Stormy's mind. Sometimes I can't read her, and it worries me that we aren't in the same place.

"What's your problem? Something happen between when I talked to you this morning?" Miles asks. I walk into the gym and the lights illuminate as I walk through. I head straight for the boxing bag and give it a swift punch without my gloves. "Hey, are you alright, bro?"

"I don't know. Sometimes I feel like Stormy is at the same place I am and then I get glimpses that says she isn't. I don't know what to do. Am I moving too fast? I want her here with me. I want to be able to protect her. I love her for fuck's sake. I feel like I am going insane," I respond, sitting on the bench and cradling my hand in my other. I know it's going to bruise. I wasn't thinking and just let my anger get the best of me.

"Listen to me. You can't rush her. It will make her run. I know from experience. She knows how you feel, and she hasn't left yet. If she didn't feel something then she still wouldn't be there. Just take a breather and calm the fuck down," he says.

"You're right. It's just these feelings and shit are for the birds. I hate feeling vulnerable," I confess. I let out a deep breath and scrub my hand over my face.

"Get your workout in and then shower your sweaty ass. Lizzie and I will be there in about an hour or so. You know women, who knows when she will be ready," He chuckles.

"Alright, thanks man. See you soon." I hang up the phone and set it on the bench. Popping in my EarPods, I wrap my hands. Hitting my bag will take out the aggression and confusion that I'm feeling. Setting a timer on my phone, I begin pounding away. All thoughts leave me allowing me to concentrate on my punching bag. I get lost in the rhythms and my chest feels lighter with every swing. This is exactly what I needed.

TWENTY EIGHT

Stormy

T he shower feels amazing on my tense muscles. I was going to tell him I loved him until his phone rang. It pulled me back to reality and scared me. I know I love him but knowing it and telling him are two very different things. I know he's probably wondering if I feel the same way and I do. It's just so hard to tell him. And it's not because I think he will hurt me. I don't know what my problem is. I feel like a bomb ready to go off. I almost want to take my anxiety medicine. Not that he is giving me anxiety, just this situation is. I can't keep using my medicine as a crutch like I do. My therapist would be upset with me.

As I step out of the shower, I listen for Sebastian, but I don't hear him. I wrap myself in a towel and brush my teeth. Going to my new closet, that feels weird to say, I pick out a deep plum sweater dress with a plunging neckline I'm sure Sebastian will love. I also grab my black knee-high boots, as well. Laying the dress out on the bed, I notice the breakfast tray is still in here. I take it to the kitchen and clean off the plates. Walking back to the room, I hear Sebastian's grunts coming from somewhere in the apartment. I follow the noise and find him working out in his gym. I stand and watch him hitting the punching back with such force it sounds like it will bust. I wonder if he always hits it this hard or if he is upset about something. Namely about me not telling him I love him yet.

Turning around, I leave him to do his workout and head back to the bedroom. I'm not sure what time Lizzie will be here, but I want to be ready when she is. I put on a matching set of bra and panties and walk back into the bathroom with my brush, blow dryer and curling iron. I don't feel like straightening my hair today so I'm going to curl it instead. I brush out the tangles and dry my hair. Before I start curling my hair, I go back to the closet and get my makeup.

I finish getting ready by putting on my dress and boots. I'm just finishing up when Sebastian walks into the room. He whistles as he comes over to me and twirls me around.

"I don't think I should let you out looking like this. Damn, baby. You're stunning," he says with a crooked smile on his face. He looks so sexy all sweaty in a pair of low hanging shorts. I would jump him right now if I didn't need to be dressed already.

"Well thank you. When is Lizzie supposed to be here?" I ask, as he rubs a towel over his face and chest, ridding himself of the excess sweat.

"Anytime now. That's why I need to jump in the shower." He drops my hand and walks toward the bathroom. I feel like I should say something to him but before I know it, I hear the shower running and I've lost my window.

Cursing myself, I go back into the closet to retrieve a jacket. I saw on my weather app that it might snow today. I've never seen snow and I can't wait for the first snow of the season. Either way, even if it doesn't snow, it's supposed to be cold and wet. I take one last look in the mirror to apply some dark plum lipstick. Taking a step back, I look at my reflection and I'm happy at what I see. I love the way this dress hugs my curves and shows off my ladies up top.

As I turn around and see the unmade bed, I decide now would be a good time to make it. I have some extra time and Sebastian is still in the shower, so I don't really have anything else to do. I guess I'm a little nervous to be meeting Miles and his wife. I truly hope they like me. If they don't, I'm not sure what that would mean for Sebastian and me. Would he take their advice, or would he not talk to them anymore? My anxiety levels rise as I think about everything that can go wrong.

Sebastian's shower cuts off and it isn't long before he is coming out of the bathroom with a towel tied around his waist. I'm sitting on the bed and getting my fill of his spectacular body as he moves past me.

"Is everything alright?" I question.

He looks at me for a moments and nods. "Yeah, just a hard workout today." He replies as he goes into his closet for some clothes.

"I know. I heard you so I followed the sound since I haven't gotten a tour of this huge place yet. I saw you punching that bag. Does that hurt your hands?" I ask, trying to figure out what's going on in his head. He seems like he is shutting me out. He doesn't want to hang out with me today and he didn't shower with me. It just seems like I have done something wrong, and I need to know what so I can fix it.

"I didn't see you come down there. You could have said something, but I probably wouldn't have heard you since I had my

EarPods in," he says from the closet. He doesn't even come out to talk to me. He gets dressed while he is in there. I take a deep breath and ask him what I want to know.

"Is there something wrong? Did I do something?" I ask, wringing my hands together. Since my hand is mostly healed, I'm able to get back to my nervous habit. He comes out of the closet dressed in a navy Henly, jeans and boots. He looks absolutely edible. He has his long sleeve pushed up to his elbows, showing off some of his ink. He didn't tell me what all of his tattoos represent but I hope to one day find out unless he is about to break up with me. "You can tell me if you want me to go back to my apartment if you're getting tired of me. You started acting weird and I don't really know how to act now," I confess.

He comes over to where I'm sitting on the bed and leans down in front of me, taking my hands in his. "You didn't do anything wrong. I got caught up in my head and I needed to get down to the gym and blow off some steam. I'm sorry you thought you did something wrong. I'm not good with communicating except to my brother, but I will try and be better for you." He presses his lips to both my hands and looks up from me with a sad look on his face. I don't ever want to see that look on his again and I'm the one that put it there.

"I did do something wrong if you had to run away from me. Please tell me so I can fix it. I don't want to lose you, Sebastian," I rush out.

"Hey, don't talk like that. I'm not going anywhere. I promise you. I just got stuck in my head and I needed to work some things out. Please don't think I am going anywhere. I love you, Stormy." He squeezes my hands and then leans up and kisses me. It's gentle but possessive at the same time. It's hard to explain but it feels like a promise. He's giving me this opening and I don't want to waste it. I'm going to tell him I love him. It's scary but it feels right. *He* feels right.

Just as I open my mouth, the doorbell rings and I curse under my breath. I cannot believe this is happening for a second time. Fucking hell. Sebastian stands from his place on the floor, kissing my head on the way up.

"Have I told you how magnificent you look? I can't wait to take this dress off you later." He says with a wink. He holds his hand out for me to take and lifts me from the bed. We walk together toward the living room, and I begin to get butterflies in my stomach. Sebastian opens the door and a tall hulking man steps through that looks so much like Sebastian it's scary. This must be Miles obviously. Lizzie comes in next, and I realize how gorgeous she is. She makes me miss having my black hair.

Sebastian clears his throat and introductions are made.

"Stormy, this is my brother Miles and his wife, Lizzie."

"Miles, Lizzie, this is my Stormy." We all shake hands with various "it's nice to meet you's" thrown in along with some "happy birthdays".

Lizzie comes over and gives me a tight hug and at first I tense but something about her seems familiar and I take in the embrace. Miles comes over and wants a hug as well but his is more of a side hug which is perfectly fine with me.

Sebastian speaks first. "So, what are you ladies doing today?" he asks Lizzie. I guess she is in charge since it is my birthday, which is fine with me because I don't feel like making any decisions.

"Well, I thought we could go to SOHO and look around then grab some lunch. Does that sound good to you?" she asks, looking at me.

"Sure, I actually went there with my roommate not too long ago. It was great except for this one shoe store we went into didn't want to help me because they didn't think I could afford the shoes. The woman was a real bitch," I remark, thinking back to that woman who thought she could treat me like trash just because we came in wearing rain-soaked clothing.

"Oh, you will have to show me where that store is, and we will go in there again. Hopefully she will be working," Lizzie replies.

"I guess we could. I did ruin a pair of Louboutins I got from there in the rain," I state.

"You didn't tell me someone was mean to you. Do you re-member her name? I'll get her ass fired," Sebastian cuts in.

"It's not a big deal. I handled it. I made her go get another pair for me and then told her to get another person to check us out because I didn't want her to get the commission. It really wasn't that big of a deal," I reply.

"Oh, we are totally going to be the best of friends. We already like the same type of shoes, and you can back talk all the bitchy salespeople," She squeals, and it makes me smile. These are the types of people I need to surround myself with. I'm sure they already know who I am, and they don't care. Lizzie links her arm in mine.

"Got everything you need?" she asks. I make sure I have my phone in my purse and jacket.

"Yep, I've got everything," I say.

Sebastian comes over and gives me a kiss. Thankfully I used lip stain, or he would be wearing my lipstick on him. "I'll see you later. Call if you run into any trouble," he says with a stern voice. "Nicolas will be driving, so there shouldn't be a problem," he states. I just nod my head.

"You all have fun with whatever secrets you're doing today," I remark, looking up into his eyes. Lizzie and Miles say their goodbyes and we are heading down the elevator a moment later. I feel a sense of freedom being able to leave the apartment without Sebastian freaking out, but he was the one that made this day possible. I smile at the thought of him going through the trouble of getting his sister-in-law to take me out today.

We get down to the lobby and I see a black Bentley waiting for us. When the driver sees us approach, he gets out and opens the door for us.

"Nicolas, this is Stormy Brooks. She is Sebastian's girlfriend, so you will be seeing a lot of her," Lizzie remarks.

"How do you do, Miss Brooks. My name is Nicolas Irmani, but you can call me Nicolas," he says.

"Thank you, Nicolas, you can call me Stormy, as well. Thank you for taking us around today."

"It's my pleasure." I slide into the car behind Lizzie and buckle up. Nicolas shuts the doors and walks around to the driver's seat. He rolls the middle window down. "Where am I taking you ladies?" he asks.

Lizzie pipes up and answers. "We want to go shopping in SOHO."

"Yes, ma'am," he answers and rolls the window back up.

"So, tell me everything about you and Sebastian. Miles thought he would be the forever bachelor," she remarks and my cheeks flame. I'm not sure what all I should tell her, definitely nothing about the scorching hot sex between us.

"We actually met at a fundraiser. I was there with the catering crew, and I didn't know who he was. He came back into the catering tent right as I was walking out with a tray of entrees, and we ran into each other. We both started yelling at each other and that was really it. I got fired and he walked off. Then Mary with HR hired me to work for him, which I didn't know at the time, or I probably wouldn't have taken the job. I thought he was an asshole." I take a breath and continue. Lizzie sits enthralled like I'm telling her the most interesting story ever. "We physically ran into each other in the lobby of the company as well and he followed me to Mary's office where we argued with her that we couldn't work together but by the end of the day, we were. I remained indifferent towards him until one night he took care of me in the pouring rain, and I guess like they say, the rest is history," I finish.

Lizzie claps her hands together and smiles. "I love that. So, an enemies to lovers story. That gives me an idea for a new book." She remarks and that sparks my memory that she is a writer.

"I forgot that you were an author. What's that like? Do you use your name or a pen name? I want to know if there is something I've read by you." I question.

"I use the pen name E. M. Austen. And have you read *The Write Knight*? It's kind of based off how Miles and I met. Of course, its fiction and names were changed but..." She trails off. "It's part of a series so I have been working on the third one. I love writing. Miles mentioned that you are in school for art. I would have done that if writing fell through." She rambles on about different art schools and the kinds of things she enjoys. She talks most of the way to SOHO and I'm fine with that. I don't like being this talkative.

Once we arrive, we thank Nicolas and he says he will be close by in case we need him, Sebastian's orders. I roll my eyes at his over-protective side but then again, I remember last night when he came to my rescue. Lizzie sees me and laughs out.

"Miles is the same way. He doesn't like me going anywhere alone. And half the time there is security with me. I wouldn't be surprised if someone is following to make sure no one messes with us." She says.

"I could see Sebastian doing something like that without telling me for sure. He is definitely the alpha caveman type." I remark.

"That's so weird because I've never seen that side of him until we came to the apartment. I could see it in his eyes that he didn't really want you to go even though it was him that put this all together." She states.

"Do you know what he has planned?" I ask. I can give it a shot and see if she will tell me or not. I'm sure she knows.

"Nope, I'm not telling. You'll have to wait and see." She says, as we walk into a clothing store.

"So, what are we looking for today? Anything in particular?" I ask because there isn't much that I need. Maybe some new lingerie for Sebastian. I know he'd love that.

"I am under strict orders to buy anything you like, no exceptions." She must see the shock in my eyes because she adds, "I know, it's a lot to get used to dating a billionaire but they want to spoil us, and I had to get over it quick because Miles' love language is gift giving. It was hard in the beginning because I didn't think

I needed the things he was buying me." She remarks as she goes down an aisle looking at mini dresses.

"I'm not letting him buy me anything, besides I don't need anything." I reply.

"You need something to wear to the funeral." She comes back with a dress and holds it up to me. Lizzie is a little taller than me, but she is absolutely stunning. I can see why Miles married her. She is the whole package, beautiful, smart, and outgoing.

"I don't think I'm going to the funeral. Sebastian didn't mention it to me, other than to help plan it." I confess.

"Of course, you will be going. You are a couple now. He isn't going to want to let you out of his sight." I shrug but she just nods her head. A sales woman walks over to us while I'm browsing the racks.

"Is there anything I can help you ladies with?" She asks, looking at Lizzie, not me. I don't know what it is about salespeople not giving me the time of day. Maybe it's my hair color. I have no idea.

"Yes, we need a room started and do you have champagne? We will need two glasses. Also, please start taking these dresses to our room. Thank you. What was your name?" Lizzie asks.

"Vivian and I will be right back with your champagne. Let me take those items for you." She grabs the dresses from Lizzie's arms and takes them toward the back of the store.

"Wow, I don't know why you were impressed with me. You just handled her like a pro." I state.

"I had to learn quick. It's either sink or swim in these stores. They turn their noses up at us if we aren't wearing the perfect outfit or if we aren't wearing makeup. I hated shopping at the beginning of Miles and my relationship. You will get the hang of it." She says.

"I'm not so sure about that." I mutter to myself. I look around and find a few things that I would like to try on but not nearly as many things as Lizzie. I wish we could go somewhere with jeans and t-shirts in stock. This stuff isn't my usual wardrobe. However, I can wear it to work. I decide to pick up a few more things and then we head to the back room to try on everything. I take a minute and shoot Sebastian a text.

Stormy:

> You aren't paying for my clothes.

It doesn't take him long to reply, probably because he is wearing his Apple watch.

Daddy:

> Is that any way to talk to Daddy? I *am* buying whatever you decide you want today.

I laugh that I still have him in my phone as Daddy. I probably need to change that in case someone sees it.

Stormy:

> Then I won't get anything.

I know I am being a brat, but I don't want him to spend all this money on me. I don't want him to think he can buy me.

Daddy:

> I'm going to text Lizzie. She has my card anyways and has specific orders to buy anything you like. I'll see you when you get home, Angel.

I know that was the end of the discussion, but I want to keep arguing. Another thing he said stuck out to me. He called his apartment home. I haven't had a home in so long. I suppose when I was really young I considered my parents' house a home but as I grew up it was more of a place I lived in, not called home. Sebastian saying home makes my stomach fill with butterflies.

Once we have tried on everything, Lizzie gathers everything up and tells Vivian that they are the items we decided on. I choose not to argue with her. She is just the messenger after all. I will pay Sebastian back later.

We ring everything up and head out the door. Nicolas is waiting for us to take our bags. Then we are on to the next store. More shopping and more clothes and more and more money we spend until I start to feel guilty. Nicolas is always on the curb waiting for us to take our bags when we finish in a store. Lizzie must text him when we are checking out or something.

We walk down the sidewalk, and the temperature seems to be dropping so I pull my jacket together tighter. We walk up to the shoe store that I was talking about, and I stop Lizzie from going in.

"Hey this is the store I was telling you about. Maybe we can go down to the next shoe store we see." I tell her.

"This is where they were mean to you?" She questions.

"Yeah, they lady was a real bitch." I reply.

"Oh, we are definitely going in then. Come on." She takes my hand and I reluctantly follow behind her. Sure, enough when we get in there, I see the woman in question, and she sees me. Unsure how she is going to handle this, I urge Lizzie to go somewhere else, but she stands firm.

"She isn't going to walk all over you. Is that her? The one eying you?" She asks. I nod my head and look away. Another salesperson walks up to us at that exact moment.

"What can I help you ladies with?" He asks.

"We need lots of shoes and my friend here was telling me that she had a bad experience in here before. She didn't even want to come in." Lizzie explains.

"Well, I'm the manager and I'll personally take care of you girls today." Lizzie smiles at the woman across the store and then follows the man to the shoe section. We both pick out Louboutins and I get a new pair that I will make sure I don't ruin on the first day of wearing them.

"I'm getting kind of hungry. How about you?" Lizzie asks me.

"I could go for some food." I say.

We check out, spending an exorbitant amount. The saleswoman helps gather our bags and hands them to me as I give her smile. Nicolas is there waiting for us when we come out but instead of shuttling us to another store, this time we get into the car so he can drive us to a place to eat.

"That was fun. You got so many beautiful things." Lizzie says to me.

"It was fun. Thank you for getting me out of that apartment. It's been hard with everything going on in the media. I'm thankful that no one recognized me today." I confess. Once we get to the restaurant, Nicolas lets us out and says to let him know when we are ready.

"You know, I could really use a trip to the salon to fix my roots, if you know of a good place that might have an opening today." I express.

"I know the perfect place. I can call them when we get inside." Lizzie suggests.

"Yeah, that would be great. Thanks." I tell her.

We get into the restaurant, order, and eat rather quickly in order to make the appointment that Lizzie made for me. Of course, Nikolas is there waiting for us when we emerge from the restaurant.

"Can you take us to Stylez, in downtown Manhattan? It'll be our last stop before we take Stormy back to Sebastian's." Lizzie tells him as we get into the car.

"Phew, I'm exhausted. When you shop, you mean business." I chuckle.

"That's the only way to do it. Then you don't have to do it as often. I don't particularly love it unless I have someone to go with. My best friend Sarah has been busy with her new boyfriend, so I haven't seen her in a while. I was excited to come out with you." She remarks.

Once we arrive at the salon, I tell them that I need my roots touched up and a small haircut adding some layers in with it. It only takes a few hours, and we are back out in the cool New York air. I feel like a new woman. With new clothes and hair, I feel like I can tackle anything. That is until I see a magazine that has my face on it. I walk over to the street seller, picking up the magazine and reading something I have only told three people. I told Sebastian, my therapist, and Lana. She sold me out for a quick buck! Lana told the story about my experience watching my husband die on the kitchen floor that day. Her face is on the magazine as well with a microphone to her mouth. Why did she do this?

Lizzie must see the tears welling in my eyes because she buys the magazine and ushers me to the car. Once we get in, I let the tears flow not caring who sees. I reread the headline over and over.

Stormy Jacks POV of the Night Blaine Jacks Died: Insider Scoop

My phone chimes in my pocket. I pull it out seeing the last name I want to.

Picasso:

We need to talk.

I stare at the simple four words but all I can think about is throwing my phone into traffic and letting her get the picture that way. I decide to write back. With blurry eyes I type.

Stormy:

Why did you do it?

I don't expect a real reason. There isn't a valid reason to begin with. She did something she promised me she wouldn't do. Did I misjudge her? I'm usually a good reader of someone's character. Although now that I think of it, people started taking pictures of me right as I got on stage the night we went out. How am I just remembering this now? How would those people have known unless they were tipped off?

Picasso:

> Just let me explain.

Stormy:

> There is nothing to explain. You got what you needed. I do have one question for you. Did you tell people who I really was the night we went out?

I see dots appear then disappear over and over until she finally writes back.

Picasso:

> Yes.

One word has never packed a punch more in my whole life.

Twenty Nine

Sebastian

My interior designer was able to come and clear out the bedroom furniture and add bookshelves and storage for all the supplies Miles and I bought. After running around town and getting everything ready for Stormy, Miles and I sit down to drink a beer.

"Thank you for everything, man. I owe you and Lizzie. I know they have been having fun. Nicolas texted earlier and said they have been all smiles all day." I remark as I open my beer. We clink bottles and I take that first sip, loving the bubbly sensation as it goes down.

"Not a problem, brother, happy to help." He puts his beer down and pulls out his phone that just went off with a text message. Probably Lizzie telling him they are on the way back. "Fuck, you are going to want to read this." He hands me the phone and my stomach drops.

Lizzie:

> Stormy just saw a news article about her that her roommate wrote and sent in. She was then interviewed for more information. We are on the way back. Be there in five.

"Fuck." I slam my beer down on the table, the foam overflowing from the top and going everywhere. She can't catch a fucking break. I'm going to sue Lana. She messed with the wrong man. I put on my shoes and jacket because I want to be downstairs when they arrive. Miles does the same as we head down in the elevator. I check my phone but the last message from Stormy was hours ago. I should have known something like this was going to happen. This could mess up everything that I have set up with the Jacks. This is their son and an inside scoop on everything that happened that night. They are going to think Stormy was the one that gave the interview. Fuck. I bet she is freaking out.

We get downstairs as the Bentley pulls up to the curb. The car barely comes to a stop before Stormy has the door open and is barreling toward me. I catch her in my arms, squeezing her tight. She has the magazine gripped tightly in her hands as she cries into my chest. My heart aches at the sight of her being upset and not knowing what to do about it. In this moment, my most important job is to calm my girl, then I will deal with Lana.

"Shh, Angel, I'm right here. We will get this taken care of; I promise." I vow as I rub my hand over her back in soft, soothing circles.

"It's just I never thought she would do this to me. She was so supportive when I first met her. I never want to see her again. I need to get my things from there though, Sebastian." Stormy looks up at me with anguish in her eyes and I want to wipe it all away.

"I will get your stuff, baby. I need to grab your bags from today and we can talk about it when we get upstairs." I tell her as I lower her to her feet. She wobbles for a moment, and I hold on to her until she's stable. Nicolas hands me all of the bags and I thank him for taking care of the girls.

Lizzie comes to give Stormy a hug. "I'm so glad I got to meet you. We had fun until that bitch ruined everything. Text me later if you want to talk." She says as she takes Miles' hand.

"It was good to meet you, Stormy. We'll take care of this. This chick isn't going to get away with this." Miles says and it makes me proud to have him as my brother. He is already taking her side and I couldn't be more thankful. As they leave, Stormy and I make our way back up to our apartment. I guess since Lana pulled a bitch move, technically Stormy only has me to live with and I couldn't be more thankful for that. I want her to be with me willingly, but I also want her there as soon as possible. Now, she won't be going back to her old apartment.

"Did you at least have fun with Lizzie until everything happened?" I ask.

"I really did. She seems like someone I could really enjoy being around. I got my hair done. Did you notice?" She questions.

"Of course, I did. I love the new cut. Did you get the color done too? It looks lighter." I assess.

"Yeah, I needed to get my roots done. Lizzie knew of a salon that was able to get me in today. So, Nicolas took us over there after lunch." The elevator opens up and Stormy walks out with me behind her with all her bags. She opens the door to the apartment like she owns the place, and it makes me heart happy. I can't wait to show her what I did to the place. I take the bags to the bedroom and come back to find her staring out the windows. The first snow is falling. Coming up behind her, I wrap my arms around her waist. I bend over and kiss the shell of her ear.

"I missed you today, but I can't wait for you to see what I did for you." I whisper.

"Can we stand here for a moment. I've never seen snow before. Growing up in Florida never allowed us such weather. We would have about a week of winter temperatures and then it went back to warmer weather." She admits.

"I didn't know that you've never seen snow. You sure came to the right state for snow, baby."

"Mhm." She murmurs as she leans back against me. I'm enveloped by her warmth. We stand and stare at the glimmering flakes as they fall in a heavy succession. They begin collecting on my balcony and I'm momentarily speechless as I watch from her point of view. It's easy to take simple things like this for granted, but it's undeniably beautiful.

"Come with me, Angel." I whisper in to her ear.

"Okay." She says as she turns from the window to look me in the eyes. Her tears from earlier have dried and her eyes are full of wonder. I hope my surprise doesn't change that. I'm nervous to show her what I did. What if she thinks it's too much? All I can do is hope for the best and be prepared for the worst. I feel like I'm holding my breath as we ascend the steps to the second floor. I take her hand in mine as we make our way to the bedroom that I converted into her studio. I pull out a silk tie from my pocket that I wanted to use on her.

"I'm going to blindfold you. Is that okay?" I question. Stormy nods her head and closes her eyes. I take the opportunity to take her lips in mine. She tastes sweet like her strawberry ChapStick that she must have put over her lipstick. She moans and throws her arms around my neck, pulling me closer. I clutch the tie in my hand as I pull her body closer to mine. I need that connection with her. My tongue delves into her mouth and tangles with hers. We stand there for a few moments lost in each other. It's the only place I want to lose myself. Stormy is my beginning and end. When she came crashing into my life is when I actually started living. I was coasting along until this hurricane stirred up my whole life.

I reluctantly pull away and tie the blindfold around her eyes. Kissing her one last time, I lead her to her studio. I open the door and the natural light spills through the space. I stand Stormy in front of me so she will have the best view of everything when I remove the blindfold.

"Are you ready?" I breathe into her ear.

"Yes. I want to see." She says as she clutches my hand tighter. I undo the tie and it falls slowly to the floor. She gasps as she looks around the room. We stand in silence as she takes everything in. I set up a large easel to the side of the window so she would get the best lighting. Various sizes of canvases line the walls with hundreds of professional grade brushes. I bought acrylic and oil-based paint. I also installed lighting fixtures throughout the room so she can turn on which ever one she is working close to. There are several different stations in this room. I added a sketching desk with all supplies she could ever need. I even added a bookshelf and a reading nook area filled with blankets, pillows, and the best lighting I could buy.

Stormy walks into the studio and softly runs her fingers over the different surfaces in the room. She gets back to the floor-to-ceiling windows and puts her hand to her chest. I knew that would be her favorite part. That's why I picked this room. It faces the Hudson River and it's one of the best views in the apartment. She turns back to me with tears in her eyes.

"This is-I can't even describe it. No one has ever done anything like this for me." She finally says. I walk up beside her and take her face in my hands.

"I'm not just anyone, Angel. I'm your man. I wanted to do this for you. I wanted you to know how serious I am about us. I want you to feel at home here. This space is all for you. Everything in here is for your use and only you. It can be your own little get away whenever I'm being a jackass because I can't promise that I will be perfect, in fact, I know I'll be far from it. But I'll try my best every day to show you what you mean to me." I confess.

"Sebastian, I-I love you." She murmurs with tears streaming down her face. "I love you. And not just because of all this," she gestures to the room, "I was going to tell you earlier, but the phone call interrupted me, and I got scared and ran away. I'm sorry. I know that I upset you this morning." I put a finger to her lips to quiet her from any more apologizing.

"I love you, Stormy. You have made me the luckiest man alive by loving me." I crash my lips down on hers and devour her. She jumps into my arms, I catch her ass in my hands. Locking her legs around my waist, I carry her over to the reading nook. Leaning down, I gently place her down on the pillows and blankets that I arranged there. I didn't think of this when I was doing it, but I guess we have to christen this room somehow. I chuckle to myself as I pull my shirt over my head and lean over her body. Our lips lock again like magnets, always looking for its other side. I groan at the sheer sweetness of Stormy's mouth against mine. I will never get enough of her.

I break away kissing her cheeks, forehead, nose, chin and back to her lips. I trace my lips along her jaw and down her neck to that sweet spot behind her ear. She trembles beneath me.

"Sebastian, I need you. Please." She pleads.

"Patience, baby." I say as I lean up on my knees, looking down at the most magnificent sight I have ever seen. Stormy's lips are red and swollen, you can see where my stubble scratched along her chin. Ever so slowly, I push up her sweater dress until I can see her black thong peeking through. I groan at the sight and my mouth waters wanting a taste. "I need to get these boots off you even though they are sexy as fuck. You will wear them soon while I fuck you. But not right now." I take one leg and slowly unzip the boot, while keeping my eyes on hers. Repeating it with the other, I set them to the side and pull off her mismatched socks and I can't help but to smile at my girl.

"Don't make fun of me! I don't care what sock I have on when I wear boots. I actually like when they don't match for some reason." She shrugs her shoulders but beams up at me and I can't wait any long to sink into her warm heat. Taking the thong in my fingers, I shimmy it off her and throw it to the side.

"Sit up, baby. Let's get this dress off of you." Stormy leans up and throws her hands in the air for me to pull the dress up and over. Fuck me, she has on a matching black lace bra that barely contains her mouth-watering breasts. Reaching behind her, I unclasp it and it falls from her shoulders. She rests back down on the blankets and looks at me expectantly.

"Now, it's your turn." I nod. I stand to pull my jeans down my body. My cock is painfully hard and leaking, knowing where it's meant to be. As I lay back down, I situate my mouth at her entrance. A groan rumbles through my chest when I smell her sweet arousal. Knowing I do that to her is a heady sensation.

"Fuck, baby, you are soaked." She nods her head and I dive in to her depths. My tongue lavishes her clit in circles, slow then fast and repeat. Reaching up, I tweak one of her nipples between my fingers as she cries out from pleasure. "You like that, Angel?" I ask. My words vibrating her core. She lets out a strangled "yes" as her legs begin to shake and pull in closer to my head. I continue licking and sucking, not wanting to waste a drop of her delicious nectar. And just like that she goes off like a firecracker. Her hips rise from the floor, trying to get closer to me. I hold her down to keep on licking and eating all she has to give me.

"Yes! Oh Sebastian, that's it! I'm coming!" she shouts as she explodes around me. I switch nipples, pulling and pinching, to continue her orgasm for as long as I can. Leaning up, I lick my lips, gather some of her wetness and rub is along my shaft. She is so slippery, so ready for me. Crawling up her body, I place my arms on either side of her shoulders, holding her face in my hands.

"I love you, Angel." I murmur as I push inside of her slowly. Her eyes roll back at my cock thrusting inside her. I continue to go slow, back and forth, back and forth. This isn't fucking, it's making love and it's the most erotic yet intimate sex I've ever had. I bring my lips down on hers, having her taste herself on my tongue. Sex with her is like being outside during a lightning storm, feeling the electric current passing through you. She is electric. One touch has me coming back for more. "You're mine, aren't you? I'm not going anywhere, Stormy." I whisper into her ear.

"Yes, I'm yours, Sebastian. More than you know. I love you," She returns. I continue thrusting, having to hold off my own release. Her words make me want to shoot off right then. I kiss her with everything I have. I kiss her with more passion than I knew I had. I want to show her the desire I have for her, something words can't express, only actions. And I will keep showing her those actions for as long as we live. I want to marry this woman. I need to. I need to have her connected to me in all ways.

"Come for me. Come on my cock. I want to feel you squeezing me. Milk me, Angel. I want every last drop inside your tight cunt." Stormy whimpers at my words. It doesn't take long for her to begin clamping down on me, sending me over the edge as well. We both orgasm in unison. Her pussy hugs me tightly making it hard to continue pumping in and out. I come so heavily that I see stars and for a moment I feel like I might pass out, as it fades I come back down to Earth. That was epic. Our bodies intertwined is one of beauty. When we come together we make a perfect masterpiece.

"That's not what I intended to happen when I brought you in here. Nor was this what this spot was designated for. However, I'm not complaining," I tell her with a devilish grin.

"We had to christen the place, right? Now I can do some real art in here and every time I look over to this spot. I'll remember the first day you showed me this room." She clenches down on me one last time making chills run through my body. Never in my life has a woman captured my soul the way she has. I would follow her to the ends of the Earth.

"We did. We need to do that to the rest of the apartment. It's imperative," I tell her.

"Oh yeah? What will happen if we don't?" She asks playfully.

"Well, for one it would be a damn shame and second it's just good manners to give all the rooms the same amount of attention," I joke.

"Oh, you are full of shit." She replies and I can't help but to smile at the quick banter between us.

"I am and you have to deal with me," I remark with a wink.

"I do but I'm not complaining. I think I can make you domesticated before long," she says in jest.

"Oh, ha ha, I'm not a dog that needs to be trained. You better watch your mouth. Brats get punishments and I don't think you have had a proper one yet. You enjoyed the spankings too much." She blushes at my words, making me fall deeper in love. This woman can still blush with everything that we have done and been through together.

"Yes, sir. I'll be your good girl," She states.

"Good." I kiss her soft lips one more time and slide out of her, rolling us to our sides.

"Thank you for this room. It's better than anything I could have imagined," she says.

"Happy birthday, Angel." I reply, kissing her forehead and pulling her body closer to mine. I pull a blanket over us, and we lay there watching the snow fall from the windows across the room. Within minutes, I hear a soft snore coming from Stormy. I know she had a long day. First with shopping and then with everything that happened after she found that article. I'm sure she was physically and emotionally exhausted. I push the hair from her eyes and rest my head against one of the many pillows under me. Sleep eventually pulls me under as well.

THIRTY

Stormy

I wake to the sound of Sebastian shouting at someone. I don't hear the other person so he must be on the phone. I look around, trying to reacclimate myself to the room. I pick up my discarded clothes on the way to the en suite bathroom to clean up and get dressed. Looking around for a brush, all I find is a comb again. "I'm going to have to stock all these bathrooms with brushes." I think to myself. I finger comb through my hair, then wipe the makeup from under my eyes. Shrugging at the woman looking back at me, I exit the bathroom, gathering my boots I go off to find of Sebastian. It's not hard. I can hear him clearly as day as I follow his voice.

"That's not what we agreed on. She wasn't the one that did the interview. It was her fucking roommate," Sebastian yells into the phone.

"I'll go seventy-five thousand and not a cent more. I will deal with this Lana person myself," he says.

"Yes, I will contact my attorney and have them draw up new papers. Do you still agree to keep her name out of your mouths?" He seethes.

"Good. Then this conversation is over. My attorney will be in touch," he hangs up the phone and throws it to the couch. Scrubbing his hands over his face, he looks out the window at the snow or maybe just looking at nothing as he stands there motionless.

I drop my boots at the bedroom door and walk down the stairs. Sebastian turns and looks at me and his face goes from livid to happiness in one glance. I love having that effect on him, but I need to know what he was talking about and who he was talking to.

"Who was that?" I ask, gesturing to his phone.

"I didn't mean to wake you." He replies, dodging the question. Now I really want to know who he was talking to.

"Sebastian, tell me now. I know you were talking about me, and I want to know why," I hiss.

"Alright, come here." He sits on the couch and pats the seat next to him. "I didn't want you to find out like this, but I couldn't control my anger when he called and started accusing you of shit." My stomach drops and I know who he is talking about before he even says it. "I have been taking to Dennis Jacks. I called him to get him to stop talking to the press about you. I had to bargain with him for fifty thousand dollars." He takes a breath and continues, not taking his eyes off me. "I wanted to take care of this for you, but then he was made aware of the article circulating now that Lana put out and he thought you had gone to the press and thrown them under the bus." I don't even know what to say, but Sebastian isn't done speaking. "He called me furious this afternoon. He wants more money and I finally agreed only because I want to put this behind us. Please tell me you aren't mad. I hated the things they were saying about you, and I knew it was all fake news. I just want you to have the clean slate you wanted when you moved here," I sit and try to take in everything that he said.

"Wow, I don't know what to say. You shouldn't have gone behind my back, Sebastian. If we are going to be a couple then we have to talk things out before we do them. I'm not necessarily mad at you, just aggravated that I didn't know anything about it. I don't want you to pay them that money. It's my responsibility. I'll pay for it with what I have left of my parents' and Blaine's insurance policies," I reply, thinking of the amount of money that I have left. I have just enough to cover it, then I'll have to work my ass off to finish paying for college.

"No. That's out of the question. I'm paying him. End of discussion on that. As for him talking to the press, he will give a statement saying that what he's previously said was false and that'll be the last time he speaks to the tabloids without having legal repercussions. He'll be signing paperwork binding him to that agreement. There will also be an NDA about the money he'll receive." Sebastian has everything figured out. The only thing I disagree with is that he wants to pay them the money. They wanted the insurance money from Blaine's death and so it should be me that pays that.

"I'm glad that they won't be able to speak out against me again, but I am still paying them. They're my problem and I'm the one that needs to deal with them. It's sweet of you that you want to help me." He holds out his hand for me to take, when I do, he pulls me flush against his side and then pulls me into his lap. Damn him and his strong everything.

"Listen to me. I'm not going to say this again. You are my responsibility now. I want to be that for you. It's not a burden for me. I actually want to protect you, but you have to let me. You have to trust me to take care of you. Trust me that I will make the right decisions for the both of us. And we will talk things through together, but with this, I wanted to take that pain I saw in your eyes away. This money is nothing to me and you are everything. Please let me hold the weight you have been carrying for far too long. I want to shoulder that for you." His words bring tears to my eyes. They begin to run down my cheeks before I can answer him. I want what he said more than anything. I want to be free of this weight on my shoulders so damn bad but that means trusting someone fully with everything I have been through. What if it's too much for him?

"Sebastian, what if this is all too much for you?" I question.

"What do you mean?" he asks.

"I mean, what if this is all too much for you? I have been through so much shit, Sebastian. Even my childhood was shitty. That's a lot for someone to carry. I should know. I don't want to be a burden, especially to you. I guess I'm scared that everything will get fucked up. And I don't want that to happen. I love you." I sigh as I rest my head on his chest.

"Angel, look at me." I pick my head up to look at his beautiful shining green eyes. "You trust me with your body, now it's time for you to trust me with your heart. Trust that I will keep it safe for you. Let me past all the walls you have constructed around your heart. I want to see the side of you that you don't let other people see. I promise you that I will love you even more for it. Let me do this for you. I know what I'm getting in to. Believe me when I say that I can handle it. I know you're scared to be vulnerable because you've had to be so strong your entire life. But it's time for you to rest now. I've got this." He leans his forehead against mine, looking into my eyes. I let out a deep breath and nod.

"Okay. I trust you, Sebastian. I know you will take care of me." I give him a little smile before I take his lips in mine. I need the connection right now. I need the feeling of his flesh against mine. I open up for him and his tongue dives into my mouth. Wrapping my arms around his head, I pull him closer to me. He grasps my hips, moving me along his hard cock. I think he is always hard when I'm near. I think he is always ready to take me. He pulls away.

"Thank you." He cups my face with his large hands and kisses me again. This time with fierce possessiveness. I can feel the love he has for me in the way he touches me. I know that everything will be okay.

"Wait! What are we going to do about Lana? I never want to see that bitch again. And all my stuff is there. What am I going to do?" I ask, not meaning to have cut the kiss short but those thoughts just came to me, and I need to know what our plan is going to be. We haven't figured everything out yet.

"I will hire movers to go over there and get your things. I will accompany them so I will be able to show them your room. I will take care of Lana. I've already asked my lawyers to look into what can be done about her. They will get back to me next week. Don't you worry. She'll pay for this." He replies.

"Thank you, for everything. You think of it all, don't you?" I question.

"That's what I'm here for, baby." He says with a smirk. I playfully slap his chest as he scoops me up, throwing me on the couch. "I

guess I will be peeling this dress off of you for a second time today."
I bite my bottom lip and a growl leaves his mouth.

This powerful, commanding, sexy man is all mine. His heart speaks the language of my soul. He's the person I never saw coming that is changing my life. I love him.

We arrive at Broken Halo Tattoo shop a little before eight. Walking in, I already know I'm going to like this place. The atmosphere is fun and inviting. Everything is neat and clean, and I don't feel like I'm going to get hepatitis from just walking in. A tall muscular man with steel grey eyes comes up to us, slapping Sebastian on the back.

"What's up my man. Long time no see," he remarks.

"Yeah, I've been way too busy. This is Stormy. Storm, this is Zane. Today is her birthday and she wanted to get more ink done," he holds out his hand for me to take.

"Nice to meet you, Zane," I say.

"You too, darlin' and happy birthday. Any ideas what you want done?" he asks.

"Actually yes. I want a dandelion blowing in the wind going up my forearm all the way up to my shoulder. Then I want seeds that fly off to become dragons flying away. I want one or two small dragons to be flying up the side of my neck. Then in a script I want the words, This too shall pass. I drew it up if you want to take a look." I grab the paper from my purse. Unfolding it, I hand it to Zane.

"This is gorgeous. You drew this yourself?" I nod my head as I rock back and forth on my feet. I always get nervous when people look at my work.

"Damn, I might have to make you a job offer," he halfway jokes.

"I might take you up on that. My boss now is a real asshole." I look at Sebastian and laugh. He pinches my side and I squeal in surprise.

"Very funny. Your boss is the best you're going to get, sweetheart," he says with a wink.

"Alright you two, enough of that before I puke. Let me go back and draw this up for you. I will be back," Zane says as he takes his leave and heads for the back of the shop.

Sebastian and I take our seats on the couch in the front of the store. It doesn't take long for Zane to come back with my tattoo drawing. It is everything I was hoping it would be and more.

"How is this?" he asks.

"I love it. It's exactly how I imagined it," I gush.

"Good. Let me get you to fill out some paperwork while I go get my station ready for you." He hands me a clipboard and takes my license to make a copy. Once he comes back, I'm nearly done with the papers. He walks us back to his station and begins prepping everything. I take off my long sleeve shirt, leaving on the tank top I have underneath.

Sebastian lets out a low growl only I can hear, and I smile at him. Before long, I'm in the hot seat getting another tattoo. I love the feel on my skin. The pain helps numb the negative thoughts roaming through my mind.

Two hours pass and Zane finally announces that he's finished. He wipes me clean and takes me to the mirror to admire his work.

"It's absolutely amazing. I love it so much. Thank you, Zane," I say as I turn from side to side examining the new ink.

"I'm glad. This was a unique piece, and it was a pleasure to work on it for you," he states. He puts Saniderm on my arm and shoulder to keep it clean and dry. Then we head to the front to pay. Sebastian pulls out his card before I have the chance.

"Happy birthday, baby," he says as he hands his card over.

"You have already gotten me too much," I whine. "But thank you. I love it. I want to come back when you get one." I say to Sebastian.

"You will." He states matter-of-factly. "How about let's get home. I think you need some more TLC," he says with a wink.

We leave the tattoo shop and head back to his apartment, or home I should call it. I never knew a simple word could have such a strong effect on me and yet here we are going home, and I want to cry. The apartment isn't my home, Sebastian is.

Thirty One

Sebastian

Stormy and I spent the rest of the weekend tangled in each other's arms. We cooked and talked and spent more time getting to know one another. I have to say that I fell more and more in love with her by the second. Every time I thought I can't love her anymore; she opens her mouth or does something that proves me wrong.

It's Monday morning and we are up getting ready for Marie's funeral. Stormy has been tense leading up to this day, so I woke her the best way I knew how, with orgasms.

"Does this look okay?" She asks as she steps out of the closet in one of her new dresses. It's a long sleeve black lace dress that falls just above her knees. She's wearing a new pair of black high heels with red soles, the same kind that were ruined the day we were stuck in the rainstorm.

I walk over to her and bend down, catching her lips in mine. "You look ravishing. I can't wait to take this off of you later," I whisper in her ear.

"Stop that! We are going to be late!" She squeals as she ducks away from me laughing. "You need to finish getting dressed, Sebastian." Stormy checks her watch and takes a deep breath. I know things are going to be hard for her today.

"Take another deep breath, Angel. I will be right there with you today. Everything will be fine. You will meet my mother and we will go over to have dinner with her tonight. Miles and Lizzie will be there as a buffer so hopefully she leaves us alone for the most part."

"I'm not worried about meeting your mother. I'm nervous about this funeral. I've been to two terrible ones in my life, and I thought I was through with those for a while." She clasps her pendant around her neck and closes her eyes.

"I got you a little something." I hold out the velvet box and hand it over, keeping my eyes on hers. She takes the box in trembling hands and looks at me quizzically.

"When did you have time to get me something? We have been here all weekend," she states. She opens the box, and a soft gasp escapes her lips. I knew this would mean a lot to her.

"They're phoenix earrings. I know how much that symbol resonates with you. I saw them and knew you had to have them. They're platinum with tiny diamonds along the tails." I comment.

"Sebastian, they're gorgeous. Thank you so much!" She leaps into my arms, I pull her tight against me. "They're so perfect for me." I kiss her forehead and let her down.

"You're welcome. I don't know if they go with the dress, I just thought they would help you get through this day knowing how much you have risen from the ashes," I say.

"I didn't know the old Sebastian Knight could be so sentimental," She teases. "But of course, I will wear them today. I won't want to take them off!" She exclaims. She takes one of the earrings out and puts it in using the mirror on the dresser. She does the same with the other. She does a little dance and turns to me with the largest smile on her face.

"I love them so much. Thank you. You don't know what this means to me." I bring her close so I can examine the earrings and they look perfect in her ears. I'm thrilled that I could make her this happy today.

"I'm glad that you like them. Now, what was that you said about me being old? I think a spanking is needed." She takes off around the room, but I am right there behind her to catch her. I pull her back against me, feeling her take a deep breath. "Why don't we finish this little cat and mouse chase later, huh?" I nip at her ear and chills run up her neck at the touch. "Now be a good girl and let me finish getting dressed. Make sure you have everything you need because we won't be coming right back here after the funeral." I mention as I tie my necktie and slide on my suit jacket. I see her staring at me from across the room and I turn to look.

"You look so handsome all dressed up like that. Here let me fix your tie." She comes over and moves it around a bit to tighten it up. Looking in the mirror, she did fix the problem I was having. I look at us standing side by side, we look like a good-looking couple. I wrap my arm around her waist to pull her closer to me. I pull out my phone to take a picture. "How about one for the books." I tell her. I angle the phone to capture us both, when I am satisfied I press the camera button.

"You'll have to send me that. It looks like a good one of us." She says as she fluffs her hair for the tenth time.

"Relax, everyone is going to love you. Are you ready?" I ask. She nods her head and I take her hand in mine as we walk down the stairs to the main floor of the apartment. I retrieve her coat from the closet and mine as well. Placing hers around her shoulders, I lead her to the elevator.

On the garage floor, I decide to take my red Porche 911. It's been a while since she was out on the road, and I fancy a drive in her today. I open the door for Stormy and clasp her seatbelt into place, against her protests that she can do it herself. Jogging around to the driver's side, I slide in and crank the ignition. Since the garage is temperature controlled, it isn't freezing in the car. I turn on the heat anyways because it will get cool on our drive over to the cemetery.

It's an overcast day, calling for more snow. Stormy was excited to see more snow but then she realized it wasn't the best conditions for a funeral.

"How long will it take us to get there?" She questions.

"About twenty minutes. Not too long. Would you like to put something on the radio?" I ask.

"No, I like the quiet, if that's okay?"

"Sure." I place my hand on her thigh as we drive down the highway.

Once we arrive, we walk over to find Thomas so we can pay our respects. With everything going on this past week, I haven't been there for him like I needed to, the thought weighs heavy on me. I know Miles has been picking up my slack, but I have known the man for most of my life. I owe him some of my time, regardless of what has been going on with me.

"Thomas, how are you?" I pull him into a tight embrace. I can see his eyes moist with tears and I wish I could do anything to bring Marie back to him. I know how much he was truly still in love with her. Much like my father, their love lasted a lifetime.

"I'm taking it one day at a time, my boy." He says as he blows his nose in his handkerchief.

"Is there anything else I can do for you? Have the meals been arriving?" I question.

"Yes, yes. We have plenty. You have done enough my dear boy. Thank you." He says with a sniffle.

"I want you to meet a very special person in my life. This is Stormy Brooks, my girlfriend." I get a flutter in my chest at the word I've never used before.

"It's nice to meet you, Thomas. Sebastian has told me so much about you. I wish we were meeting under better circumstances." She holds out her hand for Thomas to take, but instead he pulls her into a hug.

"Anyone who can tame a Knight gets a hug from me. You are part of the family now, my dear," he says with a smile.

"Thank you." She replies. A line begins to form behind us, waiting for a chance to speak with Thomas.

"We'll catch up after the service. I believe there are some people that wish to speak with you." I say as I take Stormy's hand and lead her under the awning to where Miles and Lizzie are.

"Hey brother, Lizzie. How are you all?" I ask.

"Good. Wishing we didn't have a funeral to attend but I believe it turned out nicely." Miles responds.

"Yeah, I'm so sad for Thomas. He always spoke so fondly of Marie. I wish I would have had the chance to meet her." Lizzie supplies. "How are you doing, Stormy?" Lizzie inquires.

"I'm alright. Thank you for taking me out the other day. Sorry things got a bit hectic at the end." Stormy apologizes. I squeeze her hand letting her know that I'm here for her.

"There is no need for that, Stormy. It was a bitch move from your roommate." Lizzie responds.

"Where is mother?" I ask Miles as Lizzie and Stormy continue talking.

"She was running late the last time I heard from her. She was stuck in traffic." He supplies.

"Ah, there she is now." I say when I see her heading this way. She stops by Thomas and speaks to him first then comes toward us. Here we go.

"Mother, how are you?" I give her a hug and a kiss on the cheek.

"I'm well, darling. Now let me meet this woman of yours." She replies.

"Mother, this is Stormy Brooks. Stormy, this is my mother, Amelia Knight." Mother pulls her in a tight embrace, which Stormy returns.

"It's nice to meet you, ma'am." Stormy responds.

"Oh, please call me Amelia, dear. It's nice to finally put a face to a name. I hear you are the special one to finally tame my youngest." She chuckles to herself.

"I suppose I am. I think we both have done some taming, to be honest." Stormy recalls.

"Oh, I like her, Sebastian." She says to me. "You give me a call if he gives you any trouble. Us girls have to stick together." Mother says to Stormy.

"I will do just that, Amelia." Stormy smiles at me and winks. I roll my eyes and take her by the waist pressing a soft kiss to her head. The smell of her shampoo filters through my senses and I want to take her home this instant. Unfortunately, the officiant comes forward and asks everyone to take a seat.

"Thank you all for coming here today as we celebrate the life of Marie Anderson. She was a cherished friend to many and a truly loving wife to Thomas. She spent sixty-four wonderful years upon this Earth. She will be missed every day." The officiant takes a moment to look at Thomas and he nods. "Thomas would like to come up here and say a few words." He steps down from the podium and Thomas steps up.

"Thank you, David. I have been wracking my brain for several days trying to come up with the perfect eulogy for my beloved wife. I got angry and frustrated that everything I was writing didn't do justice to my amazing wife. But you see, there is no such thing as the perfect eulogy. Anything I say, she will hear and be smiling down from above. So here it is." Thomas takes a deep breath and begins again.

"To my beautiful, loving wife,

You were my best friend and my partner in life. We shared everything – our hopes, our dreams, our lives. My life's greatest years were spent with you, Marie, the love of my life. You loved everything about life, even the downsides – you embraced it all. Life was hard, but it was also worth it for you. From the moment I met you, I knew my life would be different and that I'd found 'the one'.

I'd never believed in finding 'the one'. But boy was I wrong. My world was turned upside down the moment I met you forty-three years ago. You came into my life like a crashing wave and took me out to sea. We were never separated again. I loved you with more love than I ever knew possible. You were my soulmate and I feel like you took a piece of me with you to heaven. At least you will always have that piece of me until we meet again, my queen.

Rest in peace my beautiful angel, your pain is now gone. My heart will be yours always and forever. And to you all here today, make sure you find that special someone and never let them go. Life is too short to not be with the one you love." As Thomas steps down, *Past Lives* by DJ Agos begins to play.

"Past lives couldn't ever hold me down
Lost love is sweeter when it's finally found
I've got the strangest feeling
This isn't our first time around
Past lives couldn't ever come between us
Sometime the dreamers finally wake up
Don't wake me I'm not dreaming

Don't wake me I'm not dreaming"

The congregation rises and some begin placing flowers next to Marie's grave. Lilies in every shape and color decorate her burial place. Thomas dabs his eyes as people wait to speak with him. I don't want to ever have to go through what he is going through right now. But I suppose it's better to have loved then not at all.

"That was beautiful." Stormy murmurs as a tear slides down her cheek. "I could feel his love pouring out of him." I offer her my handkerchief as more tears begin to flow down her cheeks. She dabs her cheeks and wipes under her eyes. "Is my makeup okay? Or do I look like a sad racoon?" She sadly jokes.

"You look as stunning as ever. How about we get out of here." She nods and we say our goodbyes. We save Thomas for last because I want more people to have cleared out by the time we get to him. Thomas sees us coming and he excuses himself from who he is speaking with.

"Thank you for being here. It means the world to me and also, I know Marie was happy you came." He says.

"There is no other place we would have rather been today." I reply.

"Thank you for all the arrangements. The lilies were the best part. I'm not sure how you found so many but thank you." He responds.

"Stormy was in charge of the flowers." I squeeze her hand in mine.

"Thank you, Miss Brooks. It was truly magical." He takes his hand and places it over hers. I love how welcoming everyone has been of Stormy. I didn't think anyone would be, it's just nice to see the support I have.

"You are more than welcome. It was my pleasure. Please let us know if there is anything else we can do." She remarks.

"You've got a good one here, Sebastian. Don't let her go." He winks and then he's off talking to the next person in line.

"I don't have any intention of letting you go." I say to Stormy.

"Good. I wouldn't want to burn your apartment down." She smirks.

"You mean our apartment." I mention as she blushes and nods. Holding her hand, I lead her to my car, opening the door for her, I buckle her inside, then I run around to my side and slide in. "How about we take a drive until it's time to be at my mother's house for dinner?" I ask as I crank the engine. Small snow flurries begin to cover the windshield.

"I would like that." Stormy confesses as we pull out of the parking lot and head down the road.

THIRTY TWO

Stormy

We arrive at Sebastian's childhood home a few hours later. It's a gated entry that requires a code. Once inside, we drive down a long driveway with beautiful trees lining the road. Snowdrop plants sprinkle the grounds, a beautiful sight amongst the falling snow. As we pull up to the house, I am amazed by its beauty. It's a tall sweeping estate with a homey feel. Sebastian parks the car and comes around to let me out. A cobble stone path leads to the front steps and Amelia is there to greet and welcome us to her home.

"Welcome, welcome you two." Amelia brings me in for a hug then does the same with Sebastian. He leans over and kisses her cheek.

"Thanks for having us, Mother." He responds.

"Thank you, Amelia. We brought some wine to go with dinner." I gave her the bottle that we stopped to pick up on the way. It was my idea because Sebastian said we didn't need to bring anything. That's a man for you.

"How sweet of you, dear. Well come inside and get out of this cold weather." She gestures toward the door, and we step through. Immediately, I'm blasted with the most wonderful homecooked smell. Something I haven't had the pleasure of in a very long time. I inhale a deep breath and smile

Sebastian comes up to me and takes my jacket. I shimmy out of it, as he hangs it in the closet by the door. He takes his off and does the same, joining me in the kitchen.

"Something smells wonderful." I remark, looking around at the source.

"Mother is the best cook, unless you count grandmother. She taught her everything she knows." Sebastian whispers in my ear.

"I heard that, darling. But it's true. She did teach me everything I know while I was growing up in Italy." She supplies as she takes a large spoon and begins mixing something in a very large crockpot. "I knew we were going to have a busy day, so I put all the ingredients in here this morning. Having it simmer all day makes the flavor ten times better. I'll be serving Italian beef stroganoff and garlic bread." His mother announces.

"That sounds wonderful. I've never had that before. Do you need any assistance in the kitchen?" I inquire.

"No, definitely not. Sebastian why don't you open this bottle of wine and take Stormy on a tour of the house." She responds.

"Sure." He answers. Taking the automatic bottle opener and placing it over the wine we brought, it drills down and pulls the cork from the bottle. After filling two glasses, Sebastian hands one over me.

"Thank you." I say with a smile.

340

"You're welcome. Come with me." He takes my hand in his as we leave the kitchen. "Where would you like to start?" He questions.

"I actually want to see the room you grew up in." I answer. He twirls me around and brings me to his chest. I squeal out in laughter as I'm thrust against his hard masculine body. I'm careful not to spill my wine on us.

"My room, really? Out of everything here?" He asks with a grin.

"Yes. I want to see what teenager Sebastian was like." I laugh and pull away from him. "Lead the way, mister." I insist. We head up the stairs and he leads me to his bedroom. "Wow, very nice." I announce as I look around. "What teenager actually has a king size bed in their room?"

"I did. Look at me, I'm a big guy. I needed the space. Miles had one as well." Sebastian shuts the door behind us and turns to me with a glint in his eyes. "We could test it out if you want." He smirks as he takes my glass and sets both of ours on his desk.

"Your mother will hear us, Sebastian." I halfway argue as he pulls my waist against him and crashes his lips down on mine. The tangy taste of the red wine mixes with our tongues and he reaches deeper into my mouth.

"Fuck, I've not been able to do that all day. Are you wet baby? If I rub my fingers along your slit will I find a sticky mess?" He asks between kisses.

"Maybe you should find out." I suggest playfully.

"Are you trying to sass me, Angel? On your knees. Now." He commands as I roll my eyes. "I said, NOW! Keep it up and you will be denied orgasms. I know you don't want that, do you?" he asks with a smirk. I sink to my knees with a scoff and kneel before him.

"Is this how you want me?" I ask innocently, fluttering my eyes up at him.

"Exactly like that. You look so good on your knees before me, Angel. Now, take me out." Reaching up, I slowly let down his zipper. I can feel his hard bulge wanting to be set free. I palm at his boxers a few times as he hisses with pleasure. I take out his cock and I don't think I will ever get used to his size. It's long and thick and I'm not sure how it fits inside me every time. No wonder I feel like I'm being split open in the best way possible.

"You're so big, Daddy. Can I lick it?" I can see the precum beading at the tip about to drip to the floor.

"Yes, Angel. Take me in your mouth like a good girl and then maybe I'll let you come." I lick my lips and dive in, sucking and licking his shaft all the way to his base. "Open up." He pulls my hair in the angle he wants me and thrusts inside my mouth. He continues to pump into me as I sit there and take everything he's giving me. "You're taking me so well, Angel. Such a good fucking girl." Swirling my tongue around his cock every time he retreats, he groans out in pleasure. He starts jerkily thrusting his hips and I know he's close. I pull on his ass with every shove, urging him to go deeper. I want him to fill my mouth with his come. I taste the saltiness as soon as it hits my tongue. "Fuck, I'm about to come. Take everything I give you. Swallow me, baby." He says as streams of come hit the back of my throat. I gag almost immediately but remember to breathe through my nose. My eyes begin to water but I continue to swallow him down until his thrusts slow. I look up at him through my wet lashes and see the look on his face is one of pure pride. He slides out of my mouth, and I have to clench my pussy at the sight of his wet dick. I want it in me so bad, but we are in his old bedroom for fuck's sake. What if his mother had come looking for us. *What was I thinking?* I want her to like me. Not think of me as some whore.

Sebastian puts his hands under my arms and picks me up until I am standing. I have to stretch a bit from sitting like that for so long. He wraps his big arms around me and whispers in my ear. "You suck my cock so well." He pushes me until my legs hit the edge of the bed. Then he gently lays me down, pulling me to the center of the bed. He crawls up my body with a look in his eyes that says he wants to devour me. "I need to be in this tight pussy, Stormy, but you have to be quiet." I nod my head and he pulls my dress up to my waist. He removes my heels and thong, throwing them to the floor. His fingers skate up my legs and slow once they get close to my core. "I knew you were wet, baby. This perfect pussy is dripping for me. You need Daddy to take care of you, don't you?" He questions but he already knows the answer.

"Please fuck me," I plead. Sebastian pulls his pants down further and grasps his cock in his hand as he circles my clit with the other. He pumps and circles in synchrony. Finally, when I think I can't take it anymore, he rubs his cock along my entrance, gathering my juices. My breath hitches waiting for him to fuck me.

"You want me to fuck this pussy?" He demands.

"Yes. Yes, please!" I groan as he slips between my folds. Only his head is inside me. He pulls back out and actually laughs at my facial expression. Then without warning, he plunges in to the hilt in one swift motion. I yelp out in pain and pleasure. I don't know which is more prominent at the moment. He pulls almost completely all the way out then pushes back in with enough force to push me up the bed. Sebastian pulls one leg over his shoulder and places his hand around my throat. My pussy clamps down around him at the gesture.

"Fuck, I love this tight little pussy. This is all for me, isn't it? Tell me who owns this pussy, Stormy. Who owns this tight little cunt. Who is the only one that gets to fill it with come?" He grunts as he continues to thrust inside of me. His hand on my throat tightens and I can barely get any words out.

"You, Daddy. Sebastian, you own my pussy." I breathe out. He brushes his lips over my leg and chills erupt over my body.

"You're such a good fucking girl for Daddy. You like my cock in you. I make you gush. Do you like when Daddy talks dirty to his little girl?" He asks, but it's the truth. He owns me body and soul. Sebastian growls as my pussy flutters around him. I moan out his name and he picks up his pace. I'm already so close but his hold on me tightens and all I can do is let out a small whimper. I feel like I can barely breathe. Sliding his hand between our bodies, he finds my swollen clit and begins to rub it firmly. My legs begin to shake, and my breaths grow faster. I'm not going to last much longer. "That's it baby. Come hard for me. I want to feel you come on my cock." I whimper and mewl at his words and that's all it takes for my orgasm to rip through me. I'd scream if I could because this feels like the most explosive release I've ever had. I think that's why he has his hand around my throat. I sink my nails into his forearm, needing contact wherever I can get it. I almost pass out from pleasure but at the last possible second, Sebastian lets go of my neck and slams hard into me, spilling his come into my waiting pussy. "Shit, it gets better with you every time."

He stops his thrusts and collapses on top of me, his arms barely holding him above me. His mouth finds mine and he licks my lips until I open for him. I know he can probably taste himself on me still. He tongue fucks me until I have to move my head to the side to get a breath of air. Sebastian kisses along my neck and over the new tattoo that I got a few days ago. It twinges a bit, but the covering is still on.

"We need to go before your mom comes looking for us," I whisper. He nods in agreement and pushes himself off of me. He walks into the adjoining bathroom and brings back a cloth. Sebastian wipes me clean then himself, throwing the towel in a nearby hamper. I'm sure his mother will see it later. I do a mental face palm at this man. He bends over grabbing my shoes and placing them on each foot like Cinderella. I have to smile down at him when he looks up at me.

"The perfect fit." He knew exactly what I was thinking. Laughing I nod.

"That's what happens when you buy them in the right size." I reply.

"Of course, what was I thinking." He smirks. I scoot off the bed, wobbling a bit. I can feel his come leaking out of me and going down my thigh. I walk over to the hamper, but Sebastian stops me. "Leave it. I want to know you have my come dripping out of you while we are here. Just put this on." He hands me my thong and I'm torn between listening to him and getting that towel back out and wiping the rest of myself clean. I shake my head and snatch my underwear from him as he chuckles. Bending over, I step into it and pull it up until I can feel it catching some of our combined juices. I want to squirm at the uncomfortable feeling.

I see myself in the mirror on the dresser and am horrified by my reflection. Mascara and eyeliner are streaming down my face, not to mention my lipstick has been mostly wiped away other than the remnants that are outside my lips. I look like a fucking clown on Halloween.

"Calm down, I can see you panicking. Just use the bathroom through there and get cleaned up. Well, only your face. I'll be checking later to see if you listened to me." Sebastian says, like it will be the easiest thing in the world to fix. Men don't know anything. They will be able to tell what we were up to, I guarantee it.

"I can't just fix my makeup. I didn't bring anything with me. Your mother is going to know what we were up to." I smack my hand against my head. Sebastian comes over to me and cradles me in his arms. At least he is good at knowing when I'm about to spiral.

"Shh, it's going to be alright. My mother knows you aren't just some hookup." He says with a smile that melts my nerves away.

"How would she know that?" I ask.

He scratches his head and looks at me nervously. "Well, you are the first girl I've ever brought home. This is a special place and I've never in my life dated someone that I wanted to bring here. This is only for you," He replies sheepishly.

"Really?" I question. Not really needing an answer but to verify that I heard him correctly. "Even in high school?" I ask.

"Never, Stormy. You're it. You're the first girl that has ever been in my bedroom, other than my mother of course." He informs me.

"Wow, I don't know what to say." I state.

"Tell me you love me." He cups my face, wiping the tears from my cheeks with the pads of his thumbs.

"I love you, Sebastian," I whisper. He leans down, gently kissing me. Pushing up on my tippy toes, I try to get a deeper connection. His tongue plunges into my mouth and I moan at the connection. I can't get enough of him. He's addictive like a drug I never knew I needed. But now I need it to survive. He pulls back, looking in my eyes and presses his forehead against mine.

"I love you, too, Stormy. Thank you for coming with me today. I know it was hard for you at the funeral but I'm so proud of you. You got through it. I don't think you realize how strong you are." He murmurs in my ear. He makes me weak in the knees when he says things like that.

"I think you have something to do with that. I feel whole with you. Maybe that sounds crazy, but I know you'll be here for me. You've been my rock lately and I know you will take care of me." I place my hands over his as he pulls me in for another kiss.

"I'm not going anywhere, Angel. You are stuck with me." He announces and it makes me smile. "Now go get fixed up before someone comes looking for us. Do you want me to wait or meet you downstairs?" He asks.

"You go ahead and go. I will be down in a minute," I express. I walk into the bathroom as he leaves, wondering how the hell I'm going to fix this mess.

Sebastian

I go back down to the kitchen and see Miles and Lizzie have arrived. Miles gives me a quizzical look then smirks at me. Of course, he would know what I was up to. Mother sees me come in and smiles her bright smile, none the wiser. At least that's good.

"Where did Stormy get off to?" She asks but before I can answer, Stormy comes up beside me.

"Here I am. I had to use the little girl's room." She responds. I don't know how, but she looks the same as when we got here, except for the red mark around her neck. Hopefully, no one notices that. It would be an awkward conversation. *Hey, I like choking my girlfriend until she almost passes out so she will have the biggest orgasm ever. No big deal.* I shake my head and smile. Stormy looks up at me with a devilish look in her eyes, remembering what we were just up to.

"Stormy, where is your wine glass, honey?" My mother asks. Fuck.

"I must have left it upstairs. I can go up there and get it." She remarks, her cheeks turning a shade of pink.

"No worries, I will pour you another. Lizzie would you like some?" She asks.

"No thank you, Amelia. I won't be drinking." She brushes her hand across her flat stomach, and I look at Miles who has the largest smile on his face.

"No way! You're pregnant?" Mother asks, coming around the kitchen island to give them hugs.

"Yes ma'am. We just found out." Lizzie replies with a smile on her face.

"Congratulations." We all seem to say at the same time. Stormy goes and gives Lizzie a hug while I slap my brother on the back. The lucky bastard. He got there before me. Now more than ever, I want to knock Stormy up. Lizzie leads Stormy into the den to talk. She looks back at me and smiles. The look squeezes my heart and I know I need to get a ring on her finger as soon as possible. I want us to become a family. I want everything with her. She would never have to work if she didn't want to. She definitely doesn't need to be my assistant any longer. I can get a new one so she can focus on school. So many thoughts are running through my mind that I don't hear what Miles says to me.

"Earth to Sebastian." He says jokingly.

"Sorry, I don't know what I was thinking about." I lie. He gives me a 'yeah right' look and I have to look away before Mother suspects something. I don't want her to know my plans until I've had time to set them in place, and to talk to Stormy of course.

"I said it was a beautiful funeral today. Stormy did a great job with flowers and decorations. Elijah wouldn't have been able to do all that." Hearing that bastards name has me clenching my fists.

"She did do well. Congratulations, man. I'm happy for you." I say, bringing him in for a hug.

"You just wish it was you." He responds.

"What?" I question.

"I saw the way you looked at Stormy when you heard the news. Don't worry, your secret is safe with me. But you might want to put a ring on that finger first. Just a suggestion. Otherwise, I doubt she would go for it." Miles informs. "Just some brotherly advice."

He turns to follow the girls into the den. I'm left in the kitchen with my Mother.

"Do you need help serving the dishes?" I ask, looking at my Mother.

"Yes, that would be great, darling. Thank you." I take two plates and carry them to the dining room, setting them down on the spots that Mother has set for them. I go back and get the rest of the plates just as everyone joins us in the dining room.

We eat dinner with comfortable conversations. Miles and Lizzie talk about her pregnancy and I keep catching glances at Stormy when they mention it to see what she is thinking. She looks almost wishful or maybe that's my feelings being projected onto her.

Soon enough the dinner is over, and we are at the door saying our goodbyes. I grab Stormy's coat for her and drape it over her shoulders, knowing she won't want to wear it in the car on the way back to our apartment.

"Thank you for having us over, Mother. We'll have to do it again soon. I love you." I embrace her and kiss her cheek.

"We'll plan another time soon. It was good to meet you Stormy. Take care of my boy." She says and I roll my eyes. Stormy is the one that needs taken care of, not me. I lead Stormy to the car, placing my hand at the small of her back. Her warmth spreads through my arm and I never want to take my hands off her. Opening the door, I lock her into place and jog around to my side of the car. I slide in, dusting the snow from my hair and shoulders.

"I had a good time. Thank you for bringing me. I love your mother. She is so welcoming." Stormy confesses.

"She loves you as well. I can tell." I reply to her. A smile forms on her face.

"I guess that's good since you said you aren't going anywhere."
She teases.

"It's exciting about Lizzie being pregnant. She's thrilled."
Stormy gushes.

"Yeah, Miles is, too." I reply as we head down the long driveway.

"Do you ever think about it?" I ask, needing to know where she is.

"What? Babies?" She questions.

"Yeah, I mean you having them. Us having them. Do you want
kids?" I query.

"I've thought about it more recently than I ever have. I didn't
have a good childhood and I would never want to bring a child
into a situation like that. My parents' were always so busy working
that they never came to recitals or softball games. I just want to
be able to be present, maybe even a stay-at-home mom. But yeah,
I think about it, especially since I missed two birth control pills."
She admits.

"I didn't know you had missed another one." I speak with a little
more enthusiasm than I probably should. "What if you could be
a stay-at-home mom? What if you didn't have to work? You could
go to school if you wanted or not if you didn't. But you have the
studio now for any time you want to paint or draw or anything
your heart desires." I declare.

"I didn't tell you because I didn't want you to be upset. I didn't
do it on purpose." She explains. "So much has been going on the
past few weeks and I missed two days. I thought you might think
I was trying to trap you." she confesses.

"I would never think that about you. It's you and me now. You
know that, right?" I look over to the passenger side and see her nod
her head.

"I would love to be a stay-at-home mom, but I also would feel guilty for not pulling my weight with bills and everything. I wouldn't want that pressure on you." She says.

"Listen, I could quit working now and we would have enough to live on for the rest of our lives. I like what I do. I love working for my father's company. And I would want you to be at home with our children. They need that kind of love in the household. My mother stayed at home with us and look how great I turned out." I tease.

"I guess this is something to talk about if I don't get my period." She states, looking out the window at the snow flurries.

"I don't want you to take your birth control anymore." I command.

She turns in her seat and looks at me. "What?" She asks.

"You heard me. I don't want you to take it anymore. I haven't been joking when I mentioned it after we have sex. I want you pregnant with my child." I announce.

"I thought you were just in the moment when you would say that or push your cum back inside me. I thought maybe you had a breeding kink." She answers.

"I do when it comes to you. Never in my life have I wanted a child, but with you I do. It makes me fucking hard as fuck thinking of you pregnant with my child." I respond.

"Oh. I don't really know what to say, Sebastian. You're kind of springing this on me. I mean have you thought this through? Is this some kind of competition with Miles?" She asks.

"Hell no, it's not. If there is something I want, I go after it. I want you. All of you. I want you to be my wife and the mother of my children." Fuck it. I'm putting all my cards on the table. This probably isn't the best place to have such an important conversation, but we're here so oh well.

"Alright, call down you caveman. I was just asking." She takes a deep breath and lets it out. "I want to be engaged before we start trying to have a baby. I want that commitment. I'm not telling you to ask me now, I'm telling you that's what I want. That puts the ball in your court, big boy." She looks at me and winks. God, I love this firecracker. If she wants to be engaged, she had better be ready. I'll stop at nothing.

THIRTY THREE

Stormy

The day has come for me to move my things out of my old apartment and confront Lana at the same time. Sebastian and the movers will be coming with me, and they all signed NDAs for whatever they might see or hear. Sebastian and I head down the elevator to meet the moving crew in the garage.

"Are you sure you want to be there today? I can get your stuff and get out if you want?" Sebastian questions. He has been tiptoeing around with the idea all morning. But I need to do this. I need to see Lana and hear what she has to say. It's been driving me mad trying to figure out why she sold my story to the press.

"I'm sure. I need to talk to her, Sebastian. I need some answers." I respond, twisting my fingers in knots as the elevator opens. I'm nervous to say the least.

"I understand. I just hate to you having to go through this. If she starts a fight, I'll be more than happy to step in and finish it." He remarks. Of course, he will. I smile to myself at my caveman.

"Believe me, I know. Let's just get this over with." Sebastian opens my door then gives the crew the address to my apartment in

355

case they get stuck in traffic and can't follow us. He slides in his car, and we take off down the road. I should have taken some medicine this morning. This is making me super anxious, but I want to be strong and not use the medication as a crutch any longer.

Lana doesn't know we are coming today. I remember her school schedule and I know she doesn't have classes today. Since it's the middle of the week, I doubt she has a catering gig either. We arrive at the apartment after minimal traffic. I was kind of wishing it would have taken longer to get here. I don't know if I'm prepared enough for this.

Sebastian comes to my side of the car and opens the door for me. I take his hand and step out. It's a small gesture but it calms me. He shouts to the crew to follow us, and we all ride up in the small elevator together. Once out, I lead the way through the corridor to our apartment door. Opening it with the key, I swing open the door and there is Lana sitting on the couch watching TV. She turns to look at me, her face paling. She looks behind me at Sebastian, her face grows paler still. I don't have to look to know that he is sneering at her. He was ready to lawyer up and sue over this, but I wanted to talk to her first and get to the bottom of why everything happened the way it did.

"Lana, we need to talk." I breathe and walk toward the kitchen. Might as well make a cup of coffee while I'm here. Sebastian and the crew head to my bedroom to begin packing my things. I gave them explicit instructions on how I wanted things to be packed so I hope they follow through with that. Lana rises from the sofa, following me to the kitchen. I pour myself a cup of coffee with cream and sit at the table. Clutching the mug in my hands, I ask, "Why did you do it?"

"I'm so sorry Stormy. I never meant for any of this to happen." She takes a deep breath and tears begin to form in her eyes. "When we were at the bar that night and you got up to sing, I accidentally told someone who you were and that they needed to hear the best singer there. I was drunk and stupid. Then everything happened so quickly, pictures were taken, Sebastian showed up, you passed out. It was all too much to deal with. I don't know how you do it. The next day I found out that my father spent my college tuition gambling again. I only have a partial scholarship and the school wasn't willing to work with me. I spent all afternoon in the finance department, only to be told there was nothing they could do. I was panicking." Lana gets up to get a tissue and blows her nose. So far everything she's saying sounds feasible. She comes back to the table and sits down. "I was stopped coming into the apartment that day and asked if I would give an interview. They knew I was your roommate. I told them no several times until someone mentioned they saw me leaving campus and that if I gave them a story, they would pay me. I felt like I was caught between a rock and a hard place. I didn't think I had any more options. When they continued to harass me, I figured I would kill two birds with one stone. Get money for college and get them off my back. I'm sorry I never thought how this would affect you. I was thinking of myself the whole time. I wrote up the story you told me about the night Blaine died and then they wanted me to also do an in-person interview. Everything happened to fast." She blows her nose, wiping her eyes on her shirt. "The worst part is that I didn't get paid. They tricked me. And now the Jacks' family is coming after me for telling the press about Sean. I didn't use his name, but they figured it out. I don't know what to do. I'm scared, Stormy.

I'm no better than my father." She puts her head on the table and silently sobs. I don't even know what to say. I don't know if she is telling the truth, but she seems to be. I could always check with the school and see if she has unpaid tuition there if they would even tell me. The thing is, I still think Lana is an okay person. I'm not normally wrong about these kinds of things. Did she fuck up? Yes. Did she screw me over? Yes. But I think it was done to aid herself and not done with malice toward me.

"Do you have proof of your college tuition not being paid?" I question. She looks up at me and nods her head. "Can I see it?" She pushes back from the table and goes to her room to retrieve it. While she's gone, I look around at this apartment that I didn't have the chance to live in very long. It's a cute place. I think I would have been happy here had I not met Sebastian and had my world turned upside down. When she comes back, she hands me the paper that's dated for the day she said. I look down at the bottom and my stomach flips at the sight of how much she owes. Fuck, she did what she thought she had to do. She's so passionate about art and this school and it was about to be taken away from her. I know the feeling of being stuck and having to do something drastic. That's why I moved here in the first place. I had to get away from the stares and the constant chattering everywhere I went. "When is this due?" I ask.

"It's due by Monday if I want to keep my classes that I'm already registered for. If not, they will drop all my classes. I'm so sorry. I've messed everything up. You trusted me and I let you down. I'm going to move back home. That's the only choice I have." Lana confesses.

"What if I paid for this semester? Would you be able to save up and make payments next semester?" The question looks like it knocks the breath out of her. In all honesty, I didn't know I was going to say that either. It just flew out of my mouth.

"Why would you do that? I've been nothing but terrible to you." She argues.

"You weren't terrible the whole time. It's true that you shouldn't have done what you did but you were desperate, and you thought it was the only way to escape your fate. I get that. I want to help you, but this doesn't make us friends again. You will have to earn that trust back. But in the meantime, you'll be able to attend college. What do you think?" I ask.

"I-I mean, yes. Yes! Thank you. You don't know what you are doing for me." She states.

"I do. I'm giving you a fresh start. How about don't fuck it up this time." I reply. She puts her hand over her mouth in awe with tears streaming down her cheeks. I pull out my purse and write a check to the university in her name so it can only be used at school. I slide the check across the table and Lana jumps out of her seat to hug me.

"Thank you. You won't regret this. I promise I will earn back your friendship. Thank you, thank you, thank you." She sobs as she looks at the check in her trembling hands. "Oh! I forgot I have something for you." She runs to her room and comes right back with the pair of Louboutins that I ruined in the rain. "Here, I painted these for you. You don't have to wear them, but I thought they would be perfect for you." She hands me the shoes and I see she has painted them with scenes from the Harry Potter book covers. All seven books are represented in some fashion. They are the coolest things I have ever seen. I look back up to her and know I did the right thing. She didn't have to do this for me, she didn't know if she would see me again, but she painted these shoes for me, and I will cherish them. We may have a long road ahead of us, but this is a good start.

"Thank you, Lana. I love them. This must have taken you forever to do." I tell her, still examining the shoes and finding little details that I didn't see the first time.

"Well, I haven't been sleeping well so I would get up and paint. It helps put my mind at ease." She explains. I definitely know how she feels.

Sebastian comes out of the room and walks over to us. "The guys are almost done. They will be taking loads out soon. Everything okay out here?" He asks, looking from me to Lana.

"Yep. Everything is good." I tell him. "Let me go make sure that the guys are packing everything I came with." I get up and walk to my old room. It resembles what it did a few weeks ago with everything back in boxes. I walk over to a portrait of Blaine that I did, holding it up to the light. This portrait did not age well. The paint is chipping off in areas and the whites are turning brownish. I painted this when we were in high school, when we were happy and before the band got signed. This represents the old Blaine, my best friend.

"You were a lovely time in my life, Blaine, but that's all you'll ever be. Not all art is meant to hang on the same walls indefinitely. Sometimes we have to trash the canvas and start new." I murmur to the painting as I drop it to the floor.

Sebastian

I wait until Stormy is in her old room to speak. "I heard everything. She may believe you, but I don't. Rip up that check. I'll pay for your school but if you ever betray her trust again, you will need a lawyer for what I do to you. You revealed her secrets. I won't let you continue to hurt her. She's young and somewhat naïve but I've been around people like you. You could have found another way to pay for school or just gone back home. You didn't have to throw Stormy under the bus, but you chose to. I'll call the school and donate in your name but if you so much as utter her name in any way but positive, you will be on a bus home." Lana nods her head as a fresh set of tears spring down her cheeks. She takes the check and tears it in half. She knows I mean business. She's a money chaser like her father. They are two peas in a pod. I did a little research on Lana Jones, I know more than Stormy does. She has a history of talking to the press about things in her hometown. Only this time it didn't work out. She didn't get the money she was promised because I stopped it. "Your school is being paid for and I'm only doing that because Stormy was going to. She sees the good in you. Make me see that as well. You know, I did a background check on you, and I know this isn't the first time you've done something like this."

"I'm sorry for hurting her. She was so nice to me, and I sold her out." She replies.

"Yes, you did. And you lost that trust you built. Now sign this NDA so you can't make the same mistake again without paying a price." She signs the paper and I stuff it in my jacket just as Stormy comes back to the kitchen.

"Everything seems good to go." She says. She grabs the shoes from the table and puts her mug in the sink. "I guess I'll see you around, Lana. Good luck in school." She remarks and leaves the kitchen waiting for me to follow her. I look at Lana giving her a glare, so she knows what it means. She nods her head and I turn on my heels and walk out of the apartment with Stormy on my arm. I told her that I would always protect her and that means protecting her from bad people, even if she would never know about it. We get in the elevator as a tear rolls down her cheek.

"What's wrong, Angel?" I question.

"I just still can't believe she did it. At least it's done and I got my things from there." She says.

"Yeah, and you never have to see her again." I insist.

"Well, people can change, right? Who knows, maybe she will turn things around." I love her for her huge heart, but I disagree with her on this. People never change. They may seem like it, but old habits die hard, and Lana was probably about to try and cash in on more money with a new story had I not made her sign that NDA.

I open the car door for Stormy and buckle her in, something she still fights with me on, then I get in on the driver's side. The crew knows where we live, they will be along shortly with all of Stormy's belongings. This is the start of a new chapter in our lives. Stormy moving in with me is the best thing that could happen to us. I'm not saying I'm glad that article came out, but I'm glad it gave her the push she needed to stop dragging her feet and move in with me.

THIRTY FOUR

Sebastian

It's Monday morning, a week from the funeral, and Stormy and I are back at work. We spent the week in each other's arms when we weren't unpacking her things from her old apartment. My attorneys visited Dennis Jacks and their family. He signed the paperwork, did the official interview, and got paid the money that was promised to him. Everything seems to be back to normal.

Most people have heard about us by now. I think Mary spilled the beans to everyone, but I can't be mad at her. She was the one that essentially set us up. I owe her everything. I drafted and sent a companywide memo informing everyone that we were a couple but there would be no preferential treatment. The news was met with mostly encouraging words. There were a few women that have had their eyes on Miles and me for years now that were displeased with the news. They even went as far as to call Stormy unsavory names. Those women were terminated on the spot. Unfortunately, not everyone is going to be happy, and I don't give a fuck. It's good to be back at work, though. Having Miles back has been great as well. Now we have to deal with Elijah, to get him the fuck out of here. Unfortunately, we have to go by protocol. Taking statements and whatnot can take some time.

I decide to have a little fun with Stormy. I pull out my phone and send her a text.

Sebastian:

> As soon as I can, I'm going to pin you up against the wall with your arms above your head.

Stormy:

> Is that any way to talk to an employee, Mr. Knight?

Sebastian:

> I knew that brat would come out. Shall I go on?

Stormy:

> If you wish.

Sebastian:

> Let's just say I have no problem ripping every inch of your clothes off. Then having you look me in the eyes as I drop to my knees and put your leg over my shoulder, watching as I devour you. When you get close, I'll place my hand around your throat and squeeze.

Stormy:

> Would I get on my knees, too?

Sebastian:

Not until I tell you to. How do you like being dragged around the bed or pinned down with my hands and shoulders?

Stormy:

I want to be your ragdoll, basically. I never knew I needed this in my life until I met you.

Sebastian:

I knew it's what you needed by the way you talked to me the first time. Want to know my special skill?

Stormy:

You like being inappropriate in the workplace?

Sebastian:

That mouth is going to get you in trouble. I'm going to put my tongue on your clit and twirl it as I hum. As you get closer, to orgasming I'll slide my fingers into that tight pussy and massage your g spot until you start climaxing and I won't stop until I decide to. Don't worry, you won't be able to get away because I'll have you pinned down. You will be begging to catch your breath.

Stormy:

What if I'm a bad girl?

Sebastian:

> I'll spank that pussy until its red and swollen then I'll lick and kiss it to make it better. But you might think twice before being bad again.

Stormy:

> You're making me all hot talking about this.

Sebastian:

> Good, I'm trying to.

Stormy:

> Bastard.

Sebastian:

> Oops. That's going to cost you.

I smile as I put my phone back up. Getting back to work, I have to adjust myself in my pants and stop thinking about Stormy laid out before me. A few hours pass and my stomach rumbles.

Looking at the time, I see it's almost lunch and I promised Stormy we could go out for lunch today. It's been so hectic since we came back that we have been working through lunch, either having things delivered or running to the café downstairs. Standing from my chair, I pocket my phone and head out of my office. Stormy isn't at her desk so she must be getting something in the little kitchenette we have. As I walk over, I can hear Elijah in a heated discussion with someone. My blood boils at the thought that it could be Stormy he's talking to. I walk quickly to the kitchen but stay hidden behind the wall so I can hear. I pull out my phone just in case this is something that we can use against him.

"I think you're a little slut. Spreading your legs for the boss. What, was I not good enough for you? I don't make enough money? Is that it? You're a little gold digger. That's why you married your first husband and now you are dating the most eligible bachelor in New York City. You must have a magic pussy. I'll have to try that out sometime." I hear the sound of a slap and then, "You little bitch. I'll-" but he's cut off when I round the corner and see him choking Stormy. He takes a step back from her, releasing her to the ground in a fit of coughs. He looks frightened as he damn well should because I'm seeing red right now.

"You motherfucker. Don't you ever touch her again," I sneer as I stride to him in one step and punch the skinny motherfucker to the floor. All around gasps can be heard but I'm only concerned about the creep in front of me. I knew we should have done something with him sooner. I straddle him on the ground and continue punching his face until I feel my brother pulling me off him.

"You got him. Give it a rest, Seb," Miles says, pulling his phone out and calling security. I look at my bloodied hands, then at Stormy who is clutching her throat and crying on the floor. Mary is there trying to console her, but she needs me. I'm her rock during hard times, now. I crawl over to where she is and pull her into my arms.

"It's going to be alright, Angel. He's going to be taken care of." I pull my phone from my pocket and show her it's been recording. It recorded everything he said to her. Well, everything I heard. He probably said even more than that. At least now we have definitive proof that he can be fired, arrested, and escorted from the premises.

Miles bends down beside us. "I called security to come detain him and the cops will be here soon to take him downtown." I hand him my phone so he could listen to the proof I got.

"I knew something wasn't right, so I started recording. Thank fuck I did." I look down at Stormy who is still trembling in my hands. "Let me see your neck, Stormy." She turns and looks up at me and cringes from the angle. I see the fuckers hand print on her throat. I can see why she didn't call out for help, he was choking her to death. I don't know what the fuck happened to Elijah to go to these extremes to get to Stormy. Maybe after the news came out about her, he got more obsessed. "I can see his hand print on you still." I tell her and fresh tears begin to fall.

"He said he was going to kill you if I didn't come with him. I was so scared, Sebastian." She croaks out, unable to fully use her voice. It makes me want to punch that little shit again for what he did to her.

"Try not to use your voice, baby. We'll take you to the doctor when we leave here and get you checked out." She shakes her head no, but I'm not accepting that answer. I need to know if she's okay.

The security gets up to our floor and handcuffs Elijah, taking him to a different area so we don't have to look at him. I stand and pick Stormy up, carrying her to my office. There's a leather couch in there that I'm going to lay her on. The police can come in there and question her. I don't want all our employees knowing our business.

Retrieving a blanket from my closet, I cover her up and sit down beside her. "I'm so sorry this happened. I wish he would have already been gone by the time we came back to work today." I tell her.

"You couldn't have known he would do anything." She wheezes and I'm sure he damaged something in her neck. That motherfucker better be glad I didn't kill him for putting his hands on what's mine.

I called Dr. Peterson and asked him to meet us at the hospital. I want Stormy to have X-rays done but he's the only doctor that I truly trust. Once we got here, he was waiting for us in the waiting room. We get her checked in and he is able to take her straight back to a room. Since she can't talk well, she's having me answer most of the questions.

"So, you were choked from the front. I can see his hand print forming a contusion along the front of your throat." She nods her head and a small tear escapes. "Alright, we are going to take you back and do some X-rays. Is there any possibility that you are pregnant?" Dr. Peterson asks and all the air leaves my lungs. She looks at me and I know the answer. She never started her period like she was supposed to, but I've been enjoying having a week with her at the house that I totally forgot about it. But I see she didn't. She knows. She nods her head once and looks down to her hands wringing in her lap.

"I see. Well, in that case, let me order a test so we'll know for sure." He clicks away at the computer then leaves us alone.

I stand and walk over to the bed she's in. "Why didn't you tell me?" I question.

She shrugs her shoulders then opens her mouth. "I was scared to know. I don't know for sure but I'm pretty regular and I didn't start my period this week." She murmurs.

I sit on the edge of her bed, holding her hands in mine. "I told you that's what I wanted. Why would you be scared to tell me?" I ask. "We don't keep things from each other, ever." I try to not get my hopes up that she's pregnant but it's too late. I can see her now with a swollen belly and bare feet, painting away in her studio. Of course, we would get everything that was non-toxic. I need to research all that. I don't want anything to hurt my Angels. Yes, I said Angels because I just know it will be positive.

Dr. Peterson walks back in with a kit to take her blood. "Since you're probably too early for a urine test, we'll use a blood test to determine if you are pregnant or not." She nods her head and holds out her arm. Dr. Peterson draws the blood then labels it with her name and says he's taking it to the lab and will be back. In the meantime, I rub Stormy's back until she falls asleep I think from the adrenaline wearing off. Although she has been taking a lot more naps now that I think of it.

Once the doctor comes back with the results, I wake Stormy so she can hear. "I believe congratulations are in order. You are going to be a mom, Stormy. The test results came back positive. Unfortunately, considering how early you are, we won't be able to have an X-ray. I'll have to perform a physical exam which will be uncomfortable." He looks at me and smiles. "Congratulations, dad." I can't contain my excitement. I smash my lips to Stormy's, holding her face in my hands.

"I love you so much, baby. We're going to have a little one." I say with happy tears in my eyes.

"I love you, too. Are you truly happy?" She asks, biting her bottom lip.

"More than I can express, Angel." I kiss her forehead and get up from the bed so the doctor can get his exam over and we can get out of here. I have an engagement ring at home that I have been waiting for the right time to give her and I think tonight will be perfect.

"I'm just going to feel around your neck and see if I find anything." Dr. Peterson feels around on both sides of her neck and then the middle. She cringes a bit, but my girl is strong. She can get through anything. "Alright, I think it's just an inflamed larynx. Try not to talk as much as you can while it heals. Now, since you are pregnant and you were denied blood and oxygen to your brain for a short time, we are going to go an ultrasound of the baby and make sure everything looks alright, okay?"

"Okay." She rasps as she looks to me with true fear in her eyes. She's wondering if anything happened to the baby today, I don't think I have ever been more scared in my life until I hear the fast little heartbeat coming from the computer speakers. I look to the doctor who confirms with a head nod. I jump up and kiss Stormy. Together we share some tears as we look at the monitor that shows our little peanut on the screen.

Dr. Peterson gives Stormy directions to take it easy and a prescription for prenatal vitamins. We're out of the hospital and heading home soon after.

THIRTY-FIVE

Sebastian

S tormy passed out in the car after we talked about everything that we found out at the hospital. Dr. Peterson said it was normal for her to be tired around this time, plus with everything she went through, I can't blame her for falling asleep. I park the car and go around to her side to pick her up. She shuffles a bit until I say, "Shh, we're home. I'm carrying you upstairs. Go back to sleep, Angel." The ride up the elevator is a quiet one as I look down at the sleeping beauty in my arms. I take her back to our bed and lay her down. Taking off her boots and jacket, I cover her small body with the blanket, excited to see when her belly begins to swell. I kiss her forehead and then her stomach where our little angel is growing. My heart feels like it might burst out of my chest. I love this woman who is giving me this amazing gift. How did I ever get this lucky? I make sure the blanket is tucked in around her and leave the room, taking one last look at my loves. Closing the door, I pull out my phone and start my plans for tonight.

First, I place an order for her favorite Mexican food and tell them to deliver it at seven. That should give me plenty of time to get everything ready. I check the weather and see there is a snowstorm coming this afternoon which will be perfect since Stormy loves snow so much. I go into my Christmas closet and pull out several strands of twinkling lights. Taking them out to the balcony, I hang them under the awning where we will be. I pull the heaters closer and set out blankets and pillows on the couch outside. Next, I order some things from the grocery store that we will need over the next few days, letting them know they need to be delivered.

Once everything is delivered, I put the sparkling white grape juice in the fridge to cool. It's the closest thing to champagne she can have now that she is pregnant. Leaning against the counter, I take a minute to let that sink in. I'm going to be a dad. I can't fucking wait. Our kid is going to grow up with a cousin their age and be best friends hopefully. I can't wait to call and tell the family. I shake my head and smile at how fast things can change.

As I'm getting everything set up on trays, Stormy walks into the kitchen rubbing her eyes.

"How long was I out?" She asks.

"A couple hours, not too long." I mention. "I got your favorite." I gesture to the Mexican food.

"Yummy. You didn't have to do that." She replies as she sticks her finger in the cheese dip and sucks it off. Fuck, what a turn on and she doesn't even know she's doing it.

"I wanted to, Angel." She looks at the trays and looks up at me.

"Another night watching Harry Potter?" She asks. We still haven't quite finished our marathon. We get distracted when we put it on.

"Nope. We are eating on the balcony." I say, loving the way her eyes light up.

"Really?" She questions.

"Yep. Why don't you head on out there and I'll bring this stuff?" She reaches up on her tippy toes and kisses me then turns and walks outside to the balcony. But not before getting another finger in the cheese dip. I laugh to myself. I love that woman.

Balancing the tray in one hand and the sparkling juice and flutes in the other, I make it out without any accidents. I think it would be poetic if I spilled the trays on her since that's how we met. I place the tray down along with the champagne flutes. She gives me one of her quizzical looks, probably wondering what the hell I'm doing since we just found out we're expecting.

I pop the top on the juice and pour some in her glass along with mine. "It's sparkling white grape juice." I tell her. I shut off the indoor lights and flick on the twinkling lights at the same time. A small gasp comes from her lips, and she puts her hand to her mouth.

"What is all this for, Sebastian?" She asks and I know I won't be able to wait until the end of the meal to pop the question. I decide to do it now. I step before her on the couch and bend down on one knee. "Oh my God." She says with a smile on her face and tears already gathering in her eyes.

"Stormy, you came into my life like a hurricane, uprooting everything in its path. You made me crazy but most importantly, you made me fall in love. I love sparring with you, I love making love to you, but most of all I love loving you, Angel. Will you marry me? I promise you we will have a lifetime of hanging out like best friends, making love like soulmates, fighting like enemies, and most importantly staying together like a family. Please do me the honors." I open the baby blue Tiffany's box and a 4-carat yellow pear-shaped diamond ring flanked with white diamonds stands tall.

"Yes! Of course, I'll marry you!" She wheezes then coughs, covering her mouth and grimacing from the pain. I wish I could take the pain from her. I slide the ring on her finger and it's a perfect fit. She jumps from her seat, and I catch her midair. Twirling her around, it begins to snow. She's the most beautiful sight to behold in this moment. And in all moments. But Stormy with snow in her hair smiling and radiating love and happiness, that's the best vision.

"I love you, Angel. And I love little Angel, too." I murmur in her ear.

"We love you, too, Daddy." She says with a naughty glint in her eyes.

To hell with the food. Stormy wraps her legs around me and begins rubbing her hot pussy against my hardening cock. A groan escapes my lips, and she smiles. She knows exactly what she is doing.

She jumps down from me and darts toward the door. "You get the food. I have a surprise for you upstairs." Is all she says before she takes off through the living room and up the stairs. I bring in the tray of food and set it in the refrigerator. Then, I head in the direction my fiancé went. This woman is going to be the death of me.

Stormy

I race upstairs, undressing as I go. I wanted to put on a new lingerie set that I bought the other day with Lizzie. I haven't had the chance to try them out, but I think tonight is the night. I scramble to my dresser and pull out the black teddy with red bows. I chose this one because it matches the bows on the backs of my thighs. I slip into it and put on the famous Louboutins and sit on the bed with my legs crossed waiting for Sebastian to get up here. My heart is beating out of my chest. I can't fucking believe I'm engaged and pregnant. Who would have thought my life would take this turn when I came here. I certainly didn't. I'm thankful for one thing Lana did and that was get me the job at the catering event, without which I might not have ever met Sebastian.

He rounds the corner to the bedroom and sees me sitting there waiting for him. "Fucking hell woman, you look good enough to eat." He says as he comes closer, unbuttoning his shirt as he does.

"Well come get a taste, Daddy." I say as I spread my legs wide for him to see my wet pussy.

"You aren't supposed to be talking, Angel. How about you let me take charge." I nod as he puts his arms on the bed, caging me in. He pulls me up from the bed and crashes his lips down on mine. It's a ravenous kiss that makes me squirm. He pulls away and quickly spins me to facing the bed. Bending me over, he groans at the sight of my ass in this lacey thong. "We're going to have to get more of these." He whispers as he shreds the fabric from my body and throws it to the floor.

"Daddy, I just got those." I whine. But I know my mistake as soon as his hand comes down on my bare ass. Fuck that hurts, but he soothes it over with his palm. Then he does the other side. I'm sure to have matching prints . He gets on his knees behind me and skims his fingers over my thighs and up my back leaving goosebumps in their wake.

"Did you get this to match these sexy little bow tattoos you have? Hmm?" I nod my head, unsure if he's even able to see me or not. It doesn't matter though. I'm not talking again unless he says I can.

He spreads my leg further apart and slides his fingers through my wet pussy. "If I remember correctly, I believe someone has a punishment to pay for." He says right before he slaps my bare pussy. The sting is almost unbearable until his warm mouth glides over the spot where I was just spanked. He licks and soothes the area before he repeats. This time it takes longer for the pain to subside but I'm a wet mess. I can feel it running down my legs. Who knew I was a whore for pain? "Now, is someone going to be a good girl tonight and do as Daddy says?" He asks.

"Yes, sir." I rasp.

"That's my good fucking girl." He murmurs against my clit. The vibrations almost send me over the edge. He slams two fingers into me as he continues to lick and nip my clit. I come so hard that I almost black out. He continues pumping them inside me, not letting up and keeping my orgasm going and going. Finally, he pulls his fingers from my pussy and trails them up my backside and pushes one into my virgin hole. The sensation is strange and wonderful at the same time. He pushes deeper and uses my juices to lubricate his fingers as he sticks another one in. "You are doing so well, Angel. Daddy is proud of you. I'm going to fuck this ass tonight." Sebastian keeps thrusting his fingers inside me, stretching me, and getting me ready for his cock. His fingers scissor inside me. I hear Sebastian taking off his clothes with his other hand and soon he is naked behind me.

While keeping his fingers in place, he lines up his cock at my entrance and thrusts inside. "Fuck, you are so much tighter when my fingers are inside you." Sebastian pumps his fingers and cock inside me in tandem. "This little ass has to fit my big cock. Do you think you can do it, baby?" He asks.

"Yes, please." I rasp out my throat hurting more and more. He pulls his fingers from my ass and places them on my hips and continues pumping into me. He slides out and runs the head of his cock to my virgin rosebud, circling it before pushing in ever so slightly. I burn but the stretch feels good and I want him to just pound into me, I know he is taking it slow because I've never done this before. He rocks the head of his cock in and out over and over while circling my clit with his fingers. I'm so close to coming again just from his ministrations. He slips his fingers in my pussy and massages my g spot, making me see stars as I shatter all over his hand. He uses that opportunity to push further inside me, until I can feel him all the way in.

"Fuck, you are tighter than I thought you would be. You are strangling my cock baby." He murmurs against my ear. He continues to circle my clit and thrust into my ass at the same time. I am feeling so much all at once that I'm close to coming all over again. I slide my hands between my body and the bed to play with my sensitive nipples. I pull and twist, needing the extra pain to help me get there faster. "I'm going to come, Angel. I'm going to come in this tight little ass and watch it drip down your legs." I moan at his words and shoot off like a rocket. My orgasm ricochets through my body, hitting every nerve in its wake. I clamp down on Sebastian's cock and I can feel him jerking inside me. Jet after jet of come spurts into my ass and begin seeping down my legs. He pulls out of me and flips me over, laying me down on the bed.

He kisses me with such passion and ownership that I melt a little more for him. Throwing my arms around his neck, I pull him closer needing his body against mine. He trails kisses down my neck, over my breasts and to my belly that soon will be round with a child. He cradles my tummy and kisses it, whispering, "I love you, little one." He looks up at me from where he is, and my heart feels like it might burst from the love I feel for this man.

"Let's go take a shower, baby." He lifts me from the bed, and I wrap my legs around him as he carries me to the bathroom. Setting me down on the counter, he starts the shower. He comes back and slowly undresses me, taking off the teddy I wore for him. He removes my heels and throws them to the floor. Sebastian brings me to the shower, placing me down in the warm water. He washes my body, taking extra care of anywhere I might be sore. He soothes any pain away. We stay under the shower for a while, not speaking but letting our bodies do the talking. Once we get out, he dries my body and hair, then leads me to the bed where he tucks us both in. Kissing my forehead, he says, "I'm so in love with you. I can't wait for you to be my wife, Stormy." He pulls my hand up with the engagement ring and kisses it.

"I love you too, Sebastian. So much." He smiles with his dimple coming through and I feel a flutter in my stomach that this is my life now. I have the love of this man. We are starting a family together and I couldn't be happier than I am right now. Well, maybe when the baby is here. But right now, I am so content with my life. I'm finally home. Something I have been searching a lifetime for, I finally found. It's crazy how bad things in your life can lead you in the right direction. Life works in mysterious ways, and I will forever be thankful that the wind blew me to New York. I could have gone anywhere, but I came here. And here I'm going to stay.

Sebastian turns the light off and pulls me in close. I fall asleep with his arms wrapped tightly around me, the only place I want to be.

EPILOGUE

Sebastian

I watch as Stormy paints with one hand, while the other is rubbing her growing belly. We haven't found out what we are having but my brother and Lizzie are having a girl. I truly don't care what we have, but I think Stormy is secretly wishing for a girl. We had a small wedding soon after we got engaged. Stormy didn't want to wait and neither did I. She did give me a hard time about changing her name, like I knew she would, but I put my foot down. My wife and my children will have my last name. So, it's Stormy Leighton Knight. I chuckle when I remember the pout of her face when she realized what her name would be. My girl has been through a lot but now she has me and a place to call home.

Stormy began drawing and painting more after she found out that she was pregnant. I think it gave her the inspiration she needed. We ordered special paints that are safe for her during this time, and she hasn't stopped. Every day when I get home from work, I find her in her studio. She worked until Tracey was able to come back to work then we decided she would stay home. She's still going to classes but after the baby is born, she will take some time off. She truly wants to be a stay-at-home mother and I wouldn't have it any other way. I support my wife in all that she does. She's painted a few cover photos for books that have been published through Knight Publishing Company and I couldn't be prouder. She is getting her artwork out there like she always wanted. Right now, she is working on the cover for Lizzie's latest book. I think this will be the best one yet. I look at the paintings she has on the wall and one of them is me while I was sleeping. She said she knew she had to paint it. It came from a sketch she drew shortly after we got together. She's also painted both of us together. My girl is so talented. She's also been working on painting the nursery. She wanted a mural in there.

I hear her singing something to our child and I smile. She has been singing more and more now that she can feel the baby kicking. I haven't felt it yet. She said it just feels like little flutters, but I can't wait until I do. I love my wife today more than I did yesterday. Yes, she can still fight with the best of them, I think the pregnancy hormones have something to do with it. But we're happy.

She was broken and damaged but somehow, she found peace in the fragments scattered across the floor. She's an artist in the way she puts herself back together to create something powerful and a bit more magnificent than before. She's a whirlwind, a hurricane, a strong and sexy storm, and she is all mine. I told her during our vows, "Fuck til death do us part, if I ever lose you hell better lock its gates because I'll be coming for you." She laughed but I was serious. I surprised her with my new tattoos on our wedding day. I got "Angel" put on my ribs with her initials underneath. She will forever be a part of me. There isn't anything I wouldn't do for that woman. She's the one, just like my father would talk about. It wasn't love at first sight. More like hate at first sight but I wouldn't have it any other way. My little vixen is a fireball, and we complement each other perfectly. She needed someone to take care of her and I needed someone to care for. I didn't know what love was until we were thrust together. Now, they're both sitting before me, and I feel as though my heart could burst.

Stormy

I smile as I look down at my small baby bump. I've never been this happy and content in my life. All the puzzle pieces fell into place, making the most beautiful masterpiece I could ever imagine. I can feel Sebastian's eyes on me, so I sit a little straighter and try to concentrate on this painting that I need to get finished for Lizzie's new book. I was so pleased when she saw my work and asked if I would be willing to work with her on her book covers. It's a dream come true, getting my work out there for people to see. It's what I always wanted.

I was going down a path of destruction until Sebastian saved me from the worst parts of myself. I was broken. Even if I told him I was fine, he wouldn't believe me. He fought for me. He saved me. I was going toward my lowest point again and he pulled me back from the deep waters. I will forever be grateful for everything he did for me. He believed in me.

Life isn't always a work of art. It's messy, chaotic, and sometimes complicated, but that doesn't mean you throw away the canvas. You have to take a step back and look at it from a different angle. It's not always what it seems and more times than not it can be salvaged. Find your muse and never let it go. Mine will always be Sebastian. He resuscitated my soul, giving me purpose again.

More By L.B. Martin

Knight Publishing Series

The Write Knight – *Life isn't always a fairytale*

The Silent Knight – *Life isn't always a holiday*

The Starry Knight – *Life isn't always a work of art*

The Last Knight – *Life isn't always a battle*

Boys of Frampton University

Backstroke – enemies to lovers – *Releasing summer 2024!*

Butterfly – MFM – *Releasing Winter 2024!*

ABOUT THE AUTHOR

L.B. Martin lives in South Carolina with her husband and two children. She spends her free time reading, writing, and drinking all the coffee. L.B. majored in English literature in college with a minor in British Lit. Her husband is a professional gamer, so when he is playing, she is reading away. She loves writing MCs with mental illness in hopes to shine light on mental health awareness.

"My words spill from my mind to the pages in effort to rid myself of the demons tucked away inside. My hope is that readers will be immersed into my world and come out feeling hopeful and full of purpose."
-L.B. Martin

Linktree https://linktr.ee/lb_martin_author

MENTAL HEALTH AWARENESS

Mental health is a crucial aspect of our overall well-being. It includes our emotional, psychological, and social health, and affects how we think, feel, and act. Mental health is important at every stage of life, from childhood and adolescence through adulthood.

Mental health awareness is the ongoing effort to reduce the stigma around mental illness and mental health conditions by sharing personal experiences. It helps people understand that mental illness is not a character flaw but rather an illness like any other.

An increasing awareness of mental health helps society work toward eliminating its stigmas, but it does much more. For instance, developing a greater understanding of mental illness can allow people to recognize those in their lives who may be dealing with anxiety, depression, or other conditions that affect their mental well-being.

If you or someone you know is struggling with mental health, it's important to seek help. The National Alliance on Mental Illness (**NAMI**) provides resources and support for individuals and families affected by mental illness.

Remember, our mental health journey starts with a single moment. Let's break the stigma together!

How common are mental illnesses?

Mental illnesses are among the most common health conditions in the United States.

More than 1 in 5 US adults live with a mental illness.

Over 1 in 5 youth (ages 13-18) either currently or at some point during their life, have had a seriously debilitating mental illness.

About 1 in 25 U.S. adults lives with a serious mental illness, such as schizophrenia, bipolar disorder, or major depression.

What causes mental illness?

There is no single cause for mental illness. A number of factors can contribute to risk for mental illness, such as

- Adverse Childhood Experiences, such as trauma or a history of abuse (for example, child abuse, sexual assault, witnessing violence, etc.)

- Experiences related to other ongoing (chronic) medical conditions, such as a traumatic brain injury, cancer, or diabetes

- Biological factors or chemical imbalances in the brain

- Use of alcohol or drugs

- Having feelings of loneliness or isolation

Made in the USA
Middletown, DE
01 September 2024

60236536R00225